P9-DHF-863

FOUR GREAT STORIES FROM SILHOUETTE!

BLUEBIRD WINTER by Linda Howard

Kathleen Fields had to reach the clinic, but a Christmas blizzard left her stranded, without hope for her life—or her unborn baby's. Then Derek Taliferro arrived with his doctor's skill, his caring heart. Together they brought Kathleen's child into the world and discovered love, the greatest gift of all.

HENRY THE NINTH by Dixie Browning

Being fixed up with her landlady's brother was not Mary Pepper's idea of a good time. But when a horrible cold and a horrendous work schedule obliterated Christmas, Henry whisked her off for a late celebration on Hatteras Island, where they found themselves creating some rather unusual new traditions of their own....

SEASON OF MIRACLES by Ginna Gray

The town spinster, tenderhearted Kathryn Talmidge, had long adored Daniel Westwood in silence. The gruff widower finally proposed—but solely to give his kids a new Mom for Christmas! Though motherhood and sharing Dan's life were all Kath had ever dreamed of, now she prayed for the miracle of his love....

THE HUMBUG MAN by Diana Palmer

Montana rancher Tate Hollister had to be the grouchiest, grumpiest humbug man widow Maggie Jeffries had ever met. But, as the holiday season progressed, Maggie discovered that Tate wasn't completely immune to the Christmas spirit—his loving embrace on a cold winter's night could prove to be the gift of a lifetime....

Dear Reader:

It's hard to say who enjoyed last year's Christmas Stories more—you or the authors. I know you did because of all the wonderful letters we received; and I know the authors did, because so many called to offer us stories for the next collection. So we decided that Silhouette Christmas Stories should happen every year, just like the holiday.

Here are four all-new stories by more of your favorites. In "Bluebird Winter" Linda Howard has finally written Derek Taliferro's story. Remember him from her Special Edition *Sarah's Child*? Dixie Browning's "Henry the Ninth" is set on a North Carolina island with a Christmas tradition all its own. Ginna Gray writes about the village "spinster" who receives the gift of love in "A Season of Miracles." Lastly, in "The Humbug Man" by Diana Palmer, Maggie and Tate discover the happiness of Christmas present!

From all of us at Silhouette to all of you, we wish you the happiest of holidays. Enjoy.

Karen Solem
Editorial Director

Silhouette Christmas Stories 1987

LINDA HOWARD
DIXIE BROWNING
GINNA GRAY
DIANA PALMER

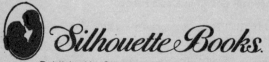

Silhouette Books.

Published by Silhouette Books New York

America's Publisher of Contemporary Romance

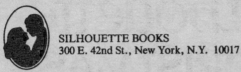

SILHOUETTE BOOKS
300 E. 42nd St., New York, N.Y. 10017

Silhouette Christmas Stories 1987
Copyright © 1987 by Silhouette Books

ISBN: 0-373-48212-4

First Silhouette Books printing November 1987
Second printing November 1988

The publisher acknowledges the copyright holders of
the individual works as follows:

Bluebird Winter
Copyright © 1987 by Linda Howington

Henry the Ninth
Copyright © 1987 by Dixie Browning

Season of Miracles
Copyright © 1987 by Virginia Gray

The Humbug Man
Copyright © 1987 by Diana Palmer

America's Publishers of Contemporary Romance

Printed in the U.S.A.

CONTENTS

BLUEBIRD WINTER   9
by Linda Howard

HENRY THE NINTH   109
by Dixie Browning

SEASON OF MIRACLES   209
by Ginna Gray

THE HUMBUG MAN   295
by Diana Palmer

BLUEBIRD WINTER

Linda Howard

CHRISTMAS SHRIMP BALL

I like the shrimp ball because it looks Christmasy when the cocktail sauce is poured over it. I also like it because it doesn't require cooking. I won't even mention the fact that I could eat the whole thing.

2 8 oz. packs cream cheese
3 cans cocktail shrimp
2 teaspoons horseradish sauce
2 tablespoons chopped onion
2 bottles cocktail sauce

Drain the shrimp and mash them with a fork until they're a fine pink crumbled mess. Combine with the remaining ingredients. (To show you how much I know about cooking, the first time I made a shrimp ball I didn't know to let the cream cheese get to room temperature before I tried combining it with anything. I had muscles like Mr. Universe by the time I had finished wrestling with the cream cheese.) Shape into a ball and chill. When you're ready to serve, pour cocktail sauce over the ball and surround it with crackers. Just thinking about it makes my mouth water.

PS: I usually need two bottles of cocktail sauce.

Chapter One

It wasn't supposed to happen like this.

Kathleen Fields pressed her hand to her swollen abdomen, her face drawn and anxious as she looked out the window again at the swirling, wind-blown snow. Visibility was so limited that she couldn't even see the uneven pasture fence no more than fifty yards away. The temperature had plummeted into the teens, and according to the weather report on the radio, this freak Christmas Day blizzard was likely to last the rest of the day and most of the night.

She couldn't wait that long. She was in labor now, almost a month early. Her baby would need medical attention.

Bitterness welled in her as she dropped the curtain and turned back to the small, dim living room, lit only by the fire in the fireplace. The electricity and telephone service had gone out five hours ago. Two hours after that, the dull ache in her back, which had been so constant for weeks that she no longer noticed it, had begun strengthening into something more, then laced around to her distended belly. Only mildly concerned, she had ignored it as false labor; after all, she was still three weeks and five days from her due date. Then, half an hour ago, her water had broken, and there was no longer any doubt: she was in labor.

She was also alone, and stranded. This Christmas snow, so coveted by millions of children, could mean the death of her own child.

Tears burned her eyes. She had stolidly endured a bad marriage and the end of her illusions, faced the reality of being broke, alone and pregnant, of working long hours as a waitress in an effort to keep herself fed and provide a home for this baby, even though she had fiercely resented its existence at the beginning. But then it had begun moving inside her, gentle little flutters at first, then actual kicks and pokes, and it had become reality, a person, a companion. It was *her* baby. She wanted it, wanted to hold it and love it and croon lullabies to it. It was the only person she had left in the world, but now she might lose it, perhaps in punishment for that early resentment. How ironic to carry it all this time, only to lose it on Christmas Day! It was supposed to be a day of hope, faith and promise, but she didn't have any hope left, or much faith in people, and the future promised nothing but an endless procession of bleak days. All she had was herself, and the tiny life inside her that was now in jeopardy.

She could deliver the baby here, without help. It was warm and somehow she would manage to keep the fire going. She would survive, but would the baby? It was premature. It might not be able to breathe properly on its own. Something might be wrong with it.

Or she could try to get to the clinic, fifteen miles distant. It was an easy drive in good weather...but the weather wasn't good, and the howling wind had been getting louder. The roads were treacherous and visibility limited. She might not make it, and the effort would cost her her own life, as well as that of her child.

So what? The words echoed in her mind. What did her life matter, if the baby died? Would she be able to live with herself if she opted to protect herself at the risk of the baby's life? Everything might be all right, but she couldn't take that chance. For her baby's sake, she had to try.

Moving clumsily, she dressed as warmly as she could, layering her clothing until she moved like a waddling pumpkin. She gathered water and blankets, an extra nightgown for herself and clothes for the baby, then, as a last thought, checked the telephone one more time on the off-chance that service might have been restored. Only silence met her ear, and, regretfully, she dropped the receiver.

Taking a deep breath to brace herself, Kathleen opened the back door and was immediately lashed by the icy wind and stinging snow. She ducked her head and struggled against the wind, cautiously making her way down the two ice-coated steps. Her balance wasn't that good anyway, and the wind was beating at her, making her stagger. Halfway across the yard she slipped and fell, but scrambled up so quickly that she barely felt the impact. "I'm sorry, I'm sorry," she breathed to the baby, patting her stomach. The baby had settled low in her belly and wasn't kicking now, but the pressure was increasing. It was hard to walk. Just as she reached the old pickup truck a contraction hit her and she stumbled, falling again. This contraction was stronger than the others, and all she could do was lie helplessly in the snow until it eased, biting her lip to keep from moaning aloud.

Snow was matting her eyelashes when she finally struggled to her feet again and gathered up the articles she had dropped. She was panting. God, please let it be a long labor! she prayed. Please give me time to get to the clinic. She could bear the pain, if the baby would just stay snug and safe inside her until she could get help for it.

A dry sobbing sound reached her ears as she wrenched the truck door open, pitting her strength against that of the wind as it tried to slam the door shut. Clumsily she climbed into the truck, barely fitting her swollen stomach behind the wheel. The wind slammed the door shut without her aid, and for a moment she just sat there, entombed in an icy, white world, because snow covered all the windows. The sobbing sound continued, and finally she realized she was making the noise.

Instantly Kathleen drew herself up. There was nothing to gain by letting herself panic. She had to clear her mind and concentrate on nothing but driving, because her baby's life depended on it. The baby was all she had left. Everything else was gone: her parents; her marriage; her self-confidence; her faith and trust in people. Only the baby was left, and herself. She still had herself. The two of them had each other, and they didn't need anyone else. She would do anything to protect her baby.

Breathing deeply, she forced herself to be calm. With deliberate movements, she inserted the key in the ignition and turned it. The starter turned slowly, and a new fear intruded. Was the battery too cold to generate enough power to start the old motor? But then the motor roared into life, and the truck vibrated beneath her. She sighed in relief and turned on the wipers to clear the snow from the windshield. They beat back and forth, laboring under the icy weight of the packed snow.

It was so cold! Her breath fogged the air, and she was shivering despite the layers of clothing she wore. Her face felt numb. She reached up to touch it and found that she was still covered with snow. Slowly she wiped her face and dusted the flakes from her hair.

The increasing pressure in her lower body made it difficult for her to hold in the clutch, but she wrestled the stubborn gearshift into the proper position and ground her teeth against the pressure as she let out the clutch. The truck moved forward.

Visibility was even worse than she had expected. She could barely make out the fence that ran alongside the road. How easy it would be to run off the road, or to become completely lost in the white nightmare! Creeping along at a snail's pace, Kathleen concentrated on the fence line and tried not to think about the things that could happen.

She was barely a quarter of a mile down the road when another contraction laced her stomach in iron bands. She gasped, jerking in spite of herself, and the sudden wrench of the steering wheel sent the old truck into a skid. "No!" she groaned, bracing herself as the truck began going sideways toward the shallow ditch alongside the road. The two right wheels landed in the ditch with an impact that rattled her teeth and loosened her grip from the steering wheel. She cried out again as she was flung to the right, her body slamming into the door on the passenger side.

The contraction eased a moment later. Panting, Kathleen crawled up the slanting seat and wedged herself behind the steering wheel. The motor had died, and anxiously she put in the clutch and slid the shift into neutral, praying she could get the engine started again. She turned the key, and once again the truck coughed into life.

But the wheels spun uselessly in the icy ditch, unable to find traction. She tried rocking the truck back and forth, putting it first in reverse, then in low gear, but it didn't work. She was stuck.

Tiredly, she leaned her head on the steering wheel. She was only a quarter mile from the house, but it might as well have been twenty miles in this weather. The wind was stronger, visibility almost zero. Her situation had gone from bad to worse. She should have stayed at the house. In trying to save her baby, she had almost certainly taking away its only chance for survival.

He should either have left his mother's house the day before, or remained until the roads were clear. Hindsight was, indeed, very sharp, unlike the current visibility. His four-wheel-drive Jeep Cherokee was surefooted on the icy road, but that didn't eliminate the need to see where he was going.

Making a mistake made Derek Taliferro angry, especially when it was such a stupid mistake. Yesterday's weather bulletins had warned that conditions could worsen, so he had decided to make the drive back to Dallas right away. But Marcie had wanted him to stay until Christmas morning, and he loved his mother very much, so in the end he'd stayed. His strong mouth softened as he allowed himself to think briefly of her. She was a strong woman, raising him single-handedly and never letting him think she'd have it any other way. He'd been elated when she had met

Whit Campbell, a strong, laconic rancher from Oklahoma, and tumbled head over heels in love. That had been ... Lord, ten years ago. It didn't seem that long. Marcie and Whit still acted like newlyweds.

Derek liked visiting the ranch, just across the state line in Oklahoma, and escaping the pressures of the hospital for a while. That was one reason he'd allowed Marcie to talk him into staying longer than his common sense told him he should. But this morning the urge to get back to Dallas had also overridden his common sense. He should have stayed put until the weather cleared, but he wanted to be back at the hospital by tomorrow. His tiny patients needed him.

The job was compelling, and he never tired of it. He had known he wanted to be a doctor from the time he was fifteen, but at first he'd thought about being an obstetrician. Gradually his interest had become more focused, and by the time he was midway through medical school his goal was set. He specialized in neonatal care, in those tiny babies who came into the world with less of a chance than they should have had. Some of them were simply premature and needed a protective environment in which to gain weight. Others, who were far too early, had to fight for every breath as their underdeveloped systems tried to mature. Every day was a battle won. Then there were those who needed his surgical skills after nature had gone awry, and still others who were beyond help. Every time he was finally able to send a baby home with its parents, he was filled with an intense satisfaction that showed no signs of lessening. It was also why he was now creeping, almost blindly, through a blizzard instead of waiting for better weather. He wanted to get back to the hospital.

The snow completely covered the road; he'd been following fence lines, and hoping he was still on track. Hell, for all he knew, he was driving across some-one's pasture. This was idiocy. He swore under his breath, holding the Cherokee steady against the gust-ing, howling, swirling wind. When he got to the next town—*if* he got to the next town—he was going to stop, even if he had to spend the night in an all-night grocery...provided there was an all-night grocery. Anything was better than driving blindly in this white hell.

It was so bad that he almost missed seeing the bulk of an old pickup truck, which had slid into a ditch and was now resting at an angle. In one sense seeing the old truck was good news: at least he was still on the road. He started to go on, thinking that whoever had been driving the truck would have sought more adequate shelter long ago, but a quick uneasy feeling made him brake carefully, then shift into reverse and back up until he was alongside the snow-covered bulk. It would only take a minute to check.

The snow had turned into icy, wind-driven pellets that stung his face as he opened the door and got out, hunching his broad shoulders against the wind that tried to knock him off his feet. It was only a few steps to the truck, but he had to fight for every inch. Quickly he grabbed the door handle and wrenched it open, wanting to verify that the truck was empty so he could get back into the Cherokee's warm interior. He was startled by the small scream from the woman who lay on the seat and then jerked upright in alarm when the door was opened so suddenly.

"I just want to help," he said quickly, to keep from frightening her any more than he already had.

Kathleen gasped, panting at the pain that had her in its grips. The contractions had been intensifying and were only a few minutes apart now. She would never have been able to make it to the clinic in time. She felt the numbing blast of cold, saw the big man who stood in the truck's open door; but just for the moment she couldn't reply, couldn't do anything except concentrate on the pain. She wrapped her arms around her tight belly, whimpering.

Derek realized at a glance what was happening. The woman was completely white, her green eyes vivid in her pale, desperate face as she held her swollen belly. A strong sense of protectiveness surged through him.

"It's all right, sweetheart," he murmured soothingly, reaching into the truck and lifting her out in his strong arms. "You and the baby will be just fine. I'll take care of everything."

She was still whimpering, locked in the grip of the contraction. Derek carried her to the Cherokee, sheltering her from the brutal wind as much as he could. His mind was already on the coming birth. He hadn't delivered a baby since he'd been an intern, but he'd been on hand many times when the newborn was expected to have difficulties.

He managed to open the passenger door with her still in his arms, and gently deposited her on the seat before hurrying around to vault in on his own side. "How far apart are the contractions?" he asked, wiping her face with his hands. She lay slumped against the seat now, breathing deeply at the cessation of pain, her eyelids closed.

Her eyes opened at his touch, the wary eyes of a wild animal in a trap. "Th-th-th-three minutes," she said, her teeth chattering from the cold. "Maybe less."

"How far is the hospital?"

"Clinic," she corrected, still breathing hard. She swallowed and wet her lips. "Fifteen miles."

"We won't make it," he said with awful certainty. "Is there anyplace around here where we can shelter? A house, a restaurant, anything?"

She lifted her hand. "My house...back there. Quarter mile."

Derek's experienced eyes took note of the signs. She was exhausted. Labor was tiring enough, without being alone and terrified, too. Stress had taken its toll. He needed to get her warm and comfortable as soon as possible. Her eyes closed again.

He decided not to chance turning the truck around and getting off the road; instead he put the Cherokee in reverse, guiding himself by the fence line beside him, because he couldn't see a damned thing out the back window. "Tell me when I get to your driveway," he ordered, and her eyes fluttered open in response.

A minute or so later another contraction curled her in the seat. Derek glanced at his watch. Just a little over two minutes since the last one. The baby certainly wasn't waiting for better weather.

A rusted mailbox on a leaning fence post caught his attention. "Is this your driveway?" he asked.

She lifted her head, and he could see that her white teeth were sunk into her bottom lip to hold back her groans. She managed a short nod, and he shifted into low gear, turning onto the faint trail by the mailbox and praying for time.

Chapter Two

The back door's open," Kathleen whispered, and he nodded as he steered the Cherokee as close to the steps as he could.

"Don't try to get out on your own," he ordered as she reached for the door handle. "I'll come around and get you."

Kathleen subsided against the seat, her face pale and taut. She didn't know this man, didn't know whether she should trust him, but she had no choice but to accept his help. She was more frightened than she'd ever been in her life. The pain was worse than she'd expected, and added to it was the numbing fear for her child's life. Whoever the man was, right now she was grateful for his company.

He got out of the Cherokee, bending his head against the wind as he circled the front of the vehicle. He was a big man, tall and strong; he'd handled her weight easily, but his grasp had been gentle. As he opened the passenger door, Kathleen started to swing her legs around so she could slide out, but again he stopped her by scooping her up in his arms.

"Put your face against my shoulder," he instructed, raising his voice so she could hear him over the howling wind. She nodded and buried her face against his coat, and he turned so that his back blocked the wind from her as he carried her the few feet to the back door. He fumbled for the doorknob and managed to turn it, and the wind did the rest, catching the door and slamming it back against the wall with a resounding crack. A small blizzard of snow entered with them.

Swiftly he carried her through the small, time-worn ranch house until he reached the living room, where the fire still burned low in the fireplace. She felt as though hours had passed, but in reality it had been only about an hour since she had fought her way to the truck.

Still with that powerful, controlled gentleness, he placed her on the sagging old couch. "I've got to get my bag, but I'll be right back," he promised, smoothing her hair back from her face. "Don't try to get up; stay right here."

She nodded, so tired that she couldn't imagine going anywhere. Why did he want his luggage right now? Couldn't it wait?

Another contraction. She curled up on the couch, giving gasping little cries at the fierceness of the pain. Before it ended he was beside her again, his voice soothing but authoritative as he told her to take quick, short breaths, to pant like a dog. Dimly she remembered reading instructions for breathing during labor, and the same description had been used. She tried to do as he said, concentrating on her breathing, and it did seem to help. Perhaps it just took her mind off the pain, but right then she was willing to do anything.

When the contraction had eased and she slumped exhausted on the couch, he said, "Do you have extra wood for the fire? The electricity is off."

She managed a wan smile. "I know. It went off this morning. I brought extra wood in yesterday, when I heard the weather report; it's in the wash room, just off the kitchen.''

"You should have gone to the clinic yesterday," he said crisply as he got to his feet.

She was tired and frightened, but fire still flashed in her green eyes as she glared up at him. "I would have, if I'd known the baby was going to come early."

That got his attention; his black brows snapped together over his high-bridged nose. "You're not full term? How early are you?"

"Almost a month." Her hand went to her stomach in an unconscious gesture of helpless concern.

"Any chance your due date was miscalculated?"

"No," she whispered, her head falling back. She knew exactly when she'd gotten pregnant, and the memory made her go cold.

He gave her a crooked smile, and for the first time she noticed how beautiful he was, in a strong, masculine way that was almost unearthly. Kathleen had gotten into the habit of not looking directly at men, or she would have seen it before. Even now, something in his golden brown eyes made her feel more relaxed. "This is your lucky day, sweetheart," he said gently, still smiling at her as he took off his thick shearling coat and rolled up his sleeves. "You just got stranded with a doctor."

For a moment the words didn't make sense; then her mouth opened in silent disbelief. "You're a doctor?"

He lifted his right hand as if taking an oath. "Licensed and sworn."

Relief filled her like a warm tide rushing through her body, and she gave a small laugh that was half sob. "Are you any good at delivering babies?"

"Babies are my business," he said, giving her another of those bright, tender smiles. "So stop worrying and try to rest while I get things arranged in here. When you have another contraction, remember how to breathe. I won't be long."

She watched as he brought in more wood and built up the fire until it was blazing wildly, adding warmth to the chilled room. Through the pain of another contraction, she watched as he carried in the mattress from her bed and dumped it on the floor in front of the fire. With swift, sure movements he put a clean sheet on it, then folded towels over the sheet.

He rose to his feet with powerful grace and approached her. "Now, let's get you more comfortable," he said as he removed her coat. "By the way, my name is Derek Taliferro."

"Kathleen Fields," she replied in kind.

"Is there a Mr. Fields?" he asked, his calm face hiding his intense interest in her answer as he began taking off her boots.

Bitterness filled Kathleen's face, a bitterness so deep it hurt to see. "There's one somewhere," she muttered. "But we aren't married any longer."

He was silent as he removed her thick socks, under which she also wore leotards that she'd put on when she realized she would have to try to get to the clinic. He helped her to her feet and unzipped her serviceable corduroy jumper, lifting it over her head and leaving her standing in her turtleneck sweater and leotards.

"I can do the rest," she said uneasily. "Just let me go into the bedroom for a nightgown."

He laughed, the sound deep and rich. "All right, if you think you can manage."

"Of course I can manage." She had been managing much more than that since Larry Fields had walked out.

But she had barely taken two steps when another contraction bent her double, a contraction so powerful that it was all she could do to gasp for breath. Involuntary tears stung her eyes. She felt his arms around her; then he lifted her and a moment later placed her on the mattress. Swiftly he stripped off her leotards and underwear, and draped a sheet over her; then he held her hand and coached her breathing until the contraction eased.

"Rest for a minute now," he soothed. "I'm going to wash my hands so I can examine you. I'll be right back."

Kathleen lay tiredly on the mattress, staring up at the water-stained ceiling with swimming eyes. The heat from the fire flickered against her cheeks, bringing a rosy glow to her complexion. She was so tired; she felt as if she could sleep for the rest of the day, but there wouldn't be any rest until the baby was born. Her hands clenched into fists as anxiety rose in her again. The baby had to be all right. It had to be.

Then he was back, kneeling at the foot of the mattress and lifting the sheet that covered her. Real color climbed into her face, and she turned her head to stare into the fire. She had never really been comfortable with intimacy, and even her visits to the doctor had been torturous occasions for her. To have this man, this stranger, touch her and look at her...

Derek glanced up and saw her flushed face and expression of acute embarrassment, and a smile flickered around his mouth as amused tenderness welled up in him. How wary she was of him, despite being forced to put her welfare in his hands! And rather shy, like a wild creature that wasn't accustomed to others and didn't quite trust them. She was frightened, too, for her child, and of the ordeal she faced. Because of that, he was immensely gentle as he examined her.

"You aren't fully dilated," he murmured. "The baby isn't in such a hurry, after all. Go with your contractions, but don't push. I'll tell you when to push. How long ago did the contractions start?"

"My back was hurting all last night," she said tiredly, her eyes closing. "The first real contraction was at about ten o'clock this morning."

He glanced at his watch. She had been in labor a little over five hours, and it would probably last another hour or so. Not a long labor, especially for a first pregnancy. "When did your water break?"

He wasn't hurting her, and her embarrassment was fading. She even felt drowsy. "Umm...about one-thirty." Now she felt his hands on her stomach; firm, careful touches as he tried to determine the baby's position. Her warm drowsiness splintered as another contraction seized her, but when she breathed as he'd instructed somehow it didn't seem as painful.

When she rested again, he placed his stethoscope against her stomach and listened to the baby's heartbeat. "It's a strong, steady heartbeat," he reassured her. He wasn't worried about the baby's heart, but about its lungs. He prayed they would be mature enough to handle the chore of breathing, because he didn't have the equipment here to handle the situation if they couldn't. Some eight-month babies did just fine; others needed help. He looked out the window. It was snowing harder than ever, in a blinding sheet that blocked out the rest of the world but filled the house with a strange, white light. There was no way he could summon emergency help, and no way it could get here, even if the phones were working.

The minutes slipped away, marked by contractions that gradually grew stronger and closer together. He kept the fire built up, so the baby wouldn't be chilled when it finally made its appearance, and Kathleen's hair grew damp with sweat. She tugged at the neck of her turtleneck sweater. "It's so hot," she breathed. She felt as if she couldn't stand the confining fabric a minute longer.

"A nightgown wouldn't be much of an improvement," Derek said, and got one of his clean shirts from his luggage. She didn't make any protest when he removed her sweater and bra and slipped the thin, soft shirt around her. It was light, and much too big, and it felt wonderful after the smothering heat of the wool sweater. He rolled up the sleeves and fastened the buttons over her breasts, then dampened a washcloth in cool water and bathed her face.

It wouldn't be too much longer. He checked again to make certain he had everything he needed at hand. He had already sterilized his instruments and laid everything out on a gauze-covered tray.

"Well, sweetheart, are you about ready to get this show on the road?" he asked as he examined her again.

The contractions were almost continuous now. She took a deep breath during a momentary lull. "Is it time?" she gasped.

"You're fully dilated now, but don't push until I tell you. Pant. That's right. Don't push, don't push."

She wanted to push. She desperately needed to push. Her body arched on the mattress, a monstrous pressure building in her, but his deep voice remained calm and controlled, somehow controlling her. She panted, and somehow, she didn't push. The wave of pain receded, the pressure eased, and for a moment she rested. Then it began again.

It couldn't last much longer; she couldn't bear it much longer. Tears seeped from her eyes.

"Here we go," he said with satisfaction. "I can see the head. You're crowning, sweetheart; it won't be but another minute. Let me make a little incision so you won't be torn—"

Kathleen barely heard him, barely felt him. The pressure was unbearable, blocking out everything else. "Push, sweetheart," he said, his tone suddenly authoritative.

She pushed. Dimly, she was astounded that her body was capable of exerting such pressure. She gave a thin cry, but barely heard it. Her world consisted only of a powerful force that squeezed her in its fist, that and the man who knelt at her spread knees, his calm voice telling her what to do.

Then, abruptly, the pressure eased, and she sank back, gasping for breath. He said, "I have the baby's head in my hand. My Lord, what a head of hair! Just rest a minute, sweetheart."

She heard a funny sound, and alarm brought her up on her elbows. "What's wrong?" she asked frantically. "What are you doing?"

"I'm suctioning out its mouth and nose," he said. "Just lie back; everything's all right." Then a thin, wavering wail rose, gaining in strength with every second, and he laughed. "That's right, tell us about it," he encouraged. "Push, sweetheart; our baby isn't too happy with the situation."

She pushed, straining, and suddenly she felt a rush, then a great sense of relief. Derek laughed again as he held a tiny but furious scrap of humanity in his hands. "I don't blame you a bit," he told the squalling infant, whose cries sounded ridiculously like those of a mewling kitten. "I wouldn't want to leave your soft, warm mommy, either, but you'll be wrapped up and cuddled in just a minute."

"What is it?" Kathleen whispered, falling back on the mattress.

"A beautiful little girl. She has more hair than any three babies should have."

"Is she all right?"

"She's perfect. She's tiny, but listen to her cry! Her lungs are working just fine."

"Can I hold her?"

"In just a minute. I'm almost finished here." The umbilical cord had gone limp, so he swiftly clamped and cut it, then lifted the squalling baby into her mother's anxious arms. Kathleen looked dazed, her eyes filling with tears as she examined her tiny daughter.

"Put her to your breast," Derek instructed softly, knowing that would calm the infant, but Kathleen didn't seem to hear him. He unbuttoned her shirt himself and pushed it aside to bare one full breast, then guided the baby's mouth to the rich-looking nipple. Still the baby squalled, its tiny body trembling; he'd have to do more than just give it a hint. "Come on, honey," he coaxed, reached down to stroke the baby's cheek just beside her mouth. She turned her head reflexively, and he guided the nipple into her mouth. She squalled one more time, then suddenly seemed to realize what she was supposed to do, and the tiny mouth closed on her mother's breast.

Kathleen jumped. She hadn't even reacted to his touch on her breast, he realized, and looked closely at her. She was pale, with shadows under her eyes, and her dark hair was wet with perspiration. She was truly exhausted, not just from the physical difficulty of labor and giving birth, but from the hours of anxiety she'd suffered through. Yet there was something glowing in her face and eyes as she looked at her baby, and it lingered when she slowly looked up at him.

"We did it," she murmured, and smiled.

Derek looked down at her, at the love shining from her face like a beacon, and the attraction he'd felt for her from the start suddenly solidified inside him with a painful twist. Something about her made him want to hold her close, protect her from whatever had put that wary, distrustful look in her eyes. He wanted her to look at him with her face full of love.

Stunned, he sank bank on his heels. It had finally happened, when he had least expected it and had even stopped looking for it, and with a woman who was merely tolerating his presence due to the circumstances. It wasn't just that she had other things on her mind right now; he could tell that Kathleen Fields wanted nothing to do with a man, any man. And yet the thunderbolt had hit him anyway, just as his mother had always warned him it would.

Teaching Kathleen to love wouldn't be easy, but Derek looked at her, and at the baby in her arms, and knew he wouldn't give up.

Chapter Three

Kathleen couldn't remember ever being so tired before; her body was leaden with exhaustion, while her mind seemed to float, disconnected from the physical world. Only the baby in her arms seemed real. She was vaguely aware of the things Derek was doing to her, of the incredible confidence and gentleness of his hands, but it was as if he were doing them to someone else. Even the painful prick of the sutures he set didn't rouse her, nor did his firm massaging of her stomach. She simply lay there, too tired to care. When she was finally clean and wearing a gown, and the linen on the mattress had been changed, she sighed and went to sleep with the suddenness of a light being turned off.

She had no idea how long it was before he woke her, to lift her carefully to a sitting position and prop her against him while the baby nursed. He was literally holding both her and the baby, his strong arms supporting them. Her head lay on his broad shoulder, and she didn't have the strength to lift it. "I'm sorry," she murmured. "I can't seem to sit up."

"It's all right, sweetheart," he said, his deep voice reaching inside her and soothing all her vague worries. "You worked hard; you deserve to be a little lazy now."

"Is the baby all right?" she managed to mumble.

"She's eating like a pig," he said, his chuckle hiding his worry, and Kathleen went back to sleep as soon as he eased her back onto the mattress. She didn't even feel him lift the baby from her and refasten her gown.

Derek sat for a long time, cradling the baby in his arms. She was dangerously underweight, but she seemed remarkably strong for her size. She was breathing on her own and managing to suckle, which had been his two biggest worries, but she was still too tiny. He guessed her weight at about four pounds, too small for her to be able to regulate her own temperature because she simply didn't have the body fat necessary. Because of that, he had wrapped her warmly and kept the fire in the fireplace hotter than was comfortable.

His calm, golden brown eyes glowed as he looked down at her tiny face, dominated by the vague, huge blue eyes of the newborn. Premature infants had both an aged and a curiously ageless look to them, their doll-like faces lacking cuddly baby fat, which revealed their facial structure in a fragile gauntness. Even so, he could tell she was going to be a beauty, with her mother's features and even the same thick, black hair.

Every one of his tiny, frail patients got to him, but this stubborn little fighter had reached right into his heart. Maybe it was because he could look at her and see her mother in her, because Kathleen was a fighter, too. She had to be; it wasn't easy to go through a pregnancy alone, as she obviously had. And when she had gone into labor too early, instead of remaining here where *she* would be safer, she had risked her own life in an effort to get to the clinic where her baby could have medical care.

He couldn't help wondering about the absent Mr. Fields, and for the first time in his life he felt jealousy burning him, because the unknown man had been, at least for a while, the recipient of Kathleen's love. Derek also wondered what had happened to put that wariness in her eyes and build the walls in her mind. He knew they were there; he could sense them. They made him want to put his arms around her and rock her, comfort her, but he knew she wouldn't welcome his closeness.

The baby squeaked, and he looked down to see that her eyes were open and she was looking at him with the intensely focused expression of someone with bad eyesight. He chuckled and cuddled her closer. "What is it, honey?" he crooned. "Hungry again?" Because her stomach was so small, she needed far more frequent feedings than a normal newborn.

He glanced over at Kathleen, who was still sleeping heavily. An idea began to form. One of Derek's characteristics, and one that had often made his mother feel as if she were dealing with an irresistible force rather than a child, was his ability to set long-term goals and let nothing sway him from his course. When he wanted something, he went after it. And now he wanted Kathleen. He had been instantly attracted to her, his interest sparked by the mysterious but undeniable chemical reaction that kept animals mating and procreating; humans were no exception, and his own libido was healthy. Her pregnancy hadn't weakened his attraction, but rather strengthened it in a primitive way.

Then, during the process of labor and giving birth, the attraction had changed, had been transmuted into an emotional force as well as a physical one. They had been a team, despite Kathleen's reserve. The baby had become his; he was responsible for her life, her welfare. She had exited her mother's warm body into his hands. He had seen her, held her, laughed at her furious squalling, and put her to her mother's breast. She was, undeniably, *his*. Now his goal was to make the baby's mother his, too. He wanted Kathleen to look at him with the same fiercely tender love she'd shown to her child. He wanted to father the next infant that grew inside her. He wanted to make her laugh, to ease the distrust in her eyes, to make her face shine with happiness.

No doubt about it, he'd have to marry her.

The baby squeaked again, more demandingly. "All right, we'll wake Mommy up," he promised. "You'll help me with my plan, won't you? Between the two of us, we'll take such good care of her that she'll forget she was ever unhappy."

He woke Kathleen before the baby began to squall in earnest, and carefully propped her in a sitting position so she could nurse the child. She was still groggy, but seemed more alert than she had before. She held the baby to her breast, stroking the satiny cheek with one finger as she stared down at her daughter. "What time is it?" she asked dreamily.

He shifted his position so he could see his wristwatch. "Almost nine."

"Is that all? I feel as if I've been asleep for hours."

He laughed. "You have, sweetheart. You were worn out."

Kathleen's clear green eyes turned up to him. "Is she doing all right?"

The baby chose that moment to slurp as the nipple momentarily slipped from her lips. Frantically the tiny rosebud mouth sought the beading nipple again, and when she found it she made a squeaky little grunting noise. The two adults laughed, looking down at her.

"She's strong for her size," Derek said, reaching down to lift the miniscule hand that lay on Kathleen's ivory, blue-veined breast. It was such a tiny hand, the palm no bigger than a dime, but the fingernails were perfectly formed and a nice pink color. Sweat trickled at his temple, and he could see a fine sheen on Kathleen's chest, but at least the baby was warm enough.

Kathleen tried to sit up away from him, her eyes sharpening as she considered his reply, but her body protested the movement, and with a quiet moan she sank bank against his muscled chest. "What do you mean, she's strong for her size? Is she doing all right or not?"

"She needs an incubator," he said, wrapping his arm around Kathleen and supporting her soft weight. "That's why I'm keeping it so hot in here. She's too small for her body to regulate its own temperature."

Kathleen's face was suddenly white and tense. She had thought everything was fine, despite the baby being a month early. The sudden knowledge that the baby was still in a precarious position stunned her.

"Don't worry," Derek soothed, cradling her close to him. "As long as we keep her nice and warm, she shouldn't have any trouble. I'll keep a close watch on her tonight, and as soon as the weather clears we'll get her to a cozy incubator." He studied the fragile little hand for a moment longer, then tenderly replaced it on Kathleen's breast. "What are you going to name her?"

"Sara Marisa," Kathleen murmured. "Sara is—was—my mother's name. But I'm going to call her Risa. It means 'laughter.'"

Derek's face went still, and his eyes darkened with barely contained emotion as he looked at the baby. "How are you spelling it? S-a-r-a- or S-a-r-a-h?"

"S-a-r-a."

It was still the same name, the name that had become synonymous, in his mind, with love. He had first seen mind-shattering, irrevocable love in Sarah Matthews's face when he had been fifteen, and he had known then that he would never settle for anything less. That was what he wanted to feel, what he wanted to give, what he wanted in return. Sarah's love was a powerful, immense thing, spilling over into the lives of everyone near her, because she gave it so unselfishly. It was because of her that he was a doctor now, because of her that he had been able to finish college at an accelerated pace, because of her that he had a warm, loving extended family where before there had been only himself and his mother. Now this new life was leading him into the sort of love he'd waited for, so it was only fitting that she should be named Sara. He smiled when he thought of Sarah holding her namesake. She and her husband, Rome, could be the baby's godparents, though they'd probably have to share the honor with Max and Claire Conroy, two other very special friends and part of the extended family. He knew how they would all take to Kathleen and the baby, but he wondered how Kathleen would feel, surrounded by all those loving strangers. Anxious? Threatened?

It would take time to teach Kathleen to love him, and all the people who were close to him, but he had all the time in the world. He had the rest of his life.

The baby was asleep now, and gently he took her from Kathleen's arms. "Risa," he murmured, trying her name on his tongue. Yes, the two of them together would overwhelm Kathleen with love.

Kathleen dozed on and off the rest of the night, and every time she woke she saw Derek with her daughter in his arms. The picture of the tall, strong man holding the frail infant with such tender concern gave her a feeling she couldn't identify, as if something expanded in her chest. He didn't let down his guard for a minute all night, but kept vigil over the child, kept the room uncomfortably warm, and held Kathleen so she could nurse her whenever that funny, indignant little squeak told them the baby was getting hungry. Sometime during the night he removed his shirt, and when she woke the next time she was stunned by the primitive beauty of the picture he made, sitting crosslegged before the fire, the powerful muscles of his damp torso gleaming as he cuddled the sleeping baby to him.

It struck her then that he wasn't like other men, but she was too sleepy and too tired to pursue the thought. Her entire body ached, and she was in the grip of a powerful lassitude that kept her thoughts and movements down to a minimum. Tomorrow would be time enough to think.

It stopped snowing around dawn, and the wild, whistling wind died away. It was the pale silence that woke her for good, and she gingerly eased herself into a sitting position, wincing at the pain in her lower body. Derek laid the baby on the mattress and reached out a strong arm to help her.

"I have to go—" she began, stopping abruptly as she wondered how she could phrase the urgent need to a stranger.

"It's about time," he said equably, carefully lifting her in his arms.

Her face turned scarlet as he carried her down the dark, narrow hallway. "I don't need any help!" she protested.

He set her on her feet outside the bathroom door and held her until her legs stopped wobbling. "I put a couple of candles in here last night," he said. "I'll light them, then get out of your way, but I'll be just outside the door if you need me."

She realized that he didn't intend to embarrass her, but neither was he going to let her do more than he deemed wise. There was a calm implacability in his face that told her he wouldn't hesitate to come to her aid if she became too weak to take care of herself. It was difficult to remember that he was a doctor, used to bodies of all sizes and shapes. He just didn't seem like any doctor she'd ever met before.

To her relief, her strength was returning, and she didn't need his help. When she left the bathroom, she walked down the hall under her own power, though he kept a steadying hand under her arm just in case. The baby was still sleeping peacefully on the mattress, and Kathleen looked down at her daughter with a powerful surge of adoration that shook her.

"She's so beautiful," she whispered. "Is she doing okay?"

"She's doing fine, but she needs an incubator until she gains about a pound and a half. The way she's been nursing, that might take only a couple of weeks."

"A couple of weeks!" Kathleen echoed, aghast. "She needs hospital care for a couple of weeks?"

His eyes were steady. "Yes."

Kathleen turned away, her fists knotting. There was no way she could pay what two weeks in a hospital would cost, yet she couldn't see that she had a choice. Risa's life was still a fragile thing, and she would do anything, anything at all, to keep her child alive.

"Does the clinic that you were going to have the facilities to care for her?" he asked.

Another problem. She swallowed. "No. I...I don't have any medical insurance. I was going to have her there, then come home afterward."

"Don't worry about it," he said. "I'll think of something. Now, sweetheart, lie down and let me take a look at you. I want to make sure *you're* doing all right."

It had been bad enough the day before, when she was in labor, but it was worse now. It had been a medical emergency then; now it wasn't. But, again, she had the feeling he would do exactly as he intended, regardless of any objections she raised, so she stared fixedly at the fire as he examined her and firmly kneaded her abdomen.

"You have good muscle tone," he said approvingly. "You'd have had a lot harder time if you hadn't been as strong as you are."

If she was strong, it was the strength given by years of working a small grubby ranch, then long hours of waiting on tables. Spas and gyms were outside her experience.

"What do we do now?" she asked. "Wait?"

"Nope. You're doing well enough to travel, and we can't afford to sit around until the phones are fixed. I'm going to start the Jeep and get it warm, and then I'm taking both you and the baby to a hospital."

She felt instant panic. "You want to take the baby *out*?"

"We have to. We'll keep her warm."

"We can keep her warm here."

"She needs a hospital. She's doing all right now, but things can change in the blink of an eye with a preemie. I'm not going to take that chance with her life."

Kathleen couldn't control a mother's natural fear of exposing her fragile child to the elements. There was no telling which roads were closed, or how long it would take them to reach a hospital. What if they ran off the road and got in a wreck?

Seeing her panic build, Derek reached out and firmly took her arms. "I won't let anything happen," he said calmly, as if he had read her thoughts. "Get dressed while I start the Jeep and fix something for breakfast. Aren't you hungry? You haven't eaten a bite since I found you yesterday."

Only then did she realize how empty she was; it was odd, how even the thought of hunger had been pushed from her mind by all that happened. She changed in her icy bedroom, hurriedly pulling on first one pair of pants after another, and growing more and more frustrated as she found that they were all too small. Finally she settled on one of the first pairs of maternity pants she had bought, when she had begun outgrowing her jeans. Her own body was unfamiliar to her. It felt strange not to have a swollen, cumbersome stomach, strange to actually look down and see her toes. She had to move carefully, but she could put on socks and shoes without twisting into awkward contortions. Still, she didn't have her former slenderness, and it was disconcerting.

After pulling on a white cotton shirt and layering a flannel shirt over it, she pulled a brush through her tangled hair and left the bedroom, too cold to linger and worry about her looks. Wryly, she admitted that he had successfully distracted her from her arguments; she had done exactly as he'd ordered.

When she entered the kitchen, he looked up from his capable preparations of soup and sandwiches to smile at her. "Feel strange not wearing maternity clothes?"

"I am wearing maternity clothes," she said, a faint, very feminine despair in her eyes and voice. "What feels strange is being able to see my feet." Changing the subject, she asked, "Is it terribly cold outside?"

"It's about twenty degrees, but the sky is clearing."

"What hospital are you taking us to to?"

"I've thought about that. I want Risa in my hospital in Dallas."

"Dallas! But that's—"

"I can oversee her care there," Derek interrupted calmly.

"It's too far away," Kathleen said, standing straight. Her green eyes were full of bitter acknowledgment. "And I won't be able to pay. Just take us to a charity hospital."

"Don't worry about paying. I told you I'd take care of you."

"It's still charity, but I'd rather owe a hospital than you."

"You won't owe me." He turned from the old wood stove, and suddenly she felt the full force of his golden brown gaze, fierce and compelling, bending her to his will. "Not if you marry me."

Chapter Four

The words resounded in her head like the ringing of a bell. "Marry you?"

"That's right."

"But . . . *why*?"

"You'll marry me so Risa can have the care she needs. I'll marry you so I can have Risa. You're not in love with someone, are you?" Numbly she shook her head. "I didn't think so. I guess I fell in love with your daughter the minute she came out of you, into my hands. I want to be her father."

"I don't want to get married again, ever!"

"Not even for Risa? If you marry me, you won't have to worry about money again. I'll sign a prenuptial agreement, if you'd like; I'll provide for her, put her through college."

"You can't marry me just because you want my baby. Get married to someone else and have your own children."

"I want Risa," he said with that calm, frightening implacability. Alarm began to fill her as she realized that he never swerved from the course he had set for himself.

"Think, Kathleen. She needs help now, and children need a lot of support through the years. Am I such a monster that you can't stand the thought of being married to me?"

"But you're a stranger! I don't know you and you don't know me. How can you even think of marrying me?"

"I know that you loved your child enough to risk your own life trying to get to the clinic. I know you've had some bad luck in your life, but that you're strong, and you don't give up. We delivered a baby together; how can we be strangers now?"

"I don't know anything about your life."

He shrugged his broad shoulders. "I have a fairly uncomplicated life. I'm a doctor, I live in an apartment, and I'm not a social lion. I'm great with kids, and I won't mistreat you."

"I never thought you would," she said quietly. She had been mistreated, and she knew that Derek was as different from her ex-husband as day was from night. But she simply didn't want another man in her life at all, ever. "What if you fall in love with someone else? Wouldn't that tear Risa's life apart? I'd never give up custody of her!"

"I won't fall in love with anyone else." His voice rang with utter certainty. He just stood there, watching her, but his eyes were working their power on her. Incredibly, she could feel herself weakening inside. As his wife, she wouldn't have the bitter, day after day after day struggle simply to survive. Risa would have the hospital care she needed, and afterward she would have all the advantages Kathleen couldn't give her.

"I couldn't . . . I couldn't have sex with you," she finally said in desperation, because it was her last defense.

"I wouldn't want you to." Before she could decide if she should feel relieved or insulted, he continued, "When we sleep together, I want you to think of it as making love, not having sex. Sex is cheap and easy. Making love means caring and commitment.''

''And you think we'll have that?''

''In time.'' He gave her a completely peaceful smile, as if he sensed her weakening and knew he would have things his way.

Her throat grew tight as she thought about having sex. She didn't know what making love was, and she didn't know if she would ever *want* to know. ''Things . . . have happened to me,'' she said hoarsely. ''I may not ever—''

''In time, sweetheart. You will, in time.''

His very certainty frightened her, because there was something about him that abruptly made her just as certain that, at some point in the future, she would indeed want him to make love to her. The idea was alien to her, making her feel as if her entire life had suddenly been rerouted onto another track. She had had everything planned in her mind: she would raise Risa, totally devoted to her only child, and take pleasure in watching her grow. But there was no room for a man in her plans. Larry Fields had done her a tremendous favor by leaving her, even if he had left her broke and pregnant. But now, here was this man who looked like a warrior angel, taking over her life and shaping it along other lines.

Desperately she tried again. ''We're too different! You're a doctor, and I barely finished high school. I've lived on this scrubby little ranch my entire life. I've never been anywhere or done anything; you'd be bored to death by me within a month!''

Amusement sparkled in his amber eyes as he walked over to her. ''You're talking rubbish,'' he said gently, his hand sliding under her heavy hair to clasp her nape. Before she could react he had bent and firmly pressed his mouth to hers in a warm, strangely intimate kiss; then he released her and moved away before she could become alarmed. She stood there staring at him, her vivid green eyes huge and confused.

"Say yes, then let's eat," he commanded, his eyes still sparkling.

"Yes." Her voice sounded dazed, even to herself.

"That's a good girl." He put his warm hand on her elbow and led her to the table, then carefully got her seated. She was uncomfortable, but was not in such pain that it killed her appetite. Hungrily they ate chicken noodle soup and toasted cheese sandwiches, washed down with good strong coffee. It wasn't normal breakfast fare, but after not eating for so long, she was delighted with it. Then he insisted that she sit still while he cleaned up the kitchen, something that had never happened to her before. She felt pampered, and dazed by all that had happened and she had agreed to.

"I'll pack a few of your clothes and nightgowns, but you won't need much," he said. "Where are the baby's things?"

"In the bottom drawer of my dresser, but some of her clothes are in the truck. I didn't think to get them yesterday when you stopped."

"We'll pick them up on the way. Come into the living room with the baby while I get everything loaded."

She held the sleeping child while he swiftly packed and carried the things out. When he had finished, he brought a tiny, crocheted baby cap that he'd found in the drawer, and put it on Risa's downy head to help keep her warm. Then he wrapped her snugly in several blankets, helped Kathleen into her heavy coat, put the baby in Kathleen's arms, and lifted both of them into his.

"I can walk," she protested, her heart giving a huge leap at being in his arms again. He had kissed her. . . .

"No going up or down steps just yet," he explained. "And no climbing into the Jeep. Keep Risa's face covered."

He was remarkably strong, carrying her with no evident difficulty. His strides were sure as he waded through the snow, avoiding the path he'd already made because it had become icy. Kathleen blinked at the stark whiteness of the landscape. The wind had blown the snow into enormous drifts that almost obliterated the fence line and had piled against the sides of the house and barn. But the air was still and crisp now, the fog of her breath gusting straight out in front of her.

He had turned the heater in the Jeep on high, and it was uncomfortably warm for her. "I'll have to take off this coat," she muttered.

"Wait until we've stopped to get the things out of your truck, or you'll get chilled with the door open."

She watched as he went back inside to bank the fires in the fireplace and the wood stove, and to lock the doors. She had lived in this house her entire life, but suddenly she wondered if she'd ever see it again, and if she cared. Her life here hadn't been happy.

Her confusion and hesitancy faded as if they had never been. This place wasn't what she wanted for Risa. For her daughter, she wanted so much more than what she had had. She didn't want Risa to wear patched and faded clothes, to marry out of desperation, or to miss out on the pleasures of life because all her free time was spent on chores.

Derek was taking her away from this, but she wouldn't rely on him. She had made the mistake of relying on a man once before, and she wouldn't do it again. Kathleen decided that as soon as she had recovered from giving birth, and Risa was stronger, she would get a job, save her money, work to better herself. If Derek ever walked away from her as Larry had done, she wouldn't be left stone broke and without the means to support herself. Risa would never have to go hungry or cold.

Five hours later, Kathleen was lying on a snowy-white hospital bed, watching the color television attached to the wall. Her private room was almost luxurious, with a full bath and a pair of comfortable recliners, small oil paintings on the wall, and fresh flowers on her bedside table. The snowstorm hadn't reached as far south as Dallas, and from the window she could see a blue sky only occasionally studded with clouds.

Risa had been whisked away to the neonatal unit, with people jumping to obey Derek's orders. Kathleen herself had been examined by a cheerful obstetrician named Monica Sudley and pronounced in excellent condition. "But I never expected anything different," Dr. Sudley had said casually. "Not with Dr. Taliferro taking care of you."

Dr. Taliferro. Her mind had accepted him as a doctor, but somehow she hadn't really understood it until she had seen him here, in his own milieu, where his deep voice took on a crisp tone of command, and everyone scrambled to satisfy him. She had only seen him wearing jeans and boots and a casual shirt, with his heavy shearling coat, but after arriving at the hospital he had showered and shaved, then changed into the fresh clothes he kept in his office for just such situations. He had seen to Risa, then visited Kathleen to reassure her that the trip hadn't harmed the infant in any way.

He had been the same, yet somehow different. Perhaps it was only the clothes, the dark slacks, white shirt and blue-striped tie, as well as the lab coat he wore over them and the stethoscope around his neck. It was typical doctor's garb, but the effect was jarring. She couldn't help remembering the firelight flickering on his gleaming, muscled shoulders, or the hard, chiseled purity of his profile as he looked down at the child in his arms.

It was also hard to accept the fact that she had agreed to marry him.

Every few hours she put on a robe and walked to the neonatal unit, where Risa was taken out of the incubator and given to her to be fed. The sight of the other frail babies, some of them much smaller than Risa, shook her. They were enclosed in their little glass cubicles with various tubes running into their tiny naked bodies, while little knit caps covered their heads. Thank God Risa was strong enough to nurse!

The first time she fed her daughter, she was led to a rocking chair in a small room away from the other babies, and Risa was brought to her.

"So you're the mother of this little honey," the young nurse said as she laid Risa in Kathleen's eager arms. "She's adorable. I've never seen so much hair on a newborn, and look how long it is! Dr. Taliferro had us scrambling like we were having an air raid until we had her all comfy. Did he really deliver her?"

Faint color burned along Kathleen's cheekbones. Somehow it seemed too intimate to discuss, even though giving birth was an everyday occurrence to the staff. But the young nurse was looking at her with bright, expectant eyes, so she said uncomfortably, "Yes. My truck slid off the road during the blizzard. Derek came by and found me."

"Ohmigod, talk about romantic!"

"Having a baby?" Kathleen asked skeptically.

"Honey, digging ditches would be romantic if Dr. Taliferro helped! Isn't he something? All the babies know whenever he's the one holding them. They never get scared or cry with him. Sometimes he stays here all night with a critical baby, holding it and talking to it, watching it every minute, and a lot of his babies make it when no one else gave them much of a chance."

The nurse seemed to have a case of hero worship for Derek, or maybe it was more than that. He was incredibly good-looking, and a hospital was a hothouse for romances. It made Kathleen uneasy; why was she even thinking of marrying a man who would constantly be pursued and tempted?

"Have you worked in this unit for long?" she asked, trying to change the subject.

"A little over a year. I love it. These little tykes need all the help they can get, and, of course, I'd have walked barefoot over hot coals to get to work with Dr. Taliferro. Hospitals and clinics from all over the nation were fighting to get him."

"Why? Isn't he too young to have built a reputation yet?" She didn't know how old he was, but guessed he was no older than his midthirties, perhaps even younger.

"He's younger than most of them, but he finished college when he was nineteen. He graduated from med school at the top of his class, interned at one of the nation's best trauma centers, then studied neonatal medicine with George Oliver, who's also one of the best. He's thirty-two, I think."

It was odd to learn so much about her future husband from a stranger, and odder still to find he was considered a medical genius, one of those rare doctors whose very name on the staff listing gave a hospital instant credibility. To hide her expression, she looked down at Risa and gently stroked the baby's cheek. "He sat up all night holding Risa," she heard herself say in a strange voice.

The nurse smiled. "He would. And he's still on the floor now, when he should be home sleeping. But that's Dr. Taliferro for you; he puts the babies before himself."

When Kathleen was back in her room, she kept thinking of the things the nurse had told her, and of the things Derek had said to her. He wanted Risa, he'd said. Was that reason enough to marry a woman he didn't love, when he could marry any woman he wanted and have his own children? Of course, he'd also said that eventually he expected to have a normal marriage with her, meaning he intended to sleep with her, so she had to assume he also intended to have children with her. But why was he so certain he'd never fall in love with someone and want out of the marriage?

"Problems?"

The deep, quiet voice startled her, and she looked up to find Derek standing just inside the door, watching her. She'd been so engrossed in her thoughts that she hadn't heard him.

"No, no problems. I was just . . . thinking."

"Worrying, you mean. Forget about all your second thoughts," he said with disquieting perception. "Just trust me, and let me handle everything. I've made arrangements for us to be married as soon as you're released from the hospital."

"So soon?" she gasped.

"Is there any reason to wait? You'll need a place to live, so you might as well live with me."

"But what about blood tests—"

"The lab here will handle them. When you're released, we'll get our marriage license and go straight to a judge who's an old friend of mine. My apartment is near here, so it'll be convenient for you to come back and forth to feed Risa until she's released. We can use the time to get a nursery fixed up for her."

She felt helpless. As he'd said, he had handled everything.

Chapter Five

Kathleen felt as if she'd been swept up by a tornado, and this one was named Derek. Everything went the way he directed. He even had a dress for her to wear for the wedding, a lovely blue-green silk that darkened her eyes to emerald, as well as a scrumptious black fake-fur coat, shoes, underwear, even makeup. A hairdresser came to the hospital that morning and fixed her hair in a chic, upswept style. Yes, he had everything under control. It was almost frightening.

He kept his warm hand firmly on her waist as they got the marriage license, then went to the judge's chamber to be married. There, Kathleen got another surprise: the chamber was crowded with people, all of whom seemed ridiculously delighted that Derek was marrying a woman he didn't love.

His mother and stepfather were there; dazedly, Kathleen wondered what his mother must think of all this. But Marcie, as she had insisted Kathleen call her, was beaming with delight as she hugged Kathleen. There were two other couples, two teenagers, and three younger children. One of the couples consisted of a tall, hard-looking man with graying black hair and a wand-slender woman with almost silver-white hair and glowing green eyes. Derek introduced them as Rome and Sarah Matthews, very good friends of his, but something in his voice hinted at a deeper relationship. Sarah's face was incredibly tender as she hugged him, them Kathleen.

The other couple was Max and Claire Conroy, and again Kathleen got the feeling that Derek meant something special to them. Max was aristocratic and incredibly handsome, with gilded hair and turquoise eyes, while Claire was quieter and more understated, but her soft brown eyes didn't miss a thing. The three youngsters belong to the Conroys, while the two teenagers were Rome and Sarah's children.

Everyone was ecstatic that Derek was marrying, and Marcie couldn't wait to get to the hospital to visit her new grandchild. She scolded Derek severely for not contacting her immediately, but stopped in midtirade when he leaned down and kissed her cheek, smiling at her in that serene way of his. "I know. You had a good reason," she sighed.

"Yes, Mother."

"You'd think I'd eventually learn."

He grinned. "Yes, Mother."

The women all wore corsages, and Sarah pressed an arrangement of orchids into Kathleen's hands. Kathleen held the fragile flowers in shaking fingers as she and Derek stood before the judge, whose quiet voice filled the silent chamber as he spoke the traditional words about love and honor. She could feel the heat of Derek's body beside her, like a warm wall she could lean against if she became tired. They made the proper responses, then Derek was sliding a gold band set with an emerald surrounded by small, glittering diamonds on her finger. She blinked at it in surprise, then looked up at him just as the judge pronounced them man and wife, and Derek leaned down to kiss her.

She had expected the sort of brief, warm kiss he had given her before. She wasn't prepared for the way he molded her lips with his, or the passion evident in the way his tongue probed her mouth. She quivered, her hands going up to grab his shoulders in an effort to steady herself. His hard arms pressed her to him for a moment, then slowly released her as he lifted his head. Purely male satisfaction was gleaming in his eyes, and she knew he'd felt her surprised response to him.

Then everyone was surrounding them, laughing and shaking his hand, and there was a lot of kissing and hugging. Even the judge got hugged and kissed.

Half an hour later Derek called a halt to the festivities. "We'll have a real celebration later," he promised. "Right now, I'm taking Kathleen home to rest. We have to be back at the hospital in a couple of hours to feed Risa, so she doesn't have a lot of time to put her feet up."

"I'm fine," she felt obliged to protest, though in truth she would have appreciated the chance to rest.

Derek gave her a stern look, and she felt inexplicably guilty. Sarah laughed. "You might as well do what he says," the older woman said in gentle amusement. "You can't get around him."

Five minutes later Kathleen was sitting in the Jeep as he expertly threaded his way through the Dallas traffic. "I like your friends," she finally said, just to break the silence. She couldn't believe she'd done it; she had actually married him! "What do they do?"

"Rome is president and CEO of Spencer-Nyle Corporation. Sarah owns Tools and Dyes, a handcraft store. Two stores now, since she just opened another one. Max was a vice president at Spencer-Nyle with

Rome, but about five years ago he started his own consulting business. Claire owns a bookstore.''

His friends were obviously very successful, and she wondered again why he had married her, because she wasn't successful at all. How would she ever fit in? "And your mother?" she asked quietly.

"Mother helps Whit run his ranch, just across the Oklahoma border. I'd spent Christmas with them, and was on the way back to Dallas when I found you," he explained.

She didn't have anything else to ask him, so silence reigned again until they reached his apartment. "We'll look for something bigger in a few weeks, after your doctor releases you," he said as they left the elevator. "I've shoved things around and made closet space, but feel free to tell me to rearrange anything else you'd like moved."

"Why should I change anything?"

"To accommodate you and Risa. I'm not a bachelor any longer. I'm a husband and a father. We're a family; this is your home as much as mine."

He said it so simply, as if he were impervious to all the doubts that assailed her. She stood to the side as he unlocked the door, but before she could move to enter the apartment he turned back to her and swept her up in his arms, then carried her across the threshold. The gesture startled her, but then, everything he'd done that day had startled her. Everything he'd done from the moment she met him had startled her.

"Would you like a nap?" he asked, standing in the foyer with her still in his arms, as if awaiting directions.

"No, just sitting down for a while will do it." She managed a smile for him. "I had a baby, not major surgery, and you said yourself that I'm strong. Why should I act like a wilting lily when I'm not?''

He cleared his throat as he carefully placed her on her feet. ''Actually, I said that you have great muscle tone. I don't believe I was admiring your strength.''

Her pulse leaped. He was doing that to her more and more often, saying little things that made it plain he found her desirable, or stealing some of those quick kisses. Five days earlier she would never have found those small advances anything but repulsive, but already a secret thrill warmed her whenever he said or did anything. She was changing rapidly under his intense coddling, and, to her surprise, she liked the changes.

''What are you thinking?'' he asked, tapping her nose with a fingertip. ''You're staring at me, but you aren't seeing me.''

''I was thinking how much you spoil me,'' she replied honestly. ''And how unlike me it is to let you do it.''

''Why shouldn't you let me spoil you?'' He helped her off with her coat and hung it in the small foyer closet.

''I've never been spoiled before. I've always had to look out for myself, because no one else really cared, not even my parents. I can't figure out why you should be so kind, or what you're getting out of our deal. You've done all this, but basically we're still strangers. What do you want from me?''

A faint smile touched his chiseled lips as he held out his hand. ''Come with me.''

''Where?''

''To the bedroom. I want to show you something.''

Lifting her brows in curiosity at his manner, Kathleen put her hand in his and let him lead her to the bedroom. She looked around. It was a cheerful, spacious room, decorated in blue and white and with a king-size bed. The sliding closet doors were mirrored, and he positioned her in front of the mirrors with himself behind her.

Putting his hands on her shoulders, he said, "Look in the mirror and tell me what you see."

"Us."

"Is that all? Look at yourself, and tell me what I got out of our deal."

She looked in the mirror and shrugged. "A woman." Humor suddenly sparked in her eyes. "With great muscle tone."

He chuckled. "Hallelujah, yes. But that's only part of it. That's not to say I'm not turned on by your fantastic legs and gorgeous breasts, because I am, but what really gets me is what I see in your face."

He'd done it again. She felt her entire body grow warm as her eyes met his in the mirror. "My face?"

One arm slid around her waist, pulling her back to lean against him, while his other hand rose to stroke her face. "Your wonderful green eyes," he murmured. "Frightened and brave at the same time. I sometimes see hurt in your eyes, as if you're remembering things you don't want to talk about, but you don't let it get you down. You don't ask me for anything, so I have to guess at what you need, and maybe I overdo it. I see pleasure when I hold you or kiss you. I see love for Risa, and compassion for the other babies. I've turned your life upside down, but you haven't let it get to you; you've just gone along with me and kept your head above water. You're a survivor, Kath. A strong, valiant, loving survivor. That's what I got out of the deal. As well as a great body, of course, and a beautiful baby girl.''

The eyes he had described were wide as Kathleen heard all those characteristics attributed to herself. He smiled and let his fingers touch her lips. ''Did I forget to mention what a kissable mouth you have? How sweet and soft it is?''

Her mouth suddenly felt swollen, and her lips moved against his fingers. ''I get the picture,'' she breathed, her heart pounding at her aggressiveness. ''You married me for my body.''

''And what a body it is.'' He bent his head to nuzzle her ear, while his hands drifted to her breasts and gently cupped them. ''While we're being so honest, why did you marry me? Other than to give Risa all the advantages of being a doctor's daughter.''

''That was it,'' she said, barely able to speak. She was stunned by his touch to her breasts, stunned and scared and shocked, because she was aware of a sense of pleasure. Never before had she enjoyed having a man touch her so intimately. But her breasts were sensitive now, ripe and full of milk, and his light touch seared through her like a lightning bolt.

''Forget about what I can give Risa,'' he murmured. ''Wasn't part of your reason for marrying me because of what I can give you?''

''I . . . I can live without luxury.'' Her voice was low and strained, and her eyelids were becoming so heavy she could barely hold them open. Her mind wasn't on what she was saying. The pleasure was so intense it was interfering with her breathing, making it fast and heavy. Frantically she tried to tell herself it was only because she *was* nursing Risa that her breasts were so warm and sensitive, and that, being a doctor, he knew it and how to exploit it. He wasn't even touching her nipples, but lightly stroking around them. She thought she would die if he touched her nipples.

"You look gorgeous in this dress, but let's get you out of it and into something more comfortable," he whispered, and his hands left her breasts. She stood pliantly, dazed with pleasure, as he unzipped the lovely dress and slipped it off her shoulders, then pushed it down over her hips to let it fall at her feet. She wore a slip under it, and she waited in a haze for him to remove it, too, but instead he lifted her in his arms and placed her on the bed, moving slowly, as if trying not to startle her. Her heart was pounding, but her body felt liquid with pleasure. She had just had a baby; he knew she couldn't let him do *that*...didn't he? But he was a doctor; perhaps he knew more than she did. No, it would hurt too much.

Perhaps he had something else in mind. She thought of his hands on her naked skin, of feeling his big, muscled body naked against her, and a strange excitement made her nerves throb. Slowly the thought filled her mind that she trusted him, truly trusted him, and that was why she wasn't afraid. No matter what, Derek would never hurt her.

His eyelashes were half-lowered over his eyes, giving him a sensually sleepy look as he slipped her shoes off and let them drop to the floor. Kathleen watched him in helpless fascination, her breath stilling in her lungs when he reached up under her slip and began pulling her panty hose down. "Lift your hips," he instructed in a husky voice, and she obeyed willingly. When the nylon was bunched around her knees, he bent and pressed a kiss to her bare thighs before returning to his pleasant task and removing the garment.

Her skin felt hot, and the bed linens were cool beneath her. She had never *felt* so much before, as if the nerve endings in her skin had multiplied and become incredibly sensitive. Her limbs felt heavy and boneless, and she couldn't move, even when his hands stroked her thighs and pleasure shivered through her. "Derek," she whispered, vaguely surprised to find that she could barely speak; she had slurred his name, as if it were too much effort to talk.

"Hmm?" He was bent over her, the warmth of his body soothing her as he lifted her with one arm and stripped the cover back on the bed, then settled her between the sheets. His mouth feathered over her breasts, barely touching the silk that covered them.

Incredible waves of relaxation were sweeping over her. "You can't make love to me," she managed to whisper. "Not yet."

"I know, sweetheart," he murmured, his deep voice low and hypnotic. "Go to sleep. We have plenty of time."

Her lashes fluttered down, and with a slow, deep sigh she went to sleep. Derek straightened, looking down at her. His body throbbed with the need for sexual relief, but a faint, tender smile curved his lips as he watched her. She had called it "sex" before, but this time she had said "make love." She was losing her wariness, though she still seemed to have no idea why he had married her. Did she think she was so totally without charm or appeal? Did she truly think he'd married her only because of Risa? He'd done his best to convince her that he was attracted to her, but the final argument would have to wait about five weeks longer.

Her thick lashes made dark fans on her cheeks, just as Risa's did. He wanted to lie down beside her and hold her while she slept. He'd known she was tired; since Risa's birth, Kathleen had been sleeping a great deal, as if she had been pushing herself far too hard for far too long. Her body was insisting on catching up on its healing rest now that she no longer had such a pressing need to do everything herself.

The telephone in the living room rang, but he'd had the foresight to unplug the phone by the bed, so Kathleen slept on undisturbed. Quickly he left the room, closing the door behind him, and picked up the other extension.

"Derek, is she asleep yet?" Sarah's warm voice held a certain amusement, as if she had known he would somehow have gotten Kathleen to take a nap by now.

He grinned. Sarah knew him even better than his mother, better than anyone else in the world, except perhaps Claire. Claire saw into people, but she was so quiet that it was easy to underestimate her perception.

"She didn't think she needed a nap, but she went to sleep as soon as she lay down."

"Somehow, I never doubted it. Anyway, I've had an idea. Now that I've opened up the other store, I need to hire someone else. Do you think Kathleen would be interested? Erica is going to manage the new store, so I thought Kathleen could work with me, and she'd be able to have the baby with her."

Leave it to Sarah to notice that Kathleen needed a friend, as well as the measure of independence the job would give her while she adjusted to being his wife.

"She'll probably jump at it, but it'll be a couple of weeks before she's able to drive, and at least that long before Risa will be strong enough."

"Then I'll hold the job for her," Sarah said serenely.

"I'm going to remind you of this the next time you accuse me of 'managing' people," he informed her, smiling.

"But hadn't you already thought of it?"

His smile grew. "Of course."

Chapter Six

The day they brought Risa home from the hospital, Kathleen could barely tolerate having the baby out of her sight for a moment. Risa was thirteen days old, and now weighed a grand total of five pounds and six ounces, which was still two ounces short of the five and a half pounds a baby normally had to weigh before Derek would allow it to be released from the neonatal unit, but, as he'd noted before, she was strong. Her cheeks had attained a newborn's plumpness, and she was nursing vigorously, with about four hours between each feeding.

Derek drove them home, then left the Cherokee with Kathleen so she would have a way of getting around if she needed anything, a gesture that eased a worry she hadn't known she had until he gave her the keys. The hospital was only a few blocks away, and the January day was mild, so he walked back.

She spent the day playing with Risa when the baby was awake, and watching her while she slept. Late that afternoon, Kathleen realized with a start that she hadn't given a thought to what she would prepare for dinner, and guilt filled her. Derek had been a saint, coddling her beyond all reason, letting her devote all her time to Risa, doing all the household chores himself, but Risa's homecoming marked a change in the status quo. It had been two weeks since Risa's birth, and Kathleen felt better than she had in years. She was rested, her appetite was better; there was no reason to let Derek continue to wait on her as if she was an invalid. He had given everything, and she had given nothing, not even her attention.

She rolled Risa's bassinet, which she and Derek had bought only the day before, into the kitchen so she could watch Risa while she prepared dinner. The baby slept peacefully, with the knuckles of one fist shoved into her mouth, undisturbed by the rattling of pots and pans. It was the first time Kathleen had cooked, so she had to hunt for everything, and it took her twice as long to do anything than it normally would have. She was relieved when Derek didn't come home at his usual time, since she was running behind schedule, but when half an hour had passed she became concerned. It wasn't like him to be late without calling her himself or having a nurse call to let her know that one of the babies needed him. As short a time as they had been married, she had already learned that about him. Derek was always considerate.

Derek was . . . incredible.

She wanted to give him something, even if it was just a hot meal waiting for him when he came home. She looked at the steaming food, ready to be served, but he wasn't there. She could keep it warming on the stove, but it wouldn't be the same.

Then she heard his key in the door, and she was filled with relief. She hurried out of the kitchen to greet him, her face alight with pleasure.

"I was worried," she said in a rush, then was afraid he would think she was complaining, so she changed what she had been about to say. "Believe it or not, I actually cooked dinner. But I couldn't find anything, and it took me forever to do. I was afraid you'd be home before everything was finished, because I wanted to surprise you.''

His eyes were warm as he put his arm around her shoulders and hugged her to him for a kiss. He kissed her a lot, sometimes with carefully restrained passion, and she had stopped being shocked by her own pleasure in his touch.

"I'm more than surprised, I'm downright grateful," he said, kissing her again. "I'm also starving. Where's Risa?"

"In the kitchen, where I could watch her sleep."

"I wondered if you'd spend the day hanging over her bassinet."

"Actually, yes."

His arm was around her waist as they walked into the kitchen. Risa was still asleep, so he didn't disturb her by picking her up. He set the table while Kathleen served the food, then they ate leisurely, one of the few times they'd had a chance to do so. Kathleen knew she was a good cook, and it gave her a great deal of satisfaction to watch Derek eat with evident enjoyment.

When they had finished, he helped her clean up, then, as sort of an afterthought, took a set of car keys out of his pocket and gave them to her. She took them, frowning at him in puzzlement. "I already have keys to the Cherokee."

"These aren't for the Jeep," he explained calmly, going into the living room and sitting down to read the newspaper. "They're for your car. I picked it up on the way home this afternoon."

Her car? She didn't own a car, just the old truck. The truth burst in her mind like a sunrise, robbing her of breath. "I can't take a car from you," she said, her voice strained.

He looked up from the newspaper, his black brows rising in a question. "Is there a problem? If you don't want the car, I'll drive it, and you can have the Jeep. I can't continue walking to the hospital, so buying a car seemed like the logical thing to do."

She felt like screaming. He'd hemmed her in with logic. He was right, of course, but that only made her feel more helpless. She'd felt so proud of preparing dinner for him, the first time she'd contributed anything to their marriage, while he'd stopped on the way home and bought a *car* for her! She felt like an insatiable sponge, soaking up everything he had to give and demanding more just by her very existence, her presence in his life.

Licking her lips, she said, "I'm sorry. I'm just ... stunned. No one ever bought ... I don't know what to say."

He appeared to give it thought, but his eyes were twinkling. "I suppose you could do what anyone else would do: jump up and down, squeal, laugh, throw your arms around my neck and kiss me until I beg for mercy."

Her heart jumped wildly. He was as splendid as a pagan god, powerfully built and powerfully male; that wasn't a twinkle in his eyes, after all, but a hard, heated gleam, and he was looking at her the way men have looked at women since the beginning of time. Her mouth went suddenly dry, and she had to lick her lips again.

"Is that what you want me to do?" she whispered.

He carefully put the newspaper aside. "You can skip the jumping and squealing, if you want. I won't mind if you go straight to the kissing part."

She didn't remember moving, but somehow she found herself on his lap, her arms around his strong neck, her mouth under his. He had kissed her so often in the week they'd been married that she'd become used to it, expected it, enjoyed it. In a way his kisses reassured her that she would be able to give something to give, even if it were only physical ease. She couldn't even do that completely, at the present, but at least the potential was there. If he wanted her to kiss him, she was more than willing.

His arms closed around her, holding her to his strong chest as he deepened the kiss, his tongue moving to touch hers. Kathleen felt very brave and bold; she had no idea that her kisses were rather timid and untutored, or that he was both touched and highly aroused by her innocence. He kissed her slowly, thoroughly, teaching her how to use her tongue and how to accept his, holding himself under tight control lest he alarm her.

Finally she turned her head away, gasping for breath, and he smiled because she had forgotten to breathe. "Are you ready to beg for mercy?" she panted, color high in her face.

"I don't know anyone named Mercy," he muttered, turning her face back to his for another taste of her mouth. "Why would I beg for a woman I don't even know?"

Her chuckle was muted by his lips as he turned passion to teasing, kissing her all over her face with loud smacking noises. Then he hoisted her to her feet and got to his. "Wake up the tiny tyrant so I can show you which car is yours," he said, grinning.

Kathleen threw an anxious look at the sleeping baby. "Should we take her out in the cold?"

"Do you want to leave her here by herself? Unless you want to try the key in every car in the parking lot, you have to know which one is yours. It won't take a minute; just wrap her up and keep her head covered. It isn't that cold outside, anyway."

"Are you certain it won't hurt her?"

He gave her a very level look, and without another word she turned to get a jacket for herself and a blanket for Risa. She felt like kicking herself. Did he think she didn't trust him to know what would harm the baby and what wouldn't? He was a doctor, for heaven's sake! He'd taken care of her and Risa from the moment they'd met. She'd really made a mess of it again, kissing him as if she could eat him up one minute, then practically insulting him the next.

When she returned with the blanket, he'd already picked Risa up, waking her, and he was crooning to her. Risa watched him with a ridiculously serious expression, her tiny face intent as she stared up at him, her hands waving erratically. To Kathleen's surprise, the baby was working her rosebud mouth as if trying to mimic Derek's actions. She seemed totally fascinated by the man holding her.

"Here's the blanket."

He took it and deftly wrapped Risa in it, covering her head. The baby began fussing, and Derek chuckled. "We'd better hurry. She won't tolerate this for long; she wants to see what's going on."

They hurried down to the parking lot, and Derek led her to a white Oldsmobile Calais. Kathleen had to swallow her gasp. It was a new car, not a used one, as she'd expected. It was sleek and sporty looking, with a soft dove-grey interior and every optional convenience she could think of. Tears burned her eyes.

"I...I don't know what to say," she whispered as she stared at it in shock.

"Say you love it, promise me that you'll always wear your seat belt, and we'll take the baby back inside before she works herself into a tantrum. She doesn't like this blanket over her face one bit." Risa's fussing was indeed rising in volume.

"I love it," she said, dazed.

He laughed and put his arm around her waist as the fussing bundle in his arms began to wail furiously. They hurried back inside, and he lifted the blanket to reveal Risa's red, tightly screwed-up face. "Stop that," he said gently, touching her cheek. She gave a few more wails, then hiccuped twice and settled down, once more intently staring up at his face.

He was perfect. Everything he did only compounded the imbalance in the deal she'd made with him. He not only took care of everything, gave her everything, but he was better at taking care of Risa. The parents of his tiny patients all thought he ranked right up there with the angels, and all the nurses were in love with him. He could have had anyone, but instead he'd chosen to saddle himself with a...a *hick* who didn't know anything but how to work a ranch, and a child who wasn't his. Kathleen felt like a parasite. If nothing else, she could begin to repay him for the car, but to do that she'd have to get a job.

She took a deep breath and broached the subject as soon as he'd laid Risa down. Kathleen didn't believe in putting things off. She'd learned the hard way that they didn't go away; it was better to meet trouble head-on. "I'm going to start looking for a job."

"If you feel well enough," he said absently as he tucked a light blanket around the baby. "You might want to call Sarah; she mentioned something about needing more help in one of her stores."

She'd been braced for objections, but his matter-of-fact acceptance made her wonder why she'd thought he wouldn't like the idea. Then she realized she had expected him to act as Larry would have; Larry hadn't wanted her to do anything except work like a slave on the ranch, and wait on him hand and foot. If she'd gone out and gotten a job, she might have been able to get out from under his thumb before he'd finished bleeding her dry. Derek wasn't like that. Derek wanted her to be happy.

It was an astounding revelation. Kathleen couldn't remember anyone ever going out of their way to give her any sort of happiness. Yet since Derek had appeared in her life, everything he'd done had been with her happiness and well-being in mind.

She thought about his suggestion, and she liked it. She wasn't trained to do anything except be a waitress, but she did know how to operate a cash register; working in a crafts store sounded interesting. She made up her mind to call Sarah Matthews the next day.

When they went to bed that night, Derek practically had to drag Kathleen out of the nursery. "Maybe I should sleep in here," she said worriedly. "What if she cries and I can't hear her?"

Sleeping in the same bed with her without touching her had been one of the worst tortures a man had ever devised for himself, but Derek wasn't about to give it up. Besides, he was ready to advance his plan a step, which wouldn't work if Kathleen wasn't in bed with him. He'd anticipated all her first-night-with-a-new-baby jitters, and set about soothing them. "I bought a baby-alarm system," he said, and placed a small black speaker by Risa's crib. "The other speaker will be by our bed. We'll be able to hear if she cries."

"But she needs to be kept warm—"

"We'll leave the heat turned up, but close the vents in our room." As he talked, he was leading her to the bedroom. He'd already closed the heat vents, and the room was noticeably cooler than the rest of the apartment. Anticipation made his heart beat faster. For over a week he'd let her get used to his presence in the bed; he even knew why she tolerated it. She thought she *owed* it to him. But now he was going to get her used to his touch as well as his presence, and he meant more than those kisses that were driving him wild. He wanted her so much he ached with it, and tonight he would take another step toward his goal.

She crawled into bed and pulled the covers up over her. Derek turned out the light, then dropped his pajama bottoms to the floor and, blissfully nude, got in beside her. He normally slept nude, but had worn the aggravating pajamas since their marriage, and it was a relief to shed them.

The cold room would do the rest. She would seek out his warmth during the night, and when she woke up, she would be in his arms. A smile crossed his face as he thought of it.

The baby alarm worked. A little after one, Kathleen woke at the first tentative wail. She felt deliciously warm, and groaned at the idea of getting up. She was so comfortable, with her head on Derek's shoulder and his arms around her so tightly—

Her eyes flew open, and she sat up in bed. "I'm sorry," she blurted.

He yawned sleepily. "For what?"

"I was all over you!"

"Hell, sweetheart, I enjoyed it! Would you listen to that little terror scream," he said in admiration, changing the subject. Yawning again, he reached out to turn on the lamp, then got out of bed. Kathleen's entire body jerked in shock. He was naked! Gloriously naked. Beautifully naked. Her mouth went dry, and her full breasts tightened until they began to ache.

He held out his hand to her. "Come on, sweetheart. Let's see about our daughter."

Still in shock, she put her hand in his as he gave her a slow, wicked smile that totally robbed her of breath.

Chapter Seven

That smile remained in her mind the next morning as she drove carefully to Sarah Matthews's store, following the directions she'd gotten from Sarah only an hour before. Risa slept snugly in her car seat, having survived the first night in her crib, as well as being tended by her gorgeous, naked daddy. Kathleen had been too stunned to do anything but sit in the rocking chair and hold Risa to her breast. Derek had done everything else. And after Risa was asleep again, Kathleen had gone docilely back to bed again, and let him gather her close to his warm, muscular *naked* body... and enjoyed it.

Enjoyed seemed like too mild a description for the way her thoughts and emotions had rioted. Part of her had wanted to touch him, taste him, run her hands all over his magnificent body. Another part of her had panicked; deep in her mind she still hadn't recovered from the brutal, contemptuous way that Larry had humiliated her before walking out.

She didn't want to think about that; she shoved the memory from her mind, and found the blank space it left promptly filled by Derek's sensual, knowing smile. *That was it!* Knowing! He'd known exactly how she had felt!

She found the cozy crafts store easily enough, despite her lack of total attention to where she was going. There was ample parking, but she carefully parked her spotless new car well away from everyone else, then gathered Risa and the ton of paraphernalia babies required into her arms and entered the store.

There were several customers browsing and chatting with Sarah, as well as each other, but when Kathleen came in a glowing smile lit Sarah's face, and she came right over to take the baby from her arms. "What a darling," she whispered, examining the sleeping infant. "She's beautiful. Missy and Jed will spoil her rotten, just like Derek spoiled them when they were little. I brought Jed's old playpen and set it up in the back, where I used to keep my kids, if you want to put all Risa's stuff back there."

Kathleen carried the bulging diaper bag into the back room, which was a section of the store stocked with doll supplies, as well as a cozy area with several rocking chairs, where Sarah's customers could sit and chat if they wanted. It was the most popular area of the store, and warmer than the front section. A sturdy playpen had been set up next to the rocking chairs, and Kathleen looked at it in bewilderment.

"You drove home to get the playpen after I called you this morning? Who watched the store?"

Sarah laughed, her warm green eyes twinkling. "Actually, I've had the playpen set up for several days. I called Derek the day you were married and told him I needed help here, if he thought you'd be interested."

"He didn't tell me until last night," Kathleen said, wondering if she should be angry at his manipulation, and also wondering if it would do any good.

"Of course not. I knew he'd wait until Risa was home and you were feeling better. But don't let the playpen pressure you into thinking you have to take the job if you don't want it."

Kathleen took a deep breath. "I'd like to take the job. I don't have any training for anything except being a waitress and doing ranch work, but I can work a cash register."

Sarah beamed at her. "Then it's settled. When can you start?"

Kathleen looked around the warm, homey store. This would be a good place to work, even though she hated the idea of leaving Risa during the day. She would have to find a day-care center or a babysitter nearby, so she could nurse the baby during lunch. She supposed Risa would have to get used to a bottle for supplemental feedings, though it made her want to cry to think about it. "I'll have to find someone to keep Risa before I can start," she said reluctantly.

Sarah blinked in surprise. "Why? My babies grew up in this store. That way I could keep them with me. Just bring Risa with you; you'll have more helping hands than you can count. Whenever you feel strong enough to start work—"

"I'm strong enough now," Kathleen said. "After working on a ranch my entire life, I'm as strong as a packhorse."

"What does Derek think about this?" Sarah asked, then laughed at herself. "Never mind. He wouldn't have told you about the job if he didn't think you were well enough to handle it. It isn't hard work; the only physical labor is putting up stock, and Jed usually manhandles the boxes for me."

Kathleen searched her memory for a picture of Jed, because she knew he'd been at her wedding. "Is Jed the tall, black-haired boy?"

"Yes. My baby's almost six feet tall. It's ridiculous how fast they grow up. Enjoy every moment with Risa, because her babyhood won't last long." Sarah smiled down at the sleeping bundle in her arms, then leaned over and gently deposited Risa in the playpen. "She's gorgeous. Derek must be insufferably proud of her."

It hit Kathleen like a slap that everyone must think Risa was truly Derek's daughter, which would explain why he had hustled Kathleen into such a hasty marriage. Why wouldn't they think it? Risa's hair was the same inky shade as Derek's, as well as her own. She didn't know what to say, yet she knew she had to say something. She couldn't let his friends think he was the type of man who would abandon a woman who was pregnant with his child, not when he had been so good to her, given her so much. In the end, she just blurted it out. "Risa isn't Derek's. I mean, I'd never met him until the day she was born."

But Sarah only smiled her serene smile. "I know; Derek told us. But she's his now, just like you are."

The idea of belonging to, or with, anyone was alien to Kathleen, because she'd never known the closeness. At least, she hadn't until Risa had been born, and then she had felt an instant and overpowering sense of possession. It was different with Derek. He was a man ... very much so. The image of his bare, powerful body flashed into her mind, and she felt herself grow warm. He had taken her over completely, so in that respect she did belong to him. The odd thing was that she had just sprung to his defense, unwilling to let his friends think anything bad about him. She had felt the need to protect him, as if he belonged to her, and that sense of mutual possession was confusing.

She pushed her thoughts away, concentrating on learning about the shop with the same intensity she'd learned how to be a waitress. As Sarah had said, it wasn't hard work, for which Kathleen was grateful, because she found that she did tire easily. For the most part Risa slept contentedly, whimpering only when she needed changing or was hungry, and occasionally looking around with vague, innocent eyes. It seemed that all the customers knew Derek, and there was a lot of oohing and aahing over the baby.

In the middle of the afternoon, when school was out, Sarah's teenagers came in, with Jed dwarfing his older sister in a protective manner. Missy, who was startlingly lovely, with her father's black eyes and black hair, nevertheless had Sarah's fragile bone structure. When she saw Kathleen, she rushed to her and hugged her as if they were long-lost friends, then breathlessly demanded to know where the baby was. Laughing, Kathleen pointed to the playpen, and Missy descended on Risa, who was just waking from another nap.

Jed watched his sister, and there was something fierce in his own black eyes. "She's crazy about little kids," he said in a rumbly voice, without any adolescent squeak. "She'll be pushing you and Derek out the door every night just so she can babysit." Then he turned and said, "Hi, Mom," as he enveloped Sarah in his muscled arms.

But there was a small frown in Sarah's eyes as she looked up at her son. "What's wrong? You're angry about something." He was too much like his father for her ever to mistake his moods.

"A pipsqueak punk has been hassling Miss," he said bluntly.

"There's nothing to it!" Missy insisted, approaching them with Risa cuddled to her shoulder. "He hasn't really said anything. He just keeps asking me out."

"Do you want to go?" Sarah asked calmly.

"No!" Missy's answer was too swift, denying her casual attitude. "I just don't want to make any big deal about it; I'd be too embarrassed."

"I'll talk to Rome," Sarah said.

"Oh, Mom!"

"I can handle it," Jed said, his voice deadly calm. He reached out and tickled Risa's chin, then deftly scooped her out of Missy's arms.

"Give her back!" Missy said, breathing fire.

They wandered into the back room, still arguing over who would get to hold the baby, and Sarah shook her head. "Teenagers. Just wait," she said with a smile for Kathleen. "Your turn will come."

"Jed's very protective, isn't he?"

"He's just like Rome, but he isn't old enough yet to know how to control all that intensity."

Ten minutes later Missy returned, having regained possession of Risa. Jed had settled down in the back room, watching the portable television and doing his homework at the same time. "Mom, please don't say anything to Dad about that guy," she began earnestly. "You know how Dad is. You almost couldn't talk him into letting me date, and I was *fifteen*!"

"What guy?" a deep voice asked calmly, and they all whirled to face the newcomer.

"Derek!" Missy said in relief, reaching to give him a hug which he returned, cradling her head against his shoulder for a moment.

Kathleen couldn't say anything; she just stared at him with her tongue glued to the roof of her mouth. The light wind had ruffled his black hair, and with his naturally dark complexion it gave him a raffish look that almost literally stopped her heart. His broad shoulders strained the light jacket he wore, his only concession to the January weather.

Sarah was frowning at him. "Why didn't the bell ring when you came in?"

"Because I reached up and caught it," he answered calmly as he slid his arm around Kathleen's waist and drew her to him. His golden eyes went back to Missy. "What guy?"

"Some scuzzball keeps pestering me to go out with him," she explained. "Jed's gone all macho, and Mom is threatening to tell Dad, and if she does he'll *never* let me date anyone again."

Derek lifted his eyebrows. "Is this scuzzball dangerous?"

An uncertain look flitted over Missy's delicate features. "I don't know," she admitted in a small voice. "Do you think Dad should know?"

"Of course. Why would he blame you for something that isn't your fault? Unless he wants to blame you for being a traffic-stopper."

She blushed, then laughed. "All right. I guess he'll let me go to the prom . . . if I can get a date."

"No boyfriend?" Kathleen asked, having finally found her tongue. Talking to Missy seemed safe enough, though her attention was splintered by the heat of Derek's body against her side.

Missy shrugged. "No one special. They all seem so *young*." With that scathing denunciation of her peer group, she allowed Derek to take Risa from her and went to join Jed.

"You're off from work early." Kathleen finally managed to talk to him, since he had released her when he lifted the baby to his shoulder.

"I'm on call. We have a mother trying to go into labor three months early. If they can't get it stopped, I'll have to be there when the baby is born. I decided to take a break while I can, and see my women."

She felt a pang at the thought that she might not be sleeping with him that night, and even a little jealousy that it was Risa who was cuddled so lovingly on that broad shoulder. Well, he'd made it plain from the start that it was Risa he wanted. Why should she be jealous? Did she want Derek to demand more from her than she could give?

Maybe she just wanted him to demand *any*thing from her, so she would know *what* to give.

"What time do you leave work?" he asked as he checked his watch.

Kathleen looked at Sarah. They hadn't even talked about hours. It had been more like visiting with friends than working, anyway. "Go on," Sarah said, smiling. "You've been on your feet a lot today, and the kids are here to help. See you in the morning at nine. Wait, let me get a key for you." She fetched an extra key from the bottom of the cash register, and Kathleen put it in her purse.

Derek got the blanket and diaper bag from the playpen and wrapped Risa snugly in the blanket. Predictably, she began fussing when her face was covered, and he grinned. "We have to go," he told Sarah as he ushered Kathleen out the door. "Having her face covered makes her mad."

Quickly he carried the baby to the car and strapped her into her seat; she settled down as soon as he whisked the blanket from her face. Then he came around to Kathleen's side and bent down to kiss her. "Be careful on the way home," he said, then kissed her again. "I'll pick up dinner. What do you like? Chinese? Mexican?"

She'd never eaten Chinese food, but she liked tacos. "Mexican."

He straightened. "I'll get the food and come straight home." Then he closed her door and walked to the Cherokee without looking back.

Kathleen licked her lips as she started the car, savoring the taste of his mouth. She could feel an unfamiliar tightening inside, and her breasts were aching. She glanced at Risa. "Aren't you hungry?"

A tiny fist waved jerkily back and forth as the baby tried to find her mouth with it. She was monumentally unconcerned with her mother's agitation.

Derek was less than half an hour behind her, but they had scarcely sat down to the spicy meal when his beeper went off. Without hesitation he went to the phone and called the hospital. "All right. I'm on my way."

He barely stopped to snag his jacket on the way out. "Don't wait up for me," he called over his shoulder; then the door closed, and Kathleen sat there with refried beans lumping in her mouth, suddenly tasteless.

The hours passed slowly as she waited for him to come home. Risa was fed and put to bed; then Kathleen tried to become interested in television. When that failed, she tried to read. That was also a dismal failure, and she was furious at herself. She was used to being alone, and had never found it oppressive before. Had she become so dependent on him that she couldn't function without his presence?

At last, disgusted, she went to bed, and her body was tired enough that she went to sleep despite her restless thoughts. When Risa's first hungry cries woke her at one-thirty, the other side of the bed was still empty.

But when she entered the nursery she jumped in surprise, because Derek was sitting in the rocking chair holding the baby while she cried, his hand rubbing her tiny back. There was a terrible emptiness in his eyes that made her hurt, but she sensed that he got some comfort from holding Risa.

"The baby died," he said in a toneless voice. "I did everything I could, but he didn't make it. He wouldn't have had much of a chance even if he'd gone full term; his heart was hopelessly malformed. Damn it to hell and back, I still had to try."

She touched his shoulder. "I know," she whispered.

He looked down at the furious baby, then caught Kathleen's wrist and drew her down on his lap. Holding her against his chest, he unbuttoned her nightgown and bared her breast, then let her take Risa and guide the child's mouth to her nipple. The outraged wails stopped immediately. Derek looked down at the vigorously suckling infant and gathered both mother and child closer to his body, then leaned his head back and closed his eyes.

Kathleen let her head rest on his shoulder, her own eyes closing as she soaked up his warmth and nearness. He needed her. For the first time, he needed her.

She knew that any warm body would have done for him right now, but the warm body was hers, and she'd be there as long as her touch gave him comfort. Or maybe it was Risa who gave him comfort, Risa whom he couldn't bear to release. She was a healthy, thriving baby now, gaining weight every day. He had seen death, and now he needed to see life, the precious life of a baby he'd helped into the world.

Kathleen had to bite her lip. Why hadn't he come to their bed? To her? Why didn't he need *her*?

Chapter Eight

Four weeks later, Kathleen could feel a secret smile tugging at her lips as she unlocked the front door and carried Risa inside to her crib. The baby grunted and waved her fists, then broke into a quick, open-mouthed smile as Kathleen tickled her chin. Even Risa was happy, but Kathleen thought her daughter was smiling at the world in general, while *she* had a very personal reason.

The obstetrician had given her a clean bill of health earlier in the day, and since then she hadn't been able to stop grinning. These past four weeks had been almost impossible to bear as she fretted the days away, impatient for the time when she could truly become Derek's wife. He was a healthy, virile man; she'd seen the evidence of it every day, because he had no modesty around her. She couldn't say that she'd gotten used to seeing him nude; her heart still jumped, her pulse still speeded up, she still grew warm and distracted by all that muscled masculinity. She was even... fascinated.

Marital relations with Larry hadn't been a joy. She had always felt used and even repulsed by his quick, callous handling; she hadn't been a person to him, but a convenience. Instinctively, she knew that making love with Derek would be different, and she wanted to experience it. She wanted to give him the physical ease and enjoyment of her body, a deeply personal gift from her to the man who had completely changed her life. Derek was the strongest, most loving and giving man she could imagine, but because he was so strong it sometimes seemed as if he didn't need anything from her, and being able to give him something in return had become an obsession with her. At last she could give him her body, and sexual fulfillment.

He knew of her appointment; he'd reminded her of it that morning. When he came home, he would ask her what the doctor had said. Then his golden eyes would take on that warm intensity she'd seen in them sometimes, and when they went to bed he would take her in his powerful arms, where she felt so safe and secure, and he would make her truly his wife, in fact as well as in name. . . .

Risa's tiny hands batted against Kathleen's arm, jerking her from her exciting fantasy. "If I give you a bath and feed you now, will you be a good girl and sleep a long time tonight?" she whispered to her daughter, smiling down at her gorgeous offspring. How she was growing! She weighed eight pounds now, and was developing dimples and creases all over her wriggling little body. Since she had begun smiling, Missy and Jed were in a constant state of warfare to see who could get her to flash that adorable, smooth-gummed grin, but she smiled most often for Derek.

Kathleen checked her wristwatch. Derek had called the store while she'd been at the doctor's office and left a message with Sarah that he would be a few hours late, so she had time to get Risa settled for the night—she hoped—and prepare dinner before he'd be home. Would candles be too obvious, or would it be a discreet way of letting him know what the doctor's verdict had been? She'd never prepared a romantic dinner before, and she wondered if she would make a fool of herself. After all, Derek was a doctor; there were no physical mysteries for him, and how could there be romance without some mystery?

Her hands shook as she prepared Risa's bath. How could there be romance between them anyway? It was payment of a debt, part of the deal they'd made. He was probably expecting it. The only mystery involved was why she was letting herself get into such a lather over it.

Risa liked her bath and with the truly contrary nature of all children, chose that night to want to play. Kathleen didn't have the heart to hurry her, because she enjoyed seeing those little legs kick. How different things might have been if it hadn't been for Derek! She might never have known the joy of watching her child splash happily in the bathwater.

But finally the baby tired, and after she was dried and dressed she nursed hungrily, then fell asleep at Kathleen's breast. Smiling, Kathleen put her in the crib and covered her with a light blanket. Now it was time for her own bath, so she would be clean and sweet-smelling in case Derek came home in an impatient mood, ready to end his period of celibacy.

She bathed, then prepared dinner and left it warming in the oven until she heard Derek's key in the lock, then hurried to pour their drinks and serve the food while he hung up his coat and washed. Everything was ready when he joined her at the table.

As always, he drew her to him for a kiss; she had hoped he would deepen the kiss into passion, but instead he lifted the warm pressure of his mouth and looked around. "Is Risa already asleep?" He sounded disappointed.

"Yes, she went to sleep right after her bath." She felt disappointed, too. Why hadn't he kissed her longer, or asked immediately what the doctor had said? Oh, he had to know everything was okay, but she still would have liked for him to be a little eager.

Over dinner, he told her about the emergency that had kept him at the hospital. Just when she had decided that her visit to the doctor had slipped his mind and was wondering how to mention it, he asked casually, "Did the doctor release you from her care?"

She felt her heartbeat speed up. She cleared her throat, but her voice was still a little husky as she answered. "Yes. She said I'm back to normal, and in good health."

"Good."

That was it. He didn't mention it again, but acted as if it were any other evening. He didn't grab her and take her off to bed, and a sense of letdown kept her quiet as they read the newspaper and watched television. He was absorbed in a hockey game, which she didn't understand. Football and baseball were more her style. Finally she put down the newspaper she'd been reading and tried one more time. "I think I'll go to bed."

He checked his watch. "All right. I'm going to watch a little more of the game. I'll be there in half an hour."

She waited tensely in the dark, unable to relax. Evidently he didn't need her sexually as much as she'd been counting on. She pressed her hands over her eyes; had she been fooling herself all along? Maybe he had someone else to take care of his physical needs. As soon as the thought formed, she dismissed it. No. Not

Derek. He had sworn fidelity in their marriage vows, and Derek Taliferro was a man who kept his word.

Finally she heard the shower running, and a few minutes later he entered the bedroom. She could feel the damp heat of his body as he slid between the sheets, and she turned on her side to face him.

"Derek?"

"Hmm?"

"Are you tired?"

"I'm tense more than tired." She could see him staring through the darkness at the ceiling. "It's hard to unwind after a touchy situation like we had this afternoon."

Kathleen moved closer to him, her hand going out to touch his chest. The crisp curls against her palm gave her a funny, warm feeling. Her head found the hollow of his shoulder, and the clean, masculine scent of his skin surrounded her. His arms went around her, the way they had every night for the past four weeks. It was going to be all right, she told herself, and waited.

But he didn't do anything other than hold her, and finally she decided he was waiting for her to give him the go-ahead. Clearing her throat, she whispered, "I...the doctor said it's okay for me to...you know. If you want to, that is," she added hastily.

Slowly Derek reached out and snapped on the lamp, then lifted himself onto his elbow and looked down at her. There was a strange expression in his eyes, one she couldn't read. "What about you?" he asked in that even tone that sometimes gave her chills. "Do *you* want to 'you know'?"

"I want to please you." She could feel her throat closing up under his steady gaze. "We made a deal... and I owe you so much it's the least I—"

"You don't owe me a damned thing," he interrupted in a harsh voice she barely recognized as his. Moving abruptly, he rolled away from her and got out of bed, standing there glaring down at her with golden eyes molten with fury. She had never seen Derek angry before, she realized dimly through her shock, and now he wasn't just angry, he was raging. Being Derek, he controlled his rage, but it was there nonetheless.

"Before we got married, I told you we wouldn't make love without caring and commitment; I never said a damned word about keeping a deal or paying a debt. Thanks, sweetheart, but I don't need charity." He grabbed a blanket and slammed out of the bedroom, leaving Kathleen lying in bed staring at the spot where he'd stood.

She shook her head, trying to deal with what had just happened. How had it blown up in her face like that? She had just been trying to give back some of the tenderness he'd given her, but he hadn't wanted her. She began to shake, lying there in the bed that gradually became cool without his body to keep it warm, but it wasn't just the temperature that chilled her. His absence chilled her; she had come to rely on him so much that now she felt lost without him.

She had been fooling herself all along. She didn't have anything to give him, not even sex. He didn't need her at all, despite his words about caring and commitment. She *did* care about him, and she was committed to making their marriage work, but he still didn't want her, not the way she wanted him to. But then, why should he? He was extraordinary in every way, while she was worse than ordinary; she had been, and still was, unwanted.

Her hands knotted into fists as she lay there, trying to control her convulsive shaking. Her parents hadn't wanted her; they had been middle-aged when she was born, and her presence had almost embarrassed them. They hadn't been demonstrative people, anyway, and they'd had no idea what to do with a curious, lively child. Gradually the child had learned not to make noise or trouble, but she had been so starved for love that she'd married the first man who had asked her, and gone from bad to worse, because Larry hadn't wanted her either. Larry had wanted to live off her and the ranch she'd inherited, and in the end he'd bled the ranch to death, then left her because she'd had nothing else to give him.

It looked as if she didn't have anything to give Derek, either, except Risa, but it was Risa he'd wanted, anyway.

Derek lay on the sofa, his jaw clenched and his body burning as he stared through the darkness. Damn, he wanted her so much he hurt, but it was like being punched in the gut for her to tell him he could use her body because she "owed" him! All these weeks he'd done everything he could to pamper her and make her love him, but sometimes he felt as if he were butting his head against a stone wall. She accepted him, but that was it, and he wanted more than mere acceptance . . . so much more.

She watched him constantly, with wary green eyes, as if trying to gauge his mood and anticipate his needs, but it was more the attention of a servant trying to

please than that of a wife. He didn't need a servant,
but he desperately needed Kathleen to be his wife. He
needed her to touch him with the fierce want and love
he could sense were bottled up inside her, if she would
only let them out. What had happened to her that she
suppressed the affectionate side of her nature with
everyone except Risa? He'd tried to tell her how much
she meant to him without putting a lot of pressure on
her, and he'd tried to show her, but still she held back
from him.

Maybe he should take what she'd offered. Maybe
emotional intimacy would follow physical intimacy.
God knew his body craved the pleasure and release of
lovemaking; at least he could have that. But she had
told him, when he'd asked her to marry him, that
things had happened to her, and she might never be
able to accept lovemaking again; when he calmed
down, he realized that she had come a long way to
even be able to offer him the use of her body.

It just wasn't enough. He wanted to erase the shadows from her eyes, to watch her smile bloom for him.
He wanted her slim body twisting beneath him in
spasms of pleasure; he wanted to hear her chanting
love words to him; he wanted her laughter and tenderness and trust. God, how he wanted her trust! But
most of all, he wanted her love, with the desperate
thirst of a man stranded in the desert.

Everything had always come so easily for him, in-
cluding women. He'd scarcely reached his teens before older girls, and even women, had begun noticing
him. It was probably poetic justice that he had fallen
in love with a woman who protected her emotions behind a wall so high he couldn't find a way over it. He
had always known what to do in any situation, how to

get people to do what he wanted, but with Kathleen he was stymied. Wryly he admitted to himself that his emotions were probably clouding his normally clear insight, but he couldn't detach himself from the problem. He wanted her with a force and heat that obscured all other details.

He was so wrapped up in his rage and frustration that he didn't hear her enter the room. The first he knew of her presence was when her hand touched his shoulder briefly, then hurriedly withdrew, as if she were afraid to touch him. Startled, he turned his head to look at her as she knelt beside the sofa; the darkness hid her expression, but not the strain in her low voice.

"I'm sorry," she whispered. "I didn't mean to embarrass you. I know I'm not anything special, but I thought you might want to..." Her voice fumbled to a halt as she tried and failed to find the phrasing she wanted. Finally she gave up and simply continued. "I swear I won't put you in that position again. I'm not much good at it, anyway. Larry said I was lousy...." Again her voice died away, and the pale oval of her face turned to the side as if she couldn't face him, even in the darkness.

It was the first time she'd mentioned her ex-husband voluntarily, and his name brought Derek up on his elbow, galvanized by this abrupt opportunity to learn what had happened between Kathleen and the man. "What happened?" His voice was full of raw, rough demand, and Kathleen was too vulnerable at the moment to deny it.

"He married me for the ranch, so he could live off it without having to work." Her words were almost prosaic, but her voice shook a little in betrayal of that false calm. "He didn't want me, either; I don't guess anyone ever has, not even my folks. But Larry used me whenever he had the urge and couldn't get to town; he said I might as well be some use, because even though I was lousy in bed, I was still better than nothing. Then finally he couldn't get any more money out of the ranch, and he filed for divorce so he could move on to something better. The last time I saw him, he...he used me again. I tried to stop him, but he was drunk and mean, and he hurt me. He said it was a goodbye present, because no other man would ever be interested in me. He was right, wasn't he?"

Slowly, shakily, she rose to her feet and stood beside him in the darkness. "I just wanted to do something for you," she whispered. "You've done so much, given me so much, and I don't have anything to give you except that. I'd give you my life if you needed it. Anyway, I won't let loving you the way I do embarrass you again. I guess all you want from me is to be left alone."

Then she was gone, walking silently back into the bedroom, and Derek lay on his cold, lonely sofa, his heart pounding at what she'd said.

Now he knew what to do.

Chapter Nine

Kathleen had had years of practice in hiding her emotions behind a blank face, and that was what she did the next day at work. She talked to the customers as usual, played with Risa and chatted with Sarah, with whom she had developed a warm friendship. Being friends with Sarah wasn't difficult; the older woman was serene and truly kind. Within a few days Kathleen had easily been able to see why her children adored her and her big, fierce husband looked at her as if the entire world spun around her.

But Sarah was also keenly intuitive, and by lunchtime she was watching Kathleen in a thoughtful manner. Knowing those perceptive eyes were on her made Kathleen withdraw further inside her shell, because she couldn't let herself think about what a terrible mess she'd made of things.

She couldn't believe what she'd said. It horrified her that she had actually blurted out to him that she loved him, after he had made it so painfully plain that he wasn't interested in her even for sex. She hadn't meant to, but she had only just discovered it herself, and she'd still been reeling from the shock. The hardest thing she'd ever done had been to leave the bedroom that morning; she had steeled herself to face him, only to discover that he had already left for the hospital. Now she had to steel herself all over again, but her nerves were raw, and she knew she couldn't do it if she kept replaying the mortifying scene in her mind.

Sarah placed a stack of embroidery kits on the counter and looked Kathleen in the eye. "You can tell me it's not any of my business if you want," she said quietly, "but maybe it would help to talk about it. Has something happened? You've been so...*sad* all day long."

Only Sarah would have described Kathleen's mood as sad, but after a moment of surprise she realized that was exactly how she felt. She had ruined everything, and a choking sadness weighed on her shoulders, because she loved him so much and had nothing to give him, nothing he wanted. Old habits ran deep, and she had just opened her mouth to deny her mood when her throat closed. She had received nothing but kindness and friendship from Sarah; she couldn't lie to her. Tears stung her eyes, and she quickly looked away to hide them.

"Kathleen," Sarah murmured, reaching across the counter to take Kathleen's hands and fold them in hers. "Friends are for talking to; I don't know what I'd have done all these years without my friends. Derek helped me through one of the hardest times of my life, even though he was just a boy then. I would do anything for him . . . and for you, if you'll only tell me what's wrong."

"I love him," Kathleen croaked, and the tears overflowed.

Sarah looked perplexed. "Of course you do. Why is that a problem?"

"He doesn't love me." Hastily she withdrew one of her hands and wiped her cheeks. "He only tolerates me."

Sarah's green eyes widened. "*Tolerates* you? He adores you!"

"You don't understand," Kathleen said, shaking her head in despair. "You think he married me because he loves me, but he doesn't. He only married me because of Risa, because it was the only way he could get her."

"Derek loves children," Sarah admitted. "He loves all children, but he doesn't marry all their mothers. He may have told you that for reasons of his own, and you may have believed it because it was something you wanted to believe, but *I* don't believe it for one minute. Surely you've noticed by now how he *manages* things; if something doesn't suit him, he works things around until it's just the way he wants it. He talked you into marrying him by using the only argument he thought you'd listen to, but Risa wasn't his main objective; you were."

"You wouldn't say that if you had seen him last night," Kathleen said in bitter hurt. She stared at Sarah, wondering if she should complete her humiliation by admitting everything, only to find that, once she had begun talking, it was more difficult to stop than to go on. "I told him that the doctor had released me—" She drew a deep breath. "I tried to get him to make love to me, and he b-b-blew up like a volcano. He was so angry it scared me."

Sarah's eyes were huge. "Derek? *Derek* lost his temper?"

She nodded miserably. "He doesn't want me, Sarah; he never has. He just wanted Risa. He's practically perfect; all the nurses at the hospital would lie down and let him walk on them if he wanted. He's strong and kind, and he'd done everything he could to take care of us; I owe him so much I can never begin to repay him. I just wanted to give him s-s-sex, if nothing else, but he doesn't even want that from me. Why should he? He can have any woman he wants."

Sarah folded her arms and gave Kathleen a long, level stare. "Exactly," she said forcefully.

Kathleen blinked. "What?"

"I agree with you. Derek can have any woman he wants. He chose you."

"But he *doesn't* want me!"

"In all the years I've known him, I've never seen or heard of Derek losing his temper. Until now," Sarah said. "If he lost his temper with you, it's because you touch him more deeply than anyone else has before. Few people ever cross Derek, but when they do, he never loses his temper or even raises his voice. He doesn't have to; one look from him can shrivel you. His control is phenomenal, but he doesn't have that control with you. You can hurt him; you can make him angry. Believe me, he loves you so much it might frighten you if you knew how he feels. That may be the reason he fed you that line about wanting to marry you so he could have Risa. Risa is adorable, but Derek could have any number of his own children, if children were what he wanted."

"Then why wouldn't he make love to me last night?" Kathleen cried.

"What did he say?"

"He said he didn't need my ch-ch-charity."

"Of course he doesn't. Of all the things Derek would want from you, that wouldn't even be on the list. He wouldn't want gratitude, either. What else did he say?"

Kathleen stopped, thinking, and suddenly it was as if a door opened. "He said something about caring and commitment, but he wasn't . . . I didn't think he meant . . ." Her voice trailed off, and she stared at Sarah.

Sarah gave a very unladylike snort. "Kathleen, you crawl into bed with him tonight and tell him you *love* him, not how grateful you are or how much you owe him. Believe me, Derek will take things from there. He must be slipping, or he'd have handled things better last night. But then, he's never been in love before, so his own emotions are in the way right now."

Sarah's absolute certainty lifted Kathleen out of the doldrums, and for the first time she began to hope. Was it true? Could he possibly love her? She had never been loved before, and it scared her to think that this strong, perfect, gorgeous man could feel the same way about her that she felt about him. She shivered at the thought of putting Sarah's plan into action, because she would be putting her heart, her entire life, on the line, and it would be more than she could bear if he rejected her again.

Her heart was pounding so violently as she drove home that afternoon that she felt sick, and she forced herself to breathe deeply. Risa began fussing, and she gave the child a harried look. "Please, not tonight," she begged in an undertone. "You were so good last night, let's try for an encore, all right?"

But Risa continued fussing, and gradually worked herself into a real fit. Kathleen was only a few blocks from the apartment house, so she kept driving, but her nerves frayed at the effort it took her to ignore her child's crying for even that short time. When she pulled into the parking lot and cut off the motor, she

felt a painful sense of relief as she unbuckled Risa
from her seat and lifted the baby to her shoulder.

"There, there," she crooned, patting the tiny back.
"Mommy's here. Were you feeling lonesome?" Risa
subsided to hiccups and an occasional wail as Kathleen gathered everything in her arms and trudged up
to the apartment. She had a sinking feeling Risa wasn't
going to have a good night.

Just as she reached the door, it opened and Derek
stood there. "You're early," she said weakly.

She couldn't read his expression as he reached out
to take the baby. "I heard her fussing as you came
down the hall," he said, ignoring Kathleen's comment as he put the baby on one shoulder and relieved
Kathleen of the diaper bag. "Why don't you take a
bath and relax while I get her settled; then we'll have
a quiet dinner and talk."

She stepped into the apartment and blinked her eyes
in astonishment. What was going on? There was a
Christmas tree standing in the corner decorated with
strands of tinsel and hand-painted ornaments, while
the multicolored lights blinked serenely. There were
piles of gift-wrapped boxes under the tree, and fresh
pine boughs lent their scent to the air, while glowing
white candles decorated the table. An album of
Christmas music was on the stereo, sleigh bells dancing in her ears.

The apartment had been perfectly normal when she
had left that morning. She put her hand to her cheek.
"But this is February," she protested, her voice blank
with astonishment.

"This is Christmas," Derek said firmly. "The
month doesn't matter. Go on, take your shower."

Then they would talk. The thought both frightened and thrilled her, because she didn't know what to expect. He must have spent most of the day doing this, which meant he had someone covering for him at the hospital. And where had he found a Christmas tree in February? It was a real tree, not an artificial one, so he must have cut it down himself. And what was in those boxes under the tree? He couldn't possibly have found a tree out in the country somewhere, decorated it and done all that shopping, too. It just wasn't possible. Yet it was done.

Despite his instructions to relax, she hurried through her shower, unable to tolerate any delay. When she entered the nursery, Derek had finished bathing Risa and was dressing her. Risa had settled down and was waving her fists around while she gave the little half cooing, half squeaking noises she had recently learned to make. Kathleen waited until he was finished, then took the baby to nurse her. As she settled herself in the rocking chair she looked at Derek uncertainly, wondering if he intended to remain in the room. Evidently he did, because he propped himself against the wall, his warm, golden eyes on her. Slowly she undid her robe and bared her breast, putting Risa to it. The baby's hungry little mouth clamped down on her nipple with comical greed, and for a moment she forgot everything but the baby and this special closeness. Quiet filled the small room, except for the sounds Risa made as she nursed.

Kathleen kept her eyes down, cuddling the baby to her and rocking long after the tugging on her breast had ceased. Derek moved away from the wall, and at last she had to look at him as he leaned down and, with the gentle pressure of one finger, released her nipple from the baby's mouth. "She's asleep," he murmured, and put the baby in her crib. Then he turned back to Kathleen, hot need in his eyes as they moved over her bare breast, and she blushed as she quickly drew the robe around her again.

"Dinner," he said in a strained voice.

Afterward, she was never certain how she managed to eat, but Derek put a plate in front of her and told her to eat, and somehow she did. He waited until they had finished before taking her hand and leading her into the living room, where that impossible Christmas tree still blinked its cheerful lights. She looked at the nostalgic scene, and her throat was suddenly thick with tears. She could never remember truly celebrating Christmas before; it just hadn't been a part of her family's tradition. But she could remember looking at pictures of a family gathered around just such a tree, with love shining in everyone's faces as they laughed and opened gifts, and she could remember the painful longing she had felt for that kind of closeness.

She cleared her throat. "Where did you manage to find a tree?"

He gave her a mildly surprised look, as if wondering why she would think finding a Christmas tree would be difficult for him. "I have a friend who grows them," he explained in that calm manner of his.

"But . . . why?" Helplessly, she gestured at the entire room.

"Because I thought this was what we needed. Why should Christmas be restricted to one certain time, when we need it all the time? It's about giving, isn't it? Giving and loving."

Gently he pushed her down to the floor in front of the tree, then sat down beside her and reached for the closest present, a small box gaily wrapped in scarlet, with a trailing gold ribbon. He placed it in her lap, and Kathleen stared down at it through a veil of hot tears that suddenly obscured her vision. "You've already given me so much," she whispered. "Please, Derek, I don't want to take anything else. I can never begin to repay—"

"I don't want to hear another word about repaying me," he interrupted, putting his arm around her and drawing her close to his side. "Love doesn't need repaying, because nothing can match it except love, and that's all I've ever wanted from you."

Her breath caught, and she stared up at him with liquid green eyes. "I love you so much it hurts," she said on a choked-back sob.

"Shhh, sweetheart," he murmured, kissing her forehead. "Don't cry. I love you and you love me; why should that make you cry?"

"Because I'm not good at loving. How could you possibly love me? Even my parents didn't love me!"

"That's their loss. How could I *not* love you? The first time I saw you, there in that old truck with your arms folded around your stomach to protect your baby, staring at me with those frightened but unbeaten green eyes, I went down for the count. It took me a little while to realize what had happened, but when I put Risa in your arms and you looked at her with your face lit with so much love that it hurt to look at you, I knew. I wanted that love turned on me, too. Your love is so fierce and strong, sweetheart; it's concentrated from being bottled up inside you all those years. Not many people can love like that, and I wanted it all for myself."

"But you didn't know me!"

"I knew enough," he said quietly, looking at the tree, his eyes calm with a deep inner knowledge few people ever attained. "I know what I want. I want you, Kathleen, the real you. I don't want you tiptoeing around, afraid of doing something in a different way from how I would have done it. I want you to laugh with me, yell at me, throw things at me when I make you mad. I want the fire in you, as well as the love, and I think I'll lose my mind if you don't love me enough to give it to me. The last thing I've ever wanted is gratitude."

She turned the small box over and over in her hands. "If loving is giving, why haven't you let me give anything to you? I've felt so *useless*."

"You're not useless," he said fiercely. "My heart wouldn't beat without you. Does that sound useless?"

"No," she whispered.

He put one finger under her chin and tilted her face up, smiling down into her eyes. "I love you," he said. "Now you say the words back to me."

"I love you." Her heart was pounding again, but not because it was difficult to say the words; she barely noticed them. It was the words he'd said that set the bells to ringing. Then she realized bells really were ringing; the stereo was now playing a lilting song about Christmas bells. A smile tilted her lips as she looked at the twinkling lights. "Did you really do this just for me?"

"Umm, yes," he said, bending his head to nuzzle her ear and the curve of her jaw. "You gave me the most wonderful Christmas of my life; I got you and our pretty Christmas baby all at one time. I thought I should give you a Christmas in return, to show you how much you mean to me. Open your present.''

With trembling fingers she removed the wrapping paper and opened the small box. An exquisite gold locket in the shape of a heart gleamed richly on its white satin bed. She picked it up, the delicate links of the chain sliding over her fingers like golden rain.

''Open it,'' Derek whispered. She used her nail to open it, and found that it wasn't just a simple two-sided locket. There was more than one layer to it. There was room for two pictures; then she lifted a finely wrought divider section and found places for two more. ''Our picture will go in the first section,'' he said. ''Risa's will go in the side opposite ours, and our future children will go in the second section.''

She turned the locket over. On the back was engraved, *You already have my heart; this is just a symbol of it—Your loving husband, Derek.*

Tears blurred her eyes again as she clasped the locket in her hands and lifted it to her lips.

He put another, larger, present in her lap. ''Open this one,'' he urged gently.

There was a small white card uppermost in the box when she opened it. She had to wipe the tears from her eyes before she could read the inscription: *Even during the night, the sun is shining somewhere. Even during the coldest winter, somewhere there are bluebirds. This is my bluebird to you, sweetheart, so you'll always have your bluebird no matter how cold the winter.* Inside the box was a white enamel music box, with a small porcelain bluebird perched on top, its tiny head tilted upward as if ready to sing, the little black eyes bright and cheerful. When she lifted the top, the music box began to play a gay, tinkling tune that sounded like bird song.

"Open this one," Derek said, putting another box in her lap and wiping her tears away with his hand.

He piled box after box in her lap, barely giving her time to see one present before making her open another. He gave her a bracelet with their names engraved on it, a thickly luxurious sweater, silk underwear that made her blush, bunny-rabbit house shoes that made her laugh, perfume, earrings, record albums and books, and finally a creamy satin-and-lace nightgown that made her breath catch with its seductive loveliness.

"That's for *my* enjoyment," he said in a deep voice, looking at her in a way that made her pulse speed up.

Daringly, she lifted her head, stopping with her lips only inches from his. "And for mine," she whispered, almost painfully eager to taste his mouth, to know the feel of his body on hers. She hadn't known love could feel like this, like a powerful river flooding her body with heat and sensation and incredible longing.

"And yours," he agreed, taking her mouth with slow, burning expertise. Her lips parted for him automatically, and his tongue did a love dance with hers. She whimpered, her hands going up to cling behind his neck as blood began to pound in her ears. She felt warm, so warm she couldn't stand it, and the world seemed to be tilting. Then she felt the carpet under her, and Derek over her. His powerful body crushed her against the floor, but it wasn't painful. His mouth never left hers as he opened her robe and spread it wide, his hands returning to stroke slowly over her bare curves.

Never in her imagination or her dreams had she thought loving could be as wildly ecstatic as Derek showed her it could. He was slow, enthralled by her silken flesh under his hands, the taste of her in his mouth, the restless pressure of her legs around his hips as she arched mindlessly against him, begging for something she didn't fully understand. Her innocence in that respect was as erotic to him as her full, love-stung lips or the entranced look in her green eyes. He took his time with her despite his own agonizing tension and need, soothing her whenever some new sensation startled her. Her rich, lovely breasts were his, her curving hips were his, her silken loins were his.

She cried out, her body surging against his as he finally entered her with exquisite care, making her his wife in flesh as well as heart. They loved each other there on the carpet, surrounded by the presents he'd given her and the strewn, gaily-colored paper that had wrapped them. The candles burned with their serene white flame, and the joyously colored lights on the tree cast their glow on the man and woman, twined together in the silent aftermath of love.

Derek got to his feet and lifted Kathleen in his muscled arms. "I love you," she whispered, lacing kisses across his throat.

Her naked body gleamed like ivory, with the lights casting transparent jewels across her skin. He looked down at her with an expression that both frightened and exalted her, the look of a strong man who loves so much that he's helpless before it. "My God, I love you," he said in a shaking voice, then glanced around the living room. "I meant to wait; I wanted you to wear the gown I bought you, and I wanted you to be comfortable in our bed."

"I'm comfortable wherever you are," she assured him with glowing eyes, and he cradled her tightly to him as he carried her to their room. Most of his presents to her remained on the living room floor, but two were clutched in her hands: the heart-shaped locket, and the bluebird music box. The winter was cold, but not her heart. She would always have her bluebird and the memory of her first real Christmas to keep her warm while her bluebird sang her lover's song to her.

A Note from Linda Howard

In my family it takes us three days to properly celebrate Christmas. My husband, Gary, and I both come from large families, and when it's taken into account that some branches of our families have lived in this area for at least a hundred and fifty years, that gives us an enormous extended family of aunts, uncles, cousins, nieces, nephews, in-laws and out-laws, as well as kissing cousins of various degrees. It takes a while to see that many people.

Gary and I begin small, with our own immediate family: Mike, Donna, Tammy, Jeff and Mark. Seven people isn't bad; this is our quiet time. From there, though, it quickly becomes something resembling either a three-ring circus or a riot.

Then we move on to our parents' houses. Christmas with my parents involves only three generations under one roof, and even though it's an army, it's a small one. The toddlers are thoroughly petted and spoiled, and everyone keeps an eye out because the babies could get lost in the sea of discarded wrapping paper.

At Gary's parents' we have our four-generation Christmas celebration. Forget about chairs; just find a bare spot on the floor to sit and don't dare get up. Bribe people to bring things to you. If a trip to the bathroom is necessary, you've lost your place to sit. Kids are everywhere, like puppies, their excited laughter adding to the din of conversation. We all eat so much we just want to lie down, but there isn't room. Actually, we start munching on the extra goodies like stuffed dates and the shrimp ball as soon as we get there. I usually don't get hungry again until about the twenty-seventh.

Just thinking about it makes me smile. Merry Christmas.

Linda Howard

HENRY
THE NINTH

Dixie Browning

MORAVIAN CHRISTMAS COOKIES

2 cups shortening
2 ¼ cups brown sugar
1 quart molasses
8 cups flour

1 tbsp. ground cloves
1 tbsp. cinnamon
1 tsp. ginger
½ tsp. baking soda
dissolved in 1 tsp.
vinegar

Sift flour and spices together. Add sugar and mix well. Work in shortening with fingertips or pastry blender. Add baking soda/vinegar solution and molasses and mix thoroughly.

Chill dough for several hours.

Roll as thin as possible on floured board. Cut with cookie cutters, carefully removing with spatula to ungreased cookie sheets.

Bake at 350° about 7 or 8 minutes until lightly browned. Remove cookies from pan *immediately* or they'll stick. They harden very quickly.

It's a good idea to take out of the refrigerator only as much dough as you can roll at one time. The colder it is, the easier it is to work. Store cookies in airtight tins to retain crispness, but if they get limp, they can be recrisped in the oven or the microwave, like crackers.

In our family these are a welcome treat after too much fruitcake and mincemeat pie. They're great with tea or coffee.

Chapter One

"Did I happen to mention that my brother Henry's coming to stay with me for a while?" Jesse Hildebrandt asked casually.

"Hmm," Mary replied noncommittally. She was concentrating on applying pale pink polish to a toenail. "Did I happen to mention that Kenneth's taking me to the opening of that new sculpture exhibit at the Chrysler Museum?"

"Humph!" Jesse's response was rather more expressive than Mary's had been. "I don't know what you see in that man. I know the type, believe me—all show and no go."

Mary's conscience stirred uneasily. So maybe she had exaggerated her involvement with Kenneth Bradshaw just a little. So far, the relationship had hardly had time to go anywhere, but a woman had to have *some* protection against well-meaning friends.

Besides, the more Jesse raved about her studious and successful twin brother, the professor, the more convinced Mary was that he must be a wimp. A nice one, of course, but a wimp all the same.

"You work too hard, Mary," Jesse persisted. "You need to find someone who can show you a good time. Henry needs to relax, too."

Let it drop, Jesse, Mary urged silently, starting on the other foot. "So . . . how long have you and Henry been twins?"

"Oh, shut up," the older woman said with a reluctant chuckle. "Go ahead—marry your cardboard Prince Charming. Just don't come crying to me when your neck gets stiff from trying to balance your darned tiara."

Mary glanced up through a curtain of fine caramel-colored hair that had just begun to dry. There were times when Jesse was a bit too shrewd for comfort. The first time Kenneth had come into the shop, she'd thought of him in those exact same terms—a real Prince Charming. By the third date, she'd dared to wonder if glass slippers really did come in size seven triple A.

Well, what was so wrong with that? Cinderella probably had dishpan hands, but she'd managed to snare her prince. If Kenneth should happen to fall in love with her, why not go for it? She had long since stopped expecting to be swept off her feet, but miracles could still happen. Why not give it a chance?

"Mary, we've always gotten along together, haven't we?"

"Mmm-hmm," Mary wriggled her gleaming toes appreciatively. Pedicures made her feel pampered, and goodness knows, she could do with a bit of pampering.

"And Henry and I are twins. Not identical of course, but close enough. The two of you would hit it off perfectly."

Mary looked up at the tall, thin woman in a white uniform, taking in the medium-brown hair, the olive complexion, and the intelligent hazel eyes. She had liked Jesse Hildebrandt from the first day they'd met when she'd come to look at the other side of the duplex Jesse owned. Since moving in, they had come to be good friends, and Mary found her to be dependable, responsible and kind.

But a male version? No thanks. When it came to her male friends, Mary wanted something a little more... exciting. She owed herself that much. After working hard for as long as she could remember, she was finally free to enjoy a little of the icing on the cake of life, and Henry sounded more like whole wheat bread than cake, let alone icing.

"Jesse, I appreciate your concern, but things are just beginning to get interesting with Kenneth."

"Are you in love with him?"

"He's a marvelous catch," Mary said evasively. "You said it yourself—he's a prince."

"Yes, but are you in love with him?" Jesse balled her hand into a fist and pushed it into the toe of one of the white stockings she wore as hospital dietitian, then reached for her threaded needle. She was the only woman Mary knew who actually darned her nylons.

"Jesse, I was in love when I was younger. At thirty-five, I think I've been immunized against the more virulent strains of the disease. Kenneth is handsome, successful, charming—"

With typical bluntness, Jesse said, "And rich as cream. Now, you take Henry—"

"I know, he worked his way through college, worked some more and took another degree, worked some more and—"

"He's a good, steady, hard-working man, and they're pretty rare."

"It's not the money, Jesse, and you know it. I earn a good salary. Money's never been especially important to me—except when I've needed it and haven't had it." She grinned, crinkling the freckles on her short, straight nose. "I've simply discovered how nice it is to be treated as if I were a piece of fine crystal. Kenneth makes me feel—well, like he's not just out for what he can get. You know what I mean."

"In other words," Jesse observed dryly, "He hasn't wrestled you into his bed yet."

"There *are* other things in life," Mary said with a haughtiness that didn't quite come off. "Oh, Jesse, I know Henry must be the salt of the earth. After all, he's your twin. If I weren't practically on the verge of getting seriously involved with Kenneth..." She sighed. When it came to men, she preferred a little less salt and a little more spice. Even Kenneth was too bland at times, but she had hopes. Once she broke through that starchy reserve of his, there was no telling what she might discover.

"What about your career? I can't see a wife of one of *the* Bradshaws managing a dress shop, even one as snooty as yours."

"Nice Things Unlimited isn't snooty," Mary defended, sidestepping the issue of marriage. She capped the nail polish bottle, and flopped down on her back on Jesse's sensible beige tweed carpet to wait for her toenails to dry. "It also isn't mine. That reminds me, I've got bushels of holly left over from decorating if you want any. Tomorrow I've got to get started on scheduling everybody's holiday time off, and frankly, I'd rather chase a greased pig up a flagpole. How is it possible for someone who loves Christmas to dread it so much?"

"Don't blame me, I'm not one of the thundering herd. I did all my Christmas shopping during the August sales." There wasn't a shred of smugness in the observation. Jesse's practical traits were wonderful, but Mary wasn't so sure they would be her first priority.

Not that she wasn't practical herself. She'd had to be, whether she was meant to be or not. She was the oldest of six children, born to an outstandingly *im*-practical farmer and an elementary school teacher who had died when the youngest was only thirteen. It had been left to Mary to hold the family together. She'd been twenty then, newly engaged and in her first year at college, having worked and saved for years to pay her way.

Now, fifteen years later, she was still single. She had a wild assortment of college credits that would never add up to anything more than personal satisfaction, but with a little financial help from her, two of her brothers and one of her sisters had earned marketable degrees. Both younger girls had married right out of high school, and all five were doing well, juggling mortgages and babies with every indication of enjoyment. Her father had finally given up trying to raise exotic crops that were never meant to thrive in the foothills near Poplar Grove, Virginia, and had married a woman who owned a catfish ranch in Arkansas.

And Mary, straight off the farm with no outside working experience other than running an egg and vegetable stand and a part-time job as a sales clerk, was managing one of the smartest boutiques in Norfolk, Virginia. Furthermore, she'd done it all without any fancy degrees or fairy godmothers.

So if a charming prince happened to look her way, why should she step back and let another Cinderella walk off with the crown?

Kenneth met her after work the following day. With ten minutes in the ladies' room, Mary had repaired the ravages of a day spent hanging holly swags and red velvet bows, and tracking down a misshipped delivery of gift boxes. She turned off the music box that played a quiet medley of Christmas tunes, adjusted the lights, set the alarm, and let herself out. For a moment, she almost wished she could go home and change into her pajamas and robe and curl up with a book and a bowl of soup.

After a ten-minute ride in the luxurious comfort of Kenneth's Bentley she was almost asleep, but she rallied quickly when they pulled up in front of a plush new restaurant. Lunch had been a hastily gobbled sandwich in her office, a long, long time ago. Kenneth did most of the talking, requiring little but an occasional appreciative murmur. Mary's eyes focused on the gleam of gold at his wrist as it appeared and disappeared each time he reached for his wineglass.

Suddenly, she blinked and took a deep breath. Had she actually dozed, or had she only imagined herself asleep? "This is a lovely place, Kenneth," she said brightly. "One of your clients, you say?" Kenneth's family had been in law for generations and the string of letters that followed his name on his letterhead included half the alphabet.

After she'd successfully covered her third yawn, Kenneth suggested they call it a night. "I'm truly sorry, Kenneth—it's the Christmas schedule. It seems to start earlier and last longer every year. Maybe I need to start taking vitamins."

He drove her back to the shop for her car and then followed her home, such courtesies having been bred into him by generations of punctilious Bradshaws. Standing on the sidewalk in the quiet residential neighborhood, Kenneth took her hand. "You're tired, my dear. I won't come in tonight."

"I'm sorry to be such a drag," Mary said, not commenting on the fact that she hadn't invited him. "Dinner was lovely."

"I thought you'd like it. My firm handled the incorporation." His smile was a gleam of white in his lean, handsome face.

Mary stifled another yawn, and to her dismay, her stomach rumbled. Actually, she thought irritably, she hadn't said she liked it, she'd said it was lovely. The way a silverpoint drawing was lovely—in a spare sort of way. If that was nouvelle cuisine, she would take chicken and dumplings any day.

Kenneth adjusted his white silk scarf, touched a button on his black topcoat, and placed his gloved hands on the shoulders of her heavy wool cape. "I'm sorry I had to cancel our date last week, my dear. Something came up and I had to go out of town."

Out of town? Mary happened to know he'd been in Paris, having called his office and been told as much by his secretary. Would she ever be blasé enough to consider Paris merely "out of town"?

Kenneth took a deep breath, signaling that he was about to kiss her good-night, and Mary closed her eyes. Her thoughts strayed to the refrigerator and before she could help herself, she mentally ran an inventory on the contents.

Dear Lord, she *must* be tired! She was being kissed by one of the most eligible bachelors in the Commonwealth of Virginia, and all she could think about was cold, leftover spaghetti? Never mind, she though fuzzily. Things would get a little steamier once the weather warmed up and the Christmas rush was over. She was tired and hungry, and blue Bradshaw blood just took a bit longer to come to a boil.

Henry Hildebrandt turned away from the window. So *that* was the wonderful Mary Pepper his sister had been raving about for the past few months. What was it Jesse had said about her? Hardworking, nice-looking, a serious woman with sound values and a good head on her shoulders? She'd sounded like a real dud, and he'd thought long and hard before even accepting the visiting professorship at Old Dominion University, knowing he would be putting himself directly into his sister's well-meaning but meddlesome clutches. For years she'd been after him to settle down again.

Mary Pepper, hmm? If the tall, willowy blonde in the flowing cape who was draped all over the guy under the streetlight was the same woman Jesse had been throwing at him for months now, then his twin needed her eyes examined. He couldn't tell much about Ms. Pepper's working habits from this range, but she didn't seem to be expending a whole lot of energy at the moment. As for the good head on her shoulders, "nice-looking" was hardly the term he would have used to describe it.

Stunning, perhaps. Or gorgeous. Maybe in a better light she would turn out to be a nice, sensible turnip, but somehow, he doubted it.

Stroking his chin thoughtfully, Henry turned away from the window just as the woman, her pale hair gleaming smoothly as she passed from streetlight to porchlight, mounted the front steps and let herself into the other side of the duplex.

Mary hung her clothes carefully, then scrubbed off her makeup with soap and water. She was out on her feet. Thank goodness tomorrow was Sunday. She could laze around, catch up on her letter writing, and cook herself a decent meal. She'd almost been too tired to eat, but all the same, three artfully arranged shreds of zucchini tied with a strip of carrot, plus a brace of smoked shrimp carefully balanced atop four coiled strips of linguini, did not constitute a decent meal. Hardly a decent appetizer!

The next morning Mary slipped out to retrieve the Sunday paper from the hedge, leaving a big slab of country ham sizzling in the skillet, and a small pot of grits just waiting for the redeye gravy. Her hair was tied back with a cotton sock. A silk scarf might have looked more attractive but it wouldn't have lasted long on baby fine strands. She wore one of her father's old blue work shirts over a pair of baggy, threadbare yellow corduroys. As manager of a fashionable boutique, she dressed the part six days a week, but on her day off, she reverted to type.

Jesse's door opened the minute she set foot on the communal porch. "Mary, come in here and meet Henry."

"Sorry, Jesse, I left breakfast cooking. Maybe later, okay?"

"It won't take a minute. I've got to run by my office at the hospital for a few hours this morning, so it's a perfect time for you two to get acquainted."

Mary closed her eyes and gritted her teeth. For a dear, dutiful, salt-of-the-earth type, Jesse Hildebrandt could be remarkably dense at times. "Uh-oh, I think my ham's burning!" She spun around, letting the door slam shut behind her.

Her ham wasn't burning; her temper was.

Dammit, Mary knew her own brothers and sisters felt guilty because she'd been dumped by a fiancé who hadn't been willing to accept her with all her encumbrances; they'd all been clumsily trying to make it up to her ever since. But what was Jesse's problem? Why this sudden interest in her love-life?

She was still fuming as she dished up her ham, grits and stewed apples. When the doorbell rang she was tempted to ignore it, but knowing Jesse, she would just let herself in anyway. Mary was coming to think that sharing a duplex with a close friend was a mixed blessing.

She threw open the door. "Jesse, I'm—" Her eyes widened as they confronted a broad chest clad in a sweater of a particularly nasty shade of green. "Sorry?" she ended weakly.

"Me, too, for what it's worth. I'm Henry Hildebrandt. Here's your paper. You forgot it, and Jesse said the dog next door would eat it unless someone collected it fast."

He had nice eyes, Mary thought irrelevantly as hers darted upward to escape the startling sweater. His sun-streaked hair needed cutting. It needed combing too, for that matter, and he definitely needed a shave. But behind a pair of plastic-rimmed glasses that had been mended with adhesive tape, his large hazel eyes sparkled with the same sort of warmth and humor that had first drawn her to Jesse.

She took the thick Sunday paper, her gaze still entangled with his. "Thanks. I'm Mary Pepper, and . . . uh . . . what are you sorry about?"

Henry decided that the woman he'd seen last night must have been a figment of his imagination. They were both tall and willowy, with flawless cheekbones and hair the color of ripe wheat, but women with socks in their hair, who smelled of fried ham, didn't usually wear flowing capes and kiss gentlemen who drove Bentleys.

"What am I sorry about?" Henry blinked rapidly behind his glasses. "Oh—for interrupting you, I guess. Jesse said you always read the paper with breakfast. She asked me to bring it over."

They were standing in the open doorway. Mary could hardly shut the door in his face, but he showed no inclination to move. "Would you . . . ah, have you had breakfast yet?"

"I thought I'd pick up a Danish somewhere. Jesse made coffee, but you know how she is about food."

Mary certainly did. For a dietitian, Jesse's personal eating habits were atrocious. Her idea of a well-rounded breakfast consisted of coffee, a cigarette and a candy bar. "I only cooked one slice of ham, but it's a whopper. There's plenty of grits and stewed apples, and I have some cold muffins we could butter and run under the broiler." Mary heard the words issuing forth and was appalled. She'd not only just invited a strange man for breakfast, she had even offered the menu for his approval.

Wishing he'd taken time to shave, Henry finger-combed his hair a little self-consciously. He'd just stepped out of the shower when his sister had started banging on the bathroom door, yelling something about a nine-thirty appointment at the hospital. "That's kind of you, but I'm sure you don't want to be bothered."

Embarrassed, Mary hastily backtracked. "You'd probably rather have your Danish." Dammit, just because he looked so shaggy and rumpled and sounded so hungry, she had to go and play directly into Jesse's conniving hands! Jesse knew she had a weakness for stray mutts. That same shaggy, wistful look, usually accompanied by an ingratiating flap of the tail, had conned her out of more than one good soup bone.

Besides, the neighbors didn't even own a dog!

Henry counted eleven freckles on her short, straight nose. She had the thickest, longest lashes he'd ever seen. They matched her hair. There was something rather entrancing about dark blue eyes in a thicket of pale gold lashes. "Hmm?" he murmured absently. "Oh, the Danish. I guess I'll just wait for lunch. I noticed a hamburger place a couple of miles from here on my way in from the airport last night."

"You're as bad as your sister," Mary grumbled, swinging the door open wide enough to start the old furnace rumbling again. "You may as well join me. I always cook far too much, and Jesse fusses at me for attracting possums and raccoons whenever I put out the scraps."

The trouble was, he was so much like Jesse. The same coloring, the same square jaw, the same slightly crooked smile and level gaze.

Henry followed her into a long, narrow living room similar to the one he'd just left. His gaze was not on the comfortable assortment of furnishings, however, but on the slender figure in baggy corduroys that swayed so tantalizingly before him. He'd lost count of the times his twin had tried to "fix him up" with a girlfriend after Lisa had died. He'd gotten to be an expert at evasive tactics.

For once she just might have done him a favor. All his instincts told him this one was different, but only time would tell.

Henry was a patient man.

Chapter Two

Six wives and no alimony payments? The man was a creep!" Mary exclaimed. "What about poor Anne Boleyn? Wouldn't divorce have been more humane?"

"Okay, so his methods might've been a bit extreme." Henry dried the last of the silver and dropped it into the drawer.

"Extreme!" Mary scoffed. "Banishment is extreme. Beheading is plain nuts. What got you hooked on that period of history in the first place? Don't tell me it was just because of your name?"

Henry grinned as he smoothed the dish towel over the rack. He'd peeled off the bilious green sweater, leaving an open-necked white shirt that deepened the shade of his rich tan. With a modesty bordering on shyness, he had told her about the treatise he had just written on the social and hereditary influences that had produced the eighth Henry.

"He was a fascinating man—brilliant, selfish, talented. He, ah...well, he had a large appetite for life."

"Appetite! The man was a pig!"

"Yeah! Well...maybe. But it took a pretty robust guy to accomplish all that he accomplished."

"If you call destroying the lives of two Annes, three Catherines and a Jane an accomplishment, I suppose he was quite a hero."

"Actually, I was thinking more of what he did for England's naval power, but I'm afraid you have a point there. Henry had a tendency to take life into his own hands and shape it to his liking."

Mary's gaze fell unthinkingly to Henry's hands. Square-palmed and long-fingered, the backs of them were lightly covered with short, golden hair. They looked surprisingly... physical. For such an intellectual man, that was. Kenneth's manicured hands were far softer.

Moving abruptly, Mary switched off the kitchen light and led the way into the living room. There followed a rather awkward silence, as if neither of them knew quite what to do next. Henry, who had collected his sweater from the back of a chair, shifted it from one hand to the other, and Mary licked her lips nervously as she tried to think of a way to get the derailed conversation back on track.

Why on earth had she invited him in for breakfast? There was something intimate about sharing breakfast, especially with a man she didn't even know! Was it because he was so much like Jesse? The first time she had looked up into those twinkling hazel eyes of his, she'd felt an instant spark of... something. Recognition? Probably.

At any rate, she'd practically dragged him in, and now it was beginning to look as if she was stuck with him for the rest of her one free day in the week. Darn it, why hadn't she just taken her paper, thanked him politely, and left him on her doorstep where she'd found him?

"Mary, I hate to eat and run this way, but I have some calls to make. While Jesse's out seems like a good time."

It was *not* disappointment she felt. It couldn't be! It was relief disguised as disappointment. "Oh. Well, sure." Mary shrugged. "I mean, I have laundry to do, and letters to write, and then I always walk on Sunday afternoons. It's been nice meeting you, Henry."

Surprisingly enough, it was true. After her initial resistance, she'd thoroughly enjoyed his company. He was enough like Jesse to put her at her ease; besides, who could stand on ceremony with a shaggy, bespectacled, unshaven professor whose greatest enthusiasm was early sixteenth-century British royalty?

A few hours later, letters written and laundry finished, Mary changed the blue chambray work shirt of her father's for a red wool hunting shirt of her brother's, laced on her purple sneakers and tugged an orange stocking cap down over her hair. Hardly fashionable, or even flattering, but on her day off, it didn't matter. She slathered on moisturizer and lip-balm and let herself out, scanning the sky with a knowledgeable squint. She hadn't spent the first half of her life in the country without learning a thing or two about the weather.

If it snowed before Christmas this year, she promised herself she'd go all out with her decorations. Lately, she'd been skimping. Living alone, it hardly seemed worth the bother.

Before she'd even passed the hedge that bordered their skimpy lawn, Jesse called after her. "Hey, wait up a minute, will you? Let me get my shoes on, and I'll be right with you. Boy, do I need an airing. Have you ever ruined a perfectly good day trying to translate IRS-ese without an interpreter?"

Mary watched her breath drift out on a cloud of vapor and waited. She didn't mind walking alone, but it was always more fun with Jesse along. "Hurry up before my battery runs down."

"I'll be right with you." Jesse zipped her fleecy jacket and called over her shoulder, "Come on, Henry, you're holding us up!"

Oh, rats, Mary thought with a sinking feeling. So this was the way it was going to be from now on. Love me, love my brother.

But by the time they'd covered three miles of Norfolk's picturesque Ghent district with its lovely winding streets, pausing occasionally to admire a particularly striking example of architecture, she had to admit that having Henry along more than doubled her pleasure. He had the same dry sense of humor she loved in Jesse, plus a fascinating knowledge of period architecture, horticulture, ornithology and ancient puns.

Mary paused to retie her shoestrings, and as she hurried to catch up, she had time to study the pair from behind. Henry was taller—a few inches over six feet, probably—but they were so much alike in so many ways. Their gait was almost comically identical, allowing for Henry's longer legs and narrower hips.

The legs and hips, plus a few other interesting parts, held her attention a bit too long for comfort, and Mary decided that it must be that awful green sweater that made his shoulders look so broad. Just as it had to be the fit of those worn khakis that made his hips look so taut and narrow and his thighs so muscular. If she hadn't known that he was just Henry—just Jesse's brother—she might have been fooled by the deep tan, the strong features, and that thick, sun-streaked hair into thinking he was something he obviously wasn't.

Professor Henry Hildebrandt was precisely what his sister had claimed: a decent, steady, serious, hardworking man.

Well, so was Kenneth Bradshaw. And Kenneth had the added advantage of being classically handsome with a courtly brand of charm that was a real rarity these days. What's more, he knew how to make a woman feel like a lady.

Yes, a small, traitorous voice whispered, *but does he know how to make a* lady *feel like a* woman?

Mary's phone was ringing when she let herself inside the house after a four-mile walk, during which she had laughed herself helpless more than once. Henry, she'd decided long before they had turned back, was a diamond in the rough. She only hoped the lucky woman who won his love some day would appreciate him for what he was, and not feel cheated by what he wasn't.

"Kenneth!" she exclaimed, tugging off her stocking cap and unbuttoning the wool shirt as she tried to catch her breath and speak on the phone. "If I sound a little breathless it's because we've been out walking, talking a mile a minute, and laughing over nothing at all. D'you ever have one of those days when everything strikes you as hysterically funny?"

She could tell by the way he quickly changed the subject that he hadn't the foggiest notion what she was talking about. Pity, she thought absently, easing her sneakers off and wriggling her toes. Why was it that some of the handsomest men were so completely devoid of a sense of humor? Could it be nature's way of compensating?

A few minutes later she hung up the phone and started tearing off the rest of her clothes. She had exactly thirty-five minutes to shower and change. It seemed that Kenneth had been trying to reach her all afternoon. He was picking her up at five to drive to Richmond, where they were to meet with a client and his wife for dinner.

If Kenneth had a flaw—besides his lack of a sense of humor, that was—it was his penchant for last-minute dates. One would think a lawyer, especially one with his social background, would plan ahead. Maybe that was the problem; his whole life was so structured, these impromptu dates were the only touch of spontaneity he could afford.

Mary honestly didn't know where their relationship was heading. Was she only fooling herself into thinking they had a future together? She was hardly desperate...and yet, she didn't exactly relish the idea of growing old alone. She'd seen how lost her father had been after her mother had died, even in a house full of children.

It was probably just the season, she told herself. Christmas meant family and children and traditions, and now that her family had families of their own, it was only natural for them to have their own traditions.

Or maybe it was biological. This odd restlessness she'd been feeling lately could be nature's way of reminding her that the clock was running and she was standing still.

Mary was ready on time, but just barely. Prompt by nature, she was usually early for everything, but thirty-five minutes to go from sweat socks and Chapstick to silk stockings and French perfume was pushing the limits, even for her.

The buzzer sounded right on the dot of five, just as she located her other white glove. Snatching up her cape, she settled it over her jade silk dress and hurried to the door.

Only it wasn't Kenneth.

"Oh," Henry said blankly. With maddening deliberation, he examined her shadowed eyelids, the subtle blush on her cheeks, and the softly gleaming lips that parted in surprise as she stared up at him.

"Uh—did you want something?" Mary asked, collecting her wits with a visible effort.

"I'm not sure."

"Then stop staring at me that way, or I'll suspect you of measuring my neck for the chopping block. Did Jesse send you?"

"Jesse?" he repeated blankly, and Mary shook her head in exasperated amusement.

"Look, whatever it is, can it wait until tomorrow? Kenneth's picking me up any minute now, and there's no telling what time I'll be back tonight. We're driving to Richmond for dinner. With a client," she added for good measure, wondering all the while why she felt compelled to explain herself to this unkempt creature who was staring at her as if she were the last plane out and he'd just missed her.

"Kenneth. That would be the gentleman with the Bentley?"

"Not that it's any concern of yours, but Kenneth does happen to drive a Bentley. Why? Does it offend your sense of patriotism?" Mary challenged.

"Not particularly." Behind the slightly smudged lenses, Henry's eyes glowed with a look of amusement.

For reasons she couldn't begin to fathom, Mary grew even more belligerent. "Then what's the matter, do you feel threatened by any man who happens to dress well?" *Mary, shut up! You're not only being irrational, you're being insensitive!*

"I don't think so." His grin was slightly lopsided, the gleam of his strong white teeth making his eyes look more green than hazel.

"I'm sorry, Henry, I don't know why I said that. I've been rushing to get ready and then, you took me by surprise. Oh, darn, how do I know why I'm such a witch? Sometimes I just get that way—mean as a snake."

"Jesse already warned me about your unstable emotional condition. Has to do with a vitamin deficiency, I think she said—or was it hormones?"

She sent him a withering look. "Nothing so dramatic. Retailers get slightly frantic between Black Friday and Christmas Eve."

"Black Friday?"

"The day after Thanksgiving. Businesses that operate in the red all year go into the black then—it's the official start of the Christmas shopping season."

"I've never been much of a shopper," Henry admitted diffidently.

Mary valiantly refrained from looking at his threadbare khakis and that dreadful sweater. "Henry, I'm sort of in a hurry."

"Oh. Yeah—well, you see, Jesse has a date tonight, and I was sitting there all alone, and I got to wondering if—"

Mary's eyes closed briefly as she felt a heavy lump form in her throat. This overgrown clown was crumbling her defenses at an alarming rate! What was she supposed to do, adopt him?

"—if I might borrow something to read," he finished apologetically. "I noticed you had a shelf full of mysteries."

Kenneth's car pulled silently up to the curb, and Mary opened her eyes. Books. For a moment there, she'd thought he was wanting something else. "Murder mysteries, huh? I might have known. You Henrys do have a taste for mayhem, don't you?"

"Among other things." His smile was gently teasing.

"You're sure Agatha Christie won't be too tame for you?"

"Henry the Eighth would've preferred something a bit lustier—power, gore, sex—not necessarily in that order. Christie's more to my taste."

Mary's eyes danced with laughter. "I doubt if old Hank had much time for popular fiction. Look, I've got to run now. Help yourself to anything you fancy and lock the door on your way out, okay?" She could feel his gaze following her as she hurried down the steps.

"Thanks, Mary. I believe I might do just that," he said softly.

Chapter Three

They were on their way home from Richmond after a pleasant, if unexciting evening, when Kenneth asked about her plans for the Christmas holidays.

"Plans? Who can plan with three people wanting time off at our busiest season of the year?"

"What about you? Don't you have any family to visit, my dear?" He always called her his dear. Some women might have considered his tone a bit condescending, but Mary found it charmingly old-fashioned.

All the same, she sent him a slightly puzzled look. She distinctly recalled telling him about her family on their second date. He had certainly looked attentive enough, but perhaps a description of her siblings and their assorted offspring didn't hold the same fascination for a brilliant legal mind as it did for her.

"I'm from a big family with lots of children. If I can snatch a day off, I'll go. Otherwise, I'll settle for phone calls and try to get home after Christmas."

"My parents usually spend Christmas at their place on St. Croix."

"How lovely," Mary murmured. Somehow the old Pepper homestead, scene of her father's many spectacular agricultural failures, sounded a bit dull compared to a vacation home in the Virgin Islands.

"I thought perhaps you might enjoy spending your Christmas vacation there." Kenneth sounded so off-hand he might have been offering her a lift to the nearest bus stop.

It took a few moments for the words to register. "Is that an invitation?" she finally managed to croak.

"It is," Kenneth replied urbanely.

"I can't believe it," she breathed. "Christmas in St. Croix!" With you and your parents, she added silently. She would consider all the ramifications of such an invitation later, after the shock wore off.

"I take it that's a qualified affirmative?"

"There's nothing qualified about it. If I have to beg, bribe and bully, I intend to arrange my schedule so that I can take off for—when did you say?"

"I thought we'd fly over on the twenty-first and come back the day after Christmas, if that suits you. I've had my secretary arrange my schedule accordingly, but if there's a problem . . ."

"Oh, no! No problem. No problem at all," Mary hastened to assure him. The Virgin Islands. With Kenneth and his parents, no less! In a man as circumspect as Kenneth Bradshaw, that was tantamount to a declaration of intent, wasn't it?

Oh heavens, how was she going to manage it? Scheduling time off had been bad before, when her own plans had been flexible. It was going to be absolute chaos now. And there was the matter of clothes. The Bradshaws' life-style would probably call for something a bit more elaborate than jeans, tops, a couple of wash-and-wear skirts and a bathing suit.

Imagine spending Christmas, which was a family holiday if there ever was one, with one of Norfolk's most eligible and sought-after bachelors—*and his family!* Men like Kenneth Allistair Bradshaw III didn't take just *any* woman home to meet the folks.

The next morning Mary sat in bed, arms wrapped around her knees, a dreamy smile spreading over her sleep-flushed face as she relived the moment when Kenneth had issued his invitation. She wouldn't say anything to Jesse yet. Call it superstition, like not telling your wish when you blow out the candles on your birthday cake. Mrs. Kenneth Bradshaw. Mary Bradshaw. A career, a husband, a family of her own. They would start their own holiday traditions.

Mary couldn't remember a time when she hadn't worked but she'd always carried a dream in the back of her mind. After so many years, it had grown almost too dim to recognize, but lately it had started to shine again.

"Move over, Cinderella, it's my turn to waltz," she said firmly, throwing back the covers.

All through a hectic morning, she found herself smiling as she pictured the two of them on a beautiful, sun-baked beach. She would be wearing her skimpiest bikini, and he'd be wearing whatever prominent attorneys wore on balmy beaches. At least it wouldn't be a black chesterfield and a white silk muffler.

"We'll see what that fancy law school of yours taught you about basic biology, Mr. Bradshaw, LL.B., J.D., F.F.V." There was more to life than Mozart and nouvelle cuisine.

The next day Mary had just come in the back door of the shop after wrestling an enormous box of plastic packing chips out to the trash when she heard Julie's distinctive giggle mingling with the deep, attractive sound of a man's laughter.

She knew that laughter. Brushing a streak of dust from her skirt, she sauntered into the showroom to discover her petite assistant laughing up into the face of Professor Henry Hildebrandt.

"Why didn't you tell me about Henry?" Julie exclaimed. "He just spent the last six months less than three blocks from the house where I grew up."

Mary knew for a fact that Julie was one of those rare creatures, a native of Key West. She turned to Henry, taking in the neatly creased whipcord slacks, the Harris tweed jacket, and the gaudy tropical tie.

Florida. So that explained the tan. "How nice." He had never mentioned the fact to her—but then, she'd never asked.

Henry shifted his weight, inadvertently drawing attention to the fit of his well-cut trousers. Even his shoes were shined! He'd had his hair trimmed, too, and for the first time since she'd met him he was clean-shaven.

"Good morning, Mary," he said, eyes sparkling through the lenses of a respectable pair of horn-rim glasses. No adhesive tape on the frames of these, she noted sourly. "I thought we might have lunch together."

"No thanks."

"You've already eaten?" If he was put out by her blunt refusal, it didn't show.

"I'm...ah, too busy to go to lunch today." Mary did her best to ignore a wildly gesticulating Julie. She couldn't very well tell either of them that she'd been expecting Kenneth to call and ask her out to lunch to discuss further plans for their trip.

"I guess I should've asked in advance. The thing is, I had an appointment with this fellow from the history department, only he cancelled at the last minute—something about his wife and traffic court—so I'm at loose ends."

Terrific, Mary thought, her narrow foot tapping silently on the carpeted floor. Any port in a storm. You're at loose ends? Why not try good old Mary, she's always available at short notice.

Thanks to having waited all morning for Kenneth to call and assure her that she hadn't dreamed last night's invitation, it wasn't hard to work herself into a fine fury.

But then Henry had to go and ruin it by being charming. "You know how silly you feel when you're all dressed up with nowhere to go?" He grinned that lopsided, irresistible grin of his, and Mary could almost see Julie begin to melt and flow into a sodden puddle.

"No, I guess you wouldn't," he continued, managing to look incredibly boyish for a man of his age and size. "You always look perfect but it's nearly a year since I've worn a necktie." He tugged at the collar of a shirt that was only a few years out of style. "I keep expecting to find myself on a gallows. I stayed too long at Key West, I suppose—had to fight the moths for possession of my winter clothes."

Dear heavens, how was it possible for some stodgy old professor with all the élan of a stray hound dog to get under her skin this way? "Oh, all right," Mary said ungraciously. "Let's go eat lunch." If the truth were known, she felt like gathering the big hulk in her arms and comforting him for no reason at all that she could fathom.

It must be because he was Jesse's brother that she felt some sort of responsibility toward him. How could any man his age, and his size, with his considerable accomplishments, be so... *vulnerable,* she thought, for lack of a better word.

Mary deliberately steered them away from her favorite restaurant, and they walked four blocks to a cafeteria. She had an idea Henry would insist on paying for her lunch, and she wasn't sure how much he could afford. He'd been on sabbatical, according to Jesse, which meant he was probably scraping the bottom of the barrel.

They passed several people she knew. Mary returned their greetings, and clutching Henry's arm, hurried them along without pausing. If just one of them had so much as *smiled* at Henry's shiny yellow-and-turquoise palm-tree necktie, she just might have decked them!

Men like Henry Hildebrandt needed someone to look after them.

Lunch turned out to be a hilarious affair. They were lucky to find a relatively quiet corner, and Henry soon had her in stitches as he related a few incidents from his and Jesse's childhood in West Virginia.

"Growing up as twins sounds almost as hectic as growing up in a family of six kids," Mary observed as she polished off the last of the coconut cream pie Henry had insisted she have.

"Jesse was pretty wild. It was all I could do to keep her out of trouble."

"Jesse? *Wild?* She's the sanest, most sensible person I know, present company excepted."

"Are you sane and sensible, Mary Pepper?" Henry asked. He leaned back, his wide shoulders and broad chest dwarfing the chrome-and-leatherette chair. "Did you know that it's a historical fact that women with dark blue eyes and pale gold lashes are so passionate and headstrong there've been wars fought over them?"

Pushing aside her dessert plate, Mary knocked over the salt shaker, and righted it with hands that were suddenly unsteady. A reaction to too much sugar in her system, she told herself. "Historical fact, huh?" she said, scoffing. "Hysterical fiction is more like it. Who knows what color women's lashes were? Even Cleopatra used kohl, and she was probably a brunette to start with. Look, this has been great, Henry, but I've got to get back to the shop."

If she hadn't been in such a hurry, it never would have happened, but she'd rushed out, leaving Henry to follow after her if he chose. A car had pulled away from the curb in front of her and she'd stepped right onto the grill of a storm drain.

Henry caught her before she could fall, but the heel that had gone down in the grate had broken completely off.

"Oh, blast!" she cried into the shiny palm-tree necktie as he closed his arms around her. "My heel is halfway to Chesapeake Bay by now!"

Henry drew her back up onto the sidewalk, his arms supporting her as he leaned over and examined the foot she held up behind her. "How about your ankle, did you twist it?"

Suddenly, she felt inordinately tired, as if the strain of having to deal with holiday mania at the shop, the excitement of Kenneth's unexpected invitation—life in general—were simply too much. Just for the moment, all in the world she wanted to do was lean against Henry's hard, warm body, supported by his strong arms, and let him worry about the stupid heel on her very best pair of shoes.

Good old Henry. Her eyes began to burn for no sensible reason at all, and she wedged her hands between her breasts and his chest and gave a halfhearted shove. "Sorry to create such a scene, Henry. If you'll just prop me up against the lamppost and see if you can snag a cab, I'll be fine. I have another pair of shoes at the shop."

"If I were Sir Walter Raleigh, I'd have flung my cape down for you to walk across," he said, easing his hold, but not quite releasing her.

"I'm the one wearing a cape, and if you try flinging it into the gutter I'll break your body." She had to laugh, and a moment later they were both chuckling.

Mary tipped her forehead against his chest again, and Henry rested his chin against the top of her head. That didn't happen too often with a man, for Mary was fairly tall, and her heels—or at least the remaining one—added a few more inches.

Later, she thought she must have imagined his brushing his lips against her hair. The same way she had imagined that odd sort of tension that sprang up between them at unexpected moments, causing her to lose her train of thought.

Henry flagged a cab and settled her in as carefully as if she were a spun glass Christmas tree ornament. Wedging himself into the opposite corner, he crossed his arms over his chest and lapsed into complete silence.

Somehow, Mary thought morosely, losing a shoe heel and losing a glass slipper weren't quite the same thing. Especially when she was with the wrong prince.

Chapter Four

Mary hadn't planned to tell Jesse about her Christmas plans quite so soon, but as it turned out, she had no choice.

"My Aunt Marvel just called. She's in the hospital with a broken hip," Jesse announced, plopping a basket of clean laundry down onto the coffee table. "And she's due out the week before Christmas—talk about lousy timing!" She grabbed a pillow slip by the corners and snapped it in the air. "Well, I can hardly let her go home alone, can I? Medicare doesn't pay for home help, and Henry and I are the only family she's got, so it looks like I'm elected."

"Oh, Jesse, that's a shame," Mary commiserated.

"It could be worse. Aunt Marvel lives in Aspen, and I've got three weeks' vacation saved up. Besides, you'll be here to keep Henry company."

"Oh, but . . ."

After that, there was nothing to do but explain.

"What can you possibly see in that stuffed Brooks Brothers shirt?" Jesse exclaimed.

"Kenneth is not a stuffed shirt," Mary defended quickly. "Just because a man dresses well and happens to have impeccable manners . . ."

"What about Henry?"

Mary snatched a towel from the basket and folded it angrily. "What about him? He's everything you said he was. Kind, serious—'' Well, not *exclusively* serious, she amended silently. She certainly seemed to laugh more than usual when she was with him. "I think of him the same way I do you—as a good friend. Sort of like a brother."

Well not *exactly* a brother, either, she was forced to admit.

The two women folded in silence. "Things must be getting pretty serious," Jesse ventured, when the job was done and she'd put on a pot of coffee. According to her, Henry had gone to keep a rescheduled appointment on the local university campus.

Mary slipped off her shoes and made herself comfortable. "I think so," she said cautiously. "I mean, after all, when a man invites a woman to spend Christmas with his parents, it's hardly a casual date."

"You're certain that's what you want?"

"Are you kidding? Show me a woman who doesn't want to be swept off her feet by a handsome, charming, successful man. Not that I've been swept yet," she added candidly. "I think Kenneth's just waiting to get his parents' approval before he takes the next step. You know how people like the Bradshaws are."

"No, I can't say as I do," Jesse replied. "In the circles I move in, if a fifty-year-old man likes a woman, he damned well tells her so without waiting for permission from his parents."

"Kenneth's not fifty! I doubt if he's much older than Henry, and anyway, it's not a case of—well, it's not like that!"

Jesse lifted a sardonic brow, her hazel eyes uncomfortably like those of her brother. Mary had taken pains to stay out of Henry's way since lunch the day before. Even so, he'd kept on cropping up in her mind, usually at the most inopportune moments. It wasn't as if she had nothing better to do. Or to think about.

"I bought a couple of dresses for St. Croix today, wanna see?"

"Do I have a choice?"

Mary went next door and brought two plastic-shrouded garments on padded hangers. With suitable flourish, she peeled off the protective coverings to reveal two dresses—one a sleeveless, white crepe dress and the other a splashy flowered cotton with a halter top and a circular ankle length skirt.

"What d'you think, too much skin showing? I don't know exactly how stuffy—I mean how conservative these people are."

"If our boy Kenny's any indication," Jesse remarked dryly, "I'd say they were set in concrete around the turn of the century."

"Jesse!"

Mary spread the dresses across the back of the beige sofa, carefully arranging the folds of the full skirt. "Never mind, tell me the truth, are these enough to make Kenneth forget about writs and torts?"

"If you haven't thawed him out yet, I'd toss him back and try somewhere else. The man's obviously deficient in zinc, selenium and vitamin E."

"Did I miss a fashion show?"

Neither of them had heard Henry come in. "We were just getting to the interesting part," his sister said.

"How'd your meeting go?" Mary inquired, shoving aside a box of Christmas cards and a stack of neatly folded towels to make room for him to sit down.

"Great," Henry said easily. He peeled off the same offensive tie he'd worn the day before and stuffed it into his pocket. "Met several nice people today. I'm looking forward to getting started. Since they're giving me my own parking place, I'd better see about getting something to drive."

"How'd you get around in Florida?" Mary asked.

"Bike and boat. I worked part-time on a commercial fishing boat."

Mary could more easily picture him standing on a windswept deck, his body braced against the heavy seas, than riding a bike under gently swaying palms, but then, Henry was full of surprises. "What kind of a car are you looking for?"

They discussed the merits of various makes and models of cars for several minutes, and then Jesse yawned widely and stood up. "Henry, you've done your duty by that horrid tie, so throw the thing out before it ruins your whole career, okay?" Turning to Mary, she explained. "Henry's friend down in Key West who lent him his house for the summer bought him a special good-luck necktie to wear for his first official visit to the University. The man's a complete rumpot but my stubborn brother insisted on wearing the tie. He'd have looked better wearing a rabbit's foot," Jesse said, rolling her eyes.

Once again Mary felt that odd sensation she'd experienced when Henry had turned up unexpectedly at the shop. There was something remarkably disarming about a man with abominable taste in clothes and a strong sense of loyalty toward his friends.

"It isn't such a bad tie, actually," she muttered, and Henry smiled his thanks. He'd been eyeing her new purchases curiously ever since he came in. There was nothing faintly intimate about a dress on a hanger; why did she suddenly feel as if his gaze were moving over her body?

She gathered them up with scant regard for the delicate fabric. "I'd better be going. I've got a million things to do," she said hurriedly as Jesse excused herself to put away the rest of the laundry. "Henry, thanks again for coming to my rescue yesterday. I might've broken a leg if you hadn't grabbed me in time."

Henry stood thoughtfully stroking his square jaw. He studied the section of Mary's ankle bared by a pair of jeans that had shrunk with years of service. "It was my fault you lost a heel," he said, his slightly raspy baritone gently teasing. "Don't make me feel worse than I already do."

"*Your* fault! That I'm such a klutz? How do you figure that?"

"If you hadn't been in such a rush to get away, you'd have watched where you stepped. If you hadn't been embarrassed, you wouldn't have been in such a rush to get away, and if I hadn't mentioned your eyes in context with heedless passion, you wouldn't have been embarrassed. Ergo, it's my fault. I owe you a heel."

Her mouth fell open as she stared at him. Then she burst out laughing. "I haven't the foggiest notion of what goes on in that convoluted brain of yours, but you're the most outrageous man I've ever met," she said when she could speak again. To her astonishment, there wasn't a hint of laughter in his face.

Well...perhaps a glint of it in his eyes. He was just like Jesse, pulling her leg without even cracking a smile. She should have known.

"Outrageous, you say. Is that a fault or a virtue?" he asked.

"I'm not sure," Mary said, shaking her head in resignation. "Jesse does it to me all the time. She pretends to be such an old sobersides, and then bingo! She's got me."

"I'll remember that," Henry said, still without a trace of amusement except for that suspicious twinkle in his eyes.

There was no way she could get out the door without passing too close to him, but Mary didn't flinch. She was no longer afraid of this overgrown version of her best friend. Now she had two best friends. "Henry," she said, pausing to look up into his tanned, reliable, decent—and actually, very attractive—face. "Henry, I'm glad you're here."

"So am I," he replied, equally soberly. "Bingo—is that the right word?"

"What?"

"'Bingo, she's got me?' That's what you said, isn't it?"

"Look, if you're going to start pulling Jesse jokes on me, wait until after the holidays. I've got all I can handle until then, but afterward, I'll take anything you can dish out, I promise you."

It was remarkably easy to fall into the habit of dropping by the Hildebrandt side of the duplex each evening, sometimes for coffee and a chat, sometimes for a late supper. With the shop open until nine during the pre-Christmas season, her schedule was hectic. Evidently, Kenneth's was, too. They had a quick lunch once. As usual, Bronwyn swooned over his classically handsome features, Ann ventured a guess as to the cost of such sartorial splendor, and Julie lifted a skeptical brow.

Mary tried to draw him out about the vacation plans, but other than the fact that there would be several other guests along with them—a disappointment she tried valiantly to conceal—and that she would definitely need a fairly extensive wardrobe, he had little to say.

But that was Kenneth. An incredibly intelligent man, he had once confided that small talk bored him. Since learning that, she'd tried to think of suitably large topics to discuss, but nothing came readily to mind.

Funny, she thought one night as she and the Hildebrandts sat around discussing such weighty topics as mud wrestling and thick vs. thin-crust pizza. Henry was obviously an extremely intelligent man, too, yet he never made her feel inferior because her college education consisted of whatever she happened to be interested in during the odd times when she'd been able to spare time and money to take a course at the local college.

By the time Jesse was ready to leave for Aspen, Mary had wrested her work schedule into some sort of order. It hadn't been easy, for everyone wanted to be off during the same time. As a rule, Mary covered for everyone else, taking the scraps that were left and fitting her own plans around them.

This time it was different. By a combination of bribery, coercion, and working fourteen-hour days, she was also able to secure her own time off. She was also able to secure a dreadful cold.

Jesse hated to leave her ailing. "Good grief, if there's one thing I *can* do it's cure a common cold! I'm not a licensed dietitian for nothing, you know. Everybody knows that the only miracle cure is scalding hot chicken soup loaded with garlic, onions and black pepper.''

"So much for science," Mary wheezed. "So I'll open a can."

But in the end, she didn't have to. Henry took Jesse to the airport in his new camper truck, and Mary slathered on makeup, dosed herself with aspirin and vitamin C, and went to work. She had a lunch date with Kenneth, which she had no intention of missing. He'd called the night before, commiserated briefly with her over her cold, and explained that he hadn't been in touch lately because he'd been out of town.

"Paris again?" If she'd sounded a bit snide, it was only because she felt snide. Aspen. Paris. Key West! All *she'd* been able to manage for the past three years was an occasional trip back home to Poplar Grove, usually to babysit while one or another of her siblings produced another heir.

"As a matter of fact, yes," Kenneth had said in that perfectly modulated voice of his. Her own voice sounded like an unoiled frog. "Shall we say one tomorrow?"

She'd said one tomorrow, and now she wished she hadn't. Her chest felt as if it had a concrete block on it, and her head ached abominably, and all hands were needed at the shop. At least she'd been able to spend the morning in the back room where she could be miserable in peace as she wrapped gifts and answered the phone.

Lunch was a disaster. Kenneth all but tied his handkerchief over his face to keep from being infected, and Mary felt tired and unattractive and weepy.

"Jingle Bells" jingled in her head until she felt as if her brain were rattling, and she scowled at the massive Christmas tree that stood in one corner, surrounded by handsomely wrapped gifts.

Gift *boxes*, that was. Mary knew very well that they were empty. All the trees in all the stores and banks and lobbies were heaped with gaily wrapped empty boxes. It had never bothered her before, but for some reason, it rankled now.

At least the nouvelle cuisine suited her just fine. Her sense of taste had fled, along with her appetite.

"Will you be able to get away for the holidays?" Kenneth asked over dessert, which consisted of three teaspoons of raspberry sorbet.

"I'b pladdi'g to," she said. Oh, darn, as if it weren't enough to look and feel so awful, now she even *sounded* like death warmed over!

"Excellent, excellent," he murmured, touching his lips fastidiously with a crisp linen napkin. "I'd better get you back to work. This is bound to be a busy season for you shopkeepers. My own schedule is extremely backed up, but you know how it is when you have to make a quick trip abroad. I understand there are ways of combating jet lag, but I must admit, I've never been able to master them. I always feel terrible for days after I cross."

That's just too, too tough, Mary thought uncharitably, searching her pockets for a tissue.

That evening Mary left work early, with no apologies. Julie all but chased her out the door. "We'll *handle* it," the tiny brunette exclaimed. "For Pete's sake, just go home and go to bed and don't come back until you can stand on your feet for two minutes without wilting. If you end up in the hospital, we'll all suffer for it.''

Mary hadn't the strength to argue. When she got home, there was a vase of half a dozen white roses on her coffee table. Well, not a vase, exactly—more like a quart jar. Her canning days were long since past, but she couldn't bring herself to throw away a perfectly good jar.

The florist's box was beside them, the green waxed paper still damp. There was a card that said simply, "Get well soon, Kenneth Bradshaw."

"How dice," she said, her eyes stinging at his thoughtfulness. Not a whole lot of emotion, but then, that was Kenneth. Lifting the jar carefully, she breathed in the fragrance. Or tried to. Dejected, she set the jar down just as Henry let himself into the apartment.

"What are you doi'g here?" she demanded irritably.

"Came to see if you're ready for supper. Hey, how about those flowers? They must be from the gent in the Bentley."

"They're frob by" —the word fiancé was too much for her congested nasal passages and besides, it wasn't actually true. Not yet, at least. "By fred Keddeth," she said with a sigh.

"Your friend Kenneth," Henry interpreted. "Right. Don't try to talk yet, honey, I think you've got a case of ingrown freckles." He eased off the cape that she hadn't even bothered to remove. "Go slip on your nightgown and robe and get into bed, and I'll bring over supper. Jesse remembered a carton of chicken soup in her freezer, and told me how to dose it up. It should do the trick, but if it doesn't, I've got a few ideas of my own.''

Chapter Five

Stay in *bed*! Do you realize what season this is? Do you have any *conception* of how busy my shop is two weeks before Christmas?'' Mary's throat hurt, but at least she could talk again. The Hildebrandts' version of chicken soup had not only cleared her nasal passages and removed the concrete block from her chest, it had practically blistered the pink polish from her toenails.

"Look, all I'm saying is that twenty-four hours in bed will have you on the road to recovery in no time," Henry told her, in that irritatingly soothing tone of voice some people insist on using with invalids and imbeciles.

He had been soothing since yesterday, when she'd come home early from work, and she'd been growing more irritated by the minute. The last thing she needed was to have someone turning her pillows, bringing her chilled fruit juice and hot spiced tea, and tucking her in again every time she so much as twitched a muscle.

She'd never been so pampered in her life. Or pampered at all. She didn't know quite how to react. She had felt weak enough before, but Henry was making her feel like a helpless little clinging vine. If there was one thing she *wasn't*, it was a clinging vine.

"If you go on pushing yourself, you'll wind up in the hospital. Is that where you want to spend Christmas?'' he asked, not one whit put out by her pink-rimmed glare.

Mary struggled to a sitting position. How the devil could she hope to hold her own against such a benevolent despot when she was flat on her back, her nose red, her eyes watering, and her hair in rattails? Darn it, no man should be allowed to see a woman in this condition. It wasn't fair!

"For your information, I intend to spend Christmas basking on a sunny beach in the Virgin Islands. Kenneth's invited me to spend the holidays with him and his parents."

"Jesse told me."

"Well then..." she said inconclusively.

"All the more reason for you to take care of yourself now. When you push yourself to the limit the way you have been recently, a cold can hang on for weeks."

Mary waved her arms wildly, losing her grip on the white wool blanket. "Haven't you understood a single word I've said? I don't have *time* to be sick! I've got the payroll to do, bills that have to be paid before I can leave. I've got ads to approve for the year-end sales, sales tax forms to fill out, and I've promised Julie she can be off next week instead of—''

Henry crossed the room and sat down on the bed, facing her. Mary groaned. One day of intensive care nursing, and he thought he was a member of her family.

She pointedly averted her head, dragging the blanket up to her chin, which covered the lace front of her rose satin gown, but didn't do a thing for the cold draft on her back. The trouble was, he *wasn't* a member of her family. He wasn't even Jesse. He was only Henry, but all the same, he was making her nervous.

She didn't care to have anyone see her looking like last year's scarecrow.

"Go water a plant or something," she grumbled.

Henry removed the blanket from her clutching fists and draped it around her. "If you insist on being stubborn about this, you could at least dress appropriately."

Cocooned as she was, it was a simple matter for him to draw her against his chest. Her head fit perfectly into the hollow of his shoulder as he wrapped his arms around her and held her there. "Mary, Mary, quite contrary," he murmured softly in her ear. "Don't fight so hard, love, this time the odds are against you."

"Nursery rhymes. Chicken soup and nursery rhymes—you're treating me like a child." Only she didn't feel like a child. She felt . . .

She didn't know *how* she felt. Confused, certainly. Any minute now she was going to kick this big bully out of here and get ready to go to work, she promised herself. Just a few more minutes, and she would put a quick end to the tyrannical reign of Henry the Hildebrandt. "I hate looking like this," she muttered into his chest.

"You look beautiful. You always look beautiful."

"Liar," she whispered. She knew exactly what she looked like. Kenneth would turn away in horror if he could see her now.

"You do understand why it's so important for me to get back to work, don't you?" she murmured into his warm throat.

"Mmm-hmm."

"They're swamped at the shop, and I have so much to do before I can leave. I'd never dream of taking off now, but this visit with Kenneth and his parents is sort of—well, it's . . . special,'' she finished lamely.

"Hmm." Henry's ambiguous response was vaguely reminiscent of the purring of a lion, but at least he'd stopped being so unreasonably reasonable.

"Try to see it from my point of view, Henry," she said earnestly, eyes shut tightly as she snuggled deeper into the comfort of his arms. "My family's been telling me for years I ought to find myself a husband, and I've been too busy having a wonderful time to pay any attention. But lately, I've begun to wonder if they might not be right. I'm not getting any younger, you know. One stocking hanging from the mantel is hardly worth the trouble. Next year, maybe I won't even get out the tree. Pretty soon, all Christmas will mean is a few cards with snapshots of other people's kids."

"Jesse and I always hung up two stockings each," Henry murmured. His fingers had found their way up under her hair, and he was gently massaging the back of her neck. "We never got away with it, though. The spares were always filled with little bags of birdseed."

"We always had the messiest trees. I used to wonder why they never turned out like those on the magazine covers." Mary sighed, stirring waves of warm, musky fragrance as she snuggled shamelessly deeper into the comfort of Henry's arms. "Too many experts, I guess. Everyone had to have a hand in the decorating. They were wonderful trees, really. My very favorite kind, only I never knew it until recently."

"Does Kenneth like messy trees?"

"You're totally missing the point." She sighed again, the sound muffled by the collar of Henry's blue striped shirt and that hideous green sweater—which wasn't all that bad, now that she'd had time to get used to it. "The point *is*, after Mom died, I took over raising my brothers and sisters. I was too busy to appreciate anything for the next few years."

"I'll bet you were," Henry rumbled deep in his throat.

Ignoring him, Mary continued. "But now all at once, I'm a fifth wheel. They don't need me anymore. Practically overnight it seems they're all married, with families of their own, and now I'm Aunt Mary, who can usually be counted on to babysit while they take vacations or have more kids."

"You're just feeling sorry for yourself. It's a phase all cold sufferers go through."

Mary lifted her head and Henry's large hand pressed it back into the niche between his shoulder and his neck. "I do *not* feel sorry for myself!"

"Okay, so you don't feel sorry for yourself. You just decided to acquire yourself another stocking on the mantel, right?"

"Well...in a manner of speaking. It simply occurred to me that it might be nice to...have someone. Of my own, I mean. And Kenneth would make an ideal companion."

Henry muttered something under his breath, but Mary was too distracted by the hand that was rhythmically stroking her back to understand the words. She lifted her head from his collarbone to gaze earnestly up at his square jaw. "Well, he's a considerate person and there's no reason why we shouldn't have a good life together."

"Sounds as if you've got it all mapped out."

Mary frowned. Had she managed to make him understand? It seemed perfectly logical to her, but whenever she tried to explain herself to Jesse—and now to Jesse's brother—it sounded sort of thin. "Henry," she ventured after several minutes had passed. "Why haven't you ever been married?"

He was silent for so long she was beginning to think he hadn't heard her, which was just as well. It was none of her business. She didn't even want to know.

Yes, she did too! Suddenly, she wanted very much to know about the women in Henry's life. It had to be her cold, she rationalized. A cold could play havoc with a woman's emotional stability.

"I was married when I was twenty-two," Henry said quietly. "We'd planned to wait until we were out of school, but Lisa discovered she had leukemia. We had eleven months together."

The pain came out of the blue, exploding inside her with numbing force. She reached out instinctively, holding on to his solid body with both arms, crooning soft, inarticulate words of comfort. "I didn't know. Henry, I'm so sorry—Jesse never told me."

"She probably knew that when the time came, I'd tell you myself."

When the time came. Long after Henry left her with a promise to look in again when he got back from seeing someone on the campus about office space, Mary mulled over the choice of words.

Her mind kept creating scenes of Henry as a lover, Henry as a husband—laughing, sharing the small intimacies that drew two people together. Dear bumbling, shaggy Henry had once loved so deeply that he'd grieved for nearly twenty years.

During her convalescence—or wasted time as Mary considered it—she'd called the shop frequently just to check on how things were going. Finally, Julie had told her rather pointedly that everything would be fine if only the darn phone would stop ringing.

Covering the dark circles under her eyes with extra foundation, she dusted blusher on her forehead, her cheeks and her chin, hoping to minimize any remaining pinkness of her nose. Her hair was dead. Not even a triple shampoo and extra-body hair spray could make it look anything but limp. She braided in a silk scarf, pinned the resulting mass on top of her head, and chose a pair of outrageous earrings to distract attention.

The shop was mobbed. Bronwyn had been drafted to do gift wrapping and she was tucking three sprays of holly into the bows instead of one, but Mary didn't care. The displays were a wreck. Someone had sold the skirt off one mannequin and the blouse off another, which meant that the back-up stock was probably in an even greater mess. Or depleted. The Christmas tree in the corner was leaning ever so slightly, and the music box seemed to have stuck on a three-note medley that sounded more like "Three Blind Mice" than "The First Noel."

Mary pitched in. It was more than an hour before she had a chance even to catch her breath. In a lull between the lunch crowd and the serious afternoon shoppers, she reached for the paper someone had stuffed under the service counter. "That ad of ours really did the trick. How does it look?"

Julie and Ann grabbed for the paper at the same time, and Mary looked from one to the other. "It is in there, isn't it? Don't tell me we're in the sports section again. They *promised* me a good spot to make up for last week!"

"It's not—" Julie began.

"Oh, Mary," Ann said mournfully.

"I can't believe it!" exclaimed Bronwyn.

The chorus was uniformly accompanied by expressions of such sympathy that Mary groaned. "All right, hand it over. I may as well know the worst. It's not the end of the world, you know, and I did run over the deadline getting the block copy in. Come on, children, I'm a big girl now. As long as they spelled our name right, I'll only kill 'em a little bit."

She retrieved the crumpled newspaper while three sets of anxious eyes watched her. "It's only one small ad, for Pete's sake," she cried, a little exasperated by the overreaction. "By tonight, it'll be wrapping garbage. Where is it—what page?"

And then her voice dwindled off. The sports section fell unheeded to the taupe carpet as Mary clutched the social section, her eyes caught by a familiar name under the featured engagement picture. The headline read, Prominent Local Attorney to Wed Daughter of French Diplomat. The photo caption was Bradshaw-Cadeaux.

Mary didn't need to read the rest of the write-up to know which attorney named Bradshaw was to marry the beautiful Mlle Cadeaux.

"Oh, Mary, I'm sorry," Julie said softly.

"That pig!" seethed Bronwyn.

Ann touched her arm in silent sympathy, and at that moment, the door opened to admit another flurry of customers. Mary took a deep, steadying breath. "If you need me for the next few minutes, I'll be in my office," she said calmly, "throwing things."

She locked the door, something she'd never done before. They were wonderful women, and they meant well, but for the call she had to make, she could do without an audience. If there'd been a window in the closet-sized room, she would have thrown it open and inhaled deeply several more times. Instead, she stood beside her tiny cluttered desk, arms crossed over her chest, chin jutting and eyes sparkling dangerously. Cool down, Pepper, she cautioned. Don't give him the satisfaction of knowing he's hurt you.

Hurt her! He'd made her *furious*! The very idea of that... Angrily, she punched out the familiar number and waited for it to ring. Imagine his wining and dining her, inviting her to spend Christmas with his family while he was practically engaged to—

"This is Miss Pepper. Is Mr. Kenneth Bradshaw available?"

"One moment, Miss Pepper, I'll see."

We'll see, all right, Mary fumed. We'll see what that two-timing, philandering, pompous so-and-so had to say about—

"Kenneth? Mary. I understand congratulations are in order."

Chapter Six

I thought I'd better call and find out just how your engagement affects our plans for the holiday," Mary said in a voice that was ominously calm.

"Why, nothing at all has changed, my dear," Kenneth replied equably. He went on, using the same tone he'd occasionally used to explain a minor point of law to her. "It's the usual open house. Friends, family, business associates. Naturally, Denise and her family will be joining us now that—" He cleared his throat. "Now that we're officially engaged."

Cozy. She was invited to join her boyfriend and his parents, plus his fiancée and *her* parents. Plus an assortment of business associates and anyone else who happened to know the difference between an oyster fork and a pitchfork.

"You're more than welcome to join us, my dear. There's golf and sailing and tennis. Bridge or dancing in the evenings, of course, and as there always seems to be a preponderance of available men, I'm sure you won't lack for partners."

A preponderance of available men? That pompous, pedantic jackass. If Kenneth Bradshaw was an example of a modern-day Prince Charming, she would settle for a chimney sweep any day of the week!

Henry had been waiting for her when she got home after work, deli soup heating on the stove. A gigantic

Christmas cactus in full bloom covered the table where Kenneth's roses had been. Having seen the announcement in the paper, he'd ignored her thunderous expression and insisted on joining her.

"No, I *don't* want any more soup, and yes, I *am* still angry! Mad as the dickens, if you want to know the truth!" Mary pushed away her empty bowl and glared at the cracker crumbs on the tray.

"I told you you should've gotten it off your chest before you ate your supper. It's not a good idea to eat while you're all riled up." Henry took the tray from her lap and tucked the afghan around her legs.

"You did no such thing; you told me I'd feel better after I ate something. Well, I don't!"

"I guess I miscalculated."

"All those trips to Paris," she muttered. "I thought they were business trips." Her shoulders slumped. "Henry, tell me the truth, am I really all that dense, or was Kenneth deliberately sending out false signals?" Her chin had developed a sudden tendency to quiver, and she clenched her teeth. She refused to cry. It was bruised pride, not a broken heart, but even bruises hurt.

Henry stacked the trays, leaving her to come up with the answer for herself. "A woman would understand," she grumbled when he came back from taking them to the kitchen. He was so much like Jesse—except for a few basic differences. Frowning, Mary examined the most obvious ones. He was wearing a pair of khakis that were better suited to a Key West summer than a Norfolk winter and had definitely seen better days. Like the faded rugby shirt that was stretched across his shoulders, they underlined the masculinity of the wearer in a way that Kenneth's custom-tailored suits never had.

Masculinity was not what she needed at a time like this. "I wish Jesse were here," she said glumly.

"Aunt Marvel picked a lousy time to show off on the ski slopes."

"The ski slopes?"

"She keeps forgetting her limitations."

"She can't ski?"

"She's been skiing all her life, but once she passed sixty, she should have stopped showing off for every good-looking young ski bum who comes along. I'm beginning to wonder if she'll ever grow up."

Mary felt an unexpected urge to giggle at the droll commentary. How on earth could she feel like laughing at a time like this?

A gurgle of laughter escaped her, and Henry smiled and shook his head. Then he was laughing with her, his deep chuckles only setting her off again. When Mary blotted her eyes, he removed his glasses and laid them aside. His gaze met hers and lingered as the laughter faded.

For a moment he might have been a stranger. Staring into those remarkably clear eyes of his, Mary felt as if the ground had suddenly shifted slightly beneath her feet.

No wonder the man hid behind glasses! Harsh green sweaters and palm tree ties notwithstanding, it occurred to her that if he'd show up in a classroom looking the way he looked right now, in those hip-hugging khakis and a clinging knit shirt, with his eyes so cool and sea-green against a golden tan, he would have had to fight off his female students with a stick.

What was the unlikely sounding legal term Kenneth had used? An attractive nuisance. In the case he referred to, it had been a client's unfenced pond that the neighborhood children had found irresistible. If it hadn't been for her involvement with Kenneth—not to mention Jesse's hardsell tactics—Mary might very well have found herself lured into deep waters before she ever recognized the danger.

Fortunately, it hadn't happened. For that, she could thank Kenneth—the wretch. "Tell me the truth, Henry, did I blow this whole thing out of proportion, or did Kenneth lead me on? And don't try to spare my feelings—I'm not your Aunt Marvel. If I'm still not old enough to know better, at least I'm old enough to learn from my mistakes."

Out in the kitchen, the coffeepot gurgled noisily as it finished its chore, and Henry excused himself, returning a moment later with two steaming mugs. Hers was precisely the way she liked it.

"A bit of both," he said thoughtfully. "I suspect he was lonely, with what's-her-name in Paris. Under the circumstances, he probably felt justified in seeing someone else on a casual basis." Mary opened her mouth to argue and clamped it shut again when she discovered that she had nothing to say. "Evidently he wasn't officially committed to her yet," he went on. "There are times when a man just wants to be with a woman."

"But if he loved her," Mary contended, "how could he even want to be with another woman?"

"Love? Are we talking about love? Because that's altogether another matter."

"All right then, leave love out of it. We'll just stick to the basics—ethics, integrity, common decency.

Dammit, he should have told me that he was practically engaged!"

"Would you have gone out with him?"

"Probably not."

"So maybe he wasn't sure which one of you he wanted. Maybe he was lonely." He shrugged, a disarming grin cutting deep grooves in his lean, tanned cheeks. "Or maybe he simply found you irresistible."

"Sure, take up for him," Mary said bitterly, eyeing the man she'd pictured grieving all alone. "I suppose you left your share of walking wounded down in Key West. Did you tell any of them about all the others? Did you ever once consider their feelings?"

"Certainly not. By the time I finish with a woman, she's not good for anything but chum bait, anyway."

Mary turned on him, ready to tear him apart. She saw the gently teasing laughter in his eyes and groaned. He'd done it to her again. "I'm sorry Henry, that was a shabby thing to say."

"I'm flattered."

"I guess I'm just blaming myself for reading more into the relationship than was ever there, but that's no reason to take it out on you. I should've known better. Here I thought I was being so sensible in choosing a life companion."

Henry appeared to strangle on his coffee. "A life companion, huh? Now why d'you suppose that sounds so much like an orthopedic device?"

"Stop deliberately misunderstanding me."

"Honey, it's not deliberate, I assure you. I expect we're all prone to misunderstanding—and to being misunderstood. We tend to see what we want to see."

What had she wanted to see? Another stocking dangling from her mantel? Prince Charming? Kenneth was simply a middle-aged bachelor, attractive, if slightly pompous, who needed someone to sit in for the someone he really wanted.

"Hindsight's a marvelous thing." She no longer felt angry, only a little sad. And slightly foolish. "Are all professors so wise?"

"Goes with the territory," he assured her gravely, and she laughed.

"You're a much nicer person than I am, Henry. I was ready to chop off his handsome head, fifty-dollar haircut and all, and use it for a doorstop."

"Henry would've loved you." At her startled upward glance, he shifted restlessly and touched his glasses. "Henry the Eighth, that is. Remember the fate of poor Anne Boleyn?"

"Wasn't she the one who was beheaded for infidelity?"

"And for producing another female. But at least he didn't use her for a doorstop. We Henrys may be cruel, but we're never crass."

Her lips quivered. A moment ago she'd been ready to weep, now he had her laughing again. Henry was a magician. "Speaking of books, I'd better get started on the ones I brought home with me. I've already wasted too much time."

"If you're not planning to take off for the Virgin Islands next week, what's the rush?"

"I rescheduled everybody and gave everyone the time off they'd originally wanted and it's going to leave me shorthanded until the end of the year. I'll be lucky to squeeze out a couple of days for myself to go home and see my family before then."

She got to her feet, folding the afghan with studious precision, trying to ignore the way the soft knit of his shirt faithfully hugged his shoulders. "You're pushing your luck," he warned. "Dr. Hildebrandt says you need to give yourself a break."

"Don't we all. But Ann's from New York, and Julie's from Florida. Naturally, they want to spend Christmas with their families. Poplar Grove's not that far away—and I see mine several times a year." She glanced at him and a warm surge of something made her voice sound slightly husky. She smiled, and the smile threatened to get out of control. "Lucky for me Bronwyn lives right here in Norfolk," she said brightly.

Legs braced apart, Henry hooked his thumbs in the pockets of his khakis. It occurred to Mary that he looked far more like an adventurer than a teacher— but then, things were seldom what they appeared.

"I didn't even thank you for the Christmas cactus, did I? It's wonderful."

Looking slightly uncomfortable, he reverted to plain old Henry Hildebrandt again. "Yeah. Well—I happened to see the thing in the grocery store, and it sorta looked like it needed a home."

"And did you also get rid of the roses?" she asked gently.

He blushed. Under a deep tan that had hardly faded at all, the forty-one-year-old professor actually *blushed*. "They looked like they were going bad to me. Kind of shriveled up, you know?"

They'd been in perfect condition, but Mary only smiled. "That was thoughtful of you, Henry. I never really cared for white roses, anyway. Too stiff and formal."

Thinking over their conversation long after he'd left her, Mary once more found herself wondering about the women in Henry's life. Or had all of his dreams of love died a long time ago with a woman named Lisa?

The rest of the week was hectic. By the time she got home at night, she was too numb to do more than fall into bed. Henry was out when she left in the morning, and when she got in at night. Evidently he was having no trouble getting into the swim of things on campus, even during the holiday break.

Jesse called late one night after the rates had dropped, and without bothering with a greeting, got right to the matter at hand. "Henry tells me you've split up with Kenneth. Best thing that could've happened. Maybe now you'll look around and see what's right under your nose."

"A tissue? That's the only thing that's under my nose at the moment. I've had this wretched cold, and—"

"I know about your cold. Henry said he couldn't keep you in bed."

The thought of Henry keeping her in bed left her reeling and she countered the feeling with asperity. "Oh, and I suppose Henry would've run the shop for me while I took it easy? Let's hear it for wonderful, reliable, decent, steady, hardworking Saint Henry!" The man hadn't even had the decency to ask how she was feeling for three days now.

There was a pause that lasted long enough for her to feel thoroughly ashamed of herself. Before she could apologize, Jesse said quietly, "You'd probably rather have Kenneth back, I suppose. Well, that's your problem."

Feeling slightly lower than a nematode, Mary stammered out some sort of an apology, but it was too little, too late. In criticizing Henry, she'd hurt Jesse.

And the worst part was, she hadn't really meant it. She was tired and confused, and sarcasm had been the first defense at hand. Although why she'd thought she needed it, she couldn't have said.

Christmas Eve came, and there was only a smattering of last-minute shoppers. Mary handled them easily. Ann had left the day before, and Julie three days earlier. Mary and Bronwyn had managed between them, but Mary felt as if her smile were frozen in place.

Somehow, she had managed to get a tree up. It was too neat, and since she'd had to mail all her gifts, the white flannel blanket beneath it looked entirely too barren. She could have done with a bit of cheering. Jesse was still gone.

As for Henry, he'd evidently found more entertaining company. She was glad for him, truly she was. Just as well she had put an end to the careless sort of intimacy that had sprung up between them when she'd been home with a cold and he'd been plying her with chicken soup. Jesse would have misunderstood, and they'd all have ended up being embarrassed.

But she refused to start feeling sorry for herself. Hundreds of people were probably alone on Christmas Eve—

The thing to do was make plans. She would slip over to Jesse's and leave Henry's gift where he'd find it when he came in, and then she would get started on her phone calls to the family. She would give anything to be there when the children woke up the next morning. Christmas was for children, for those who still had the courage to dream.

That darned tree! She was beginning to understand why stores and banks and restaurants decorated their trees with gaily wrapped boxes of nothing. Everyone knew the boxes were empty, but at least they looked the part.

What a sad commentary. All the glitz and glitter hiding only emptiness. There was a moral in there somewhere, Mary told herself tiredly, only she wasn't in the mood to dig for it.

She straightened a painted wooden ornament, and touched another, her gaze straying to the strangely shaped package propped against the base of her lop-sided cedar.

Why on earth hadn't she simply sent him a card? Or bought him a book or something suitably prosaic? Instead, she'd seen a secondhand musical instrument in a shop window and lost her head completely. She hadn't even known what it was. It had looked vaguely medieval, and not until she'd bought the darned thing had it occurred to her that Henry the Eighth might not be medieval. She didn't even know when medieval *was*, for Pete's sake!

She would take it back right after Christmas. At least he didn't have to know she'd made a fool of herself for the second time in as many weeks. What woman in her right mind would offer a man a bowed psaltery as a token of appreciation for chicken soup, hot tea and a comforting shoulder?

Or maybe she would keep the thing herself. She needed a hobby. Years ago, she'd played the piano, and playing a weird stringed instrument should be enough to keep her out of trouble for the next few years.

She was actually reaching for the blue-and-gold package when someone rapped on her door. "Mary? Could I come in for a minute?"

Henry! Guiltily, she clasped her hands behind her back. Why hadn't she taken time to change clothes after she'd gotten home from work? She felt about as fresh as last week's newspaper.

Unlatching the door, she opened it wide. "Hello, Henry." She gazed up at him, unable to think of another thing to say. "Oh—Merry Christmas," she added hurriedly.

Henry stopped just inside the room, looking taller and a little paler than she remembered. It occurred to her that she was incredibly glad to see him.

"I guess you've been pretty busy lately," Henry said in that deep, quiet voice of his. "I haven't seen much of you."

He held a clump of greenery in his hand as he stared down at her. Seconds passed, and they seemed like hours. Mary found her tongue cleaving to the roof of her mouth. "I, um, where..."

What was happening to her? It must be some slow sort of paralysis that afflicted first one part of her body and then another. The first to go had been her brain, and now her powers of speech were failing.

"I brought you this," he said, as he put the greenery on the coffee table, practically in the clutches of the carnivorous-looking cactus he'd brought her the week before.

It was mistletoe, Mary noted with a distinct flutter in the vicinity of her rib cage. The lungs would be going next.

Didn't the man even know what mistletoe was? Or was he just going to throw it at her cactus and run?

Chapter Seven

Mary stared at Henry, torn between amusement and frustration. Henry stared at the cluster of green leaves and waxy, pale berries. Dear Lord, she thought helplessly, for a man with a string of degrees, this one has all the savoir faire of a head of cabbage!

He cleared his throat abruptly. "I just thought you might like to know that Jesse called tonight. She'll be home in a few days."

"Oh. I mean, that's wonderful. I've missed her."

End of conversation. A hard knot was making itself felt in her midsection and she wanted to yell at someone—*anyone*. About something. Anything! Didn't this stubborn galoot even know what mistletoe was *for*, for goodness' sake?

He was studying the back of her old wing chair as if faded chintz were the most fascinating thing in the world. "My father tried cultivating mistletoe one year. We plastered the undersides of every twig on the farm with squashed berries," she said in an effort to get him off dead center.

He nodded thoughtfully. "I can see how that might be practical with the *Phoradendron flavescens* variety, but the *Arceuthobium* would've destroyed the host eventually."

She watched as he reached for the bouquet he'd tossed on the table. What now, a dissertation on the ceremonial uses of parasitic plants?

Henry reached for the cluster, then dropped it. His palms were sweaty. He was forty-one years old, and he couldn't look at this woman without falling apart. What's more, he suspected she knew it. She *had* to know it. He'd managed to stay away for three whole days, hoping it would get better. It hadn't.

"I never knew the Latin names for it," Mary told him. "All I know is that birds eat the seeds and people buy lots of it at Christmas. It—it makes a nice decoration, doesn't it?"

"Mmm-hmm. I...ah, I understand it was the Druids who discovered it." He managed to pick up the waxy bundle again without dropping it. The leaves quivered, revealing the condition of his nerves, and he clutched it tighter.

Mary moved a step closer, studying it with unusual interest. "Isn't it funny how silly superstitions get started over—over a perfectly ordinary..." Lifting her gaze from his chest, she encountered the strong column of his throat, and the squared-off jaw that could be called stubborn or firm, depending on interpretation.

She swallowed hard. Her gaze moved on to his lips—also stubborn or firm. The lower one was full, even sensuous, while the upper one remained stern and in command. A potent combination, she thought, sighing unconsciously.

In fascination, she watched the object of her scrutiny part and come closer as Henry lowered his head. With a sense of inevitability, Mary closed her eyes. A woman could spend years imagining what a man's kisses would be like and never come close to the reality. How could she possibly have dreamed this incredible gentleness? The world tilted at a crazy angle and hung suspended, as one by one, her senses succumbed to his sweet, minty taste, his hard strength, and his clean masculine scent.

He touched her mouth with a series of slow, gentle caresses, almost as if he were determined to give her a chance to escape—but escape was the last thing on her mind. Mary wrapped her arms around his waist and pressed herself even closer. Tension exploded, touching off still more tension as he slipped his tongue into her mouth.

Mary dug her fingertips into the solid muscle of his back, frustrated by the layers of clothing between them, desperate to feel that hard strength with her bare hands, her bare body. It felt as though candles of joy were being lit, one by one, in her heart. She stroked his shoulders, the curve of his neck, and ruffled his thick, sun-streaked hair. As crazy as it was, she couldn't seem to get enough of him.

Lifting his head, Henry stared down at her. He blinked, and for the first time, she noticed that his glasses were missing. When had he removed them? Or had she knocked them off?

"Merry Christmas, Mary," he said, his voice a bit uneven.

As cool air rushed in between them, Mary drew in a deep, shuddering breath. What on earth was happening to her? A few days ago, she'd been thinking seriously of Kenneth, and then Henry had kissed her. Dull, decent, dependable Henry—one kiss and she splintered into a million shimmering fragments!

Dropping his hands from her arms, Henry fumbled for the glasses he'd hooked over the back of a chair and slipped them on again. He might as well have slammed a door in her face. Gone was that endearingly nearsighted look that had left him accessible for just a moment. She felt a wild urge to snatch the things off and crush them.

If only she knew what he was thinking. That had been no innocent little mistletoe kiss. It might have started out that way, but something had happened along the way, something that had left her more bewildered than ever.

And sent him scurrying for cover, from the looks of it.

"Henry—?" Mary said tentatively.

"Um, well—Merry Christmas, Mary. Or did I say that already? I guess I did." He was backing toward the door, and as Mary watched helplessly, he reached behind him, grabbed the knob, and let himself out.

Henry crossed the porch to Jesse's door in three long strides, calling himself every name in the book. It amazed him that someone as supposedly mature and intelligent as himself could become such an idiot whenever he was within earshot of one Mary Pepper! He'd planned on giving her a little more time to get over Bradshaw, but instead he'd pounced on her, sweaty palms and all. And he was too chicken to apologize. He must have made a terrific impression on her, he thought disgustedly.

For a long time after Henry left, Mary leaned over the back of the chair and stared unseeingly at the winking lights of her tiny tree. He hadn't even given her time to wish him a Merry Christmas, much less give him his gift. Now what was she supposed to do?

Embarrass them both by chasing after him with the thing and have him stammer through an explanation of why he hadn't bought one for her?

It had never occurred to her that he would. He'd done so much for her already, bringing her that ridiculous, beautiful cactus that was threatening to take over her living room, taking away Kenneth's flowers, making her chicken soup and cuddling her like a baby.

The last time she remembered being so pampered, she'd been seven years old, home from school with the chicken pox. Her mother, pregnant with Marion—or was it Helen?—had brought home a stack of books from the school library, and read to her for hours to keep her from scratching.

So all right, maybe she had gone overboard. A secondhand psaltery wasn't exactly a gift to be embarrassed about, for goodness' sake. All the same, she wasn't going to chase after him and force it on him. If he didn't have the common decency to stick around after he'd kissed the living daylights out of her, he could stay holed up next door until he grew moss on his north side!

A few minutes later, she heard Jesse's front door close, and then the sound of Henry's new camper starting up and driving off.

Fine. Just because she had nothing to do on Christmas Eve and no one to do it with, that was no reason for him to stay home. He'd made lots of new friends—attractive young female professors no doubt.

Hadn't she been looking forward to having a full day of peace and quiet to recuperate from the mad rush of the past month? Of course she had. So now she had it.

* * *

The trouble with peace and quiet, Mary decided just before dark on Christmas day, was that it gave a person too much time to think. She'd attended midnight services the night before and slept until the middle of the morning. Christmas dinner was breakfast, which suited her just fine. Who wanted to go to all the trouble of making a huge feast for one?

Bored stiff by midafternoon, she dug out the withholding forms she had been putting off facing, only to discover that the government had finally simplified them beyond all comprehension.

Henry had obviously found greener pastures, she thought rancorously. The coward. What had he been afraid of, that she would read something in a simple kiss that might compromise him?

For the first time, it occurred to Mary that Jesse's matchmaking might have worked both ways. Was it possible that her conniving friend had been pushing her at Henry the same way she'd pushed Henry at Mary? She could just imagine that "Jesse-knows-best" tone of voice saying, "Poor old Mary's not all that young, but she's held up well. At least she still has all her own teeth. She's a hard worker and a good, plain cook if you don't mind overdone vegetables and a little too much cholesterol."

"I'll die," Mary said feelingly. "No, I'll strangle her first, then I'll die!" No wonder the poor man had run. First his sister had given him the hard sell, and then Mary had come on with that business about life companions—he'd probably been afraid she would lash him to the bedpost and call the preacher!

When Jesse came home Mary waited as long as she dared and then went next door. To her relief—at least, she hoped the sharp pang she felt was relief—Henry wasn't there.

"Jesse, have you forgiven me for what I said about Henry yet?"

"It was your tone of voice that hurt, not the things you said. Those were all true."

Mary knew they were true. Henry was exactly as she'd said—steady, reliable, hardworking, decent. The trouble was, he was so much more, and it was those little extras that were beginning to disturb her. Quite a lot. "Jesse, by any chance, did you happen to mention me to Henry before he came here?"

Jesse looked up from her unpacking. "Mention you?" She shook out the folds of a beige shirtwaist dress. "What if I did? It's only natural to mention the woman who rents half my house, isn't it?"

Mary sank down on the foot of the bed. "Care to let me in on what you told him?"

This time the look was more evasive, yet so like Henry's that Mary felt a catch in her throat. "Oh, I don't remember exactly...I probably told him that you were nice, and that you were a good friend, and that you were pretty and sensible and . . ."

"Unattached and desperate?"

"Hardly. That would be like the pot calling the kettle black."

Mary tried to be angry, but she had to laugh. Jesse sighed, tossed a handful of white cotton underwear into the top drawer, and then she was laughing, too. "All right, so I'd hoped you two would hit it off. So sue me! Gain a sister-in-law, lose a good tenant. Either way, I get the short end of the straw."

"Or the long end, depending on how you look at it."

"Yeah." Jesse resumed her unpacking. "Did Henry tell you he's found a place that suits him? He'll be moving in any day now. He's been busy *decorating*." She made a wry face. "If you can call it that. I told him to wait and let me help him with the colors, but he refuses to let a little thing like color blindness slow him up."

"Henry's color-blind? You didn't tell me that."

"Oh, did I forget to mention that he is also near-sighted, stubborn as a one-eyed mule, and constitutionally unable to turn his back on anyone he thinks might need him? Like poor little Lisa." Shoulders slumping tiredly, she plopped down on the bed.

Mary wanted to know everything about the girl Henry had once loved enough to marry, but before she could shape the first question, Jesse continued.

"For all he's my twin brother, sometimes I wonder about his judgment. I keep hoping he'll find someone else, but maybe Lisa was it. As I said, Henry's stubborn. And private. He doesn't open up much anymore, even with me. He was in Vietnam, you know, and he came back so old, so quiet. It took a long time for him to get young again. By the time he did, he wasn't—if you know what I mean."

"I'm beginning to understand that he's an extremely complex man," Mary said quietly.

Jesse nodded. "He's so wonderful, but he hides it so well that most people never appreciate him. I guess maybe I tried too hard to sell him to you, didn't I?"

"I guess you did," Mary said with a rueful smile. "Eat your liver and spinach, Mary, it's good for you," Mary said in her best schoolmarm tone.

"And there you were, dining on Bradshaw caviar. I tried to tell you all that sodium was bad for you."

They both laughed, and then Jesse scooped up her cosmetics case and headed for the bathroom. "If it's any comfort to you, I've learned my lesson. I'm just going to back off and let my dear brother live alone in the past with all those dead kings of his."

Mary sighed. It was no comfort to her at all.

Chapter Eight

The Christmas rush was over, a brand-new year just emerging, and Mary was busier than ever. There was no time to brood, even if she'd been so inclined. Only in her dreams was she vulnerable, and she'd long since learned to discount dreams.

Once she had dreamed of getting a degree in geology and traveling to exotic parts of the globe. She'd settled for a library card, a few night courses, and a job in retailing, all less than three hundred miles from the small town where she was born.

As for her brief dream of a fairy-tale romance, that had been doomed from the start. Even as a child, she had always wondered why Cinderella had been so anxious to trade in a nice, messy hearth and a lot of friendly mice for an uncomfortable-looking glass slipper that had been tried on by every woman in town.

As dreams go, she wouldn't have minded a few days on a sunny beach, but she could live without it. She'd even resigned herself to spending Christmas alone instead of with her family.

She'd planned to go home on New Year's Eve, but that hadn't worked out, either. One of the kids had picked up a flu bug, and now they were all in varying stages of misery. She'd been warned off.

Jesse was not particularly sympathetic. "You had your chance to go to the Virgin Islands with what's-his-name and his whole entourage. I can't imagine why you turned down the invitation."

Mary sent her a blighting look. "Why don't you go back to Aspen and try skiing again. Maybe some of Aunt Marvel's luck will rub off on you."

Jesse just grinned. As a matter of fact, she'd been doing a lot of that since she'd gotten back from her mission of mercy. Since their talk the night Jesse returned she hadn't mentioned her brother once, and Mary had stubbornly refused to ask about him. After kissing her senseless and walking out on Christmas Eve, he had disappeared into thin air. She could only assume he was busy with his new position, his new apartment and his new friends.

"What's the matter, Mary?" Jesse inquired, all innocence.

"Nothing! Oh, all right, I'm feeling sorry for myself because I missed Christmas this year." With a mild snort of self-derision, she went on. "I decorated everything in sight, busted my budget on the kids' gifts, broke all previous sales records at the shop, and I'm *still* waiting for Christmas to happen."

"So go put on your red flannel pajamas and ho-ho-ho your way around the block a few times. Just don't expect me to bail you out when you get picked up for disturbing the peace."

"On second thought, maybe I'll just eat a candy cane and hum a few bars of "Jingle Bells" in the privacy of my own home."

"As your landlady, it's my duty to tell you that that tree of yours is becoming a fire hazard. Next time, get an aluminum one. They're neat and efficient and fireproof.''

"But they don't smell like Christmas." Still in the suit she'd worn to work, Mary had removed her pearls, her shoes and her belt. She took down her hair and began weaving it into a lopsided braid while she told Jesse about her decision to steal away by herself for a few days of rest.

She heard the sound of a door behind her, and Jesse's expression brightened. Her voice trailed off as Henry came into the room, bringing with him the invigorating scent of cold rain and a subtle masculine cologne.

"Mary," he said easily, "Good to see you again. Jesse, I brought your waffle iron back. The woman across the hall from me says she makes waffles all the time."

"With or without strings?" Jesse inquired dryly.

"Just butter and maple syrup, I think, but I'll ask."

Mary's braid was a lost cause, but she continued to finger her hair as an excuse not to look directly at him. She'd seen enough in that first moment to know nothing had changed. Her reaction to him was still totally unreasonable. Oh, his hair was getting darker, and his tan was beginning to fade—his smile was even more devastating than she remembered—but he was still just good old Henry, Jesse's twin brother. So why was her heart pounding like a runaway horse?

"I'd better get going, Jesse," she said, standing abruptly and dumping half a dozen hairpins on the floor.

"When are you taking off on this rest cure of yours?"

"This weekend." She knelt just as Henry did, and began snatching up her hairpins. He smiled as if his sister's living-room floor was the most natural place for them to hold a conversation.

"Get that Christmas tree down before you go," Jesse reminded her.

Mary promised, and with only the hastiest of goodbyes, let herself out. She halfway expected Henry to follow her, but he didn't.

Nor did he bother to call.

Not that there was any real reason why he should, she told herself as she packed away the Christmas ornaments for another year. Her scrawny little cedar looked pathetic now that it was naked. But then she always bought the ugliest tree on the lot, knowing that no one else would. She would even drive blocks out of her way to avoid a tree lot on the day after Christmas rather than see the poor orphans no one had wanted.

The psaltery was still there, looking self-conscious in its gay wrappings. It had been an impulse buy, and like so many of her impulses, it had been a hundred and eighty degrees off course.

Perhaps one day she would be able to look at it without that nagging little ache in her heart. If she pretended she'd bought it for herself, no one would ever know how foolish she'd been.

By Thursday, the rain had turned to sleet with a few snow flurries, but by Friday, it had changed back to a gray, sullen rain. Few people ventured out to shop, and by four-thirty Mary was unable to wait any longer. "I'm going to throw a few things into a bag, lock the door, and drive until I feel like stopping," she told Julie. "No plans, no schedules, no hassles."

"Take my advice and head south," advised Ann, who had missed three flights out of Kennedy Airport on account of the weather. "Keep going until you strike sunshine, and don't be in any hurry to come back. We'll cope."

The first thing Mary noticed when she unlocked her front door was the smell of freshly brewed coffee. The second thing she noticed was one of her suitcases parked in the middle of the living-room rug.

The third thing she noticed was Henry.

"Is something going on I should know about?" she asked warily.

"I thought you might like a roast beef sandwich and a cup of coffee before we take off. Or if you'd rather, we can eat on the road." He was smiling, but the look in his eyes was guarded.

"Have you taken leave of your senses?" Mary dropped her purse and automatically stepped out of the matching shoes. Her pulse was hammering out a warning, but the message was garbled. "Henry, I want to know just what's going on and I'll give you two seconds to start talking."

His calmness seemed to increase in proportion to her agitation. It was maddening! Hadn't she already made her year's quota of mistakes? Hadn't she sworn off impulsive acts?

"You're off for the weekend," he said. It was a statement, not a question.

On the other hand, Mary rationalized, it was the beginning of a new year. "I'm free until Tuesday, not that it's any business of yours. Now if you don't mind, I have a lot to do. I haven't even decided yet where I'm going."

"I have."

"*You* have!"

"Mary do you trust me?" He held up a hand, his capable palm towards her. "Hold on, don't make any snap judgments. Think about it, do you trust me?"

She didn't have to think. It wasn't Henry she distrusted—he had given her no cause. She was the one who bore watching. "Of course I trust you," she snapped. "What does that have to do with anything?"

With her words his guarded look disappeared. Beaming like a kid with a brand-new skateboard, he said, "Then go change into something warm and comfortable for a three-hour drive. They're predicting a hard freeze before morning, but if we get a move on, we can beat it. I'll fill a thermos and pack the sandwiches, and we'll eat on the road. Jesse'll look after things here, so don't worry about your pipes."

It wasn't her pipes that concerned her, Mary thought dazedly an hour later as they sped through the night. It was her brains! Thirty-five years old, supposedly of sound mind, and she'd just delivered herself into the hands of a man she barely knew for a trip to God knows where.

"Would you mind telling me where you're taking me?" she asked grimly. "If it's ransom you're after, forget it. My family's up to its collective ears in mortgages and dentist bills."

Henry braked for a stop sign, downshifted smoothly, and picked up speed again. He was the only man she'd ever known who could grin and whistle "I'm Dreaming of a White Christmas" at the same time.

"Henry," she began threateningly.

"Want to break out the sandwiches? You like 'em with horseradish or without?"

"With!" she snapped. "Henry, I'm warning you for the last time, I don't like this one bit. You barge into my house, you slice my roast beef, you—"

"I water your Christmas cactus," he offered modestly.

"Thanks! I wasn't finished. You actually have the temerity to paw through my clothes and decide what I want to take with me!"

"Naturally," he said in that reasonable tone of voice that made her want to throw something at him. "I'm the only one who knows where we're going."

Now she really *was* alarmed. "You mean you haven't even told Jesse?"

"Nope."

"But—" In the dim glow of the instrument panel, Mary studied his profile. The high forehead with a lock of hair that insisted on tumbling forward, the thrusting nose, the mouth that was surprisingly both sensitive and sensuous, and the jaw that was . . .

She exhaled noisily. Stubborn was the only word to describe it. Just like the man himself. Stubborn, headstrong and utterly maddening. "Henry, for the last time, where the hell are we going?"

"To Christmas."

"To Christmas. Ask a foolish question," she said dryly. "Would you care to be more specific?"

"Specific? Okay. About four centuries ago, give or take a few years, a handful of English colonists settled along the Outer Banks of what's now North Carolina. While other colonists set about building a country and arguing politics, these Bankers were too busy just surviving to pay much attention to the outside world."

"Is there some point to all this, or are you just polishing up your lecture technique?"

He took the sandwich she'd unwrapped for him, squeezing her hand companionably in the process. "Years passed and things were beginning to heat up here in the New World. Then, in 1752, the British government saw fit to replace the old Julian calendar with the Gregorian version and impose the change on all its colonies."

They sped along the gleaming band of wet highway that skirted the Dismal Swamp, the darkness broken only by the occasional farmhouse or passing car. Mary poured coffee for them both. Sooner or later, he was bound to get to the point. Meanwhile, she had to admit that she wasn't actually suffering. She was warm, relaxed and comfortable, and it was really rather romantic to be whisked away in the night by a tall handsome man.

"To make a long story short, no one bothered to tell the people who'd settled on Hatteras Island in the villages of Rodanthe, Waves and Salvo that eleven days had been lopped off the calendar. They went right on celebrating Christmas same as they always had, eleven days late. Actually, it's twelve days now. In 1900 another adjustment was made."

Lulled by the lazy sweep of the windshield wipers, Mary murmured, "You really meant it when you said you were taking me to Christmas." She laid her unfinished sandwich on the dashboard and allowed her eyes a moment's rest. The combination of warmth, food and humming tires, plus Henry's deep, soothing voice, was beginning to relax her a little too much.

"Go ahead, take a nap if you want to. Might be a draft by the door, so lean over this way instead."

"I'm not sleepy, it's just my eyes are tired." Her last conscious thoughts were muddled ones—something about best friends and best lovers, and calendars with missing pages.

Some time later, Henry roused her gently. "We're here, honey. Go inside and get warm while I unload the car."

She was stiff and disoriented. Blinking awake, she saw a squatty shape perched on pilings, silhouetted against moonlit water. They'd left the rain somewhere in Virginia.

There was no traffic, only the moaning sound of the wind and something she later identified as the sound of water beating against the shore. Mary felt as if she'd come to the far edge of the world. Inside the cottage she discovered three bedrooms with an assortment of beds in each, as well as three baths, two of which were waterless. Winterized, according to Henry. Someone had been kind enough to open the shutters and turn on the heat, and Mary huddled on the sofa and watched as he brought in an assortment of boxes.

"I stocked up on canned stuff," he informed her, "but there'll be oysters tomorrow. The next day, too, if I can borrow a shotgun."

"A shotgun?" Mary asked, totally mystified.

"I did tell you about the oyster shoot, didn't I?" Henry distributed his battered flight bag, her overnight case, and the enormous canvas tote she'd hastily packed before they had left home. Then he joined her on the sofa before a small radiant heater.

Mary's gaze wandered over the strong contours of his face as he told her about his discovery several years before of the isolated village and its unique celebration. Had she actually once considered this man dull and predictable? she mused. There wasn't a predictable bone in his body. Harris tweed and shiny palm-tree neckties, chicken soup and prehensile cacti—fishing boats and Henry the Eighth. Now Christmas and oysters.

Plus a gentle strength she would have entrusted with her life.

"That's in addition to the traditional oyster roast, you understand," he was saying. "Are you a good shot, Mary?"

"I've shot a few copperheads that were hanging around the chicken house. I've never shot an oyster before."

Henry rested his head against the back of the sofa and grinned up at the ceiling. He was wearing his good glasses, she noted—the ones without the adhesive tape—and his favorite green sweater. How could any woman fall in love with a man whose favorite color was pond-scum green?

And who the dickens said anything about falling in love? she asked herself in astonishment. She began to edge away. "Look it's been a long day and I'm bushed, so if you don't mind, I think I'll turn in. I'll worry about shooting oysters tomorrow."

"Good idea, we'll both get an early night," Henry murmured, his deep voice stirring tendrils of hair on her neck.

Was it her imagination, or had he moved closer? Suddenly, the scent of his aftershave seemed to trigger an allergic reaction, making her eyelids grow heavy and her breathing become fitful.

"We've got a lot to pack into a short time—the oyster roast, the dance, Old Buck, the Bull of Trent Woods. All the traditional old Christmas festivities," he said.

He *was* closer! His thigh was pressed against hers, the arm that had been casually stretched across the back of the sofa moments before was now closing around her shoulder. Mary pretended not to notice. "Traditional?" she asked in a voice that was only an octave or so higher than normal. "What happened to caroling and stockings on the mantel?"

"Ah yes, those stockings on the mantel again." He wound several strands of her hair around his finger, neatly trapping her. His smile was not at all reassuring. "One of the locals told me that as a boy, he used to hang a stocking on the bedpost with a cold biscuit in it for Old Buck, but I expect that tradition's gone the way of the drum-and-fife parade that used to be a part of the celebration. These days, Old Christmas is strictly a social occasion."

"One of those remnants of the past you're so fond of," Mary whispered. Without thinking she reached up and removed his glasses, and then froze at her assertiveness. "I'm sorry," she said quickly. "I don't know why I did that."

She stared at the gold glints in his eyes and was more confused than ever. Eyes she'd once thought of as ordinary hazel were as dark as the swamp they'd passed earlier, and every bit as enigmatic.

"What's wrong Mary? Do you want to know what I'm thinking? Is that it?"

She scrambled to her feet, but there was no escape. Whatever happened to safe, dull Henry—the man she'd felt sorry for because he was so touchingly, endearingly awkward?

"All you ever need to do is ask," said a Henry who suddenly struck her as neither dull nor awkward. Certainly not safe!

"So all right, I'm asking." Her voice was a mere whisper.

"Right now I'm thinking that your suitcase is in one bedroom and mine's in another, and I wish to hell they were in the same room," Henry said quietly, and she moaned. "You're shocked, aren't you? Regardless of what Jesse probably led you to believe, I do occasionally think of something besides my work."

His smile was a twist of self-mockery, and impulsively, Mary laid a hand on his arm, only to feel it turn to steel beneath her touch. Snatching her fingers away, she stepped back. "My gosh, I'm tired!" she said brightly. "Aren't you tired? I've been up since six, and I didn't sleep well at all last night, and—"

She wished to goodness he would put his glasses back on. He was making her extremely nervous.

"Don't worry, Mary, I don't take after my namesake. A reigning monarch might be able to arrange life to fit his desires. A schoolteacher seldom has that prerogative."

"And if you did?" Mary heard herself daring the devil and wondered what ever happened to her sense of self-preservation.

"If I did Mary, this is the way I'd begin," he said in a deep voice, closing his hands over her shoulders as he drew her nerveless body against his own.

There was nothing at all tentative about his kiss. Right from the first, it was as though he were laying claim to a territory he considered his by conquest. His arms hardened until they bit into her sides, and Mary clutched at the shoulders of his sweater and hung on to keep from falling.

Clothes proved no barrier to his explorations. With exquisite slowness, he stroked her back, sliding his warm, hard palms up to cup her shoulders, and down again to circle her waist. When he dropped them to her hips, she began to tremble.

Alternatively aggressive and coercive, he explored her mouth, caressed the slope of her cheeks, kissed her eyelids and nibbled a tortuous trail along her throat. Her breasts ached for his touch, yet he only brushed their sides as he held her.

"Henry, please," she gasped, sagging against his chest. "I can't—I don't—"

"It's all right, Mary, I won't rush you. We have all the time in the world."

Henry might have all the time in the world, she told herself as she lay awake and listened to the wind howl around the corners of the cottage; she wasn't so sure about herself. Obviously his sense of time had been distorted by his work. Yet, he'd been the one who had kissed her. He'd been the one who had kidnapped her and dragged her off to this windy little outpost on a pretext so thin she could practically see through it. He'd been the one whose heart had been going gangbusters against her body, whose eyes had glittered like obsidian, whose face had been flushed.

Besides, there were some signs a man couldn't disguise. And Henry hadn't even bothered to try.

Chapter Nine

The house was swaying. Mary's sense of equilibrium told her that. Her sense of hearing told her the wind was still howling outside, and her sense of smell told her that someone was cooking breakfast.

Another gust of wind struck the side of the cottage, and she sat up in bed, hugging her knees. She was still trying to make sense of what had happened to her when Henry rapped on the door and opened it a crack, allowing the fragrance of freshly brewed coffee to precede him into the chilly little room. "You awake?" he whispered.

"I am now." Mary leaned over and snatched up the shirt she'd discarded the night before and pulled it on, buttoning it up to her throat. "Why bother to knock if you're going to barge in anyway?"

He ignored her peevishness and placed a tray on the bedside table. "Happy Old Christmas, Mary. Coffee and sandwiches," he said proudly. "Bacon, egg, butter and ketchup." And then he frowned. "You do take ketchup on your egg sandwiches, don't you?"

Mary detested egg sandwiches, especially with ketchup, but not for the world would she have let him know it. Furthermore, she would have liked a chance to brush her hair and wash her face; her eyes weren't even open wide yet. "So...we're having breakfast in bed, are we?"

There were two thick, untidy sandwiches and two steaming mugs on the tray. "Yeah, well—I can eat alone in the kitchen if you'd rather. I just thought that since it's already Saturday, and . . ."

He looked so crestfallen she could have hugged him. Kissed him too. In fact, to her dismay, Mary knew that there was nothing she would rather do than dispense with breakfast altogether and concentrate on another growing hunger. "Pull up a chair and let's get started before it gets any colder," she said gruffly.

When had it happened to her? Was it really what she suspected, this breathless feeling of tenderness and excitement that affected her whenever she even thought about him? She'd been blindsided!

"I thought we'd explore the beaches before the oyster shoot if that's okay with you."

It was more than okay with her. If he'd suggested crossing the Atlantic in a rowboat, she would have grabbed an oar, which only went to show how far this thing had progressed. A month ago, he had been only a name—a name Jesse had ballyhooed to the point that she'd been prepared to dislike him on sight.

After breakfast, Henry insisted on washing the few dishes while Mary got dressed. "Bundle up," he warned. "It's not all that cold, but it's blowing a gale."

"Are you sure this island's anchored down? That wind didn't let up all night." She tucked her orange stocking cap down over her ears while Henry pulled on a windbreaker over his favorite sweater.

Alternately battling and borne along by the heavy gusts, they explored the beaches, filling their pockets with sandy treasures. Mary laughed at everything— the pelicans winging their ponderous way along the shoreline, flight after weaving flight of honking geese, tiny beach birds daring the waves in search of a juicy morsel.

Henry only smiled. Smiled and watched her watching the birds. He held her hand, and once he snatched her away from an incoming wave, but he made no effort to kiss her again. By early afternoon, Mary's patience was wearing thin. Could she have misread the signals so completely? It wouldn't be the first time.

Not until late that afternoon at the oyster shoot, when she lifted a borrowed shotgun to her shoulder, did she find herself in his arms again. It hadn't seemed so difficult when he'd explained that all she had to do was hit the target, but the darn thing weighed a ton! Several men laughed and made ducking motions, which only firmed her resolve. She was determined to bag *something*, even if it was only a basket of oysters!

Henry moved in behind her while she was trying to maneuver the heavy barrel in the general direction of the target.

"Point, don't aim," he advised quietly. "Steady now."

Steady! With his chest against her back, his cheek brushing against her hair? "You're not helping, Henry." Stepping forward, she tried to squeeze the trigger the way she'd done on her father's old twenty-two. It was stiff. And then, all of a sudden, it wasn't.

Henry caught her as she fell backward. "I was afraid it was too much for you to handle. Think you bruised your shoulder?"

"Only my pride," she said dryly, handing the twelve gauge over to its grinning owner. "I take it I didn't win any prizes."

"But you didn't hit anyone, either," Henry replied diplomatically. He was still holding her, and Mary was in no particular hurry to be released.

"Tell 'em they can come out from behind those trucks now, I've surrendered peacefully."

"Have you, Mary?" The words were barely audible, but she caught them. Caught them, hugged them to her, and took hope again, like the fool she was.

"Look," she said shakily, reluctantly extracting herself from his arms, "if you're such a hotshot, let's see you do any better."

Half an hour later, they drove back to the cottage and unloaded the bushel of oysters. Mary bid on the first shower and won, promising to leave enough hot water for Henry.

Seeing his toiletries in among her own gave her the sort of thrill she thought she'd outgrown before she left her teens. "This is absurd," she whispered to the steamy mirror as she wrapped a towel around her wet hair. How was she going to make it through the rest of the weekend without giving herself away?

She could picture it now—she would blurt out her feelings, and he would get that embarrassed look on his face and mumble something apologetically, and she would excuse herself and go dig a hole in the sand and crawl in it.

That night in the small wooden building that housed the community centre, they danced to the rowdy strains of a country music band. Mary was determined to shake off her mood and enjoy the occasion. Actually, it was impossible not to join in the fun. People of all ages and backgrounds danced together, wandering outside from time to time to enjoy the feast of roasted oysters.

Henry was a wonderful dancer. A short while ago that might have surprised her, but Mary was beyond being surprised by anything about the man. There was more to Henry Hildebrandt than met the eye, and what met the eye was enough to turn the head of every woman in the crowded room.

Mary was in great demand. While Henry had drawn first one woman from the sidelines and then another, she'd whirled about the floor with half the men there, from a fifteen-year-old self-proclaimed hunting guide to an eighty-year-old man who swore his ancestors had been kin to half the crowned heads of Europe.

She would have to remember to introduce him to Henry the Ninth.

"My goodness, it's getting warm in here," she blurted when Henry rejoined her after a few rounds with a woman who could have been his grandmother.

"Why don't we go outside for a breath of air?"

At any other dance, an invitation of that sort would have had but one meaning. A chance to be alone together, to steal a few kisses and explore a few possibilities.

In this instance, it meant a chance to indulge in a few more of the delectable oysters that were roasting over a screened bed of coals just outside the building. There was nothing at all romantic about gulping down oysters, surrounded by dozens of beer-drinking fishermen, retired coastguardsmen, their wives and children, plus the few hardy tourists who attended the event yearly.

Yet Mary knew she wouldn't have traded that moment for all the fancy restaurants and glamorous escorts in the world. Henry was no fairy-tale prince, all done up in fancy wrappings like one of those empty gift boxes under the Christmas tree at Savings and Loan. The gift was in the man himself, and Mary would have given anything she possessed to be offered such a prize.

A dozen or so oysters later, they went back inside. Shortly afterward, the band took mercy on the winded dancers and played a slow number, and Mary tucked her face against Henry's neck and closed her eyes. He immediately tightened his arms around her, and she inhaled the intoxicating scent of him, smoky, salty, and utterly masculine. His thighs moved against hers in an intimate caress, and she was suddenly aware of every firm inch of his body.

A low, inarticulate sound escaped her. Henry pivoted, the inside of his thigh against the inside of hers, causing the little strength that remained in her to melt away. He moved his hands restlessly over her back, pressing her even more tightly against him. Soft against hard, heat kindling heat. And then they were no longer dancing, but swaying in place, and this time the low sound of distress came from Henry.

He murmured a soft oath, which Mary would have seconded if she'd been able to speak. Of all the places to start a meltdown!

"Time to go home, Mary," Henry said quietly, and suddenly, she was afraid. As long as she was here in his arms, knowing that at least for now, he wanted her as much as she wanted him, she could dream. But what happened when the dream ended?

Oh, he would be ever so gentle about it; unlike his famous namesake, cruelty wasn't a part of this Henry's makeup. He was still a virile male in the prime of life, even if his marriage had ended a long time ago, but lust and love were not necessarily synonymous.

"Already?" Reluctantly, she moved away. "I'm having such a wonderful time I wish it would never end," she said wistfully.

"What makes you think it's ending? Come home with me, Mary." And with that she had to be content.

The drive took only a few minutes, and Mary grew silent as she tried to interpret the signs. Henry seemed unusually relaxed. A few minutes ago, he'd been anything *but* relaxed, but now he was even whistling under his breath.

Bad sign. If he'd shown the slightest indication of being nervous, she would have held out more hope. In all her adult life, Mary had never felt less relaxed—or less secure. Which was ridiculous! She was thirty-five years old, for goodness' sake! When was she supposed to develop a modicum of self-possession? Would she simply wake up one morning, look in the mirror and see a self-confident woman who knew her own worth, one who remained completely unflappable under the most trying conditions, business or social?

Bonne chance! as they said in Paris!

"The bathroom's all yours if you'd like to wash the oyster juice off your elbows," Henry offered. "I'm going to lash a tarp over the hood of the truck to keep it from getting sandblasted in case the wind picks up again before morning."

Mary selected a yellow sweat suit from among the things Henry had packed for her. It was a good thing she'd checked before they'd left. He hadn't thought to include such luxuries as hairbrush, shoes, or underwear. She had packed a canvas tote, and at the last minute, she'd included Henry's psaltery, still in its blue-and-gold wrappings. She was determined that he should have the thing, but so far, she hadn't found the proper moment to give it to him.

Several minutes later, still flushed from a quick shower, Mary opened the door and walked directly into Henry's arms. He caught her by the shoulders, laughing down at her in a way that sent a flurry of goosebumps racing down her spine. "What are you, a voyeur?" she gasped.

"Sorry to disappoint you—just being practical. I was about to suggest that if we double up, we could save time as well as water."

"Since when have you been a conservationist?"

"Some of the men were talking tonight about the water problems here on the island. Salt water intrusion." His glasses were steamy from the cloud drifting out of the bathroom, and he removed them and tossed them on the dresser. "Oh, hell, Mary, the only thing I'm interested in conserving is my sanity." His hands slipped from her shoulders down her arms until the fingers meshed with hers. Wrapping her arms about his waist, he drew her against him. "Funny how you think you know yourself. I always considered myself a pretty patient guy," he said in a gritty whisper. "I was wrong."

Mary absorbed him with her senses. He still smelled of salt air and smoke from the oyster roast. Having just come in from outside, his skin was cool to touch, even though his face was flushed and his eyes were glittering feverishly.

"You were?" she whispered. He was what? She'd forgotten already. Why was it that every time this man touched her, he blew out every fuse in her mental circuit? So she was occasionally a bit lacking in poise— she was still an intelligent woman, not some giddy female who could be turned on by any good-looking man who came her way. Kenneth had never even come close to having this effect on her.

Henry's lips followed her hairline until they reached her temple, and she shivered uncontrollably. "Henry, would you please just tell me what's going on?"

"I thought it was pretty obvious. Am I doing it wrong? It's been awhile for me."

Backing away from the door without releasing her, he sat down on the edge of the bed and drew her down in his lap. "I had it all planned out in proper sequence," he said with a funny little half smile that wrapped itself around her heart and squeezed until it hurt. "We'd do a few things together, spend a few quiet evenings just talking. No pressure. You'd gradually come to like me—maybe a lot," he added hopefully. "Then I'd propose and give you the ring I bought for you—if you don't like it, or it doesn't fit, you can exchange it. Then I was going to seduce you."

Stunned, she could only stare at him—at the square jaw, the curve of his firm, sensuous mouth, those remarkable eyes of his. Laughter trembled on her lips as she felt the uncertain winter inside her give way to a sweet melting spring. "Henry, do I understand you correctly?"

He was moving his hands in seemingly random patterns over her back, and then somehow, one of them found its way under her shirt. At the slightly abrasive feel of his hard palm on her naked skin, she drew in a deep, shuddering breath. Another fuse blew.

"Yeah, well . . . so I had problems with my timing. I was anxious to get on with it—I've been waiting outside the door forever, but I should've known that the bathroom was no place for a formal proposal.

Then there you were, all damp and rosy, and my glasses sort of steamed up, and I sort of forgot the proper sequence and started seducing you before I'd even proposed."

"Are you seducing, Henry?"

"If I'm not, I'd better head for the beach. A long, cold swim is definitely in order."

Turning her face into his throat, Mary gave in to the laughter that had been brimming ever since she'd walked out of the bathroom and into his arms. It wasn't amusement; it was sheer joy.

"Henry, wait right here," she said suddenly, slipping off his lap and dashing barefooted across the chilly floor. "This is for you, and it's silly, and you'll probably wonder what on earth I was thinking about, but it's too complicated to explain, so if you—" She had extracted the awkward-shaped package, and now she placed it in his hands, painfully conscious of his bemused expression.

"You bought this for me?"

"Open it. I don't think it's returnable or exchangeable, but if you don't like it, I'll keep it. I think I could learn to play it."

By then Henry had carefully stripped the thick layers of paper away, exposing the spruce-and-cherry instrument. "Holy cow, a bowed psaltery," he said almost reverently. "Where did you find it?"

"It's only a reproduction," she said anxiously. He *liked* it! His hands were cradling it as tenderly as if it were a baby. She unwrapped the small bow and handed it to him.

"I saw one of these things when I was in Florida, and I've been kicking myself ever since for not getting it. It's Renaissance, you know—that is the bowed type. But in one form or another, they've been around since Biblical days."

As it turned out, Henry was a dreadful musician. On the unfamiliar instrument, Mary wasn't much better. But the high, clear sounds were accompanied by so much laughter, neither of them cared.

He closed his arms around her as she experimented with different bowing techniques. Her head rested on his shoulder as he examined the variety of different woods used in construction. Her back pressed against his chest as together, plucking and bowing, they played scales and called it "Joy to the World."

And then the psaltery was forgotten as other harmonies intruded, and they explored music of another kind.

The next morning, Mary lay in bed, her body still singing with remembered ecstasy, and waited for Henry to pour the champagne. He was totally unselfconscious in his nakedness, and totally beautiful. She gazed wonderingly at his tanned back, his narrow hips, and the powerful length of his hair-roughened legs, and sighed. "All this and champagne for breakfast, too. For such a serious man, you're surprisingly hedonistic, Professor Hildebrandt."

"The champagne was supposed to be for dinner tonight, to celebrate our engagement. Once I get out of sequence, I'm a lost cause." He slid the bottle back into the ice-filled bait bucket, placed both glasses on the bedside table, and slid back under the covers.

"Who's complaining?" Mary's voice was husky with soft laughter, and he drew her close to his side. Just as the eastern sky had turned pearly with daybreak, he had given her a small, exquisite sapphire ring. She lifted her hand now to admire it. "The important thing is that we're both out of sequence together."

A thought occurred to her, and she twisted in his arms to stare down at him. "Henry, do you realize I came *this* close to missing you?"

"No you didn't, love. I'd have been waiting when you got back," he said with a grin that stopped just short of being smug.

A Note from Dixie Browning

I'm not sure how many of my readers would be interested in learning how to prepare one of my childhood favorite treats, stewed goose with rutabagas and pone bread with goose gravy. It might be an acquired taste, so I've shared with you a taste I acquired after moving inland from North Carolina's Outer Banks.

Moravian Christmas cookies are a tradition in Winston-Salem, site of one of the original Moravian settlements. The first time I tasted one, I was intrigued. So simple, I told myself. What could be difficult about making a perfectly plain, paper-thin molasses cookie?

I'll tell you what's difficult—it's the rolling! There's no easy way to do it, and each time you turn your back, the dough seems to double in bulk. I rolled for days that first time, and finally threw out the rest of the dough. My cookies tasted good—I added the zest of an orange, and some people don't—but mine never came out quite as thin and crisp as those of the best Moravian cooks.

My daughter bakes them now for her son. Right after Thanksgiving she starts, and before long, she has stacks of airtight tins of crisp, spicy treats, ready for children and gift giving. Hers are better than mine ever were, so I've given you her recipe. Best of Luck, and Merry Christmas.

Dixie Browning

SEASON
OF MIRACLES

Ginna Gray

BRANDY FRUITCAKE

1 cup white raisins
1 cup chopped dates
½ cup candied pineapple
2 pounds mixed diced candied fruit
1 ½ cups coarsely chopped pecans
½ cup coarsely chopped almonds
1 cup coarsely chopped walnuts
1 teaspoon cinnamon
1 teaspoon nutmeg
1 teaspoon mace
1 teaspoon allspice
½ teaspoon ground cloves
½ cup molasses
½ cup peach or apricot brandy
½ pound real butter
1 cup brown sugar
3 large eggs
2 cups flour
½ teaspoon salt
½ teaspoon soda

Rinse and drain raisins and dates. Chop dates. Combine fruits and nuts, spices, molasses and brandy and *mix* well. Set aside. Cream butter and sugar until fluffy. Beat in eggs one at a time. Stir in *sifted* dry ingredients. Fold in fruit mixture. Pack firmly into a 10-inch tube pan, lined with *heavily* greased white parchment paper. Bake at 300 degrees for two hours. When cool, wet a clean white cloth in brandy and cover top and sides. Wrap tightly in foil and store in airtight cake tin for two weeks or more. When storing longer, check the cloth for dampness. It should not be allowed to dry out. Yield—one 8-pound dark *DELICIOUS* fruitcake.

Chapter One

Kathryn's spirits were as gray as the overcast Texas sky.

It was the approaching holidays, of course, she told herself as she tussled with the old lock on her back door. They were wonderful for business—already the shop's daily receipts were climbing, and it was only the first of November—but for her, the holidays were a time to be endured, a sharp annual reminder of dreams unfulfilled and the emptiness of her life.

In years past she had tried to adopt a festive attitude, putting up a tree and decorating the house, cooking a feast with all the trimmings, but somehow, with just her and her father to share it, it had never seemed like much of a celebration. Now that he was gone, she knew that this year she would not even bother to make the effort, and that saddened her even more.

Impatient with her maudlin mood, Kathryn gave the key a hard twist. The lock clicked and she opened the door, shoving the self-pitying thoughts away as she stepped inside. Following her routine by rote, she turned on the radio to fill the silence and switched on the coffee maker. As it brewed she flipped through the day's mail.

A few minutes later the rumble of an engine drew her attention. Leaning forward, she peered out the window over the kitchen sink, her eyes lighting when she saw Daniel Westwood climb from his pickup and head for her back door.

Quickly, she bent and checked her reflection in the gleaming surface of the toaster, but she barely had time to fluff her hair and inspect her lipstick before his knock sounded. The next instant the door opened and Dan poked his tawny head inside.

"Hi, Kath. You busy?"

"No, not at all." Even if she had been, it wouldn't have mattered. She was never too busy for Dan. Smiling, she fluttered a hand toward the coffee maker. "I just got home and was about to unwind with a cup of coffee. Would you like some?"

"Sounds good."

Dan shrugged out of his sheepskin-lined coat and hung it and his Stetson on the rack beside the back door. He joined her at the counter, lounging back with his lean hips against the edge, his long legs outstretched and crossed at the ankles. When she handed him the steaming mug of coffee, he accepted it with a wink and a smile.

Blustery winds had tousled the sun-streaked hair that grew just a shade too long over his ears. The fresh crispness of the outdoors clung to his skin, mingling with his scent and the delicious aroma of freshly brewed coffee. Kathryn's senses tingled, and a soft smile curved her mouth as she looked at him. He dominated her blue-and-white kitchen with his size, his tough maleness, that vital sensuality that was so much a part of him.

"Hmmm. You always did make the best coffee in Boley," he said, swigging down nearly half the scalding brew in one swallow.

She merely smiled and sipped her own, content for the moment simply to be near him.

Something was bothering him, Kathryn thought as she focused on the pulsing vein in his temple. She had known Dan all her life, and, despite his casual air, she could tell when he had something on his mind. She waited, knowing he would tell her when he was ready.

"So, how are the children?" she asked after a moment.

Dan gave a snort and shot her a wry look. "Susan creeps around the house like a little ghost, Joey sucks his thumb and whines all the time and Carla bursts into tears at the drop of a hat. I never know what I'm going to say to set her off."

"It's just the age, Dan. Fourteen is a very difficult time for a girl."

"Yeah. Especially for one without a mother."

He looked tired and dispirited, and Kathryn's tender heart went out to him. Since his wife's death three years earlier, Dan had struggled to be both mother and father to his children. Between his large veterinary practice and the demands of his family, he was run ragged most of the time.

She placed her hand on his forearm. "I know it's difficult, Dan, but you're doing a wonderful job. Really."

He took another swig of coffee and shook his head. "Lord knows I try, Kath, but those kids need more than I can give them. They deserve more. And I've made up my mind to do something about it."

Kathryn felt as though her chest were being squeezed by a giant fist. Dear Lord. Had he come to tell her he was getting married again?

Swirling the brown liquid remaining in his cup, Dan stared at it. "That's why I'm here, Kath." He looked at her then, his hazel eyes dark and serious. "I have to talk to you."

She braced herself, her free hand clenched so tightly that her nails were digging into her palm. "All right."

"I've been giving this a lot of thought, and, well...I think it would be a good idea—for both of us—if we got married."

She stared, not quite believing she had heard him right.

The cup she was holding began to rattle against the saucer, and she carefully placed it on the counter.

"You...you want to marry me?"

"I want a mother for my children, Kath," he said bluntly. "They need a woman in their life, someone gentle and understanding who'll be there for them, care for them, listen to their troubles—someone they can tell all those things that they can't tell a dad."

He could have no idea how much his proposal hurt her. She had loved Dan since she was sixteen, had dreamed of him asking her to marry him in a thousand different ways...but not like this. Never like this.

She wanted to lash out, to pummel his chest and shriek at him for trampling on her feelings, but of course she wouldn't. He didn't know of her feelings. She had taken great care to hide them from him—and from everyone else. She was simply his friend, someone who was always there, ready with a cup of coffee and a sympathetic ear when he was down and needed to talk.

"Dan, I know you love your children, but that's not a good enough reason to marry," she said in a voice that was not quite steady.

"I can't think of a better one."

Her blue eyes widened in astonishment. "What about love?"

"Aw, Kath, honey, I can't wait around for love. My kids need a mother now. And I need a wife." Startled, Kathryn blinked, and he gave a little laugh. "My reasons for wanting to marry aren't altogether self-less, I'll admit. To tell you the truth, I'm damned tired of sleeping alone in a cold bed."

Kathryn blushed hotly, her body tingling at the thought of sleeping with Dan. How would it be, lying in his arms, holding him, loving him? Oh, God, she'd dreamed of it so often!

Grinning, he touched his forefinger to her warm cheek. "What's the matter, Kath; did I shock you? I'm a man, honey, with a man's needs, and I'm tired of having to go Amarillo every time I want to satisfy them. After nineteen years of marriage I guess I'm too domesticated to enjoy playing the part of a young stud. I prefer one woman to a string of one-night stands."

The fist around Kathryn's chest squeezed tighter. She pulled back from his touch and took three jerky steps away, wrapping her arms around her middle. She didn't want to hear this. All those years she had tried not to think of him in bed with his wife, making love to her, holding her in the sweet, warm darkness. It had been too painful to bear. Since Barbara's death she had naively assumed, or maybe she had just pretended, that he led the same solitary existence as she. The thought of him sharing intimacies with another woman, a string of other women, brought a vicious, slashing pain.

She looked at him over her shoulder. "Why pick me?" she asked, her eyes unconsciously pleading for something more, some small hope that he desired her for herself.

"When I decided that marriage was the answer, you were the first one I thought of."

Then he saw the hurt in her eyes. He put down his empty mug and came to her, placing his hands on her shoulders and looking at her contritely. "Ah, Kath, I'm sorry. I didn't mean to hurt you or upset you. It's just that I thought...hell, I still think...that it would be the perfect solution for both of us."

"Solution?" For some strange reason she had an insane desire to giggle.

"Kath, you're all alone now that your dad is gone, and I know you've always wanted a family. I can give you that." His mouth quirked up in a lopsided, half-apologetic smile. "A ready-made one, true, but it's better than nothing."

And at forty, your chances of having any other kind are slim. Dan was too kind to come out and say it, but the implication was there. That it was true didn't make it any easier to accept or the pain any less.

Not that she hadn't had offers. Only two months ago Greg Richards had asked her to marry him. She had been flattered, but she'd had to refuse. Even if he weren't too young for her, she didn't love him.

Mutely, quivering with hurt pride and fighting the ache in her throat, she stared at the second button on Dan's shirt.

He placed a finger beneath her chin and tipped it up. Tenderness softened his roughhewn features. "Do you find the idea of being married to me distasteful?" he asked softly.

Distasteful! She had to stifle a sob of hysterical laughter. Oh, God, if he only knew! Marriage to Dan, loving him, sharing his life, mothering his children— it was all she had ever wanted, more than she had ever hoped to have. But...she had wanted it to be for love, not for such cold, practical reasons.

Even so, to her disgust, she could not quite bring herself to reject the offer. That was how weak she was where Dan was concerned. She closed her eyes. "No. No, of course I don't."

"Is there someone else? Someone I don't know about? I know you date several men, but I didn't think you were serious about any of them."

"No, it's not that. There's no one special. But, Dan, I—"

"We could make it work, Kath," he insisted. "In fact, I think we could have a damned good marriage. We're old friends, so we're not likely to be in for any nasty surprises. We have mutual admiration and respect going for us. The kids like you, and I think you're fond of them."

"Of course I am, but—"

"And..." He cupped his hand around her cheek and looked into her eyes, giving her a teasing smile. "...I happen to think you're one fine-looking woman, Kathryn Talmidge. Believe me, honey, I won't find marriage to you a hardship."

Kathryn's heart thumped. As compliments went, it wasn't terrific, but it was the most intimate thing he had ever said to her. Just knowing that he found her attractive made her feel weak and warm inside. Foolishly hopeful.

"So, what do you say, Kath?" He gave her a coaxing smile and cocked his head to one side. "Will you marry me?"

"Dan, I...I can't give you an answer just yet. I have to have some time to think it through. This...this is all so new."

He frowned, obviously not pleased with her answer, but after a moment he nodded and released her, stepping away. "All right, you think it over," he said, taking his coat from the rack and shrugging into it. With his hand on the doorknob he paused and settled his Stetson on his head. From beneath its broad brim he gave her a piercing look. "Just don't take too long, Kath. I made myself a promise that my children were not going to go through another holiday season without a mother."

With that, he left. In a daze, Kathryn slipped her hands into the deep pockets of her skirt and moved across the kitchen to the door. Night had fallen while they talked, and she watched him stride to his pickup, his broad-shouldered form barely visible in the dim light that spilled from the windows.

Long after he had gone she remained where she was. Her chest was tight with a tumult of conflicting emotions; joy, anger, sadness and hope roiled within her.

Focusing on her reflection in the windowpane, she touched her cheek with her fingertips. What did Dan see when he looked at her? she wondered. She was forty years old, but that was not such a great age, and the years had been kind. Except for a few fine lines about her eyes, her skin was smooth and clear, and as yet no gray had appeared in her shoulder-length sable hair. She was slender, maybe a bit on the thin side, but that was fashionable these days. She was no ravishing beauty or cuddly sexpot, but, with all due modesty, Kathryn knew she was attractive.

With a sigh, she turned away from the window and wandered aimlessly through the house. Whether she was attractive or not, everyone thought of her as the town spinster. If she married Dan, they would think she had done it out of desperation, an old maid taking on the responsibility of another woman's children just so she would finally have a husband.

An ironic smile tilted her mouth. All this time, she had hidden her feelings so well she doubted anyone even suspected that she had been in love with Dan since her sophomore year in high school.

He had graduated that year and gone away to college, and she had lived for those times when he came home for visits. It had been during the Christmas holidays, two years later, that she had asked him if he would take her to her senior prom in the spring. Grinning, Dan had ruffled her hair and said, "Sure, Kath. It's a date."

They never kept that date, Kathryn recalled sadly as she curled up in her father's favorite, leather easy chair before the fireplace. When Dan had come home during spring break, he had brought his bride with him.

She had spent her first year at college trying to forget him, dating dozens of young men and eventually entering into an affair. It had not lasted long; Kathryn had quickly realized that sex without love was not for her. And she loved Dan. Eventually, she'd had to accept that she always would.

Maybe if she hadn't come back to Boley to live, she would have gotten over him, but Kathryn never had the chance to find out. Her parents had been middle-aged when she was born, and by the time she'd finished college her father was a widower and in uncertain health. So Kathryn had come home to stay, and, mainly to have something to fill her days, she'd opened her dress shop.

Kathryn knew what people said about her. "Kathryn Talmidge? Oh, my, such a sweet, unselfish little thing. Devoted her whole life to taking care of her elderly father. That's why she never married, you know."

It wasn't true. Kathryn had loved her father and would have taken care of him in any case, but he was not the cause of her single state. She'd had proposals. Several of them. She hadn't married because she couldn't have Dan.

But you can have him now. You might not have his love, but you can share his life and his children.

Kathryn sighed. It wasn't much, but it was so much closer to her dreams than she had ever thought to come.

She was torn between logic and longing, and in the end, longing won out. She could well be letting herself in for more heartache, but she had no choice. If she did not marry Dan, he'd find another woman to mother his children and warm his bed, and she simply could not go through that again.

Chapter Two

When Dan made up his mind to do something, he did it.

Kathryn called him that same evening with her answer, and four days later, in his parents' living room, with only a few friends and his family present, they were married.

It wasn't that he was an impulsive man, given to rash actions. He had devoted a lot of thought to his situation, but once he had decided to marry, he had seen no reason to delay. Plus, he admitted to himself, there had been that uneasy, half-formed feeling that if he gave Kathryn too much time to think it over, she might change her mind.

Dan sipped champagne and gazed across the room at his bride of fifteen minutes. She had been the first woman he'd thought of. Which was curious, considering he'd never dated her, had never even kissed her before that brief, surprising exchange at the end of the ceremony.

He knew a lot of single women, both in Boley and Amarillo. Most were younger than Kathryn. Some were prettier. Well...as pretty, anyway, he amended as he took in the lovely picture she made in the pale blue dress, with her dark hair piled on top of her head.

A few of the women he'd considered asking had been widowed or divorced, experienced in marriage and child rearing. Yet his thoughts had kept returning to Kath. He wasn't sure just why.

Probably because you're so comfortable with her, he told himself as he watched her smile at something Ivy Thompson said. The minister's wife was a vague woman who could drive a saint crazy with her meaningless chatter, but Kathryn's attention never wavered.

There was a serenity about her, a quiet strength that soothed and reassured. It had drawn him to her countless times over the years. Whenever he had felt discouraged or angry or worried about something, he had always dropped by Kathryn's for a cup of her coffee and a chat. She would listen, really listen, her soft blue eyes filled with understanding and fastened on you as though what you were saying was the most important thing in the world.

Oftentimes he had thought that those visits with Kath had saved his marriage. Barbara had been a fiery, exciting woman, both in bed and out, and he had loved her, but she'd had little patience with—or for that matter, interest in—any problem that did not affect her or her precious quarter horses. So he had talked to Kath.

Now he realized suddenly that he had been so determined to marry Kathryn because he wanted—needed—all that warmth and caring. For himself *and* for his children.

Regardless of his reasons, he'd made the right choice. He was sure of it. There was a feeling of...rightness about the whole thing.

He only wished the kids would show more enthusiasm. Recalling their reactions when he had told them the news, Dan grimaced. Susan had withdrawn even more into her shell, and the way Carla had carried on, you would have thought Kathryn was the Wicked Witch of the West.

Only Joey had seemed to like the idea of having a new mother. He had asked hundreds of questions in the past four days, and since they had arrived for the wedding he hadn't let Kath out of his sight. Even now, he was practically hanging on to her skirt.

"Where are you going to take Kathryn for a honeymoon?"

Dan turned his head and looked at his father, surprised by the question. "We're not taking a honeymoon."

"Why not?" Charles Westwood demanded, his white eyebrows drawn together in a disapproving frown. "Kathryn is a lovely woman, and this is her first and only marriage. It seems to me that the least you can do is make it special for her. Things like a honeymoon are important to women."

"Dad, Kath and I are old friends who married for very practical reasons. It's not as though this is a love match."

Charles subjected his son to a long, intent look. "Then more fool you," he said with patent disgust.

Dan's eyebrows arched skyward as he watched his father stalk away, but before he had a chance to question the comment, someone else claimed his attention.

It did not take Dan long to circulate among the few guests, and once the cake had been cut and eaten, the champagne drunk and well-wishes received, it was time to go.

As Dan and Kathryn were saying their goodbyes, Carla, Susan and Joey appeared, all buttoned up in their coats. "We're ready, Dad," Carla announced flatly.

"Wait a minute, you three," Nora Westwood intervened with a chuckle. "You're not going. You're going to stay here with Granddad and me tonight."

The two younger children looked uncertainly from their grandmother to their father, but Carla's eyes flashed defiance. She lifted her chin, her face growing even more sullen. "We can't. We didn't bring any clothes with us."

Nora sent her son an exasperated look that told him exactly what she thought of his lack of sensitivity and planning, but when she turned to her recalcitrant granddaughter she smiled. "Nonsense. That's no problem. There are plenty of your clothes here." She put her arm around Carla's stiff shoulders and gave her a squeeze. "We'll make some popcorn and watch movies. It'll be fun."

"No thanks, Gran. We'd rather go home."

"All the same, I think it would be better if you stayed," Nora said, and this time there was a note of steel in her voice that said she would brook no argument.

"Why? So Dad can be alone with *her*?" Carla flared, glaring at Kathryn. "I can't see what difference it makes. Everybody knows what they're going to—"

"Carla!" Dan thundered. "That will be enough!"

"If you loved my mother you wouldn't ha—"

"I did love your mother, Carla. Very much. But she's gone. I'm married to Kathryn now, and as my wife she at least deserves your respect. Now, I want you to apologize to her at once."

"Dan, no, please—"

"Yes," he insisted, cutting off Kathryn's protest. "I won't have her behaving this way toward you."

An uncomfortable silence fell. Susan edged to the back of the group. Clinging to his grandmother, Joey buried his face against her thigh and began to whimper.

After a tense moment, Carla muttered a surly "I'm sorry," not quite meeting Kathryn's eyes.

"That's all right, dear. I understand," she replied, but the statement merely earned her a narrow-eyed look of intense dislike.

Nora and Charles stepped into the breach, smoothing over the awkward moment with hugs and well-wishes, and soon everyone joined in. They opened the door to blustering winds and sleet, and as Dan and Kathryn made a dash for the car they were peppered with rice and boisterous shouts of congratulations.

When they had pulled away from the curb and were heading for Dan's place on the outskirts of town, he slanted her an apologetic glance. "Sorry about that, Kath."

"About what? The send-off, or Carla's outburst?"

"Both, I guess." He reached over and gave her hand a squeeze. "But look, about Carla—please don't take it personally. It's just that...well...she was very close to her mother, and it's hard for her to accept someone else—anyone else—in her place. But she's always liked you, Kath; she'll come around eventually."

"I hope you're right."

"I am. You'll see. As you said, fourteen is a difficult age."

Kathryn gave him a wan smile and leaned her head back on the seat.

Dan glanced at her delicate profile and knew again that warm feeling he'd been experiencing ever since he had asked her to marry him.

They rode in silence, each lost in thought. The only sounds were the swish of tires on the wet paving, the rhythmic thump of the wipers, the soft whir of the heater. As it filled the car interior with warmth, Dan caught a whiff of Kathryn's subtle perfume. To his surprise, he realized that he was acutely aware of her— her warmth, her nearness, the allure of the soft feminine curves beneath the enveloping coat.

Ironically, until Carla's outburst he hadn't given all that much thought to the physical side of this marriage. He'd been too busy rushing around making the arrangements. Plus, he simply wasn't used to thinking of Kathryn in a sexual way. Not that he hadn't had a stray erotic thought about her now and then. After all, he was a normal male, and she was a beautiful woman. But, besides the fact that he believed in being a faithful husband, their friendship had always meant too much to him to risk jeopardizing it.

Now, however, he found he was looking forward to making love to her. Already he felt a stirring rush of heat in his loins as his body tightened in anticipation.

Of course, he didn't expect fireworks or steamy passion. Kathryn was a soothing woman—gentle, quiet, giving. Easy on the nerves as well as the eyes. And she was exactly what he needed. Her tender heart would make her a good mother and a pleasant companion, and she would bring order and peace to his life with that sweet calm of hers.

At that moment, Kathryn was feeling anything but calm. She had not had a calm moment in four days.

They had passed in a blur of activity and turbulent emotion, fear and doubt, hope and anticipation all churning within her. And today—today she had been a bundle of raw nerves. Everything had seemed like a dream—the music, the flowers, floating down the stairs on Charles's arm, Dan waiting for her, Reverend Thompson's mellifluous voice saying those words she had never thought to hear.

Do you, Kathryn Ann Talmidge, take this man, Daniel Roman Westwood, to be your lawful wedded husband? To have and to hold from this day forward, for better or for worse, for richer or for poorer, in sickness and in health, as long as you both shall live?

Kathryn had been quaking inside, her heart filled with such sweet pressure that she'd thought it would surely burst. She had barely been able to whisper "I do." If it had been possible to die from joy, she would have at that moment.

Dan had made the same reply in his strong, sure voice, and they were pronounced husband and wife. He had gathered her in his arms then, and for the first time, their lips met in a slow, soft, stunningly sensual kiss that surpassed every dream she'd ever had. She had almost shattered with delight, her heart booming, her body going weak and warm, melting against him as his hard arms supported her.

Even now, just thinking about it made her giddy.

Surreptitiously, Kathryn extended her left hand and gazed at the wide gold band on her finger. It gleamed in the dim light from the dash. *Kathryn Westwood. Mrs. Daniel Westwood.*

She closed her eyes again, a tiny smile curving her mouth. Those few precious moments would stay sharply etched in her memory forever, even if she lived to be a hundred.

Carla's tantrum had been the only sour note. It had added to Kathryn's doubts and briefly made her wonder if she had done the right thing in marrying Dan. But it was too late to turn back now, and in any case, she doubted that she could have mustered the strength to refuse him.

It did not take long to reach Dan's home. The rambling old house had been built in the previous century by a local rancher, and though it was of no particular period, it had charm and character. Dan and Barbara had purchased it ten years ago, along with the surrounding hundred acres of land, but the locals still referred to it as the Ebersole place.

Since childhood Kathryn had been enchanted by the house. It was built with quality and craftsmanship, full of interesting nooks and crannies, lovely hand-carved wood and molding and extravagant decorative flourishes from a bygone era.

After parking the car in the garage, Dan took her small case from the back seat, then grabbed her hand, and they sprinted through the blowing sleet and rain to the back veranda.

"Well, this is it. Welcome to your new home, Kath," Dan said, unlocking the door.

Kathryn hesitated, hoping he would carry her over the threshold, but when he pushed the door open and gestured for her to precede him, she swallowed her disappointment and stepped into the old-fashioned kitchen.

As he led her through the downstairs she was surprised and faintly dismayed. The house had stood vacant for a few years before he had bought it, and in those days Kathryn had fantasized about living there, what she would do to spruce it up and return it to its former glory. She assumed that Barbara had done all that, but the interior was just as forlorn and shabby as it had been ten years ago.

The wallpaper was darkened with age and buckling in spots, the dull oak floors had not seen a coat of wax in years, and ancient, heavy curtains hung in limp folds over the windows. The house was clean and fairly neat, but there was no sign of a woman's touch anywhere.

Kathryn knew that Dan's wife had been a tomboy, more interested in the quarter horses she raised than in decorating or fashion or any of the other things most women enjoyed. Still, it surprised her that Barbara had not bothered to put her personal stamp on the home she had lived in for so long.

It was yet another stark reminder of the differences between herself and Dan's first wife. Depressed, Kathryn wondered, as she had so many times before, if she was even remotely Dan's type. Certainly she was nothing like Barbara. Never had two women been more different, in looks, personality and style.

"Sorry about the house, Kath," Dan said beside her, and she looked at him, blushing as she realized that her dismay had shown on her face. "It needs a lot of work, I know, but...well, Barb just never took any interest in that sort of thing."

"Oh, Dan, I'm sorry. I didn't mean to be rude. I just—"

"That's all right, honey. I've grown used to it like this, but I know it's a mess." Putting an arm around her shoulders, he hugged her to him and smiled. "But at least this way, starting from scratch, you'll be able to decorate it as you please."

Surprise raised her eyebrows. "You wouldn't mind?"

"Mind! Honey, I'm hoping you'll turn this moldy old barn into a home." He leaned down and kissed her, and Kathryn felt the bottom drop out of her stomach. When he raised his head his gaze roamed over her face, surprise glittering in his hazel eyes, along with something darker, more intense, that sent shivers up Kathryn's spine. "This family needs you, Kath," he said in a husky murmur. "I need you."

Kathryn's heart boomed like a kettledrum. He didn't love her, but surely need was the next thing to it. And in time . . . maybe . . .

Her mind shied away from completing the thought, but it was there all the same, a small kernel of hope to which her heart clung fiercely.

He kissed her again, his tongue slipping between her lips to touch the tip of hers. The contact sent fire streaking through her, and she shivered within his embrace.

When their lips parted Dan drew back and cupped her cheek with his palm, his expression tender. "Are you nervous, Kath?"

"I . . . a little," she admitted.

"There's no reason to be. We'll still be friends. Just more . . . intimate friends." He brushed his thumb over her lower lip, his eyes growing dark and heavy lidded as he watched it tremble. "Friends . . . and lovers," he whispered as he slipped his arm around her and led her up the massive oak stairway.

In the master bedroom he placed her case on the bed. "I've cleared some space in the closet and the dresser. The bath is right through there," he said, pointing to the door in the far wall. "I'll use the one across the hall." He kissed her quickly and left.

Standing in the middle of the room, quivering with almost unbearable excitement, Kathryn stared after him.

A short while later, Dan lay propped up in bed, waiting. As he listened to the soft sounds coming from the bathroom he was both amused and amazed at how eager he was for Kathryn to join him.

Eager. He shook his head, giving a rueful chuckle at the understatement. Since leaving his parents' house, he'd been in a constant state of arousal. It was beginning to hit him that along with the change in their relationship, his feelings for Kathryn had shifted subtly. How, he wasn't quite sure yet, except that he was aware of her in ways he never had been before.

The bathroom door opened, and Dan's breath caught. Kathryn stood in the doorway wearing a delicate confection of rose silk and cream lace, and for a moment, backlit by the bright light from the bathroom, her shapely curves were visible through the sheer gown. Except for two thin straps, her shoulders were bare, and her shining hair tumbled against her skin like dark silk.

Kathryn turned out the light and took a hesitant step, then stopped. She gazed at him, her soft blue eyes wide and vulnerable and filled with uncertainty, and Dan felt his heart turn over.

Throwing back the covers, he rose from the bed and went to her. He forgot that she was his lifelong friend and confidante. He forgot that he had asked her to marry him for the most practical and prosaic of reasons. He forgot that he was naked.

He stalked toward her, drawn by her alluring, fragile beauty. Kathryn gasped. Her eyes grew round as they slid over his large muscular body, but he didn't notice her discomfort.

Stopping in front of her, he framed her face with his hands, his long, blunt fingers threading into the hair at her temples. "Oh, Kath." Her name was a sigh on his lips, breathy and full of wonder. His thumbs brushed the hollows beneath her cheekbones as he gazed into her wide, startled eyes. "Sweetheart, you're so beautiful."

The steam rolling from the bathroom was redolent with the feminine scents of bubble bath, floral soap and talc. They clung to her skin, but mixed with them was her enchanting woman smell, which made their effect all the more potent. Dan breathed deeply, delighted, intoxicated.

With utmost tenderness, he kissed her forehead, and when her eyes fluttered shut he pressed his lips to first one satiny lid, then the other. Making a tiny sound of pleasure, Kathryn swayed and grasped his waist for support.

The feel of those small soft hands on him drew a low groan from Dan, and his mouth found hers, rocking, rubbing, nipping with barely restrained hunger.

Blindly, Kathryn sought to deepen the kiss, pressing closer, her mouth open, seeking. A wild, almost unbearable pleasure shuddered through her, making her heart pound and her knees turn to water.

Feeling her quivering reaction, Dan wrapped his arms around her, molding her to him as the kiss became hot and hungry and urgent. His hands smoothed over her, sliding downward to fondle her waist, the enticing rounded hips, before grasping her buttocks and pressing her against his aroused body with a slow, undulating rhythm.

The explosion of pleasure was almost more than Kathryn could bear. Years of longing surged to the surface, and she wrapped her arms around him, her hands moving restlessly, her fingers digging into the hard, flat muscles that banded his broad back.

Plastered together, their mouths still joined in feverish passion, Dan eased them toward the bed, sinking with her onto the wide mattress. He lay half over her, his hand beneath the plunging bodice of her gown cupping her breast, his callused palm rotating against the engorged nipple. His crooked knee pressed between her legs.

Kathryn writhed beneath him, crying out at the tension building inside her, so sweet and hot it was almost pain.

"Easy, sweetheart. Easy," Dan crooned, feeling his control slipping perilously. He was stunned and delighted by her response, but her innocent movements were pushing him over the edge. He wanted to draw it out, to ensure her pleasure, too. It surprised him, but he also wanted to see that lovely, gentle face flushed with passion, feel her going wild beneath him. "This is new ground for us, Kath," he whispered, stringing kisses along her arched neck. "We can take it slow and easy. There's no need to rush."

Kathryn was too caught up in the spiraling need to heed his words. And she had waited years already.

She reached for him, her hands frantic, her expression rapt. She touched him everywhere, his ears, his shoulders, the hollow at the base of his throat, lightly raking his nipples with her nails, threading her fingers through the mat of hair on his chest.

"Love me, Dan," she urged. "Love me."

With a helpless groan, Dan shoved aside her gown and bent his head. Kathryn cried out and arched her back when he took her nipple into the warmth of his mouth. As he drew on her with a slow, sweet suction, his hand slipped under the lower edge of her gown and glided up her silky inner thigh to stroke and caress the moist petals of her womanhood.

In a frenzy of need, Kathryn's exploring hands followed the narrowing path of chest hair downward to his flat, quivering belly. Sucking in his breath, Dan went perfectly still, his jaw clenched, but when he felt her intimate touch he shuddered violently and his restraint snapped. "Oh, God, yes. Yes!"

With swift, desperate motions, he stripped the gown from her, tossing it aside to flutter soundlessly to the floor, and moved into position between her thighs. Braced above her, he looked into her slumberous eyes, stunned anew by her ardency, the rapturous expression on her face. His hesitation lasted only a moment, for his aroused body demanded satisfaction. Following the urging of her soft hands, he thrust into her, slowly, deeply, the intense pleasure of it taking their breath away.

The sensuous rhythm caught them, carrying them quickly beyond reason, beyond all but the exquisite pleasure they shared.

Long moments later Dan braced up on his forearms and smiled at her. "You amaze me, Kathryn Westwood," he said, but there was deep satisfaction in his voice. "All these years I had no idea there was a passionate woman hiding behind that serene exterior."

He was the first to call Kathryn by her new name, and the sound of it on his lips thrilled her. She slid her hands up his arms and over his shoulders, giving him a beguiling look. "Are you complaining?"

"Hardly." Chuckling, he rolled from her and pulled her close, tucking her head against his shoulder. "Just surprised." With a hand under her chin, he tipped her face up and looked at her, his expression tender and serious. "And pleased. Though I should have known we'd be good together; we've always been compatible." He brushed her mouth with a soft kiss, then settled her head back on his shoulder. "We're going to have a good marriage, Kath. I'm going to do my damnedest to make you happy."

Kathryn snuggled closer, and he reached out and turned off the lamp. In the darkness he absently rubbed his jaw against her temple and stared at the window, where tiny pieces of ice clicked against the pane.

She hadn't been a virgin. That had surprised him, and because it had, he felt like a ridiculous fool. In truth, he'd never really given a thought to whether or not Kathryn had had any sexual experience, but, he supposed, like everyone else in town, he had assumed she had not. Which was absurd. She was forty years old, a vibrant, lovely, normal woman, not some neurotic old maid. It was to be expected that at some point in her life she had cared enough for some man to make love with him.

Dan wondered who the man was. It had probably happened a long time ago, and he was sure it couldn't have been anyone in town, or he would have heard about it. In a town the size of Boley it was impossible to keep something like that a secret.

It was normal, Dan told himself. Natural.

Still, though he silently chided himself for it, somehow the thought of Kath lying in the arms of some nameless, faceless man made him feel like punching something.

Unaware of the trend of her new husband's thoughts, Kathryn sighed, blissfully content. She closed her eyes and smiled, absorbing the feel of his warm flesh pressed against hers. Lord, she loved him so! At that moment Kathryn was happier than she had ever been in her life.

The only way she could be happier would be if she had his love. Still, she wouldn't be greedy. For now she would concentrate on their marriage, on making him happy. To do that she was going to have to win over the children, especially Carla. And she would. Somehow.

In time he might even come to love her. Already, by some miracle, she was his wife. Who knew how many more miracles were in store?

Chapter Three

The next morning Kathryn was disappointed when she awoke alone.

"What did you expect?" she chided herself as she slid out of bed and headed for the bathroom. "An early morning cuddle session? Did you really think that one night of lovemaking would make Dan fall head over heels for you? That he would want to linger in bed like a besotted bridegroom?" She bent over the old-fashioned pedestal sink and splashed icy water in her face, then grimaced at her reflection in the mirror as she patted her skin dry with a towel. "Don't be a fool, Kathryn."

Over and over, as she dressed and made her way downstairs, she reminded herself that Dan had married her for practical reasons. He had been open and honest about that, and she had no right to expect more.

She knew that Dan felt affection for her. He would honor her, care for her, be a thoughtful companion. She vowed that she would not be greedy, that if that was all the future offered, then she would be happy with it.

Her spirits took another nose dive, however, when she stepped into the kitchen and discovered that it, too, was empty. Then she spotted the note on the table, anchored beneath the sugar bowl. Reluctantly, she picked it up.

Sorry, Kath, but I got an early call. Colby's prize mare is about to foal, and she's in trouble. I'll be back as soon as I can.

That he had gone out on a call on this particular morning told Kathryn exactly how little sentiment he attached to their marriage. Dan's practice was large and demanding, but there were two other vets in the clinic, and either would have covered for him if he had bothered to ask.

She allowed herself a moment of self-pity, standing there in the middle of the kitchen, her shoulders drooping, feeling hurt and abandoned. But only a moment. With quiet determination, Kathryn squared her shoulders and shook off the mood, reminding herself of her earlier vow.

Deciding there were better ways to spend her time than moping around waiting for Dan to return, she located the keys to his car and drove to her house. Everything had happened so quickly, she had not had time to move her things or even decide what to keep and what to get rid of, and now was as good a time as any to start on that chore.

Two hours later she was bent over, dragging a box that she'd filled with shoes and purses from her closet, when a pair of hard, masculine hands cupped her bottom.

"Hmmm, Mrs. Westwood, I presume."

Kathryn let out a shriek, straightened and whirled around. "Dan!" Weak with relief, she sagged against his chest, and his arms closed around her.

"Who else were you expecting?" he asked with a chuckle.

"No one. Least of all you," she mumbled into his shirt.

She had not meant it to sound like an accusation, but apparently it had. He grew still, and his strong arms tensed around her. "Kath." He said her name hesitantly, his voice touched with wariness and regret. "I'm sorry about this morning."

Kathryn pulled free of his embrace. Their wedding night had been wonderful, marvelous, and she loved Dan to the depth of her soul, but suddenly, recalling the passion, the intimacies, her own abandoned response, she felt self-conscious and ill at ease. And despite the bracing lecture she'd given herself, she harbored some residual hurt and anger over his cavalier treatment. "Oh, don't worry about it," she said. "I understand." She went to the dresser and snatched out items willy-nilly, then added them to the suitcases spread out on the four-poster bed.

Frowning, Dan watched her agitated movements. "I didn't have a choice, Kath," he said quietly. "We're shorthanded at the clinic. Bob is out with the flu, which is why he didn't make it to the wedding. Eli is on call this weekend, but when Colby phoned this morning he was already out on an emergency, so I had to go."

Kathryn looked up, hope she was powerless to hide lighting her eyes. "Really?"

Dan came around to her side of the bed and cupped her face between his palms. "Kath, did you really think I would leave you alone, today of all days, unless I had to?" he asked softly. She bit her lower lip and stared at him, her eyes filled with uncertainty, and he shook his head. "Honey, I may not be the most sensitive guy in the world, but I wouldn't leave my bride of less than twelve hours unless I had no choice. This marriage is important to me, Kath," he stressed in a low, husky voice. "*You're* important to me."

He lowered his head and kissed her, and because she wanted to believe him, *needed* to believe him, she melted into his embrace and let her doubts slip away.

His lips were warm and soft on hers, exquisitely arousing, and Kathryn trembled beneath the tender assault. When he raised his head she blushed. She wasn't used to Dan kissing her, touching her so intimately, and though she loved it, she was terrified of giving herself away.

A teasing glint entered his eyes, and he touched her warm cheek with one finger but made no comment.

To hide her embarrassment Kathryn stepped away from him and bent over one of the open cases on the bed. Sliding his fingers, palms out, into the back pockets of his jeans, Dan looked around with interest. "So this is your room."

"Yes." It had been hers since the day she was born. During the past forty years it had sported everything from a child's clowns and teddy bears to a young girl's frills and flounces to a teenager's posters, mobiles and assorted junk, but for the past eighteen it had looked as it did now, with delicate blue floral wallpaper, graceful period furniture and her mother's plush cream and pale blue Oriental rug covering most of the polished oak floor.

"You know, I've probably been in this house a thousand times over the years, but I've never been upstairs before," Dan mused as he took in the antique bed with its lacy, hand-crocheted canopy and the graceful Philadelphia highboy. He looked at her and smiled. "It looks like you—peaceful, in good taste and elegantly beautiful."

Kathryn was both warmed and flustered by the compliment, but before she could reply, Dan calmly shut the suitcases and set them on the floor. Her eyes widened as he tossed back the candlewick bedspread. "What are you doing?"

"I'm going to make love to my wife." He walked toward her. The weak light filtering in through the lace curtains struck his face, and Kathryn's heart began to thud when she saw his intent look, the heavy-lidded eyes that were fixed on her with blatant desire. Her body grew warm, and a trembling started deep inside her. It was a fantasy come true, one she'd had countless times over the years, seeing that hunger and heat in Dan . . . for her.

He stopped in front of her. "I want you, Kath," he said in a velvety murmur. "Right here. Right now. In this lovely room." Reaching out, he slowly unbuttoned her blouse. "For hours."

So excited she could scarcely breathe, Kathryn stood docilely and allowed him to strip her. When he eased her onto the bed and stepped back to remove his own clothes, she lay watching him, fascinated by his male beauty, the lithe perfection of his hard, fit body. Enthralled as she was, she even forgot about guarding her emotions.

Smiling, Dan lay down beside her and gathered her to him, and Kathryn gave a helpless little moan as he pulled her into his heat. He kissed her temple, her cheek, her arching neck. "You, my sweet Kath, are like an addicting drug," he whispered in her ear. "One taste, and I can't get enough."

Winter's early darkness was already settling in when they returned home hours later. Feeling sated and smug and filled with soaring hope, Kathryn drove Dan's car, and he followed in the pickup, both vehicles loaded with her belongings.

Those hours of passion had been delicious. Dan might not love her, but he desired her. She didn't know how the miracle had come about, but she accepted her good fortune gratefully. Feminine instinct told her that desire that strong could eventually lead to love. If they could make the transition from friends to lovers, surely anything was possible.

As they drove through town, Kathryn noticed that already the merchants were getting into the holiday spirit. A few shops had Thanksgiving decorations in the windows—cornucopias, pilgrims, cardboard turkeys with fanned out crepe paper tails—but most had bypassed that holiday in favor of the glitter and tinsel of Christmas. The bay window of Janine's Hobby Shop boasted a display of handmade ornaments and wreaths, and the bakery, the drugstore and Pruit's Shoe Emporium were all decked out in blinking lights. Sprayed in artificial snow on the plate-glass window of Bowden's Hardware on the corner of Main and Pine was a sign that read Pre-Christmas Sale! Soon, Kathryn thought, the city fathers would hang those huge silver bells tied with red velvet bows to the town's three traffic lights and string gold garlands from lamppost to lamppost, as they did every year.

The decorations, the thought of Christmas, brought home to Kathryn that she no longer had any reason to dread the holidays, and her heart swelled with elation. This year, and for all the years to come, she had a family with whom to share it. A husband. She had Dan.

When they reached the house Dan unloaded her things, then left to pick up the children while Kathryn prepared dinner.

It was the first meal Kathryn had ever cooked for her family, and she wanted it to be special, but she soon discovered that the kitchen was stocked with only the most basic ingredients. Either Dan was not much of a cook or they were all accustomed to very plain fare, indeed.

Making a mental note to grocery shop the next day, Kathryn made do with what she could find and managed to put together a chicken Florentine of sorts, rice pilaf, a salad, rolls and a cherry pie made from canned filling.

She was setting the table in the kitchen when the back door flew open and Joey came barreling in. At the sight of Kathryn he stopped short, relief, then joy chasing across his babyish face. "You're here. Just like Daddy said you'd be. I wanted to come home this morning to see, but Gran wouldn't bring us."

The innocent words revealed a world of fear and wrung Kathryn's tender heart. She put down the silverware and ruffled his tawny hair. He looked so much like his father, she thought, smiling into the dark-fringed hazel eyes gazing up at her with adoration. "Yes, I'm here, Joey," she reassured him softly. "I live here now."

"And you'll be here every day when I get home from kindergarten? Just like a real mommie?" he asked hopefully.

"I . . ." Until that moment Kathryn had not given a thought to making any drastic changes regarding her business, but Joey's expression caused her to rearrange her entire work schedule without a second thought. Kneeling in front of him, she took both his hands in hers. They were soft and warm, still pudgy with baby fat, and slightly sticky. "Yes, Joey. I'll be here."

She would cut back on her hours and work mornings only, make Sarah, her one full-time clerk, store manager, and get her part-time helper to come in more, she decided quickly. It would mean smaller profits, but Joey's needs came first.

"And I can call you Mommie?" he asked eagerly.

"She's not your mommie," Carla snapped from behind him.

Kathryn looked up to see the girl standing just inside the door, glaring at her with undisguised dislike, her stout young body rigid with fury. Susan stood behind her, staring at the floor and twisting one blond braid around and around her fingers.

"Is, too!" Joey insisted whirling on his sister. "Daddy said so!"

"Just because she married Dad doesn't mean—"

"That's enough, Carla." Dan's stern voice cut across his daughter's. "If Joey wants to call Kathryn Mommie, he can, provided it's all right with her."

Four pairs of eyes turned on Kathryn. Dan's were bland and noncommittal, Joey's bright with expectancy. Susan clasped her hands behind her back and shuffled her feet, but every few seconds she risked a wary, curious glance at the woman kneeling before her baby brother. Carla's brown eyes burned with resentment.

Kathryn looked back at Dan in silent censure for putting her on the spot, but when her gaze once again encountered Joey's she knew she was going to have to risk Carla's ire; there was no way she could resist the plea in those big hazel eyes. Nor did she want to.

With a gentle smile, she touched his cheek and pushed the unruly sun-streaked curls off his forehead. "Of course it's all right with me," she said softly. "I've always wanted a little boy."

Before the words were out of her mouth Joey gave a delighted cry and flung himself against her, his chubby arms clamping about her neck in a strangling hug.

Kathryn wrapped her arms around his warm little body and cuddled him close. She could scarcely breathe for the lump in her throat. Over his shoulder, her eyes met Dan's. His smile held approval and gratitude. Emotion quivered through Kathryn. Her chin wobbled and her throat ached, and she closed her eyes against the sudden rush of tears.

"Hey, sport, if you want to eat, you're going to have to let go of her," Dan said, untangling his son from her arms.

The child relinquished his hold with reluctance, but as Kathryn rose to her feet she silently thanked Dan for saving her from making a complete fool of herself; in another minute she would have been weeping.

When they sat down to dinner, Carla took one look at the meal and announced that she didn't like any of it.

"How do you know?" Dan inquired. "You've never had it before."

"I just know, that's all."

He frowned when Carla rose and headed for the pantry. "What are you doing?"

"I'm going to make a sandwich."

"You'll do no such thing. You're going to eat the meal Kathryn cooked for you."

"Daaad!" Carla wailed.

"Dan, I don't think you should—"

"Don't interfere, Kath," he snapped, never taking his eyes from his daughter's petulant face. "I will not tolerate rudeness."

Kathryn felt as though she'd been slapped. Carla sent her a smirking look of triumph, but it faded quickly into anger when her father ordered her to return to the table. With a furious toss of her blond hair, she flounced back across the room and threw herself into her chair.

The first meal with her new family turned out nothing at all the way Kathryn had envisioned. Dan and the girls ate in silence, while Joey, oblivious to the tension in the air, dug into his dinner with gusto, keeping up a cheerful barrage of chatter between bites. Quivering with hurt, Kathryn kept her eyes downcast and did little more than rearrange the food on her plate.

Pleasure moved through Dan as he watched Kathryn. Wearing only a towel knotted about his lean hips, he stood in the bathroom doorway, a shoulder propped against the jamb.

She was sitting at the antique dressing table, which he'd carried upstairs just a few hours ago, her head tilted to one side, methodically brushing her hair. It crackled about the brush and shimmered in the lamplight.

She was a beautiful, desirable woman. Why had it taken him so long to notice? No, that wasn't quite right. He'd noticed. But now...now he was seeing her from a different perspective. Now she was his. His wife. Dan smiled, the thought pleasing him.

Her rose silk gown was cut in a deep V all the way to her waist, and as his gaze tracked the elegant curve of her spine he felt a hot surge of desire. His mouth quirked. Considering the hours they'd spent twined together in her delicate four-poster bed, he hadn't expected to want her again quite so soon.

He'd enjoyed making love to her in that exquisitely feminine room where he was absolutely certain no

other man had ever been. There had been something
erotic about it, something deeply satisfying.

And she had surprised him, last night and again this
afternoon, with all that flaming passion. He was still
having a difficult time relating soft, sweet, serene
Kathryn Talmidge with that sensual woman who'd
caught fire in his arms. He shook his head. Still waters.

He pushed away from the door and crossed the
room to stand behind her. When his hands settled on
her shoulders she jumped and stiffened.

"What's the matter, honey?" he asked, grinning as
he rotated his thumbs over her shoulder blades.
"You're as tense as a fiddle string. Don't tell me
you're still shy."

Her somber gaze met his in the mirror, and gradually his teasing look faded into a frown. His voice
deepened with concern. "What is it, Kath? What's
wrong?"

"Before we go any further, Dan, I want to know
exactly what it is you expect of me."

His frown deepened. "What do you mean?"

"You told me you wanted a mother for your children, yet whenever I open my mouth you shut me up,
tell me not to interfere."

"For Pete's sake, Kath, are you still fretting about
that scene at the table? Carla was behaving like a rude,
obnoxious brat, and I put a stop to it. That's it. It's
over. Settled."

Kathryn rose and faced him, her arms folded over
her midriff. "Dan, you can't *make* her like me, and
forcing the issue is only going to make things worse."

"So what am I supposed to do? I told you, I won't
have her treating you that way."

"Give her time. Let her get to know me. Once she sees that I'm no threat, either to her mother's memory or to her, everything will be fine." She stepped close and put her hand on his chest. Her eyes were soft and beseeching. "Let us work out our relationship on our own, Dan. Please."

Dan cupped his hand around the back of his neck and sighed. "All right. I guess I've had them by myself so long that I'm just not used to sharing the responsibility," he said wearily. "But the next time Carla gets into one of her snits, I promise, I'll let you deal with her."

"Good." A wistful smile wavered about Kathryn's lips. "After all, that's why you married me."

Dan frowned. He didn't like that. Yet...he couldn't dispute it. Feeling somehow at fault, he watched Kathryn walk to the bed and slip beneath the covers. Thoughtfully, he followed.

In the darkness he reached for her, and Kathryn came willingly into his arms, her sweet, soft body pliant against him. This time he took her powerfully, a little roughly, driven by a compulsive need he didn't understand.

A long while later, as Kathryn slept at his side, Dan lay staring at the darkened ceiling, filled with disquiet and a vague sense of guilt.

Chapter Four

Kathryn did not expect miracles. She could only wait and hope that Dan and his children would eventually open their hearts to her.

Because Carla, Susan and Joey were his, she loved them, but she knew it would take time for them to accept her.

She didn't push, didn't make any overt attempts to win them over. Kathryn was simply herself. With patience, understanding and gentle determination, she eased herself into their lives, quietly doing the hundred and one things that wives and mothers do and families take for granted.

Whether or not they noticed, under Kathryn's hand the household ran more smoothly. Suddenly the refrigerator and pantry were always stocked with delicious things to eat, there were always fresh towels in the bathrooms, clean linens on the beds, pressed clothes in the closets, neatly folded underwear in the drawers. The beds were always made, the kitchen always spotless. The stacks of old newspapers and magazines had disappeared from the living room, and fresh flowers and leafy plants were scattered throughout the house.

The children came home to a warm house and were greeted by delicious smells wafting from the kitchen and the sweet scent of potpourri that Kathryn had placed everywhere in little jars and dishes. She was always there to meet them with a smile and a soft word. Caring was in her eyes, and implicit in her manner was the silent offer of support and love—if they wanted it.

Joey, of course, had been her devoted slave from the first, and Kathryn doted on him. He was a bright, affectionate child, as starved for a mother's love as she was to give it. She adored it when he climbed into her lap and cuddled close, and at night when she tucked him into bed and he clamped his chubby little arms around her neck and gave her a wet, smacking kiss she never failed to get a lump in her throat. She even found bath time delightful. Amid the squeals and giggles and splashing she usually ended up as wet as Joey, but it was worth it. When he clambered from the tub for her to dry him, his sturdy little body all warm and rosy and smelling of soap and his wonderful little-boy smell, his hazel eyes gleeful, she knew a happiness beyond measure.

The girls were a different story. Kathryn's overtures of friendship were met with resentment from Carla and skittish withdrawal from Susan. It was distressing, but she bore it with equanimity and forbearance and kept right on trying. Time and patience. Kathryn knew they were her best weapons.

News of their marriage spread through Boley like a prairie fire in the wind. All of Kathryn and Dan's friends and acquaintances called to wish them well. People she barely knew and some she didn't know at all stopped by the shop to offer their congratulations and comments. Kathryn suspected, from the women's giggling comments and sidelong glances, that most had come out of curiosity, wondering how on earth the town's old maid had snagged its most eligible male.

A week after the wedding, Kathryn was in the shop during the noon hour when an attractive woman in her early thirties came in. She paused just inside the door and looked around. When she spotted Kathryn she headed straight for her.

Sighing, Kathryn braced herself for more gushing comments and probing stares and stepped forward to greet the woman. "Hello. May I help you?"

"Yes, I hope so. You are Kathryn Westwood, aren't you? Dr. Dan Westwood's new wife?"

Kathryn willed her smile to remain in place. "Yes, I am."

"Oh, good." At first the woman looked uncomfortable, but she drew a deep breath and began determinedly, "Mrs. Westwood, I'm Lucille Bates. Susan's teacher. I wonder if I might have a word with you."

Alarm widened Kathryn's eyes. "Is something wrong? Is Susan ill?"

"No, no. Nothing like that. It's just that...well...I was wondering if you were planning on being at school this afternoon."

"At school?"

"For the spelling bee." Kathryn gave her a blank look, and Ms. Bates's face registered surprise. "You mean you don't know that Susan has made the semifinals? She didn't tell you?"

"She didn't even mention that she had entered the competition."

"My goodness. I wonder why. I know it's very important to her. She's been studying for months, and she's very excited. You see, today's winner will go on to the district competition."

"I see."

"That's why I'm here. Mrs. Westwood, I hope you don't think I'm interfering, but...well...I think it would mean a lot to Susan if someone from her family were there. She's never had anyone to support her at these sorts of things in the past. Her father tries, but the poor man is always so busy that he seldom can make it. That's why I was so delighted to hear that he'd remarried. My first thought was, now Susan will have someone to root for her."

"Thank you so much for telling me, Ms. Bates. I assure you, I'll be there. And I'll try to reach my husband, too." Kathryn felt a little thrill as she said the words. She still could hardly believe that she and Dan were married.

"Oh, good. It will be held at two o'clock in the school auditorium." Lucille Bates glanced at her watch. "I really must run now. I'm on my lunch break, and if I don't hurry, I'm going to be late." At the door, however, she paused with her hand on the knob and turned back to Kathryn with a speculative look. "I wonder... would you consider becoming a room mother? All you'd have to do is help out with school parties, act as chaperon on field trips—that sort of thing."

Amusement glittered in Kathryn's eyes. Susan's teacher obviously thought she'd found a soft touch. Smart woman, Ms. Bates. "I'll think about it and let you know. Thank you for asking me."

As soon as the door closed behind the woman, Kathryn rushed to the phone and called the veterinary clinic. Dan was out on a call and not expected back for hours, but she left a message, anyway.

Kathryn arrived at the school early and got a seat in the third row. At precisely two o'clock the principal, the teacher who was conducting the spelling bee and the semifinalists filed onto the stage. Susan's gaze made a cursory sweep over the audience, sliding past the third row without a flicker, then stopped and flew back. Kathryn smiled and waved as she watched her stepdaughter's eyes grow round.

When Susan's first time up came her voice was shaky, and Kathryn began to worry that perhaps her presence was making the child nervous.

The initial few rounds brought no casualties, but after a while, one by one, contestants were eliminated. Each time Susan was given a word, she first glanced at her stepmother, who smiled and gave her a thumbs-up signal, then slowly spelled it. And each time Kathryn heard that quivering little voice, her heart swelled with pride, and tension knotted her stomach.

At the end, only Susan and a boy named Mike Sanders were left standing. There followed five more perfect rounds. Through them Kathryn sat forward in her seat with all her fingers crossed, gnawing her lower lip, her gaze fastened on Susan.

Then Mike missed a word.

Kathryn held her breath. When Susan spelled the word correctly the breath came out in a whooshing sigh, and she clapped so hard and so long that when the applause ended her palms were red.

"You came," Susan said when she joined Kathryn afterward. Amazement widened her eyes and made her voice a wisp of sound.

"Of course I came. I wouldn't have missed it for anything. Oh, Susan, I'm so proud of you."

"But how did you know?"

"Ms. Bates told me. Sweetheart, why didn't you tell us? If you had, I'm sure your father would've arranged his schedule so that he could have been here."

"I . . . I knew Daddy would be busy."

"You could have told me."

"I thought you'd be busy, too. Besides..." Susan fingered one braid, stared at the toe of her scuffed shoe and mumbled, "I didn't think you'd be interested."

"Oh, Susan." Kathryn placed her fingers beneath the girl's chin and tipped her face up. She smiled gravely, her blue eyes soft with gentle reprimand. "I'm interested in *you*. Don't you know that?"

Susan licked her lips and swallowed hard. She stared searchingly, her expression a mixture of wariness and hope, and Kathryn felt her heart constrict at the stark vulnerability in that thin, painfully young face. "R-really?" she finally managed.

Kathryn wanted to hug the child to her breast and tell her what was in her heart, but she resisted the temptation. Not yet. Not yet, her common sense urged. It's too soon.

"Yes, really." Striving for a lighter mood, she gave Susan's braid a teasing tug, put her arm around her shoulders and led her toward the auditorium doors. "Come on. Let's go find your brother before he gets on the school bus, and I'll give you both a ride home."

Susan acquiesced without a word, her expression thoughtful. As they walked down the hall toward Joey's kindergarten class Kathryn glanced at her and said, "By the way, your teacher asked me if I would be a room mother."

The girl's head jerked up, her startled gaze flying to Kathryn's face. "Are you gonna?"

"I thought I would." Casting her a sidelong look, she cocked one brow. "Unless, of course, you'd rather I didn't."

"No, I'd li—" Susan stopped. Schooling her features, she gave an elaborately casual shrug and replied, "Makes no difference to me."

"Then it's settled," Kathryn said, fighting back a smile.

Taking Dan at his word, Kathryn started right away on redoing the house. The entire project was going to take months, but she was determined to have at least the living room, dining room and entry hall finished in time for Christmas. Having known for years exactly what she would do with each room, she was able to skip the planning stage and plunge right in.

She hired Jake Riley, the local handyman, to do the work. He walked through the house with her as she explained what she wanted done, and he made up a list of supplies he would need. Armed with the tally, Kathryn drove into Amarillo, where she rented a floor sander and bought varnish, solvent, paint, wallpaper and various tools. Two days after Susan's spelling bee, work began.

The children arrived home from school that afternoon to chaos. All the furniture had been removed from the living room, dining room and foyer; the floors were littered with shreds of wallpaper that had been stripped from the walls; the air was thick with dust and reeked of old paste, age and the pungent fumes of varnish remover. In the center of the living-room floor, two sawhorses with a sheet of plywood over them formed a work surface, and scaffolding was set up along the walls. Standing on the raised platform, wearing a cap on his bald head and paint-spattered white coveralls that hung on his lanky frame like wet wash on a windless day, Jake Riley was slopping solvent onto the ceiling molding. Dressed in faded jeans and one of Dan's old shirts, with a bandanna tied over her hair, Kathryn watched him from below.

As usual, the children burst into the house in a storm of clattering footsteps and boisterous chatter, but as soon as the door slammed behind them absolute silence fell.

Surprised, Kathryn glanced at her watch, then spun around and stepped to the doorway. "Hi, kids. My goodness, I had no idea it was so late."

They were standing stock-still, their expressions dumbfounded, looking around at the bare walls and the mess littering the floor. Carla's gaze, angry and accusing, turned on Kathryn. "What are you doing?" she demanded.

"I've started redecorating. I know it looks awful now, but just wait. It's going to be beautiful when—"

"You have no right! No right!"

"Carla, please, listen to me. It will be lovely when I'm through, I promise you. I'm sure you'll like it. And think how pretty it will be for the holidays to have it all fixed up."

"No! I'll hate it! I hate it already. How dare you come in here and start changing everything? This is my mother's house, and we like it just the way it is." With a sob, she bolted for the stairs, taking them two at a time, the anguished cry trailing behind her.

They heard her footsteps pounding down the upstairs hall; then a door slammed. In the uncomfortable silence, Kathryn looked back at the other two and found that Joey was biting his lip, his eyes round as saucers, and Susan was watching her uncertainly. Kathryn recalled how happy the child had been after the spelling bee, how last night and again this morning she had seemed to draw tentatively closer. And now this.

Kathryn sighed. "Perhaps you'd better go up and make sure she's okay," she suggested, and Susan nodded and flitted up the stairs like a wraith.

"Why's Carla crying? What's she mad about?" Joey asked in a quavering little voice.

"She's just upset, Joey, but it's nothing for you to worry about. Now, why don't you run out to the kitchen and get some cookies while I talk to Mr. Riley. I'll be there in a few minutes."

"Okay," he muttered as he trudged away through the litter toward the door at the end of the hall, glancing back over his shoulder at her every few steps.

When Kathryn reentered the living room, Jake paused in the act of dipping his brush into the can of solvent and looked at her with his bushy eyebrows raised. "You want I should stop?"

"No, of course not. It's too late for that now, anyway."

"Jist wondered. That little gal was shore upset." He spit a stream of brown tobacco juice into the empty can sitting on the end of the scaffolding and wiped his mouth with the back of his hand. "But then, I reckon she'll get over it," he said, picking up the brush again.

"I'm sure she will."

Kathryn folded her arms around her middle and looked sadly at the stairs. It seemed that for every step forward, she took another back.

Dan's reaction to the remodeling was not much better than Carla's.

Due to an emergency he had to work late that night, and sometime after eleven Kathryn was awakened from a sound sleep by a tremendous crash, followed by a string of curses. Without taking time to put on her robe or slippers, she dashed downstairs to find

Dan standing in the middle of the hall, his booted feet braced wide, fists propped on his hips, scowling at the mess. Jake's extension ladder lay drunkenly across the floor, one end tilted up on the bottom step of the stairs.

"Dan! What happened?"

His furious gaze turned on Kathryn, where she hovered halfway up the stairs, one hand on the rail, the other curled into a fist and pressed against her chest. "I knocked the damned ladder over," he said in a grating voice. "Now, would you mind telling me just what in the name of hell is going on here?"

Kathryn shifted uneasily from one bare foot to the other. "I, uh . . . I hired Jake to do the renovating and redecorating. He started today."

"You what!"

"You told me to fix the place up."

"Good Lord, Kathryn, I didn't mean right now! It's less than six weeks until Christmas! And Thanksgiving is just nine days away! How are we supposed to enjoy either one in this mess?"

Hurt pierced her. In all the years she'd known him, Dan had never talked to her in that tone of voice before. Nevertheless, she lifted her chin and replied, "We can have Thanksgiving at my house. And Jake assured me that he'll be finished in four weeks. Five at the most."

"Uh-huh, sure." Dan jerked up the ladder and propped it against the wall, then started to climb the stairs.

"Dan, please." Kathryn put her hand on his arm as he went to move past her, stopping him. "I'm sorry. If I had known it would upset you, I'd—"

"Look, Kathryn . . ." He sighed and raked a hand through his hair. "They've got problems out at the

Abbott spread, and I've been inoculating cattle and horses for the past seventeen hours. Tomorrow promises to be more of the same. I've been stepped on, kicked, bitten and butted. I'm tired, I'm dirty and not in the best of moods, so let's just drop it. Okay? It's too late to do anything about it now, anyway.'' He shook off her hand and climbed the remainder of the steps without another word, the set of his shoulders and his stiff carriage telegraphing his anger.

Kathryn gazed after him, feeling guilty and hurt and disappointed. The wooden stair tread was cold beneath her bare feet and coated with a fine layer of grit from the day's activities. She had turned the heat down before retiring, and the chill raised gooseflesh over her arms and shoulders. She noticed neither. She turned her head and studied the littered floor and the ugly stripped walls, and her spirits plummeted lower. Too late she realized that she should have discussed her plan with Dan before putting it into action, should have at least asked his opinion. ''That's what comes of being single so long and making all your own decisions,'' she muttered to herself glumly as she turned and trudged up the stairs.

When Dan awoke the next morning and glanced at Kathryn sleeping peacefully beside him, he felt guilty for the sharp way he had spoken to her. He wasn't happy about the house being torn apart, especially now, with the holidays coming up, but to be fair, he *had* told her to do whatever she wanted with it.

Bracing himself on one elbow, Dan studied his wife in the weak predawn light, his expression growing tender as his gaze traced the incredibly fragile eyelids and the sweep of dark lashes that lay against her cheeks like feathery fans. Her skin was scrubbed clean and silky soft, her pink lips sweetly curved, slightly parted in slumber and very inviting. With a grimace, he resisted the urge to kiss her and instead smoothed a dark lock of hair off her cheek.

It struck him there in the quiet stillness of early morning that Kathryn was the most utterly feminine woman he had ever known. Soft. Nurturing. Without an ounce of guile or coyness. It was part of what had drawn him to her over the years. He found it infinitely more appealing and arousing than overt sexuality.

And beneath that tranquil surface were secret depths that fascinated him more each day.

With a sigh, Dan eased from the bed and headed for the bathroom. When he was shaved and dressed he paused beside the bed, debating whether or not to wake her and apologize. He ran a callused forefinger over the elegant curve of her cheek and smiled foolishly when she made a sleepy sound and shifted away from the feathery touch. No, he'd let her sleep, he decided finally and bent to brush her forehead with a kiss. He'd talk to her when he came home.

But the day turned out to be a repeat of the previous one. The situation at the Abbott ranch was critical, and it was after midnight when Dan arrived home. Kathryn was asleep when he tiptoed into the bedroom and asleep when he left the following morning before dawn. It took almost four days to finish inoculating the Abbott stock and complete treatment on the ailing animals, but when he was done he headed his pickup for home.

It was a little after noon when he turned into his driveway. He was tired, hungry and needed a shower, but that wasn't the reason he was there. He wouldn't lie to himself. He was there because he couldn't stay away a minute longer. The admission brought a wry twist to Dan's mouth as he killed the engine and climbed from the pickup. Turning up the collar of his sheepskin coat against the blustery wind, he hurried toward the house, anticipation building in his chest.

Kathryn was running something through the food processor and didn't hear him step into the kitchen. He leaned back against the door and watched her, his expression softening into tenderness.

He hadn't expected this fierce attraction, this deep yearning to see her. Touch her. Be near her all the time. He had expected peace with this marriage, that their lives would settle, become routine. Wasn't the familiarity of marriage supposed to create, if not boredom, exactly, then a sort of comfortable complacency?

Hell. Since he'd married Kath life had been anything but comfortable. He was forty-two years old, but she made him feel about twenty—eager and hot and lusty and able to take on the world. He felt foolish admitting it, but he was becoming obsessed with his wife. A woman he'd known all his life, for heaven's sake!

But foolish or not, it excited him to know that beneath that calm exterior was a sultry passion that could burn a man right to his soul—and that it was all for him.

Still, it wasn't enough. Sex with her was fantastic. It was better than fantastic; it surpassed anything he had ever known. Yet he sensed that there was a part of herself she was holding back. Despite all those years that bound them in friendship, and despite the new physical intimacy and sweet sensual awareness between them, there were times when she retreated from him behind those gentle smiles. And the longer they were married, the more it bothered him. He wanted it all. Everything Kath had to give.

She turned off the food processor, and into the silence he said softly, "Hi. Remember me?"

Kathryn gasped and spun around, a spatula in her upraised hand. "Dan!" She closed her eyes and sagged against the counter. "You scared the life out of me."

"Sorry." He looked around. "Where's Jake?"

"He had a dental appointment, so he could only work half a day."

Dan crossed the room and stopped in front of her. In silence, his gaze roamed her upturned face. Then his big hand curved around the side of her neck, his thumb beneath her chin, fingers tunneling under the fall of dark hair as he lowered his mouth to hers. The kiss was soft and hot and hungry, his lips rocking over hers with a slow, sweet passion. Beneath his hand, Dan felt the quiver that ran through Kathryn, felt the throbbing beat of her pulse that so exactly matched his own.

When the kiss ended their lips clung, parting slowly. He raised his head, his hazel eyes intent and filled with male satisfaction as he studied her dazed expression. He rubbed his thumb back and forth across her chin and smiled when her lips trembled. "I missed you," he whispered.

"I missed you, too," Kathryn managed in a breathless little voice.

He bent to kiss her again, then stopped and drew back, a rueful smile kicking up one corner of his mouth as he glanced down at his soiled chambray work shirt. "As enjoyable as this is, I think I'd better hit the shower. I'm not exactly socially acceptable at the moment." He touched her cheek with his forefinger and winked. "I'll be right back."

Kathryn leaned against the sink and watched him go, her heart in her eyes. She would not have cared had he been covered in mud; he looked wonderful to her.

With trembling fingers she touched her lips. The last time they had spoken he had been angry, but there had been nothing angry about that kiss. Hope burgeoned inside Kathryn, thrusting up within her breast with the fragile insistence of a flower unfolding. Surely, *surely*, he couldn't kiss her that way unless he was beginning to love her. Just a little.

A short while later Dan returned, bringing with him the fresh, woodsy scent of the soap he used, and when Kathryn turned to greet him her throat went dry. He was barefoot and wearing a pair of snug jeans. He had pulled on a shirt but neglected to tuck it in or button it, and it hung loose and open. His hair was wet, the tawny strands darkened to brown and hanging in soft tendrils across his forehead. Moisture beaded the mat of gold curls that covered his chest and arrowed downward to swirl around his navel and disappear beneath the low-slung waistband of the faded jeans. He looked big and bold and impossibly virile.

With an effort, Kathryn dragged her gaze away from his body and found that he was watching her intently. She squirmed and fluttered a hand toward the table. "Would you, uh...would you like some lunch?"

"Yes. I'm starving." His unwavering gaze remained fixed on her.

"Would you like a sandwich?"

"No."

"Then how about some soup? I made some yester-day." She stepped toward the refrigerator, reaching for the handle. "It won't take but a minute to warm it."

"No."

"Oh." Kathryn stopped and blinked at his flat re-fusal, then brightened. "I know, how about a salad?"

"No."

"Then what do you want?" she demanded with faint exasperation.

Dan moved toward her with that slow, sexy, loose-limbed saunter, his bare feet silent against the tile floor, and Kathryn's heart began to thump as she watched his eyes grow heavy-lidded and hot. He stopped in front of her and smiled. In a low, dark voice that vibrated with need and sent fire streaking through her, he said, "I want you."

Chapter Five

Much later, they lay in the jumbled bed, luxuriating in the quiet aftermath. Even with their passion spent, Dan kept her beneath him, their intimate embrace unbroken. A feeling of utter contentment filled Kathryn as she gazed dreamily at the ceiling and stroked his back. Outside, the November day was gray and cold. A fine mist was falling, like a gossamer veil, giving the bleak winter landscape the look of an impressionistic painting. In the shadowy room Kathryn felt warm and secure, wrapped in Dan's arms. She loved the feel of his skin against hers, the heavy weight of him crushing her into the mattress. Over the years, when she had dreamed of them together, it had been like this—a storm of passion, then this lovely, quiet closeness, a blending of souls. For the moment she almost felt loved.

Dan nuzzled her neck, inhaling the sweet fragrance of her skin, her hair. "Kath?" he murmured as he mouthed her earlobe.

"Hmmm?"

"About the other night . . . I'm sorry."

Her hands stopped their absent rotation, then started up again. "That's okay. You were right."

"No. No, I wasn't. You were just doing what I'd told you to do. My only excuse for being such a sorehead is that I was beat and out of sorts. Forgive me?"

"Of course." There was a smile in her voice, and her arms tightened around his back. Though briefly she wondered if the exquisite loving they had just shared had simply been an apology, she quickly thrust the thought away. Even if it were true it wouldn't matter, she admitted to herself with a touch of sadness; she would always forgive him anything—everything—so deep and abiding was her love for him.

"Mmmm, my sweet Kath," Dan murmured sleepily as he slid lower. With lazy satisfaction, he kissed her nipples and cupped his hands around her breasts before settling his head against her soft flesh.

A moment later he fell asleep, his moist breath eddying against her skin, warming it. Kathryn sifted her hands through his tawny hair, ran them over his strong back and shoulders, traced a thick silky eyebrow with her forefinger, relishing the freedom to touch him, hold him close. In the peaceful quiet of the dim afternoon she felt happy and cosseted, and after a while she, too, slept.

Over an hour later, Kathryn awoke. She blinked at the clock on the bedside table and gave a startled cry, her eyes growing round with panic.

"Dan! Dan, wake up!" she said, shaking his shoulder. "The children will be home from school any minute."

He raised his head and gave her a crooked grin, his sleepy, sexy smile teasing. "There's no need to panic, Kath. The kids know we sleep together."

"Dan!"

She shoved harder and squirmed from beneath him. As she pawed through the jumble of clothing scattered on the floor, she glanced back at the bed and blushed when she discovered him eyeing her nakedness with possessive satisfaction, a lascivious, purely male gleam in his eyes.

"Dan, will you *hurry*!" Kathryn admonished as she scrambled into her clothes and swiped at her tangled hair with a brush.

Finally, chuckling, he climbed from the bed.

They'd barely made it to the landing when Carla burst through the front door. It hit the wall with a crash as the girl ran for the stairs, sobbing as though her heart would break.

"What the devil—" Dan loped down to meet her, with Kathryn at his heels, but they might as well have been invisible. The distraught girl took the steps two at a time and passed them without a glance, heading for her room.

The two adults exchanged bewildered glances, and at the same time Susan and Joey ambled in through the open door.

Joey's face lit up at the sight of them. "Hi, Mommie! Daddy!" he called with innocent enthusiasm.

After glancing at her sister's retreating form, Susan looked at her father and stepmother, grimaced, rolled her eyes and shut the door behind them.

"What's wrong with Carla?" Dan demanded.

"I think she's crying over some dumb boy," the younger girl said with patent disgust.

"Yeah," Joey agreed. He hooked his satchel over the newel post and took off for the kitchen at a run, calling over his shoulder, "She's silly!"

"Oh, Lord. I should have known," Dan muttered. He heaved a sigh, then turned to Kathryn and smiled tightly. "Well, honey," he announced, sweeping his hand toward his daughter's room with a flourish. "She's all yours."

"Oh, but—"

"No, no. You wanted to deal with Carla's problems your way, so here's your chance. But don't worry.

I guarantee you'll handle this situation better than I could.''

Kathryn had serious doubts on that score. In the two weeks since the wedding her relationship with Carla had not improved one iota. Still...she had made an issue of accepting her share of the responsibility, so she had to at least try.

As she drew near Carla's room the heartrending sounds coming from inside banished Kathryn's reluctance. When her tap on the door brought no response she opened it partway and stuck her head inside. "Carla? May I come in?"

"G-go...a-away. J-just...go away," Carla wailed between broken sobs.

But one glimpse of those heaving shoulders made that impossible for Kathryn. Carla lay huddled on her side in the middle of her bed, her body drawn up in a tight ball, a clenched fist jammed against her mouth. Anguish contorted her features, and her cheeks were slick with tears. Beneath her head they formed a dark blotch on the aqua bedspread.

Kathryn sat down on the bed and touched Carla's shoulder, but the girl flinched away. "Leave m-me alone!"

"Carla, won't you tell me what's wrong?" Kathryn asked gently. "I'd like to help you if I can."

"No one can help me. N-no one! I'm...f-fat and...and ugly...a-and no boy is...e-ever going to notice m-m-me."

The statement brought on another burst of tears, and Kathryn let her cry it out. When the sobs finally abated she said quietly, "I'm sorry you feel that way, but you're wrong, you know."

Carla gave her a sullen glare and swiped at her nose with the back of her hand. "Oh, yeah, sure," she sneered, though her attempt at belligerence was spoiled by the pathetic quiver of her chin.

"I mean it. You're a bit overweight, yes, but that's not an irreversible problem."

"H-how would you know?" Carla demanded resentfully. "You're as s-slender as a model."

"Only because I eat right and exercise." Kathryn reached out and touched a pale curl at Carla's temple. "You have lovely hair and a pretty face. If you lost weight, maybe got a new hairstyle, you'd be every bit as pretty as your mother was."

Carla sucked in a quavering breath and eyed her suspiciously. "You...you thought my mother was pretty?"

"Very. And you can be, too. If you're willing to make the effort, I'll help you with your diet. I'll even exercise with you."

"Why?" Sitting up, Carla scrubbed her cheeks with the backs of her hands and swiped at her nose again. "Why would you do that?"

"Several reasons." Kathryn rose and crossed the room. "Regardless of what you think, I like you. And I'd like for us to be friends." She snatched a wad of tissues from the box on the dresser, walked back and handed it to Carla. "But most of all, I want you to be happy with yourself."

"And you really think it will make a difference?"

"Yes, I do. But I'm warning you, dieting won't be easy, especially with the holidays coming up, because I don't intend to stint on the goodies I make for the rest of the family. It's going to take a lot of willpower and hard work, but if you're willing to give it a try, I'll help you all I can. Okay?"

Carla plucked at a bump in the nubby bedspread and stared at it, her expression sulky. Finally, she dabbed at her swollen eyes and gave a bored shrug. "Sure. Why not?"

The next few weeks were busy, frantic, exhausting...and the happiest of Kathryn's life. Rising an hour earlier than usual, she dragged a sleepy Carla from her bed and took her jogging, each day gradually increasing the distance they covered. Then it was home to make breakfast. About the time everyone was leaving for work and school, Jake arrived, and after getting him started on the current project, Kathryn spent the remainder of each morning at the shop.

Because of the remodeling mess, they had Thanksgiving at Kathryn's house. Carried away by the holiday spirit and the special joy of having a family, she invited not only Dan's parents but also his brother and his family and assorted aunts, uncles and cousins to share the feast. Then she panicked at the thought of feeding so many and spent every afternoon for a week prior to the holiday frantically cooking.

"Good grief, Kath," Dan complained in amused exasperation when he dropped by the house one afternoon and found her baking yet another batch of pies. "You're not feeding an army, you know."

But to Kathryn, thirty people was an army, and at the last minute she decided to bake a ham as well as a turkey. Just in case.

They ended up freezing half the enormous spread, but everyone seemed to enjoy the meal, even Carla, for whom Kathryn had cooked special low-calorie dishes.

Afterward, the men groaned their accolades, then, rubbing full stomachs, gravitated toward the den to watch football on television. The women exchanged recipes and gossip as they tackled the cleanup, while small squealing children darted among them, playing games only they understood. Susan and two cousins her age commandeered Kathryn's old room for a game of Monopoly. Teenagers gathered in the living room to listen to music. For the first time in Kathryn's memory the rambling old house rang with voices and laughter. Life.

The boisterous Westwood clan gathered Kathryn into their midst with the ease and firmness of a mother hen tucking a stray chick under her wing. By the time they all left she was bone tired but gratified beyond measure, and when Dan hugged her close against his side and said, "You did great, Kath," she felt so ridiculously happy that tears sprang into her eyes.

The Christmas shopping season started in earnest the day after Thanksgiving. That meant Kathryn had to put in more hours at the shop, but she always made it a point to be home when the children got back from school, even if it meant returning to work later, in which case she always took Joey, and sometimes Susan, with her. After a while Carla began coming along, too.

If Kathryn showed enthusiasm for Thanksgiving, she pulled out all the stops for Christmas. She was determined that this first Christmas with her new family was going to be as beautiful and as perfect as she could make it.

She bought dozens of gifts, giving each a lot of thought, wrapping them with care and hiding them away in the attic as soon as she brought them home. She sent out Christmas cards to everyone they knew, thrilling each time she signed her name along with Dan's and the children's.

Kathryn drew the children into the festivities by enlisting their help for a marathon of baking. She put

Joey to work shelling nuts and snipping candied fruit and taught Carla and Susan to measure, mix and stir. Together they made Christmas cookies, which the children cut out and decorated themselves, popcorn balls, pumpkin bread, pies and more than a dozen fruitcakes, which they wrapped in brandy-soaked cheesecloth and packed in tins to be given to friends and family.

She worked like a demon to get the house ready for Christmas. A search of the attic turned up a treasure trove of decorations and ornaments, to which Kathryn added the best from her own collection. She hung a huge wreath on the front door, strung colored lights in the shrubs in the front yard and evergreen and holly garlands from the banisters. The scent of bayberry candles filled the house, mistletoe hung over every doorway, and the Nativity scene Susan had made in art class occupied the mantel. In between, Kathryn helped with homework, put on a Christmas party for Susan's class, nursed Joey through a cold and attended aerobics class with Carla two evenings a week.

Though she was bone weary most of the time, it seemed to Kathryn that the closer Christmas loomed, the more things improved at home. Joey, though he was still affectionate, grew secure enough that he no longer clung to her like a limpet, nor did he suck his thumb or whine. He was a happy child and the joy of her life.

Susan spent less and less time holed up in her room and more with the family, often chattering freely to Kathryn as they worked in the kitchen.

The hectic pace of the holidays kept Kathryn from seeing much of Dan, but her nights were spent blissfully wrapped in his arms. Though she cautioned herself against wishful thinking, it seemed to her that his lovemaking became more intense, more ardent, by the day, and a small flicker of hope burned inside her like an eternal flame.

Even Carla was coming around.

To her credit, she stuck to the diet and the rigid routine of jogging and aerobics Kathryn had instigated, and in the first month she lost seventeen pounds and two dress sizes.

To celebrate, Kathryn took her to the shop and told her to select any outfit she wanted.

"You mean it?" Carla squealed, darting from one rack of clothes to another.

"Yes I mean it," Kathryn said, laughing.

Carla tried on one outfit after another, and while Kathryn waited for her to make a choice she helped wait on customers. By the time they left the shop she was so tired that she suggested they stop by the City Café for hot chocolate.

Carla looked at her sharply. "Are you feeling bad again?"

"Just a bit woozy, that's all."

"That's what you said yesterday when we went to aerobics. And this morning you were dizzy while we were jogging."

"I'm just tired." At Carla's skeptical expression she said, "Look, it's nothing. But if it'll make you feel better, as soon as we have some hot chocolate we'll buy a Christmas tree and go home. Okay?"

"We could go home now. Dad and I can come back for the tree."

"Are you kidding?" The bell over the door of the City Café tinkled as she took Carla's elbow and shepherded her inside. "Let a man pick out a Christmas tree? Never!" They settled into a booth in the corner. As Kathryn stripped off her gloves she leaned across the Formica table and whispered in a confiding tone, "Sweetheart, it takes a woman's discerning eye to handle these things. Let a man pick out a tree, and every time he'll come dragging in a monstrosity that's flat on one side, has gaps you couldn't fill with an ornament the size of a basketball and is so tall it overshoots the ceiling by four feet."

Amusement danced in Carla's brown eyes, and the corners of her mouth twitched. "That sounds like the one we had last year."

"Which, no doubt, your father picked."

"Uh-huh," Carla confirmed, and promptly burst out laughing. "Oh, Kathryn, you should have seen it. It was *awful*!"

"Well, don't worry. As soon as we've had our chocolate you and I will go over to Floyd Tully's lot and pick out a beautiful tree."

Five minutes later, as they were sipping their warm drinks and discussing where to put the tree, a man stopped beside the booth.

"Hello, Kathryn," he said, and she looked up, a pleased smile lighting her eyes.

"Greg! How nice to see you." She scooted over and patted the padded bench beside her. "Won't you join us?"

Carla scowled as he slid onto the seat.

"I'm sure you know Mr. Richards, Carla," Kathryn said. "He's the new football coach at your school. Greg, this is Carla Westwood, my stepdaughter."

Greg acknowledged the introduction with a smile and a polite "Hello. It's nice to meet you," to which Carla mumbled a barely civil reply.

Ignoring the sullen girl, Greg turned to Kathryn. "I was surprised to hear that you had married," he said softly. Unspoken, but clear all the same, were the ad-

ditional words, *especially since you turned me down.*
It was there in his hurt look, in the hint of accusation
in his voice.

Regret and pity created a heaviness in Kathryn's
chest, but she refused to feel guilty. She had told him
from the beginning that she didn't want to get serious. To start with, he was too young for her. But Greg
had not heeded her warning, and when he'd proposed
she'd had to explain that she didn't love him, would
never love him in the way he wanted. He was a nice
man, good-looking, pleasant. But he wasn't Dan.

"It happened very suddenly," she said with a gentle
smile.

His sad eyes searched hers. "Are you happy, Kathryn?"

Kathryn sighed. She was beginning to regret asking
him to join them. She stole a glance at Carla and saw
that the girl was glaring daggers. "Yes. I'm very
happy," she assured him and steered the conversation
onto safer ground.

They talked about inconsequential things for several minutes, until Greg noticed their empty cups.

"Here, let me buy you both another round." He
started to raise his hand to signal the waitress, but
Kathryn stopped him.

"No, really. We must be going. Carla and I have to
stop and buy a Christmas tree before we go home."

They slid out of the booth, and Greg held Kathryn's coat as she slipped her arms into it. "That
sounds like fun. Why don't I come along with you? I
can carry it to your car for you."

She was about to refuse when Carla jumped in.

"Floyd will do that. Besides, picking out Christmas trees is a job for women. C'mon, Kathryn. Let's
go." She threw Greg another challenging glare. "My

Dad's probably waiting at home. He worries when Kathryn's late coming home.''

Why, she's warning him off! Kathryn realized as she stared at the girl's black scowl and aggressive stance. She was both stunned and warmed...and a bit amused at the display of jealousy and possessiveness.

Reading the signs of imminent eruption in Carla's eyes, Kathryn excused them as quickly as possible and, with an arm around her shoulders, guided the girl from the café.

Dan wasn't home when they arrived, and Kathryn was too weary to drag the tree into the house, so they left it in the garage, propped in a corner, the trunk in a pail of water. When she went upstairs to change clothes before dinner she sat down on the edge of the bed to remove her shoes and gave in to the temptation to lay her head on the pillow for just a minute.

The next thing she knew Dan was bending over her, unbuttoning her blouse.

"Wha-what? What is it?"

"Shhh. Lie still," he said, going to work on the waistband of her slacks. "You fell asleep with your clothes on. I'm trying to make you more comfortable."

"What time is it? Oh, my Lord!" she exclaimed when she glanced at the clock. "Look at the time! And I haven't even started dinner!" She struggled to sit up, but her puny strength was no match for Dan, and he pushed her back down.

"Don't worry about it. Carla's making soup and sandwiches." He finished undressing her, slipped a gown over her head and tucked her beneath the covers. Kathryn was too exhausted to even protest. He sat down beside her and tenderly caressed her cheek with the backs of his knuckles. "She tells me you haven't been feeling well for a couple of days now."

"No, no. I'm fine. Just a bit tired."

"You're overdoing it, Kath. Pushing yourself too hard. You don't have to be supermom, you know."

"Dan, I'm okay. Really."

He studied her in silence, then bent and kissed her forehead. "All right, then, you rest while I go get you something to eat. I'll be right back."

"Okay," Kathryn agreed, giving in to the awful lethargy. With a sigh, she allowed her heavy eyelids to drift shut and snuggled her cheek into the pillow.

When she next opened her eyes sunlight was pouring in through the curtains at the window. Amazement and guilt were her first reactions. Kathryn couldn't believe that she'd left Dan and the kids to fend for themselves, or that she'd slept like a stone for over twelve straight hours. Even so, she still felt exhausted. It was all she could do to crawl from the bed and dress for work.

"You can't be coming down with something, Kathryn," she told her pale reflection in the mirror as she applied extra blusher to her cheeks. "Not five days before Christmas!"

Fearful that she was doing just that, Kathryn wheedled her way in to see the doctor that afternoon. She hoped he would tell her that the problem was a simple one and that he could give her something to at least stave off the malady for a few days. Instead, his diagnosis knocked her for a loop.

"Pregnant?" Dazed, Kathryn stared across the desk at Dr. Fisher's kindly face, her mouth hanging open. Her heart was booming, and her body tingled all over. "I'm really pregnant?"

Chapter Six

Kathryn sat glassy eyed through Dr. Fisher's lecture on prenatal care and the precautions recommended for a first-time mother of her age, taking in only bits and pieces. When he finished she accepted his congratulations and the prescription for vitamins, made an appointment for the following month and walked out like a robot.

She didn't remember driving home, but fifteen minutes later she was turning into the driveway. By then, however, the numbness was beginning to give way to excitement and burgeoning joy. Kathryn parked the car in the garage, but when she shut off the engine she simply sat there, gripping the steering wheel with both hands.

A baby. A child of her own. She couldn't believe it. She was forty years old and had long ago given up hope of ever becoming a mother. And now... Kathryn placed her palm against her flat stomach. Her throat ached. Her nose burned. She was going to have a baby! Dan's baby.

Overcome, she closed her eyes against the sting of tears and pressed her quivering lips together.

But a moment later she scrambled from the car and dashed through the freezing cold toward the back door, so excited that she was halfway across the yard before she realized it was snowing. She stopped and raised her face. Icy crystals stuck to her lashes and melted on her skin. She caught one on the tip of her tongue and laughed, her heart as light as the feathery flakes that drifted down from the leaden sky.

Dan was not in the best of moods. He stared straight ahead through the falling snow, his jaw clenched. The steady *thump-thump* of the wipers brushing aside the accumulating flakes seemed magnified in the silence.

From the corner of his eye he saw his father take out his pipe and fill it. Since retiring two years before, the elder Westwood occasionally went along on calls just to get out of the house. Dan didn't mind; he enjoyed the company and often welcomed an extra pair of hands to help with a fractious animal. But today he almost wished his father had not come along.

They hadn't spoken a word since leaving the Mason farm, but Dan knew they were both thinking about the same thing.

Damn the woman! In a town the size of Boley very little went unnoticed, and discussing other people's business was the favorite pastime, but Clodine Mason was the biggest gossip of all. They had barely stepped down from the pickup when she sidled up, clapped Dan on the back and—with great delight, it seemed—informed him and everyone within earshot that Kath and Greg Richards had met for a cozy discussion at the café the previous evening.

"Saw 'em myself," she'd bellowed in that foghorn voice of hers. "Sittin' side by side in one of them booths with their heads together." She'd poked him in the ribs then and cackled gleefully, "You'd better watch it, Dan. That there's a mighty good-lookin' young fella, and he's been sweet on Kathryn ever since he hit town. And from the looks he was givin' her, he ain't give up yet."

Malicious old busybody, Dan thought as he reached out and turned on the radio. The country-western lament about cheating love that poured from the speakers made him grind his teeth, and he snapped the radio off, giving the knob a furious twist.

"I heard talk that he asked her to marry him," Charles said out of the blue.

Dan shot his father a hard look. "Who? What are you talking about?"

"Richards. I heard he proposed to Kathryn."

"That's ridiculous. He must be five years younger than Kath."

"Seven. But what's that got to do with anything? Kathryn is a wonderful woman. Anyway, she obviously turned him down." Charles puffed thoughtfully on his pipe for a few seconds, then added, "Of course, that doesn't mean he's stopped loving her."

Dan scowled. He trusted Kath completely. If she'd had coffee with Richards, he knew it had been perfectly innocent. But he didn't like the idea of a man— any man—mooning around after his wife. Kath was *his*, dammit!

After dropping his father off, Dan headed the pickup toward home. Two miles from the house the left front tire blew out, and when he got out the spare it was flat, too. By the time he hitched a ride back into town, bought another tire and hitched a ride back, it was dark and snowing harder. He scraped three knuckles and nearly froze to death putting the new tire on the truck, and when he finally climbed back inside and started for home again, his dark mood had worsened.

Kathryn was wound as tight as a spring by the time Dan arrived. When his mother had dropped the children off she'd been tempted to blurt out her news, but she wanted to tell Dan first. The hours of waiting for him to come home had seemed interminable.

She met him at the back door, her face alight with eagerness. "Dan, we have to talk. I—"

"Not now, Kath," he snapped, tossing his coat over the back of a kitchen chair.

"Dan, I have something to—"

"I said, not now." He strode past her and pushed through the swinging door. On the other side he bumped into a sawhorse sitting in the middle of the hall and cursed fluently. "What the devil is this doing here? Don't tell me Jake isn't finished yet."

"He promised me he would be tomorrow. He only has a few little things left to do."

"Where are the kids?"

"Susan and Joey are watching TV, and Carla went to a matinee with Julie Crenshaw. Mrs. Crenshaw will bring her home," she told him quickly. "But, Dan, listen to me. There's something—"

At that moment, Carla stormed in and slammed the door. She raced for the stairs, her distraught face blotchy and streaked with tears.

Concern for the girl wiped every other thought from Kathryn's mind, and she stepped toward her, her hands outstretched. "Carla, darling, what is it? What's wrong?"

Carla stopped with one foot on the bottom stair and glared. "I starved for weeks and did all that exercising just so Jason would like me, but he hasn't even noticed. And today he was at the movie with another girl," she wailed. "All your so-called advice was worthless! I hate you!"

"Carla, dear, listen to—"

"No! I won't!"

"All right, that's enough! Quiet! Both of you!"

Kathryn jumped at Dan's angry shout. Carla turned reproachful eyes on him, let out an anguished cry and raced up the stairs, her feet pounding the treads like hammerblows.

"Dammit!" Dan thundered. "I don't know where I ever got the idea that marriage to you would solve anything." He swung on Kathryn, glaring fiercely, and flung his arm out in a sweeping arc. "You promptly tore apart my house. My daughter bawls more than ever. Hell, I've hardly had a moment's peace since you moved in."

Kathryn was too stunned and hurt to reply, and after a moment he made an aggravated sound and took the stairs three at a time.

Squeezing her eyes shut, Kathryn stood rooted to the spot, rigid, as though afraid she would shatter at the slightest movement. She listened to his footsteps recede along the upstairs hall, heard the bedroom door bang with an awful sound of finality. Inside she quivered with pain and utter desolation. She had been such a fool. Such a hopeless, romantic fool. Despair welled up inside her, so intense it wrung a silent cry of agony from her soul, and in an unconscious, protective gesture, she hunched her shoulders and folded her arms over her abdomen. Her chin trembled and her throat worked as she fought to hold back tears. One after another they seeped through her tightly closed eyelids and trickled down her cheeks.

"Mommie, Mommie! Come watch TV with us," Joey called from the living room. "They're gonna show 'The Grinch That Stole Christmas'!"

Kathryn's eyes snapped open and darted around. She had to get out of there! She couldn't cope with the children right now. She had to be alone.

Panicked, she snatched her coat from the hall closet and ran. Thrusting her arms into the garment, she grabbed the car keys from the peg beside the back door and raced out into a world of blackness and blowing snow.

In less than a minute she was speeding away, with no thought to where she was headed or the worsening weather conditions. All she could think of was the mess she'd made of everything. You were a fool to be happy about this baby, she told herself scathingly. Dan married you to help raise the children he has, not saddle him with more. And face it, you're not doing a very good job of that.

It occurred to her that he might not even have intended for the marriage to last forever but only until the children were grown and gone. In which case he'll probably be horrified to learn about the baby and that he's inextricably tied to you. And the kids will probably hate the idea, resent the baby. Tears blurred her vision, and she swiped at them impatiently with the back of her hand as she leaned forward to peer through the swirling clouds of white. Oh, Lord, Kathryn, why don't you face it? You don't belong in this family. You're nothing but an intruder. And you're a complete failure as a wife and mother.

It was the last semicoherent thought she had, for at that instant the car hit a patch of ice, slid sideways and nose-dived into a ditch. Kathryn's instinctive scream ended with startling quickness as the world suddenly went black.

Dan's temper cooled before he finished his shower, and when he thought about the things he'd said to Kathryn, guilt and remorse riddled him. "God, what a dumbass you are, Westwood," he muttered to himself as he hurriedly dressed and went in search of her. "Kath doesn't deserve that kind of treatment."

She wasn't in Carla's room, as he had half expected. When he didn't find her downstairs he stopped at the door to the living room, where Susan and Joey were sprawled on the floor watching television. "Does anyone know where Kathryn is?"

Susan spared him a distracted glance. "She may have gone out. I thought I heard the back door slam a few minutes ago."

Out? A chill of unease gripped Dan as he headed for the kitchen. When he saw that her keys were missing from the peg beside the door, his gaze went to the swirl of white beyond the window, and his uneasiness became real fear.

He darted back down the hall, shouted up the stairs for Carla to look after her brother and sister, then took off, grabbing his coat on the way out.

Less than a quarter of a mile from the house he spotted the rear end of Kathryn's car jutting up out of the ditch. Dan's heart lurched. He slammed on the brakes, threw the gearshift into Park and bolted from the pickup almost before it stopped rolling.

He leaped into the ditch and tore open the car door. Fear clawed at him when he saw she was slumped over the steering wheel. "Kath. Oh, Kath, sweetheart. I'm sorry. I'm so sorry," he murmured over and over as he frantically searched for a pulse. His relief was so great when he found one that he almost sagged to his knees.

Quickly, he ran his hands over her. There was a bump on her head and the sticky wetness of blood on her temple, but there didn't appear to be any broken bones. As carefully as possible, he pulled her from the car. With her limp body cradled against his chest, he staggered up out of the ditch and carried her to the idling pickup.

An hour later, Dan was counting endless minutes in the hospital waiting room. He sat on a vinyl-covered bench, leaning forward with his elbows resting on his knees, his hands clasped in a fisted prayer. *Oh, God, please let her be all right. Please.*

In that first instant when he'd seen her car sticking up obscenely from that ditch, it had hit him that he loved Kathryn. More than he had ever loved anything or anyone in his life. If he lost her now, he didn't know how he would bear it.

The casual, undemanding love he'd always felt for Kathryn had deepened and grown into something vital and all-consuming without his knowing quite how or when, though he suspected it had begun long before he'd asked her to marry him.

The sound of footsteps brought his head up. Dan was hoping it would be the doctor, but he wasn't surprised when his father sat down beside him on the bench. He had called his parents the moment the attendants wheeled Kathryn away.

Charles Westwood put a hand on his son's shoulder. "How is she?"

Dan shook his head, his eyes bleak. "There's been no word yet."

"I took your mother over to stay with the children. She said to tell you not to worry and to call her the minute we know something."

"Thanks."

Propping his elbows on his spread knees, Charles assumed the same posture as his son. "So what happened?"

"I yelled at her. Blew up because I was tired and angry—"

"And jealous."

Dan turned his head and met his father's steady gaze. His mouth twisted. "And jealous. And like a fool, I let fly at Kath. I shouldn't have, I know, but . . . dammit, Dad, I just don't understand. Lots of husbands get angry and say things they don't mean without their wives running off into a snowstorm."

"Maybe so." Charles filled his pipe from a leather pouch and tamped down the aromatic tobacco with his thumb. "But then, most wives have the security of knowing that they're loved."

Dan's skin paled even more, and he hung his head. "And I've never said those words to Kath," he murmured guiltily. He wondered if he would ever get the chance, now.

Dr. Fisher appeared in the doorway, and Dan lurched to his feet. "How is she? Will she be all right?"

"Calm down, Dan. She has a nasty bump on her head and a colorful assortment of bruises, but nothing a few days' rest won't cure."

"Thank God." Dan closed his eyes and released a long breath as a shudder rippled through him.

"And equally important," Dr. Fisher continued, "no harm came to the baby."

"Baby?" At first Dan looked confused; then his eyes widened, and his face went comically slack. His knees buckled, and he dropped down hard onto the bench.

"Well, I'll be!" his father whooped, thumping him on the back, but Dan paid no attention.

"Kathryn's pregnant?"

"Yes. Six weeks. She didn't tell you?"

"No, she—" He stopped, remembering her eagerness when she'd met him at the back door.

Dan, we have to talk.

"Oh, God." His expression stricken, he slapped his forehead and slid his hand down over his face wearily. "No. No, she didn't tell me," he said in a voice weighted with self-recrimination. Then his head jerked up, his eyes filled with sudden panic. "Is she all right? I mean, at her age, is it safe?"

"She's fine," Dr. Fisher assured him. "Naturally, we'll take all necessary precautions and monitor her closely, but Kathryn should breeze through this with no problems." He gave his best benign smile. "She's going to be a wonderful mother."

"She *is* a wonderful mother," Dan replied staunchly, and his father's hand tightened on his shoulder in silent approval.

When Dan was finally allowed into Kathryn's room, his heart reeled at the sight of her, so small and still in the hospital bed. She lay with her eyes closed, her hands folded over her abdomen atop the covers. A bandage covered most of her forehead. Her hair seemed darker against the pillow, its sterile whiteness almost matching her pale face.

Dan swallowed hard, love swelling in his chest as he stared at her. With an unsteady hand, he reached out and tenderly stroked her cheek.

Kathryn's eyes fluttered open. "D-Dan."

Gently, he slipped his hand beneath one of hers and brought it to his mouth. He kissed each fingertip and pressed his lips to the center of her palm. Kathryn watched him, bewilderment in her eyes, but when she opened her mouth to speak Dan placed two fingers against her lips.

"Shh. Before you say anything, there's something I have to tell you." He pressed her hand to his cheek.

"I love you, Kath," he said softly. "I love you more than anything in this world. More than life itself."

The astounding statement seemed to set off an explosion in the region of Kathryn's heart, and she caught her breath, her eyes widening.

"I should have told you before this," Dan continued as she stared at him in wonder. "But, fool that I am, I didn't realize it myself until I thought I had lost you."

Two diamond-bright tears welled up in Kathryn's eyes and spilled over. "Oh, Dan," she managed in a small choked voice that quavered with emotion. "Do you really mean that?"

"I mean it."

"Oh, Dan." Her chin wobbled, and more tears followed, streaming down her cheeks unheeded. She lifted her other hand and framed his face between her trembling palms. "I love you, too," she declared tearfully. "So very much. I always have."

Dan bent over and kissed her with such tenderness that Kathryn thought her heart would surely burst. For long, breathless moments his lips caressed hers lovingly, sweetly, while her heart thrummed and the world seemed to spin away.

When at last he raised his head to look at her, his hazel eyes were dark with love and concern. "Forgive me for the things I said, Kath. And for not letting you tell me about the baby."

Alarm flared in her eyes. "You know?"

He nodded. "The doctor told me."

"Do...do you mind very much?"

"I was surprised." He gave a little laugh and shook his head. "No, *surprised* isn't the word; I was stunned." He sat down beside her on the bed and, bending forward, laid his head on her stomach. "But mind? No." He rocked his head against her, and she felt him smile. "Knowing that you're having my baby is the best Christmas present I've ever received." He slid his hand up over her rib cage to cup her breast. "And you? How do you feel about it? Do you mind? Are you worried about having children now?"

Kathryn ran her hands through his hair and smiled, luxuriating in the weight of his head against her, the moist warmth of his breath filtering through the cotton hospital gown, dewing her skin. "I've loved you, wanted you, wanted to have your babies since I was sixteen. How could I be anything but happy?"

Dan raised his head and looked at her, his stunned expression filled with wonder. "Oh, Kath," he whispered as he reached out and touched her cheek with his fingertips. "My Kath."

On Christmas Eve Dan brought Kathryn home. With the second snowfall of the season fluttering around them, he carried her from the car as though she were made of glass.

The instant his footsteps sounded on the porch the front door opened to reveal three anxious faces.

"Mommie! Mommie!" Joey cried, bouncing up and down as though trying to jump into Kathryn's lap.

"Joey, stop that," Carla commanded, dragging him out of the way. "At least let Dad put her down before you pounce on her." Taking charge, she led the way to the living room, shooing the other two children ahead as she called over her shoulder, "This way, Dad. We have a place all set up for her on the sofa."

"But close your eyes, Kathryn," Susan instructed excitedly. "And don't open them until we tell you."

"Yeah," Joey chimed in. "'Cause we got a surprise for you!"

"Don't peek! Don't peek! Keep 'em closed," they all chorused as Dan carried her into the room and set her down.

"I won't. I promise," Kathryn said, laughing.

When she was finally settled, there was silence; then Carla said, "Okay. You can look now."

Slowly, Kathryn opened her eyes, and gasped, joy lighting her face as she looked around. "Oh, kids," she whispered in an awed tone. "It's *beautiful*!"

This part of the house was exactly as Kathryn had always pictured it. The new lighter colors opened it up, giving it a fresh look. Gone was the shabby furniture and the heavy old swags of velvet at the windows. In their place were the graceful period pieces from Kathryn's home, and crisp linen draperies in pale blue and eggshell stripes that blended with the blue-and-cream wallpaper and cream-painted woodwork. The Oriental rug that had been her mother's most prized possession was centered on the polished oak floor before the sofa, which faced the fireplace. Flanking it were her father's red leather easy chair and ottoman and two Queen Anne wing chairs in a beige, blue and cream floral print. Visible through the arched entrance to the dining room was her great-grandmother's rosewood Duncan Phyfe table, bearing a centerpiece of thick red candles, pinecones, nuts, berries and greenery.

Five knit stockings hung from the mantel, and there in the corner of the room, twinkling with hundreds of lights and glittering ornaments, with dozens of gaily wrapped presents spilling outward from its base, was the Christmas tree that had been propped in the garage the last time Kathryn had seen it.

For a moment she was too overcome to speak. She looked at the children and found them standing in a tight little group, watching her. "Do you really like it, Kathryn?" Susan ventured doubtfully. "We didn't know where you wanted the furniture, so we can move it if you want us to."

"No. Everything is perfect. Just perfect." Dan sat beside her on the sofa, and she squeezed his hand as she gazed up at them, touched beyond words. "You all did a marvelous job. It's beautiful. All of it."

The children looked at one another and shifted restlessly, still oddly constrained, even Joey. Eyeing Kathryn's bandage, he asked, "Does your bump still hurt, Mommie?"

"It wouldn't if I could have a hug," Kathryn said, holding her arms out to him.

With a muffled little cry, Joey flung himself into her lap and burrowed close.

Then suddenly, to her surprise, the girls knelt on the floor on either side of her knees. "Kathryn," Carla began hesitantly. "We just want you to know that...well...we're glad to have you home. And...and we're real happy about the new baby."

"When it gets here, we're going to help you take care of it," Susan said earnestly. "We'll feed it and change it and everything."

"Why, thank you, girls." Kathryn squeezed Carla's hand and smoothed a loose tendril of hair away from Susan's face. "I appreciate that."

"And," Carla added, watching Kathryn cautiously, "since the baby will be our brother or sister, we talked it over and...well...we decided it would be best if we all called you Mom."

Dan's arm tightened around Kathryn's shoulders, but she didn't dare look at him or she would break down and cry. Her chest grew so tight that she could barely breathe, and her lips trembled as she murmured over the lump in her throat, "I would love that. Truly."

As though uncomfortable with the emotion-charged atmosphere, Carla jumped up, announcing as she took off for the kitchen that she had dinner ready and would serve Kathryn's on a tray.

It turned out that they all ate from TV trays in the living room. Afterward, Dan and Kathryn gave in to the children's wheedling and allowed them to open one present apiece. As they tore at the gay ribbons and foil wrappings, Dan pulled Kathryn closer against his side and whispered in her ear, "Merry Christmas, my love."

With her heart in her eyes, she reached up and kissed him softly. "Merry Christmas."

The faint peal of church bells sounded in the distance. Outside, snow fell with silent insistence, piling in drifts about the old house. Inside, a fire crackled in the hearth, and children laughed and bantered, while in the background the soft strains of "O Little Town of Bethlehem" flowed from the stereo.

Her heart overflowing, Kathryn snuggled against Dan's chest and gazed at the tree, but its lights became mere blurry spots of color through the wall of tears banked against her eyelids.

Christmas. It really was the season of miracles.

A Note from Ginna Gray

When my editor asked me to write a Christmas story, I was thrilled. But what to write? As I cogitated, it occured to me that, as an adult, I hadn't really appreciated the special magic of Christmas until I met my husband.

The first Christmas Brad and I were together, onerous chores—battling the shopping crowds, tromping through muddy Christmas-tree lots, wrapping gifts and addressing endless cards—all became a joy, simply because they were shared with my beloved. That year the store Santas seemed jollier, the decorations lovelier, the smells of fir and wassail and mince pies more heavenly than ever before. And our holiday enjoyment multiplied a hundredfold as our family grew.

I considered how sad a solitary Christmas would be, and my writer's "what if?" stage began.

What if you were alone because the man you loved had married someone else? What if you saw him daily, yet he never knew of your feelings and considered you a friend? What if you longed for children but were, say... forty, and had given up hope? Then, what if your beloved was single again and asked you to marry him, but for all the wrong reasons? Would you? Could you?

Of course! Christmas, after all, is the *Season of Miracles*. By now Kathryn and Daniel had come alive for me. And after such lonely, gentle steadfastness, it seemed only right that Kathryn would finally win Dan and know all the joys of a family and a Christmas shared. So I had her experience many of the things I enjoy with *my* family, among them, baking my mother's favorite fruitcake.

I hope that this Christmas all of you will find your own special miracle and be as happy and fulfilled as Kathryn and Dan.

Ginna Gray

THE HUMBUG MAN

Diana Palmer

Happy Holidays

Chapter One

Tate Hollister lived alone, which wasn't surprising to his nearest neighbor. He had a temper like black lightning and seemed to hate people in general, and boys in particular. Maggie Jeffries had gotten an earful about the taciturn rancher from her late father-in-law, and her son Blake was an ongoing verbal documentary on his life. If she hadn't loved the boy so much, she might have had some terrible fights with him over the incredible case of hero worship he had for Hollister. Maggie had seen their black-eyed neighbor from time to time over the years, but he avoided her the same way he tried to avoid Blake. But he didn't have a lot of success with the boy; Blake was almost ten and Hollister was his hero.

It was hard to overlook Blake's constant chatter about the man, but Maggie loved her son, so she tried not to be annoyed. She also kept in mind that Blake had never known his father. Bob Jeffries had been a war correspondent. He'd died in Central America covering a story, leaving Maggie destitute and three months pregnant. She'd supported herself by working as secretary to a printing corporation executive. When the company had moved its headquarters from Tennessee to Tucson, Arizona, Maggie had decided to go along with little Blake. Her parents were dead and her three brothers were scattered all over the country, but Grandpa Jeffries had still been alive. She wanted to be close enough that Blake could spend some time with him on his rural Montana ranch.

Over the years, Maggie had rapidly climbed to executive secretary and held a responsible job. Then Grandfather Jeffries had died unexpectedly in the fall and had left this small ranch to Maggie.

Blake, who'd been in military school for the past year, had jumped at the chance to go to Montana. Couldn't they, he pleaded, just for the Christmas holidays? Then Maggie could decide if she wanted to sell the place, couldn't she? After all—he played his trump card with a dejected expression that was only partially faked—they hardly saw each other anymore.

That had done it. Maggie missed her son, despite the fact that she wanted him to be independent and not tied to her apron strings. She'd asked for two weeks leave from her job, just through the Christmas and New Year's holidays. Then she'd found them a temporary secretary to take her place, and she and young Blake had left for the wilds of Montana.

And here they were. In two feet of drifting snow, on a rickety, run-down ranch facing the Bitterroot mountains, with no close neighbors except for the elusive and unfriendly Mr. Hollister, whom Blake seemed to worship from afar for God alone knew what reason.

The ranch house was more of a large cabin than a house, but it wasn't uncomfortable. It had just four rooms, two of which were bedrooms. The living room and dining room were combined, with a small kitchen in one corner and a bathroom that was definitely an afterthought. The furnishings were wood, and all of it had a definite Indian influence, from the blankets and rugs to the paintings that decorated the rough wood walls. The only difference now was the few

Christmas decorations that Maggie and Blake had added, like the pine boughs around the fireplace with their red velvet bows and the cheerful red and green candles and the artificial holly on the coffee table.

Maggie found the idle pace of life in Montana familiar. It brought back memories of her childhood spent in the mountains of southern Tennessee, so close to the Georgia line that it had once been disputed border territory. She'd lived in the backwoods with her parents and three brothers, and it had been a satisfying life until Bob had passed through covering a story and had wooed Maggie out of her mountains and into Memphis and a small apartment.

Sometimes that part of her life seemed like a long-ago dream. If it hadn't been for the photos, she would hardly remember what Bob looked liked, although she'd loved him desperately at the age of eighteen. Now she was twenty-eight, and there were faint threads of silver in her wavy, dark brown hair. She was tall and slender as a willow, but her eyes had a haunted look these days. She was restless lately, and sometimes she felt like she was searching—but she didn't know for what.

"It's fun here." Blake was grinning as he stared out the window at the snow. "I don't miss prickly pear cactus and creosote and roadrunners and dry washes, you bet."

"At least in southern Arizona we didn't have all that snow, or haven't you glanced out the window lately?" she asked, smiling, and her eyes crinkled at the corners. She had an elfin face, very mischievous, and an elegant carriage, which had come from her mother's insistence on proper posture. Those contradictions, added to the faint traces of her southern mountain drawl, made her something of an enigma. She did attract men occasionally, but her rigid Scotch-Irish up-bringing didn't allow for a casual outlook on life, and most of the city men she ran across were as easygoing about sex as they were about letting a woman buy them a meal. It was a kind of life that suited many, but Maggie had too many hang-ups. So she was still single.

She wondered sometimes if Blake was being deprived of male companionship solely because of her attitudes. It bothered her, but she didn't want to change.

"Snow is awesome," he sighed, using a word that he used to denote only the best things in his life. Cherry pie was awesome. So was baseball, if the Atlanta Braves were playing, and football if the Dallas Cowboys were.

She smiled at his dark head, so like her own. He had her slender build, too, but he had his father's green eyes. Bob had been a handsome man. Handsome and far too brave for his own good. Dead at twenty-seven, she sighed, and for what?

She folded her arms across her chest, cozy in the oversize red flannel shirt that she wore over well-broken-in jeans. "It's freezing, that's what it is," she informed her offspring. "And it isn't awesome; it's irritating. Apparently, the electric generator goes out every other day, and the only man who can fix it stays drunk."

"That cowboy seems to know how," Blake said hesitantly.

Maggie agreed reluctantly. "I know. Things were running great until our foreman asked for time off to spend Christmas with his wife's family in Pennsylvania. That leaves me in charge, and what do I know about running a ranch?" she moaned. "I grew up on a small farm, but I don't know beans about how to manage this kind of place, and the men realize it. I suppose they don't have any confidence in working for a secretary, even just temporarily."

"Well, there's always Mr. Hollister," Blake said with pursed lips and a wicked grin.

She glared at him. "Mr. Hollister hates me. He hates you, too, in fact, but you don't seem to let that stand in the way of your admiration for the man." She threw up her hands, off on her favorite subject again. "For heaven's sake, he's a cross between a bear and a moose! He never comes off his mountain except when he wants to cuss somebody out or raise hell!"

"He's lonely," Blake pointed out. "He lives all by himself. It's hard going, I'll bet, and he has to eat his own cooking." He sat up enthusiastically, his thick hair over his brow. "Grandpa said he once knew a man who quit working for Mr. Hollister just because the cook got sick and Mr. Hollister had to feed the men."

Maggie glanced at her son with a wicked gleam in her eyes. "He probably fed them some of his razor blades," she murmured.

"Oh, shame on you," Blake said with a chuckle. "How did I wind up with a mother like this?" he asked the ceiling.

"Well, they ran out of ugly, mean ones, and here I was," Maggie sighed, striking a pose.

Blake laughed harder. He would have agreed with her if he could have stopped laughing. He thought she was the best mom in the whole world, even if she did have this annoying hang-up about his beloved Mr. Hollister. "But really, Mom, you're going to have to do something about the cattle and the men pretty quick," he finally said, sounding grown-up and almost knowledgeable. "The cattle are straying real bad. I saw some down on Mr. Hollister's place just this morning."

She drew in a breath. "Why didn't you say so? For God's sake, don't just sit there. Get some barbed wire, and I'll send for a few land mines...." She shuddered.

"He's a nice man. You just don't understand him," Blake said.

She lifted her eyebrows. "Are we talking about the same Mr. Hollister? The one who looks like a hat and mustache sitting on a rock?" she asked, turning away from Blake's amused grin. "I'll bet if he ever smiled, his face would break."

"Grandpa liked him," he reminded her. "I do, too. You just don't know him, that's all. He's a real jake guy."

"I don't want to know him. That's why I spent every minute I came up here hiding out from him. And I will never learn to understand the language you speak," she informed him. "It goes from mumble to street jive to unintelligible—" A loud knock at the door stopped her in midsentence. "Maybe it's the man who can fix the generator," she said hopefully and went to open the heavy oak door.

A rush of cold air hit her in the face, temporarily blinding her. Montana in winter was uncomfortable, even for natives. The windchill factor was nearly unbearable, and the snow never seemed to stop. This small ranch that she'd inherited from her father-in-law was located between the Bitterroot mountain range on the west and the Pryor mountains on the east, with the Wyoming border to the south. Tate Hollister's much larger ranch and enormous house were on her north border and only about a quarter of a mile from the small frame house she shared with Blake.

She wasn't really surprised to find Tate Hollister on her doorstep when she got her eyes cleared of snowflakes. He was tall already, but he seemed to have grown two feet since Maggie last saw him. He glared down at her from black eyes in a thin-lipped, deeply tanned face, which was all hard lines and sharp angles. He looked to be in his late thirties, and he was as wild a man as Maggie had ever seen. In his battered black ranch hat and sheepskin jacket, worn jeans and black boots, he looked like an outlaw. He needed a shave and his mustache needed trimming. His thick, shaggy hair was disheveled. Just the sight of him was enough to intimidate most men, much less Maggie.

"Yes?" she asked with forced pleasantness, he head cocked warily as he removed his gloves and slapped them into his palm.

"Ten head of your cattle are grazing on my winter feed supply," he said without preamble. "What are you going to do about it?"

"Award them the Croix de Guerre for bravery above and beyond the call of duty," she answered without hesitation.

He stared at her as if he wasn't quite certain that he'd heard her. His head tilted slightly and his dark eyes narrowed, while Blake struggled with suppressed laughter. "I don't think you understand the situation," he tried again. "If you don't get them off my land and out of my hay, I'm going to throw down on them."

"That is an old Western expression," Maggie explained to Blake. "It means he's going to shoot them." She looked back at Tate Hollister. "I hope you plan to give them a sporting chance. They are, after all, unarmed.'' She smiled vacantly.

Hollister's dark eyes were shadowed with surprise, and his mustache actually twitched, but there was no smile on his lips. ''Mrs. Jeffries, this isn't a laughing matter.''

''Yes, sir.'' She curtsied. ''What would you like me to do about the cattle?''

He looked as confused as a man could. He glanced at Blake, glowering at the boy's grin, which was quickly erased.

''Oh, for God's sake, where's Jack Randall?'' he demanded, his deep voice like a bass fiddle with the wind howling outside the door.

She stared at him. ''Jack who?''

''Your foreman, lady!''

She sighed. ''Oh, him. He left two days before we got here.''

''Left!''

She put a hand to her ear. ''Please. I have sensitive ears. Yes, he left. He took his wife back east to visit her people for Christmas.''

''Christmas!'' he muttered, and Maggie stared at him wide-eyed, waiting for him to come out with a hearty ''Bah, Humbug.'' The sentiment was in his expression, even if he didn't say the words, and she had to stifle a giggle. That made him scowl even more. ''Are you really this boy's mother?''

Her eyebrows arched. Just because they'd never spoken to each other before was no reason for him to pretend he didn't know who she was. He'd at least seen her a time or two. ''Of course,'' she said.

''I found her under a cabbage leaf,'' Blake volunteered with twinkling green eyes.

Hollister wasn't amused and after a moment, returned to the subject. "What about the other men?" he asked.

"They're out doing God knows what." She sighed. "We've only been here three days and I can't get one of them to stand still long enough to listen to anything I say. And the man who fixes the electrical generator is—" she hesitated, eyeing Hollister "—indisposed."

"He's out in the bunkhouse drunk," Blake countered, grinning when she glared at him. "Well, he is. I looked in the window."

"Honest to God, you'll die up here in a week," Hollister muttered, glaring at both of them. "City greenhorns! Why in hell didn't you stay in New Mexico where you belong?"

"Arizona," Maggie corrected. "And we don't really belong there. Blake and I moved there from Tennessee."

"Southerners," Hollister grumbled. "Easterners."

She hated that cold, arrogant black stare. She drew herself up to her full height and still had to tilt her head back to look at him. He made her home state sound like the worst kind of insult. Maggie lifted her chin, and her gray eyes sparkled like flint chips. "Well, let me tell you, Mr. Hollister, if I was back home, I'd have plenty of willing help," she replied. "These men seem to think they're being paid by the tooth fairy, and the only mechanic I've got can't walk unless he's carrying a bottle of beer!"

He didn't even flick an eyelash. "No cowboy in his right mind is going to take orders from a city woman with no savvy about ranching. As for the generator, I can fix that."

He antagonized her as no man in her life ever had. She wanted to tell him what he could do with his offer. Damned bossy so-and-so . . . !

"Well?" he asked, glaring. "I can't work and shine a light all at once. Get me a flashlight, boy."

Blake didn't hesitate. "Yes, sir!" he said smartly and rushed off to look for one.

"Don't order my son around," Maggie said quietly. "I don't like other people telling him what to do."

"If you didn't, you wouldn't have jailed him in a military school," he returned coldly, shocking her because she hadn't realized he knew so much about Blake.

She caught her breath, but before she could say anything, Blake was back with the flashlight. "I'll come and hold it for you," he offered.

"Your mother can do that," he replied with an arrogant smile. "Or don't you know how?"

Her gray eyes flashed, and it was a good thing she didn't see the expression of unholy glee on Blake's face as all his secret plans for bringing these two together seemed to be coming true.

"I'm an executive secretary for a printing corporation," she informed him with blatant hostility. "I can do a lot more than hold a light."

"Oh, I can see how valuable you'd be in an emergency, with all that specialized knowledge," he agreed and turned to open the door. "Get a coat on."

She absolutely gasped. In all her life, she'd never run into anybody like him. He threw out orders like a drill sergeant. And it didn't help that Blake was sitting there with a book on his lap, looking the picture of a studious, polite boy. She stuck out her tongue at him as she put on her leather jacket, and he grinned like a Cheshire cat.

"I'll get you for this," she mouthed at him and left him giggling on the sofa.

She followed the big man around the house, because he hadn't even bothered to wait for her to trudge through the snow with him. He had the flashlight in one enormous gloved hand. He paused by the housing that protected the generator, then thrust the flashlight at her while he uncovered the apparatus and then studied it silently.

"Hold the light on the damned thing, if you please," he shot at Maggie. "I can't see in the dark."

"My God." She whistled. "And you're actually admitting it?"

He muttered something she was glad she couldn't understand.

She grinned as she leveled the flashlight. Odd how refreshing it was to have a man actively dislike her. Most men seemed to feel obliged to chase her. This one wouldn't chase anybody, she mused. He wasn't a marrying man or a particularly romantic one, and it was really fun to antagonize him. She'd never tried to deliberately upset a man before, but it was wildly exhilarating. She felt alive in a way she hadn't for over ten years. Strange, really, since Hollister was the last man in the world she could feel an attraction for.

Hollister paused and scowled down at the generator. "This damned thing came over with the Ark," he muttered. "I don't understand why your father-in-law didn't replace it."

"He probably liked eating," she remarked, pulling her stocking cap over her ears. Snow was falling again. "He wasn't a wealthy man."

"Could have been," he murmured as he stripped off his gloves to reveal huge but elegant hands, which were long-fingered and darkly tanned—capable hands, with calloused ridges on the finger pads. "But he kept putting off things."

"Maybe he thought money would corrupt him," she suggested.

His big shoulders shrugged. "It can." He caught her hand that was holding the light and positioned it where he wanted the beam with no regard for her posture. His hand was warm over her own, and curious little tingles went down her spine until he released his brief hold. "Keep it there," he said absently, scowling under the brim of his hat. "Damn. I hope I can splice that wire...."

He pulled out a pocketknife while Maggie watched with fascination. He was a fixer. Most men were, but this one did it with such style. She studied his profile in the faint radiance of the flashlight, fascinated with its hardness, the uncompromising nature it revealed.

He seemed to feel her intent scrutiny because his head turned. His black eyes caught hers and held them, penetrating, questioning. "Well?" he asked curtly.

"You have an interesting hairline," she improvised. Her voice sounded odd. Probably because lightning was running down her spine from that intent black stare.

He lifted a shaggy eyebrow as if he thought she might need immediate mental counseling. "That's a new one."

"Thanks," she said with a grin. "I thought it up all by myself, too."

He tilted his hat back as he worked with the generator. "What the hell are you and the boy doing up here by yourselves?" he asked suddenly.

It was none of his business, and she almost said so. But she stopped herself in time—it wouldn't do to antagonize a man when he was that close to fixing her generator.

"It's almost Christmas. Blake wanted to spend some time with me," she said finally. "He doesn't really like military school, and I think he's out to convince me that I can run a ranch in the wilds of Montana while he sits on a fence and hero-worships you."

He looked at her with wide, disbelieving eyes. "I beg your pardon?"

"Sorry. It slipped out." She leaned against the wall, holding the light steady.

But he wasn't moving. His dark eyes were fixed on her face. "I said: I beg your pardon, lady."

How in the world could a man make an insult of the word lady, she wondered absently. She shifted. "Blake likes you."

"Well, I'm not much on boys," he returned shortly. "Or city women. Or even neighbors. I live alone and I like my privacy. I don't intend having it invaded by your son."

"That's plain enough," she returned, feeling her temper start to rise. "Now let me tell you something. I don't like men in general and you in particular, and what I think of your type of man would fill a book! As for my son, he's only nine years old and he never knew his father. His grandfather is the only male besides you that he's ever spent any time around. And Papa Jeffries was kind and gentle and loving—the exact opposite of you. Blake doesn't know what a man is, so you'll have to forgive his attachment to you!"

His left eye had narrowed and his jaw was clenched. "You are playing one dangerous game, lady," he said shortly.

"I'm so sorry if I've offended you, Mr. Hollister," she replied coolly. "And I promise you Blake won't be allowed within a mile of you for the entire two weeks we're in residence.''

''You won't last two weeks if you don't get this outfit into shape,'' he said shortly as he looped a wire and stayed it with a screw. ''There. Let's try it now.''

He replaced the cover and started the generator. Maggie had to concede that Hollister was good with his hands. He was lucky, she thought venomously, that he had something to make up for his lack of looks.

Hollister slid his gloves back on and didn't glance at her. She brought back painful memories, she and her son. It had been six years, but he still grieved for his own family. He didn't want or need complications, but this woman could get under his skin. And that irritated him. She opened his wounds and made them bleed. The boy rubbed salt in them.

Blake opened the door and let them back in. ''The heater's running!'' He grinned up at the big, unsmiling man. ''Thanks, Mr. Hollister. We'd have frozen to death but for you.''

Hollister's black eyes went over that boyish face with something less than affection. The boy looked like a boy—all uncombed hair and eyes that sparkled with mischief. Just like his mother. The pair of them were going to give him problems. He could feel it in his bones. He missed the old man, because Jeffries had never bothered him. But Blake had, at every opportunity. When he'd come to visit Jeffries for the summer, Tate couldn't walk for bumping into him. It had been irritating at first, and then frankly painful. He'd been glad when the boy left at the end of summer and went back to school. Now here he was back again, and Hollister was feeling the same old stabs of memory, only they were worse. Because now she was here, too, and he'd been a hell of a long time without a woman.

She aroused sensations that he'd forgotten he could feel, and he hated them. Damn it, he hated the world...!

Maggie glanced at him, surprised by his cold reaction to Blake's gratitude. He was a cold man, though, she thought as she got out of her cap and jacket and boots. Thank God he wasn't going to be around very much.

"Yes, thank you for fixing the generator," Maggie agreed. "I suppose you need to get home, so I won't offer to make coffee...."

She didn't want to, she meant. Oddly enough, that irritated Hollister. He didn't like the way she reacted to him. He knew he wasn't pretty, for God's sake, but did she have to make it so obvious that she found him ugly?

"Those cattle have got to be moved. I'll find your men and set them to it."

"Thank you," she said, deciding against arguing because it would only keep him here longer, and she didn't want that.

"Wouldn't you like a cup of coffee?" Blake invited, while Maggie felt herself choking. No, Blake, she moaned inwardly.

Hollister saw that look in her eyes and just for the hell of it, he said yes.

Maggie forced a smile to her lips. Be generous, she told herself. He fixed the generator. You won't freeze. The least you can do is give the poor cold man a cup of hot coffee. If only she could have managed to get him in the pot with it....

"What do you take in your coffee, Mr. Hollister?" she asked with forced sweetness.

He took off his hat, revealing his thick black hair. Snow flaked from the hat as he placed it on the hat tack and shed his thick coat. Under it he was wearing a red flannel plaid shirt and as near as she could tell, no undershirt. The flannel was unbuttoned halfway down his brawny dark chest, and it had the thickest covering of hair she'd ever seen on a man.

She stared at him. She couldn't help it. Despite her very brief marriage, she knew almost nothing about men. Bob had been as inexperienced as she, and as shy, so she'd learned little during those few fumbling encounters in the dark. But Hollister had a savage masculinity, an untamed look that made her blood run crazy and her pulse do unexpected things. She didn't even like him, but he had a dangerously sensual appeal. She forced her eyes back to the white mugs she was pouring coffee into.

"I take my coffee black, Mrs. Jeffries," Hollister said quietly.

She'd known that somehow before she'd posed the question. He looked that kind of man. No frills, no embellishments. She'd have bet that he drank his whiskey straight and never put catsup on his meat. She looked up as he came close to take the cup, smelling of wind and fir trees and leather.

"I'll bet you never put catsup on a steak," she said without thinking.

He searched her eyes curiously. "As a matter of fact, I don't," he agreed. His heavy brows moved together faintly. "What brought that on?"

She dropped her eyes to her coffee. "I don't know." She lifted it, even though it was hot. Involuntarily her gaze went to Hollister's hands. They fascinated her, now that she knew how capable they were. They were huge. Lean. Darkly tanned, with thick hair on the wrists and hard muscle in the long fingers. Flat nails, very clean. She could imagine those hands doing anything that was necessary on a ranch, from fixing generators to helping a calf be born.

"Do you still have that big Aberdeen Angus bull, Mr. Hollister?" Blake asked. He'd joined them at the table and was sipping a cola from a can he'd gotten out of the refrigerator.

Hollister hated having the boy ask him questions. But the youngster had a natural feel for ranching, and he remembered vividly the ease with which Blake had helped old man Jeffries deliver a calf and doctor one of the bulls. "I've still got him," he replied tersely. He glanced at Blake, his eyes suddenly curious, losing their sharp edge as he realized that the boy was really interested and not just asking inane questions. "And I've brought a new Hereford crossbreed bull as well. I'm doing a three-one cross this next year. Angus to Beefmaster, Beefmaster to Hereford, and back to Angus again."

"Angus are easy calvers," Blake said knowledgeably. "And Herefords are hardly. And Beefmasters are good choice grade beef."

"With good weight gain ratios," Hollister agreed. The boy had been putting in some study to learn all that. He was impressed despite himself. "I had to sell my Brangus bulls. After two years of inbreeding, you can create some problems for yourself if you don't introduce some new blood into your herd."

"That's a fact," Blake said, sipping his cola.

Maggie, lost, glared at both of them. Hollister happened to glance her way and lifted an eyebrow. He came as close to smiling then as he had in six long years. "Something bothering you, Mrs. Jeffries?" he asked in his deep, slow tone.

"She doesn't know a lot about cattle," Blake said. "But she's a whiz at math and accounts payable and organizing things. She's the top secretary at Skyline Printing Services and a computer expert.''

Maggie shifted restlessly. ''Don't brag about me that way,'' she told her son. ''I only learned accounting to get out of typesetting. And I learned computer programming to get out of accounting.''

''Most women aren't good at math.'' Hollister's dark eyes narrowed in his hard face. ''My mother could barely count hens.''

''It was always my best subject in school,'' Maggie replied. ''My dad was a farmer. He kept a tally book, and I was his payroll clerk. He taught me to add columns of figures in my head.''

''Her parents are dead now,'' Blake volunteered. ''I have three uncles, but they're spread all over the country and I never see them.''

''A farmer?'' Hollister persisted. ''What kind of livestock did he have?''

''Cattle and hogs,'' she answered. ''He had some high pastures, too. Right on the side of the hills, but he did very well. We had Jersey cows and a few Holsteins.''

The tall man finished his coffee. ''But you don't know how to breed cattle?''

''A handful of cows, mostly milk cows, doesn't qualify anyone to handle several hundred head of beef cattle,'' she reminded him. ''It's a totally different proposition. And I was only eighteen when I married Blake's father and left the country for the city. I've forgotten most of what little I knew about the management of it.''

Hollister's big hands toyed with the empty cup. ''I went to school with Bob Jeffries,'' he said. ''He was a grade behind me.''

She sat very still. "He died in Central America before Blake was born. We'd been married less than six months." She sighed. "It seems like a dream sometimes. Except for the talking proof sitting there trying to look invisible while he drinks his soda," she added with a dry grin at Blake.

Blake just grinned back, but he was listening.

"Bob loved danger," Maggie reminisced, aware of Hollister's narrow gaze on her face. "He fed on adrenaline. Just after we were married he tried to give it up." She smiled sadly. "It didn't work out. For him it was like trying not to breathe."

"I never knew him," Blake sighed. He looked up at Hollister. "You aren't married, are you, Mr. Hollister?"

Hollister stared into the empty coffee cup. "I was." He put the cup down on the table and turned. "Thanks for the coffee. I'll round up your hands and point them in the right direction." He put on his coat and cocked his hat over one eye, glancing back at Blake and his mother without smiling. "If I were you, I'd stay inside until this snow lets up. And I'll have that fence fixed before I let your men come home."

"Thanks for fixing the generator," she said, alternately relieved and irritated by his shouldering of her own problems.

He opened the door. "No problem. Good night."

He was gone in a whirl of wind and snowflakes, and Maggie stared after him feeling oddly empty and alone. How strange to feel that way about a man she disliked.

"He must be divorced," Maggie said absently.

Blake joined her in the kitchen, draining his can of soft drink. "No, he's a widower," he told her. "Grandpa said his whole family was killed in an accident in the Rockies. Mr. Hollister was driving. His wife and son died, and he didn't.'' He shrugged, oblivious to the shock and horror on his mother's soft face. "Grandpa said that was why he lived like he does, alone and away from everybody. That he was punishing himself because he didn't die, too. Too bad. He sure is a nice man.''

He glanced at his mother and did a double take at the look on her face. She actually looked interested. And that made him smile, but he was careful not to let her see him doing it.

Chapter Two

With the electrical generator fixed and the snow diminishing, thank God, Maggie spent a day going over the ranch's financial statement. Blake busied himself with a new computer game while listening to Christmas music on a local country and western radio station. She wondered how Grandfather Jeffries had ever made a go of ranching in the first place, having spent so much on adding new land to his ranch when interest rates were sky-high and spending so little on herd improvement.

What little she'd gleaned from Hollister about crossbreeding had piqued her curiosity. She wondered if her father-in-law had been trying that angle, or if he'd just raised beef without worrying about bloodlines or grades at auction.

The really big problem, though, wasn't what the ranch's past had been. It was what its future was going to be. She hated to sell it. There was something majestic and real about rural Montana. About mountains that touched heaven and trees almost that tall. There was space here, not unlike the Arizona she'd come to love, and there were basic values. Blake would love staying on the ranch, having cattle to raise, and he'd have a heritage to inherit. But how was she going to keep it solvent all by herself? As she'd admitted, she knew nothing about the daily routine of ranching, even about how to breed cattle. The worst thing in the world would be to tackle it without expertise. She'd fall flat on her face and lose everything, and where would she be then?

Blake, noting the lines of worry on her oval face, saved the game he'd been playing and, carefully removing the disks first, cut off the computer. He lowered the volume on the radio and turned to face her.

"Something's wrong, isn't it?" he asked.

She smiled. "I'm no rancher," she sighed. "That about sizes it up. This place needs a cattleman, not a vacationing secretary."

"There's always—"

"Mr. Hollister," she bit off with a glittering stare in his direction. "Don't you know any other words?"

Blake grinned, not at all chastened. "His first name is Tate."

She rolled her eyes toward the ceiling and went back to the figures. "I'll never be able to make it work."

"We have a great foreman," Blake said sensibly. "And that's mainly all we need."

"You make it sound so easy," she replied and smiled wearily at him. Probably at his age everything was easy. It was only when people grew up that life got so complicated. "Well, I'll think about it," she promised.

But Blake went to bed that night frowning because she'd had that look on her face. The one that said: I'm quitting while I'm ahead. And at all costs, he couldn't possibly let her out of these mountains before he got a good chance to bring her and Mr. Hollister together. They were both alone, about the right age, and he doted on them. Why wouldn't it work? He turned off his light so his mother would think he was sleeping, and before he dropped off to sleep he had the answer.

Maggie made pancakes the next morning, and Blake ate two helpings before he got up from the table, put on his boots and thick parka and announced that he was going to hike down the ridge to the river and see if it was frozen.

"You be careful," she cautioned as he went out, reminding herself that young boys had to have some independence and that she couldn't keep him indoors for the rest of his life.

"Sure I will," he promised. He chuckled. "See you in a couple of hours. I've got my watch on, so I'll know when I'm due back, okay?"

She smiled gently. "Okay."

But two hours passed, joined by two more, and still he didn't return. Maggie was frantic. She tried searching, but she didn't have any idea how to find which way he'd gone. She didn't trust the men, either. Not with Blake's life. She grimaced and gritted her teeth and tried to stay calm. There was only one person in the world she did trust to find Blake. In a fever of impatience, she got into the four-wheel-drive Bronco that Blake had talked her into buying in the summer and went quickly down the road to the Hollister place.

The Hollister house was a big rugged retreat, with a varnished wood exterior, all angles and glass. Every possible view had its own window, and judging by the number and size of the chimneys, it must have as many fireplaces. Maggie had never set foot inside it, but she'd seen it often enough from the road.

She jumped out of the Bronco, tugging her leather jacket closer against the biting wind. The windchill in these parts was formidable, even in December.

The front porch was long and rambling, with plenty of chairs, but she didn't stop to admire the view. She knocked frantically at the front door and only then wondered what she was going to do if he wasn't home. What if he was gone for the day, or out on business, or . . .

The door opened. Tate Hollister eyed her over a cup of steaming coffee, his blue-checked flannel shirt the only bright and welcoming thing about him as he stared down at her.

"I don't recall inviting you to lunch," he said.

She glared at him. "Blake's missing," she said hesitantly. Now that she was here, it was even harder than she'd imagined. He did look like stone, mustache and all.

"Don't look at me," he said imperturbably. "I don't have him."

"He said he'd be gone two hours." She gnawed her lower lip. "He went down to the ridge to see if the river was frozen. That was four hours ago, and it's snowing again." Her soft gray eyes looked up at him helplessly. "I can't even find tracks."

"He's playing a prank," he told her easily. "When he's had enough, he'll come home."

"He's not," she argued. "Blake is like me. If he says he'll do something, he'll do it. He doesn't play pranks."

"You don't know much about boys, do you?" he mused.

She was freezing, and his attitude wasn't warming her at all. "No, I guess I don't," she admitted flatly. "I've been too concerned with trying to support us to have much free time to learn, either, and Blake is a handful sometimes."

His dark eyes went slowly over her face, as if he hadn't really looked at it before. Around them, the wind blew and snow peppered the porch, but he didn't seem to notice.

"He might be hurt," she said with involuntary softness. "I'm afraid."

He pursed his lips, the mustache twitching. "It's a prank," he repeated. "But I'll come. You can wait inside if you like, while I get my coat."

She didn't understand why, but she didn't want to go in that house. She thought suddenly of the wife and child he'd lost, and her feet froze to the porch. It would be like trespassing.

"No," she hesitated. "I'll... I'll just wait out here, thanks."

He frowned slightly, puzzled, but he shrugged and went off after his coat.

She was standing by the Bronco when he came out, his torso and lean hips covered by the thick shepherd's coat, his thick black hair under the wide brim of his black Stetson and what looked like a rifle in one hand. At closer inspection, it was, and she frowned.

"You can drive if you like..." she began, but he was going the other way. "Where are you going?" she called, running to keep up with him as he went toward the stables down the road from the house.

"You're crazy if you think I'm taking a vehicle, even with four-wheel drive, down that ravine," he said easily. "I'm going out on horseback."

"With a rifle? What are you going to do with it?"

He spared her an impatient glance. "Oh, for God's sake, woman. I'm not going to shoot the boy."

"I didn't say so," she faltered.

He made a sound that reputed that and kept walking while she ran along behind him.

"You can wait in the house or go home," he said. He opened the stable door, and she saw a wide alley filled with wood chips with bright, clean stalls on either side, some of which housed horses.

"He's my son. I want to come, too."

He turned, staring at her. "Can you ride?"

"Of course I can ride," she said irritably.

"Well, well. You aren't quite the lily I thought you were," he mused as he went to the tack room.

And what did that mean, she wondered, but anxiety kept her quiet. He saddled a quiet little chestnut mare for her and a huge buckskin gelding for himself. Snow was falling steadily as they stood outside the stable.

"Molly won't toss you, but she has a tendency to scrape people off against tree trunks, so keep your eyes open," he said as he held the mare for her to mount.

She swung easily into the saddle, sitting tall, the reins held lightly in her hands.

He looked up. His dark eyes approved her excellent posture and he smiled. It was the first time she recalled ever seeing him smile, and his face didn't even break.

"No hat," he said then and went back to the tack room again, returning with a beat-up old Stetson, which came down to her ears but did keep the snow off. "Let's go." He swung into his own saddle and took the lead. "Keep in my tracks," he said over his shoulder. "And don't stray off."

"Yes, sir, Mr. Hollister," she muttered under her breath.

"What was that?"

She averted her eyes from that black stare. "Not a thing."

There might have only been the two of them in the world as they rode out through the tall lodgepole pines and aspens, where the snow was less thick, and Maggie thought irrelevantly that this was the best way to see Montana. Not in a car, or on foot. But on the back of a horse, with leather creaking as they rode, and the smell of the fresh mountain air and the bite of the wind and snow on her face. If she hadn't been so worried about Blake, she might have even been able to appreciate it.

She was still tense, but somehow she knew that whatever was wrong, Hollister would be able to handle it. She glanced at him curiously, wondering at the sense of security she felt with him, even in an emergency like this one. Which brought her mind back to Blake and to the hundred things that might have happened to him, the least of which was enough to make her nauseous. He was all she had . . . !

"I said," Hollister repeated curtly, "which way did he go when he left the house?"

She looked up, to see her own cabin just before them. She had to blink twice to get her mind back on track. "Sorry." She bit her lower lip. "He went there," she nodded toward the back of the cabin, down the long hill behind.

He spared her an irritated glance before he urged his mount forward, so much at home in the saddle that he seemed part of the big buckskin. Halfway down the ridge, he held up his hand and swung down, kneeling in the snow to look. He went on foot from there, stopping to examine limbs, his eyes keen and quick as they darted around the mountainous terrain of the forest.

"He went through there," he murmured, his eyes narrowed as he studied the downward slope. His head went up, and he listened. Maggie heard it, too—a voice.

"Blake!" Hollister's deep tones cut through the wind, carrying, bellowing.

"Hellllp!"

The cry was definitely Blake's, and there was an odd note of fear in it. Maggie almost cried out herself, feeling that piercing cry to her soul.

Hollister didn't spare Maggie a glance. He whipped his rifle out of the sheath on his saddle and swung back up onto the horse, wheeling the animal in the direction of the shout.

Maggie urged her mount after him, terrified. Hollister wasn't a hysterical man. If he reacted that way, there was a reason. But even as she was thinking it, she heard the sound, and it chilled her to the bone. A sob caught in her throat. She knew the howl of coyotes, but this sound was deeper, richer, more threatening. It was the howl of a wolf....

Hollister urged his mount down the ridge at a clip Maggie did her best to follow, frustrated that the snow made it such an ordeal to get to Blake.

With her heart hammering in her throat, blind fear choking her, she held on to the reins and felt her heartbeat shaking her as she heard Blake's shrill voice.

Ahead of her, Hollister made his way quickly through another thick stand of aspens, through the thick underbrush, and Maggie, right on the heels of his mount, caught a horrifying glimpse of a small dark head far below, near the ribbon of stream that cut through the snow. Blake! And only a few yards away, stalking, a big silver wolf.

Maggie felt her heart stop. Her son. Her boy! She saw Hollister swing out of the saddle, heard his voice.

"Don't move!" he yelled at Blake and sighted down the rifle barrel with an economy of motion that was as menacing as the wolf itself.

There was a sudden report, and then another and another, the crack of rifle fire echoing with horrible violence down the ridge and up the next slope, at odds with the pastoral beauty and peace it disturbed.

"Blake!" Maggie screamed, tears sliding down her cheeks as she swung out of the saddle. There was smoke from the rifle in Hollister's hands, but even before it cleared, he was down that slope, his big frame absorbing the shock of his steps with grace and ease. Maggie was right behind him.

"Mr. Hollister! Mom!" Blake cried, his voice excited and high-pitched with pain.

Through her tears, Maggie could see the unnatural angle that Blake's left leg was lying at. Broken for sure, she thought sickly, and thanked God for Tate Hollister.

The man knelt quickly beside the boy, the rifle cast aside as he felt the lower leg, and Blake winced. Maggie got on Blake's other side, hugging him, shaking with reaction.

"Broken," Hollister murmured. "A simple fracture, thank God, not a compound one. What happened?"

"Lost my footing." Blake tried to grin. "I came out...to check the river. Gosh, Mr. Hollister, that wolf sure was a beaut. I guess that's why you didn't kill him, huh?"

"Timber wolves are damned near extinct," Hollister said as he got up and broke two limbs off a tree. "If he hadn't turned tail, I wouldn't have had a choice, but I flushed him. I hate killing when I don't have to. Maggie, I need some cloth to make a splint," he said as he pulled a folded blanket from its position just behind the saddle on his horse. He wrapped the limbs to make a cradle and then very carefully drew the cradle under Blake's leg.

It was the first time he'd ever called her by name, and Maggie couldn't understand why her heart ran wild. She let go of Blake long enough to hand him the wool scarf around her neck.

"Will this do?" she asked in a quivering tone, handing the scarf to him while Blake gripped her hand tightly and tried to reassure her that he was all right.

"Hi, guy," she said and spoiled her stiff upper lip by bursting into tears.

"Aw, cut it out, Mom," Blake muttered. "It's just a broken leg."

"Excuse me," she said, trying to laugh. "You know how mothers are."

Hollister glanced at her, but he didn't say anything. He whipped out his pocketknife and made a neat slit right down Blake's boot so that the whole thing was laid bare and easily removed. Then he positioned the sticks he'd broken on either side of Blake's leg and put his wool bandanna next to Maggie's. "OK," he told Blake quietly. "This is going to be rough. I have to straighten that leg and splint it, and it's going to hurt like hell. Want something to bite on?"

"Oh, but you can't—" Maggie was already protesting.

"Shut up," he told her, his eyes black and steady and challenging.

She did, instantly, without an argument, because that hard glare was like a dash of cold water.

"I'll be OK," Blake said through his teeth, nodding. He clenched his hands at his sides and propped himself on them. "Go ahead."

Maggie felt tears spurt from her eyes as Hollister worked, his hands deft and sure. Blake cried out just once and almost blacked out when Hollister pulled the leg straight, but the boy never let out another sound, even while the makeshift splint was put on and tied in place. But his face was as white as plaster when Hollister finished.

"OK?" Hollister asked, and his voice was different. Gentle. Deeper. He smiled at the boy.

Blake beamed. He managed a grin because it was like a turning point in his relationship with the taciturn rancher. "OK," he agreed.

"Here." Hollister handed his rifle to Maggie. "Wait a minute. Let me put the safety on." He did that and handed it back. "Don't shoot yourself in the foot," he cautioned.

She glared at him. "I know which end to point, thanks."

Tate didn't smile, but his dark eyes twinkled. He lifted Blake very carefully, but Blake's breath sucked in at the pain the movement caused. "This is doing it the hard way, I know," he told Blake as he carried him to the buckskin, "but it can't be helped. Back in the old days, the Plains Indians made a travois and pulled injured warriors back to camp on it."

"A . . . travois?"

"That's right." Hollister propped Blake on the saddle while he swung into it behind him and turned him over his knees, wonderfully gentle even though Maggie could see the pain in Blake's young face. "I'll tell you about it on the way back," he said, nodding to Maggie who'd managed to get the rifle back into Hollister's saddle horn before she'd mounted the mare.

She let Hollister take the lead, wondering at his skill as a woodsman as he led them right back up to the cabin with no fuss or side trips, talking softly to Blake the whole time, his deep voice steady and comforting. It dawned on her then that he wasn't just making conversation. He was keeping Blake calm so that he didn't go into shock.

She wondered what she would have done if Tate hadn't been around. She'd have done her best, but would it have been good enough? Just the thought of that wolf made her blood run cold. But the man she'd imagined Hollister to be would have killed the wolf without a second thought. Instead, he'd managed to run it away because he didn't like to kill things unless he had to. Her gray eyes watched his tall form quietly, curiously, and new feelings began to bud inside her.

"Keep him warm," he told Maggie after they'd gotten back to the cabin and he'd put Blake carefully on the sofa. "A couple of aspirin wouldn't come amiss until we can get him into Deer Lodge to the doctor. Keep him talking. It will help him fight off shock. I'll take the horses home and bring the Bronco back as quick as I can. You left the keys in it, right?"

She nodded and started to speak, but he was gone before she could get her mouth open.

"Isn't he something?" Blake sighed through his pain.

"He is that," Maggie agreed. She brushed back his dark hair. "Are you going to make it?"

"Sure," he said, grinning. "I'm tough."

"I guess you are, at that. I'll get those aspirin."

By the time Hollister got back, Blake was in a little less pain, although he was still groaning a little.

"I'll put him on the back seat," Hollister said, lifting Blake gently. "You'd better sit back there with him. The way the snow's coming down, we may slide a bit getting down into the valley."

"I wish I could thank you enough—" she began.

"Get the door," he said tersely, ignoring her efforts to tell him how she felt.

She sighed softly and did what she was told.

All the way to Deer Lodge, holding Blake's head in her lap, she wondered at her new acceptance of Hollister's rough demeanor. He made her feel feminine. Watching the easy, confident way he handled the Bronco, she recalled the same ease with which he'd repaired the generator, handled the emergency of Blake's broken leg, routed the wolf and got them down the mountain in deep snow. He was simply amazing. And she was suddenly hurt that he had a past that wouldn't allow him to lose his heart because it was dawning on her that she wanted it. She wanted to learn everything there was to know about him. She wanted to smooth away the hard lines from that dark face and make him laugh. She wondered if he even knew how to laugh, with all the tragedy he'd known.

Dr. Peters examined Blake's leg at the small clinic and set it, commending Hollister's knowledgeable first aid treatment as he put on a thick plaster cast. He wrote Maggie a prescription for pain pills to give the boy, praised him on his bravery and told him when to come back to have the cast removed.

Maggie didn't even think about it until they'd stopped by the pharmacy to get the prescription and were on the way back up the mountain. They'd be back in Tucson when that cast had to come off. She'd have to be back at work, but how could she possibly send Blake back to military school? She frowned, gnawing her lower lip as the thought of leaving the ranch began to make her feel sick.

"Reaction," Hollister mused, watching her. She was sitting in the passenger seat now, because Blake had a dose of sedative in him and was almost asleep on the back seat. "Don't worry. I wish I had a nickel for every broken bone I've set over the years. He'll be fine."

"What?" she asked quietly.

"Now that it's all over you're going green, Mrs. Jeffries," he murmured dryly. He was smoking a cigarette, the acrid smell of it filling the cab as he easily handled the sliding motion of the Bronco on a patch of hard ice and whipped it around the next horrible curve as they wound back up to the cabin.

"I think I'm entitled," she said gently and smiled at him.

His dark eyes studied that smile, intent on her soft mouth, and his thick eyebrows drew together. "Yes," he said after a minute, dragging his eyes back to the road. "I guess you are."

"Don't you ever smile?" she asked suddenly, the words popping out before she could stop them.

He didn't look at her. "Not often. Not anymore."

She wanted to say more. She wanted to ask him about the accident. She wanted to tell him that he shouldn't live in the past. But she didn't have that right, and she was shocked at her own forwardness. She loved her own privacy. It was odd that she should feel free to infringe on his.

She blushed as she looked out the window at the distant majesty of the mountains all around, blue and white against the gray sky.

"Now what is it?" he asked.

She shifted restlessly. "Nothing."

"You colored."

He saw too much. "I wanted to thank you for what you've done," she said. "You . . . make it difficult."

"I don't want thanks," he said simply. He lifted the cigarette to his chiseled lips. "Up here, we look out for each other. It's how we survive."

"I can't imagine you letting anybody look·out for you," she sighed.

He glanced at her with both eyebrows arched.

She shivered, putting her jacket closer. "Well, I can't," she said doggedly, and her silvery eyes glinted at him.

The mustache twitched, and his dark gaze had a twinkle in it as he turned his attention back to the road. "I'm glad the boy was all right."

"Yes, so am I." She shivered again. "Just thinking about that wolf..."

They were at the cabin now. He stopped the Bronco and cut off the engine, turning to look at her. It was almost dark, and in the going light he could see the strain in her face, the worry darkening her eyes. A woman alone with a boy was hard going, especially when she was their only support. He wondered if she'd ever let herself lean on a man since the death of her husband and figured that she probably hadn't.

"He's all right," he reminded her.

"No thanks to me," she laughed huskily and heard her own voice break.

His chin lifted while he studied her. "Come here," he said, catching her arm with his free hand. "Come on," he said when she hesitated. "I guess you need a good cry."

It seemed strange, letting him hold her when they'd been strangers. But he didn't feel like a stranger anymore. He'd saved Blake and taken care of everything, and she felt safer with him than she'd ever felt with anyone. She sighed, giving way to the tears while he held her, one lean hand smoothing her hair, his deep voice quiet and comforting at her temple.

"I'm sorry," she said after a little, embarrassed at her lack of composure. "It frightened me."

"It should have. Don't let the boy wander off like that again," he said, his tone firm and commanding. "This isn't downtown Tucson. There are wolves around here and even a few bears."

"He isn't likely to go far with a broken leg," she reminded him, her gray eyes meeting his.

"No, I guess not." He was looking into those silvery pools and forgot what he was going to say. He couldn't seem to look away. His body tautened and his breathing seemed to go haywire. God, she was pretty! His face hardened. He didn't want or need this . . . !

Maggie was having problems of her own. Her heart was going wild from that look. She felt like a young girl with her first beau. Involuntarily, her eyes dropped to his mouth under the thick black mustache, to the beautifully cut lines of his hard lips, and she wanted to kiss him.

"Oh, no," he said suddenly, and his lean hand contracted in her hair, tugging her face up to his. "No, you don't, lady. I'm not going that route again in one lifetime." He let go of her all at once and opened the door.

Maggie felt nerveless. She didn't understand what he'd said, unless he was insinuating that he'd loved his wife and didn't want to risk his heart twice. She even understood. But she hadn't been trying to tempt him . . . or had she?

She watched him get Blake out of the Bronco and thanked him tersely as he laid the boy on the bed in his room and went back out again.

"I'll bring the Bronco back later, when I get one of my men to ride with me," he said coldly. "Is there anything you need?"

He was as icy as the wind. She wouldn't have asked him for a crumb if she'd been starving. "No, thank you, Mr. Hollister," she said with remarkable calm, considering how churned up she felt. She even managed to smile faintly. "Thank you for all you've done."

He searched her face with eyes that didn't want to see the pain he'd just caused with his remoteness. He turned to the door. "No problem," he said curtly and left without a backward glance.

Chapter Three

Blake rested fairly well that night, thanks to the medicine the doctor had prescribed for him. But Maggie was wakeful and restless. Her mind kept going back to Hollister, to a day that was going to live forever in her memory, like the man who was such a part of it.

She hadn't wanted this complication in her life. For years she'd kept men at a safe distance. She'd dated, but with the careful stipulation that she was searching only for friendship. Once or twice she'd had to ask to be taken home because some of her dates had been quite sophisticated and certain that they had the perfect cure for her reserved attitude about sex. But Maggie wasn't interested in cures or even in men. Her brief marriage had left her unsatisfied and a little embarrassed at her own sexuality. She didn't understand the restlessness she'd been feeling lately or her rather frightening attraction to Tate Hollister. She knew so little about men and intimacy. Far too little to handle a violent emotional upheaval in her life. All she wanted now, she told herself, was her job and her son. Or she had. The trouble was that Tate Hollister was suddenly coloring her world.

It was the longest night in recent memory. She didn't sleep until the wee hours of the morning and woke to freezing cold. Dragging herself out of bed in her blue flannel pajamas, she went to the thermostat and tried to turn on the furnace, only to discover that there was no electricity. Again.

She moaned. Well, wasn't this just the berries, she thought gnashing her teeth. Infuriated, she went to the fireplace, where she'd laid a fire the night before and searched for matches. Then she remembered that she'd used up the last one and hadn't thought to ask Hollister for the loan of a pack. Not that they'd have done much good. She didn't have any wood except what was in the fireplace. Nobody had cut any more.

She sat down on the sofa and burst into tears. Her whole life seemed to be falling apart.

The knock on the door came as a shock. She stared at it, frowning because it was barely dawn. Could it be one of the men? She went to it, hesitating because she was in her pajamas and didn't have a robe handy. She opened the door just a crack and found a familiar hard, mustached face.

Her heart jumped, and the light that came into her face seemed to paralyze the man on the porch for a split second. He studied what he could see of her with a faint twinkle in his own eyes.

"Your generator's down again," he said.

"Yes, I noticed. How did you know?"

"I wanted to see if my jury-rigging was going to hold since the temperature dropped so much last night," he said with a curious inflection that made her suspicious.

"Did you?"

"I can't fix it without the proper supplies, anyway," he said impatiently. "So I guess that being the case, you and Blake had better come home with me until this weather lets up."

Her heart ran away. She had doubts about it, and she wanted to ask more questions about that generator because he did look suspicious. But his dark eyes had found hers, and she couldn't quite look away from them.

"Come...home with you?" she faltered.

"Mmm-hmm," he murmured, as oblivious to what they were saying as she was. She was pretty even without makeup, and her gray eyes were oddly welcoming.

"Would you...like some coffee?" she asked, without realizing that if she didn't have any power, she certainly couldn't make any.

"Sure," he replied.

She opened the door, moving back, and she flushed scarlet when he came in the door and got a good look at her pajama-clad, barefoot figure.

"Oh," she exclaimed, pausing while she tried to decide what to do.

His dark eyes raked over her, and there was a faint flush high on his cheekbones.

"I...I'd better get something on," she began.

"You better had," he agreed.

But she couldn't seem to convince her legs because they wouldn't move. She stood helplessly, feeling her breasts swell, feeling her heartbeat shaking the low V of the pajama top so that he had to be able to see it. In fact, his eyes had dropped there and narrowed as he looked, and that flush on his cheekbones that was so puzzling got even darker.

Her lips parted. No, it wouldn't work. She was afraid to go with him, afraid of what was happening. "Blake and I...had better stay here," she said huskily. "But thanks anyway."

Her breath stopped as he suddenly bent and lifted her in his hard arms, carrying her straight back to her bedroom. His booted heel caught the door and slammed it. He put her down then, slowly, with her back to the door.

"What are you afraid of?" he asked quietly.

She felt the cold door at her back and the even colder floor under her feet, but her body was blazing with sensation as he paused just a foot away. "You," she confessed.

His dark eyes went over her like hands, fascinated, intent. "I guess that should flatter me?"

She moved restlessly under the pressure of his black stare. "You've been married," she said hesitantly. "So have I, but only for a few months, and I haven't dated very much since Blake was born."

That surprised him, although with what he was learning about her, it shouldn't have. He tilted his hat back, watching her face. "No sex?" he asked quietly, not dressing it up.

She blushed scarlet and her eyes dropped. She shook her head.

His lean hand went to her chin, tilting it up, and for all its cool deftness, it didn't insist. "Yes, I was married," he said gently. "To a woman who avoided the very touch of me."

She stopped being afraid and just stared, astonished. "But . . . you had a child."

He sighed heavily. "Most people think that. I've let them think it to prevent gossip for the sake of her people." He touched her hair lightly, as if its dark silkiness fascinated him, while her rapt gaze remained fixed on his hard face. "She was my brother's girl. He was killed in a skiing accident several years back, just weeks before they were to be married, and he left her pregnant with his child. She was from good stock, churchgoing people with hard ideas about anticipating marriage vows. It was my nephew she was carrying. So we married, for the child's sake.''

''She didn't love you?'' she asked gently.

His chin lifted pugnaciously. ''I'm not a lovable man,'' he said with a cold smile. ''No, she didn't love me. She loved my brother and grieved for him the whole time we were married. Even after the baby came, she could hardly bear to let me touch her.'' He studied her mouth as he spoke, as if the words were coming harder by the second. ''We'd taken Kip on a camping trip, up into the Rockies, and for the first time, Joyce was showing some interest in life. I'd let them ride in the trailer we were towing, against my better judgment.'' His eyes closed, his whole body going rigid. ''The coupling came loose. They went over....''

She didn't even stop to think. She slid her arms under the shepherd's coat, around him, and pressed close, holding him as hard as she could, rocking him. ''I'm sorry,'' she whispered, her eyes closed as she gave him what little comfort she could. ''I'm so sorry.''

He was astonished at the gesture. His hands touched her shoulders lightly as he tried to decide what to do. The feel of her lightly clad body under his coat was disturbing him. He could feel her soft breasts pressing into him. She was clinging too hard, making his mind whirl with sensation, with soft woman smells coming up into his nostrils and making him hungry in a way he hadn't been since Joyce's death.

''It was a long time ago,'' he said finally. His lean hands smoothed over her hair, holding her cheek to his chest as he stopped fighting it and gave in to the feel of her against him.

''You loved her.''

He hesitated. "I thought I did, yes," he agreed and wondered why he qualified it that way when he'd always assumed that it was love. Now it seemed more likely that he'd pitied Joyce, that he'd wanted to make up to her the loss of his younger brother. But now, with Maggie holding him, he wasn't sure anymore.

"And the boy."

He drew in a steadying breath. "Especially the boy," he confessed. "I missed him like hell. I still do, Maggie."

The sound of her name on his lips made her go warm and soft all over. That startled her into stiffening.

"Sorry," she said, starting to draw back.

But he held her. "No," he said quietly at her temple. "I haven't had a woman this close in years. It feels good."

His admission was shocking. She lifted her gaze to search his black, intent eyes. "Years?" she asked hesitantly, and with that one word, she was asking how experienced he really was.

He didn't want to tell her. But the way she was looking at him wasn't mocking or amused. He touched her cheek with the back of his hand. "Years," he confirmed, and that strange flush was back on his cheekbones.

Her lips parted because she wanted to know, needed to know, had to know. "Were there... many?" she whispered.

He swallowed. His eyes went over her face gently. "No," he whispered back. His jaw clenched. "Only one, if you can't live without having the whole truth," he added harshly, because he hated admitting it. In fact, he didn't know why he was even telling her.

She had to catch her breath. He looked so sophisticated, so worldly. And he was telling her blatantly that he was as inexperienced as she was. She felt a thrill go through her body that was beyond anything she'd ever felt.

He was rigid, waiting for the laughter. It didn't come. And the way she was looking at him made fires in his blood. His head lifted, and he looked down at her quietly, curiously. "No smart remarks?" he asked, challenge in the very set of his dark head.

"Oh, no," she whispered, her expression soft, adoring. "There was only my husband, you see," she replied. "And I was innocent and very young. He wasn't terribly experienced, either. We did a lot of fumbling, and I don't know if either of us was ever...satisfied." She buried her red face in his hard chest, feeling his heart pounding under her forehead. "I could never say that to anyone before. I could never talk to a man like this."

He felt like throwing his head back and laughing with the sheer delight of what he was learning about her. He smiled to himself, secretly, triumphantly. "And here I thought you wrote the book on city sophistication," he murmured with a soft sound that was almost a chuckle.

"Fooled you, didn't I?" she asked dreamily.

In more ways than one, but he wasn't letting his guard down that far. His hands smoothed her hair, savoring its softness. "Then come home with me, you and Blake. Until the snow's gone, at least. You'll need help bathing him, if nothing else," he persisted. "I remember how I was at his age. I'd have raised hell before I'd have let my mother give me a bath."

She laughed delightedly and lifted her head, her gray eyes sparkling, beautiful in her soft face as she looked at him. "I guess he would, too," she agreed.

"I won't hurt you," he murmured. "I don't have enough experience to seduce women. Even green little girls like you."

She smiled even wider. "Thank you, Tate," she said gently.

The sound of his name in that soft, husky tone made his heart stop beating. He searched her eyes, watching the smile falter at the intensity of the look they were exchanging. "Say my name again," he whispered.

"Tate," she obliged, her voice breathless now.

His lean hands framed her face, and holding her eyes, he bent toward her. His hard lips touched her mouth hesitantly, the mustache tickling. He was a little awkward, and his nose got in the way before he finally pressed his mouth to hers.

"God, I'm rusty," he whispered on a husky laugh. "I think I've forgotten how!"

She laughed, too, because it was delicious being with a man who was as inexperienced as she was herself. It was the sweetest kind of pleasure. She reached her arms around him and tilted her head back. "I don't mind," she whispered. "Could we try again? I'm kind of rusty, too."

He smiled, a real smile this time, and bent again. This time he wasn't awkward. His hard lips brushed hers, once, twice, and then settled, moving gently until the contact suddenly became electrically charged.

She felt the very moment when his big body stiffened, when his breath caught. She started to speak. The opening of her lips coincided with the downward movement of his, and he tasted her.

"Maggie," he groaned. He eased her back against the door, and his big body moved down, pinning her there with exquisite strength but so gently that it didn't frighten her. She felt his mouth, tasted its hard, moist crush, and her lips parted for him with a soft little cry.

She couldn't remember the last time a kiss had aroused her. Even during her brief marriage she hadn't felt this oddly weak and trembling vulnerability. Tate might be inexperienced, but there was a powerful chemistry between them if this shuddering need was any indication. She loved the hard crush of his lips, even the abrasive tickle of his mustache. And the feel of his muscular body so close was making her tingle from head to toe.

He lifted his head, and his dark eyes were black as they searched her face.

She felt drowsy, hardly capable of standing alone. "Tate," she whispered, lifting her mouth toward his blindly.

"No, honey." He moved away from her then, the endearment coming without any effort at all, although he'd never used them in his life. He held her until she got her balance back, his hands gentle but firm on her soft upper arms. "We have to stop."

She looked up at him with blank eyes that slowly darkened as she became aware of reality again. She flushed and dropped her eyes to the heavy rise and fall of his chest. "Oh, my," she said inadequately.

"You'd better get dressed," he said, fighting for reason. The bed was just behind him, and he could already feel her soft bareness against him. He shook his head to clear it. "I'll go roust Blake and help him dress."

"Thank you."

He moved her gently to one side, his hands still warm and comforting on her arms. "Maggie, are you all right?"

She forced a smile. "Just a little shaky, that's all," she said and laughed at her own weakness.

He laughed, too, because it was new to be vulnerable. And because he didn't mind if she saw that he was. She was just sweet hell to make love to. That could cause some problems, but he wasn't wasting time thinking about consequences right now.

"Me, too," he murmured, lazily studying the way her pajama top was shaking with her heartbeats. Her breasts were hard tipped. He could see their outline, and he wished for a moment that he had more experience, but since she wasn't put off by it, why should he worry?

"Stop that," she whispered, embarrassed, and crossed her arms over her chest.

He chuckled. He liked her reactions. He liked her. "Get some clothes on."

He opened the door and went out, and it was almost a minute before Maggie could even move. She tasted him on her lips, she smelled the clean scent of him on her pajama top. She and Blake were going to his house, to live with him until the snow stopped.

Until the snow stopped. She blinked. Christmas was next week, and soon she and Blake had to leave Montana. She winced. It was going to be harder than she'd expected. She didn't want to leave Montana. She didn't want to leave Tate. She turned back to her chest of drawers to get out a blouse, wondering how this sudden attachment to him had come about and how she was going to cope with it.

Tate had his own four-wheel-drive Jeep outside, and he carefully loaded Blake into it, then Maggie, along with the clothes she'd packed quickly, and they headed for his place.

Fortunately, it was a big house, and there were four bedrooms. Tate had renovated one of them and made it into an office where he did his book work, but there were three rooms with beds left. Tate had the biggest, filled with antique furniture in dark oak shades and a bed that was king-size and boasted a quilted coverlet with a Western motif.

The others were alike, pine-paneled rooms with modern furniture and trimmings in shades of brown and beige and green. Earth colors that suited him. Maggie took one room and Blake had the other.

"Who cleans the house for you?" Maggie asked as she joined him in the huge living room with its cathedral ceiling and large stone fireplace. The furniture was heavy and dark, made for comfort. There were stone ashtrays and several potted cactus plants, and even a rubber tree in one corner.

"One of my men has a compassionate wife," he murmured, smiling at her curiosity as she went around the room looking at the Indian pottery on the mantel, at the huge Hereford bull whose masculine beauty was captured in a painting above the mantel.

"Who is he...was he?" she corrected, indicating the bull.

"King's Honor," he said proudly. "He was a champion sire. Lived to be twenty years old and kept the ranch going when nothing else could. His progeny are still well-known in cattle circles."

"I wish I knew more about ranching."

"Plenty of time to learn," he said, his eyes twinkling as they met hers.

She loved to look at him. It became a habit as the day wore on. Maggie cooked supper, grilling steaks on the big expensive range in the kitchen. She made creamed potatoes and cooked some frozen beans and even made bread to go with it.

Tate was fascinated with the bread. "I didn't know women still made it," he confessed as he finished his third buttered slice.

"Mom loves to cook," Blake grinned.

"Mostly out of laziness," she confessed. "I hate eating out."

He laughed gently. "So do I." He glanced at Blake's sudden grimace. "How about something else for that leg?" he asked the boy.

"I don't really need it," Blake said.

Tate turned his chair around, staring at the boy. "I broke my leg once. Got backed up on by one of my bulls. I learned that pain hurts, and that if you don't overdo pain medication, it gets you over the bad spots. You don't have to prove anything to me," he added with a quizzical smile. "You kept your head eye to eye with a wolf. That told me all I needed to know about you."

Blake actually flushed with pleasure. "It wasn't so bad," he mumbled.

"Now how about that capsule?" Tate persisted.

Blake sighed. "OK."

Tate waved Maggie back down when she got up to get it. Instead, he rose and brought back the bottle. "Have one, then I'll teach you how to play chess. Or do you already know?"

"I can play checkers, but nobody ever taught me chess."

"No time like the present to learn," Tate said and smiled at the boy.

Maggie did the dishes and then curled up on the sofa to watch the game. Tate was patient in a way she'd never expected him to be, going over and over the moves with Blake until he understood. Her first impression of him had been that he never stopped or slowed down for anybody. But all those first impressions were undergoing change. She found that he had a dry sense of humor, that he wasn't really a bear at all and that he was rather a lonely kind of man. There was nothing in this elegant house to indicate that he was wealthy, except for the sheer size of the ranch around it. He didn't put on airs, but she imagined that he could have if it pleased him.

"It must get lonely," Maggie said absently, smoothing one of the Indian blankets that lay over the back of the sofa.

Tate looked up from the chessboard while Blake frowned in concentration over his next move. "It does," he answered her. "Especially for a woman."

She blinked, averting her eyes.

"I guess loneliness is pretty portable, though," he added, watching her. "Because I've known people who could be alone in a crowd."

"That's true enough," she conceded, trailing her finger over the design in the blanket while the fire roared like a fiery lullaby in the hearth. She was oddly sleepy. That was new, because she'd been a little jumpy at the cabin, even with Blake nearby. But here, in Tate's house, she felt safe. She smiled secretively and closed her eyes.

Tate's dark eyes wandered slowly over her face, aware of that dreamy expression on it as he tried to reconcile his misgivings with a new and staggering hunger.

Blake caught the look on the man's face before he could erase it, and he had to bite his tongue to keep from smiling. So far, so good, he thought.

Chapter Four

Blake went to sleep during a chess move, and Tate lifted him carefully, cast and all, and carried him into his room.

"Get me his pajamas," he called over his shoulder, "and I'll get him into them."

"It will take a miracle to get them over that cast," she sighed.

He smiled at her gently. "Good point. Well, get his jacket anyway, and I'll loan him a pair of my bottoms."

"I can see him now with the legs tied around his neck to hold them up," she mused.

He actually laughed. He put the boy down on the bed, hesitating as he stood watching him sleep. His dark eyes narrowed. "Nine going on ten," he said softly. "He's a hell of a boy."

Maggie caught her breath at the quiet affection in that statement and wondered if he realized how much emotion he was betraying. But after a minute he moved, frowning, and went toward his own room as if he was preoccupied.

She got Blake out of his flannel shirt and into the pajama top just as Tate came back with a pair of cotton trousers that looked new in one lean hand.

"Oh, you shouldn't let him have your newest ones...." she protested.

He gave her a faintly mocking smile. "Honey, I don't wear anything in bed. I keep a couple of pair in case of fire."

She flushed beet-red without understanding why. After marriage and a child and despite his admitted lack of experience, he could so easily reduce her to shyness.

"Sorry," she said, then added as she backed toward the door, "Well, I'll leave you to it."

He turned toward Blake, still smiling.

Minutes later, he was back. He eased down onto the sofa beside her and lit a cigarette while the fire crackled and wind occasionally whistled down the chimney.

"Does he miss not having a father?" he asked with studied carelessness.

"Sometimes I think so," she confessed. She tucked her feet under her, bare below the hem of her jeans, and folded her arms over her cotton top. It was the same shade of blue as the one Tate was wearing, and she wondered if he'd noticed that their taste in color seemed to match. "It's especially hard on him at school, although a number of the boys have divorced parents. Most of their mothers seem to have remarried or at least have boyfriends who come to the events at school."

He leaned a long arm over the back of the sofa and studied her face openly. "And there aren't any men in your life."

She smiled, not embarrassed. "I'm hopelessly old-fashioned," she explained. "I guess Blake thinks I'm a dinosaur."

"I'd bet you that he doesn't," he replied, surprising her. "He told his grandfather that he thinks you're the best mother a boy could possibly have."

Her breath caught, and she smiled. "He said that, really?"

"That's what Jeffries told me," he agreed. He took a draw of the cigarette. "I used to spend a lot of time at his place, when you and the boy were in Tucson. I heard about you until I felt as if I knew you. But I didn't, of course. Not at all. I had a totally different picture of you. I thought you probably went out a lot, but were very discreet," he added with a faint smile.

"I wouldn't know how," she sighed. "If I were involved with someone, Blake would know it instantly. I can't hide how I feel."

"Thank God," he said and meant it.

Her eyes came up, curious.

"I hate lies," he said unexpectedly. "I hate social convention and subterfuge and polite verbal warfare. I say exactly what I think, and I appreciate it when other people do. You and I got off to a rough start, but after what we said to each other back at your house, I think we're on the way to something good."

"What kind of...something good?" she asked, still a little wary of an intensity in him that she didn't quite understand.

"You tell me, Maggie," he replied quietly. He bent then and brushed his mouth very softly over hers. "Sleep tight."

He got up in one smooth motion, leaving her staring after his broad back.

"It's only eight o'clock," she said to the room at large.

"I get up before dawn. Cattle don't keep city hours," he added with a slow smile. "Turn out the lights when you're sleepy."

"OK."

She sat a little longer by the fire, spinning dreams, thinking about how it would be if they were a family, she and Tate Hollister and Blake. But they were only dreams, she reminded herself, and soon enough she'd be back at her desk at work, with only memories.

The next morning, something woke her before daylight. A sound. A movement. She got up, feeling bright eyed because she was accustomed to rising early when she had to work. She dressed in jeans and a pullover gray jersey, pausing to run a brush through her hair before she tiptoed down the hall to Blake's room and peeked in.

He was still sound asleep. She smiled, closing the door, and went into the kitchen in search of coffee. Only to find somebody else bent on the same course.

Tate was there, in his stocking feet wearing nothing but his blue jeans. She stopped dead in the doorway, her eyes helplessly drawn to a body that would have made a male centerfold look anemic. Muscles rippled under darkly tanned skin as he rose from peeking into the oven, and when he turned toward her, she wondered if it was permissible for a modern woman to swoon.

His chest was completely obscured by thick black curling hair. Muscles rippled in his big arms, down his flat stomach, and she knew there wasn't an ounce of fat anywhere on him. She'd never liked hairy men, but this one was a work of art. He didn't have tufts of hair on his arms and shoulders as some men did. No, it was all on that broad chest, thick and gleaming with faint moisture, as if he'd just come from a shower. Probably he had, because his shaggy head was a bit damp as well, his straight hair falling roguishly over his forehead.

"Good morning," he murmured, his eyes running over her face with blatant interest. "No makeup?"

"I hate the stuff," she blurted out.

He laughed. "So do I. Get some cream out of the refrigerator and I'll pour you some coffee."

"I didn't think you were so handy in the kitchen," she remarked as he took up the toast he'd been watching under the broiler and added it to a platter of thick bacon and scrambled eggs.

"Oh, Jeffries used to tell a story about one of my hands quitting because I fed him, but I'm handy enough, I guess. I was a marine, honey," he added with a quick glance as he filled two thick white mugs with coffee. "Cooking is one of the easy things you get taught."

She opened her mouth to make a comment but thought better of it. He put the coffee on the table and sat down.

"I didn't expect you to be up and about this early," he said as he filled his plate.

"I like to watch the sun come up," she confessed. "It's magic in Tucson, when dawn hits the Santa Catalina mountains. They change color. Sometimes they're red, sometimes black, then they turn pink and rust . . . they haunt me."

"I've seen my own mountains change, but from blue to purple," he told her. "And dead white in winter. Have some eggs. You need feeding up."

"I never gain weight," she confessed as she reached for a piece of toast to go with her slice of bacon. She watched as he dumped eggs on her plate. "That's too much," she told him.

"If you're going to live on a ranch, you have to keep up your strength. Blake will tell you that." He was through his eggs already and working on homemade jam and toast.

"I won't be out pitching hay and fixing fences and checking on cattle," she reminded him.

"What did you plan to do?" he asked curiously.

"I thought I'd clean the house, if you don't mind— not that it needs it, but the beds will have to be made." She dropped her gaze. The sight of his bare chest at close range was making her weak in the knees. "I wouldn't want to interfere with your cleaning lady, of course."

"You won't interfere. Do whatever you like. Within reason, of course. I get funny about lace on my undershirts."

"Do you wear one?" she blurted out, and blushed as she realized how intimate the question sounded.

He was watching the way her eyes glanced off his chest, and she couldn't know how much a man her shy appreciation made him feel. His dark eyes narrowed on her face. "No, I don't," he answered the question. He finished his toast and swallowed the rest of his coffee. "Want a second cup?"

"Yes. I'll get it." She got up, but as she went past him, his lean hand shot out and caught her wrist.

"No, you won't," he murmured dryly, and jerked.

She fell across his lap, gasping, one slender hand coming into sudden, shocking contact with all that bare chest. She couldn't even protest. Her gaze fell to where her hand was half-buried. She didn't want him to see how vulnerable she was, but it took too much work to try and hide her blatant interest.

He pressed her hand flat against him, looking at the small ovals of her nails without polish. She had nice hands, very slender and graceful. "Stop hiding from me." He tilted her face to his so that he could see all the doubts and nervousness. His black eyes were kind for all the darkness growing in them. "This is as new for me as it is for you, so don't think I'm going to make fun of the way you're looking at me. I'd be staring just as hard at you if your shirt was off."

Her lips parted. "Really?"

"Really." He moved her hand against the thick hair and hard, warm muscle beneath it, watching the movement, feeling its instant effect on him. He laughed, the sound deep and low and pleasant in the early morning stillness. He looked up to see an arrested fascination in her eyes. "I thought I was immune. Feel." He put her hand over his heart and let her feel its hard, heavy beat.

"I guess none of us are...immune, that is," she whispered.

"Is yours beating that hard?" he asked softly and, still holding her gaze, his lean hand pressed just under the soft breast. But his other arm came up at the same time, arching her, and he eased her down into the crook of it while his long fingers spread. The tips of them just touched the soft underswell of her breast, bare under the jersey, and she couldn't breathe. She began to tremble and her eyes darkened to old silver, staring up into his black ones.

"Tate," she whispered huskily, her breath catching.

"I suppose there are rules about this sort of thing," he said tautly, holding her eyes as his fingertips traced the swell of her breast. "Back in the Dark Ages when I was a boy, nice girls would slap a man for what I'm trying to do to you."

"I'm a widow, not a girl," she breathed shakily. "And I...like...what you're doing to me."

"You aren't supposed to tell me that, Maggie," he whispered as his head bent toward her. He brushed his lips over hers once, twice, and then they settled on her mouth. His hand searched for the hem of the jersey, found it and went up until it found a warm, soft mound with a hard tip that arched into his palm even as she shuddered with rapt sensation.

She moaned under his mouth. He tasted her, felt her hunger, drowned in her yielding softness.

When she tensed again, without taking his mouth from hers, he pushed the jersey out of the way and pulled her against his bare chest. She tensed, gasping as her breasts melted into the thick hair and warm muscle of him. His head lifted, because he wanted to see her face.

His dark eyes narrowed. She looked... wild. Abandoned. Her lips were swollen, her eyes half-closed, misty and faintly savage all at once. She was flushed and her body arched toward his.

His eyes went down to her breasts, and he looked at the contrasts between what he could see of her pink and mauve flesh and his hair-matted darkly tanned chest. His arm tightened, but he lifted a little away, because it had been years since he'd seen a woman without clothes, and he wanted to look at Maggie's soft breasts.

She saw him visibly start at his first real sight of her that way. His face hardened, his eyes began to glitter. He frowned slightly, looking intently at her body. As if fascinated, one lean, dark-fingered hand came up to touch the round contour with its blatant hardness, and she gasped at that tender tracing because the excitement she was feeling was so intense.

His black eyes moved back up to hers. "You fascinate me," he whispered tautly. "All of you. Your body, your heart, your mind. I've always thought of women in physical terms until now. But, I touch you and I wonder..."

"Wonder what?" she asked in a soft whisper, because it was almost reverent with him.

"I wonder how it would be if I gave you a child," he whispered, his tone full of awe.

She stopped breathing. His words held that kind of impact. Her eyes searched his face, and she lifted her hand to touch his mouth, to trace the thick mustache, the hard cheek, the thick brows. His eyes closed and he sat quietly and a little tensely while her soft hand went over him, learning the contours of his face.

She arched then and touched her mouth with aching tenderness to his. Her fingers found his, pressing them down over the softly mounded flesh, holding his palm there while her mouth made slow, sweet love to his.

"You're killing me," he whispered on a tortured laugh.

"You aren't doing my metabolism much good, either," she whispered at his lips. She was sitting up on his lap, with both hands on his chest, and her eyes were full of emotion. Their color was soft, like gray doves.

He took a deep breath and forced himself to pull her jersey down, smoothing it around her waist. "I've got to go to work," he groaned. "My God, I hope I can pitch hay bent over double."

He was laughing, though, and her eyes blazed with triumph, with delighted knowledge of her part in his downfall. She smiled at him, and her hands smoothed back, his thick dark hair, lingering at his temples.

"What would you like for lunch?" she asked.

"Anything," he replied. "As long as I get to look at you while I eat it."

"Oh, Tate." She put her mouth over his and clung to him, feeling him move, feeling his lean hand gather her hips suddenly against his.

He felt her tauten. His head lifted and he looked into her wide, frightened gray eyes. "I won't hurt you, Maggie," he whispered. "I just want you to know how much a man I am with you. It isn't a threat. It's..." He paused. "I don't know. Pride, I think," he decided finally, and it was in his eyes, in his whole look.

She met his level gaze and the fear was gone, all at once. She relaxed into him, forcing her taut muscles to give, forcing her body to trust him. "It's difficult," she said softly. "I've spent years holding back."

"I understand." He kissed her closed eyelids and then he let her go, helping her back onto her feet as he rose and towered over her. "I didn't bring you here to seduce you," he added, framing her face in his warm, strong hands. "There's nothing to be afraid of."

"But I am afraid," she whispered, frowning as she looked up at him. "Tate, I... We mustn't..."

He put a long finger against her soft lips. "I have to go." He brushed his hard mouth over her forehead, and the mustache tickled. "Let's live one day at a time. OK?"

She forced herself not to panic. "OK," she agreed.

He smiled. He seemed to do a lot of that lately, she thought, watching him go down the hall to his bedroom. But, then, so did she.

The days that followed were magic. Tate didn't touch her again, although she could see the banked-down fire in his eyes when he looked at her; she could read the hunger there. He spent time with Blake at night when he wasn't working, talking cattle and marketing, things that went right over Maggie's head, but that Blake seemed to understand and really enjoy. And when Tate loaned him his *Stockman's Handbook* to study, the boy was over the moon.

"It's got a whole section on feedlot management," Blake said enthusiastically.

"We could use a feedlot around here. I just never seem to get time to look into the possibilities," Tate said, leaning back on the sofa with a cup of black coffee and smoking a cigarette. "But it's interesting all the same to see how they're operated. There's more to it than just grouping numbers of cattle together and feeding them twice a day."

"This is interesting, about the danger of explosive gases," Blake murmured.

Maggie looked up from her *Ranch* magazine, where she was going over a recipe for a beef casserole. "Gases?"

Blake went into a long and nauseating explanation of how the unvented waste from livestock could create explosive and toxic gases, while Tate watched, faintly amused at her wide-eyed disgust.

"Son, I don't think your mother's in raptures over the gory details," he murmured. "She might find some tips on range management a little easier to take."

"Right," Blake agreed readily, flushed because his idol had actually called him "son." He looked at Tate with more emotion than he realized, so hungry for a father of his own that he was as open as a book.

Tate, watching that expression unfold, felt a wild stirring inside himself. A protective stirring, just as he had the morning he'd shot at the wolf when it threatened Blake. The boy and the woman were getting to him, growing on him, taking him over. Once, he'd have drawn back in anger from that kind of affection. But now . . .

He looked at Maggie, his eyes quiet and tender on her down-bent dark head as she read her magazine. She and Blake were already part of his life; it was as natural as breathing. He looked forward to coming home at lunch, at night. He looked forward to every new day. That was when it dawned on him that Christmas was five days away and they'd be going back to Arizona soon afterwards. He felt sick all over.

To ward off thought of the future without them, he got to his feet. "What are we going to do about a tree?" he asked suddenly.

They both stared at him.

"Well, we have to have a tree," he explained. "It's going to be Christmas in five days."

Maggie felt the same sickness he'd just experienced at the thought of what came after the holiday, but she forced herself to smile. "What are we going to put on it?" she asked. "Do you have any decorations?"

"We could put one of my hats on top, I guess," he mused, "and whip a rope around it for a garland."

"We could put it in one of your boots," Blake chuckled and got a black glare for his pains.

"Suppose we make decorations?" Maggie pondered. "I can bake cookies in different shapes to go around it, and do you have some popcorn and thread?" Tate nodded and she grinned. "We can make garlands of popcorn. But what about Christmas dinner? Tate, can you get a ham and a turkey?"

"There are three hams in the deep freeze," Tate replied. "But a turkey. . ." He frowned. "I guess I could get one from Jane Clyde, over the mountain."

"Is it far?" Maggie asked.

"Just an hour's drive or so."

She thought of him on that winding road, of how dangerous it was in snow and ice. "We don't need a turkey," she said. "Really, I hate turkey. And so does Blake," she added, daring her son to argue.

But he was quick, was Blake. He'd already followed her reasoning and was agreeing with enthusiasm that turkeys were the curse of civilization.

Tate didn't say anything else about going over the mountain to get a bird. But he smiled to himself when he left the room. They weren't fooling anybody—he saw right through them.

For the next few days, Maggie and Blake worked on decorations and made presents. Since the nearest store was down the mountain, they decided to make do with what they'd brought with them from Tucson. Maggie had Tate run her back to the cabin to check on everything, and she dug out the shopping bags full of things she'd brought with her from the city for Christmas.

"More decorations," she murmured, tossing out tinsel and gently laying a box of colored balls on the sofa. "And this is what Blake especially wanted for Christmas." She showed him a computer game, one of the very expensive ones with graphics and three diskettes.

He pursed his lips. "Very nice. I have a PC compatible, but I hadn't realized that Blake had an interest in computers."

"You have a computer?" she asked with vivid curiosity because she was thinking up a present for Tate, since he was the one person she hadn't foreseen a need to buy one for.

"Sure. Over 600 kilobytes of storage space, double disk drive, with a modem and a daisy wheel printer." He smiled at her fascination. "I keep my herd rec-

ords on computer these days. It beats the hell out of
having to handwrite every entry.''

''Do you have a spreadsheet program?'' she fished.

''I do, indeed,'' he said and named it. It was one of
the more expensive ones, so that program was out.

''What I don't have,'' he sighed, studying Blake's
disk, ''is a good word processing program. I could use
one of those to write letters with.'' He glanced at her,
noticing her rapt expression, and he grinned again. He
had two word processors, but he wasn't about to tell
her. He'd rush home and hide those disks, fast!

''My, my, they do come in handy, don't they?'' she
mused and quickly hid the one she'd bought for Blake.
Blake could wait another Christmas for a word processing program; he wasn't getting this one.

They loaded her packages in the car after she'd
taken time to wrap them. ''Tate, I never thought,'' she
said as they got into the Jeep, ''is there anyone you
spend Christmas with? Your family?''

''My parents are long dead, Maggie,'' he said quietly. ''I have no one.''

''I'm sorry, I didn't mean to pry.''

He took her slender hand in his and pressed his
mouth to the palm. ''You and I aren't going to have
any secrets from each other,'' he said tenderly. ''I
don't mind telling you anything you want to know.''

He let go of her hand and started the Jeep, and she
thought about what he'd said all the way home.

Home. It felt like home. She finished the last of the
icing on the Japanese fruitcake she'd made, with its
one mince layer and two white layers and exotic candied fruit icing with coconut all over it. It was like the
cake her mother had always made back home. She
wondered if she could ask Tate later about phoning

her youngest brother Michael on Christmas Eve and charging the bill to her phone in Tucson. Oddly enough, she hadn't missed having a telephone at the cabin, but she knew Tate had one because she'd heard him talking on it occasionally. Michael still lived in Tennessee, and he kept in touch with the rest of the family. Maggie wanted to know how Jack and Sam and their families were, and Michael was always good about passing messages along. Dear Michael, with his hair as dark as her own and eyes almost as gray as hers.

"What are you dreaming about?" Tate asked, reaching past her to refill his coffee cup while he and Blake took a short break from one of the old computer games Maggie had brought over.

"About Michael," she said without thinking and looked up to see a flash of lightning in Tate's black eyes.

"Who's Michael?" he asked tersely.

"Oh, I like that," she said softly and smiled up at him. "I like the way you sound when you think there's another man in my life. But there isn't, you know. Michael is my younger brother. He's just twenty-two, and he looks like me, except in places."

He mellowed. His lean fingers brushed back her thick hair. "Does he?" He bent, nuzzling her cheek with his. "I'm getting possessive. Does it bother you?"

"Look at another woman and you'll see how much it bothers me."

He lifted his head, searching her eyes quietly. "I see what you mean," he mused.

"What?"

He rubbed his nose against hers. "I like it, too." His breath was on her mouth. "Like what?"

"Having you get possessive. Open your mouth."

She did and his brushed against it, open, too. He bit at her lip, his mustache abrasive, his mouth hard. He grasped the back of her neck and pulled her closer, crushing her mouth under the warm pressure of his.

"Would you bring me a cola, Mr. Hollister?" Blake called suddenly from the office, shocking them apart.

Maggie could hardly breathe. Tate seemed to be having a bit of a problem in that direction himself. He stood up, blinking. "A what?" he called.

"A soda."

"Sure." He shook his head, whistling through his teeth as he got one out of the refrigerator. "Heady stuff."

"What is, cola?" she murmured dryly, although her heart was still pounding.

"You," he whispered and kissed her again, softly, as he went past her to the study.

She leaned against the counter, watching his broad back disappear into the room with the computer, and she thought dreamily how sweet it would be if they were married and she never had to go back to Tucson.

But despite their closeness and the way Tate was with them, she had to remember that she was only a guest and in less than five days she and Blake would be in Tucson and this would only be a memory.

Tears stung her eyes as she finished icing the cake. Only a memory, perhaps, but one that would haunt her the rest of her life. The thought of being away from Tate now was worse than the threat of death. And whatever he felt, he was keeping his own counsel. He wanted her, that she knew. But there was a chasm between wanting and loving, and one was nothing without the other.

Chapter Five

Getting Blake to go to bed on Christmas Eve was like trying to put a pair of pants on an eel, Maggie thought as she watched him make his fourth reappearance.

"Mr. Hollister, is there or isn't there a Santa Claus?" he asked Tate.

Maggie stared blankly at Tate, who was struggling valiantly not to give the show away.

"Santa Claus is like a spirit, Blake," he finally told the boy as he sipped his coffee on the sofa. "So in a sense, yes, he exists."

"But he doesn't come down fireplaces?"

"I didn't say that," Tate replied.

Blake bit his lower lip, leaning heavily on the crutch Tate had loaned him. "But there's a fire in it," he groaned.

"Fire," Tate improvised, "can't possibly hurt a Christmas spirit like old Santa. He can get right through it to the stockings."

"Are you sure?" Blake asked worriedly.

Tate put his hand over his heart. "Blake, would I lie to you?" he asked.

Maggie had to bite her tongue almost through to keep from laughing at the expression on Tate's face. But Blake let out a pent-up sigh and grinned.

"OK," he said. "I just wanted to be sure. Good night. See you early in the morning!"

"You, too, darling," Maggie smiled, kissing his forehead gently. "Sleep well."

"Ha, ha," he muttered, glancing ruefully at the huge pine with its homemade decorations in the corner by the window. All lit with colorful lights and smelling of the whole outdoors, it had turned out to be a better tree than anyone had expected. But the crowning touch was some soap flakes that Maggie had found in the kitchen cabinet. She'd mixed them with water and made "snow" to go on the branches. The finished product was a dream of a Christmas tree, right down to the paper snowflakes that Blake had cut out—something he'd learned to do in art class in school.

Maggie sighed as she looked at the tree. "Isn't it lovely?" she asked absently.

"Not half as lovely as you are," Tate remarked quietly, his dark eyes possessive on her body in its sleek silver dress, a long camisole of sequins and spangles that had impressed her with its holiday spirit. With her dark hair short and curled forward, she looked like one of the twenties flappers.

"I'm glad you like it," she curtsied for him with her coffee cup held tightly in one hand. Like him, she didn't drink—rarely even a glass of wine. They were celebrating Christmas with black coffee, despite her dress and his suit slacks, white shirt and navy blazer.

He turned off the top light, leaving the winking, blinking colorful lights of the tree to brighten the room. His arms slid around her waist as they looked at the paper angel Blake had made for the tip-top. "I'm sorry we couldn't get you up there," he mused. "You'd make a pretty angel."

"I'd rather be just a woman," she said, turning. Her eyes ran over his face quietly although her heart was beating her to death. It had been forever since that morning when he'd made such sweet love to her in the kitchen. And she wanted that, and more, tonight. Her whole body ached for him.

He touched her throat with the very tip of his fore-finger, watching the pulse throb there, watching her lips part. She was his. She didn't even have to tell him. He could see it in her eyes, in her face, in the body that leaned toward his in the semibright darkness.

He took a step forward, so that he was against her, and his head bent to hers. His mouth brushed her open one, feeling with shock the sudden darting movement of her tongue against his upper lip.

He caught his breath and her eyes opened lazily, looking at him.

"It...it's something I learned when I was still in my teens," she faltered.

"It's damned arousing, do you know that?" he asked quietly. "Having Blake in the house wouldn't even slow me down, Maggie, so don't look for mira-cles if you start something tonight."

He made it sound as if she was making him a prop-osition. Well, she was, but he didn't have to make her feel cheap for it. She'd taken certain things about their relationship for granted, but perhaps she'd presumed too far. She'd wanted a memory of him, something warm and private, just for the two of them. A Christ-mas memory that she could take back to the desert with her to last all the long, lonely years that she was going to spend grieving for him.

Her head bent. Her hands clenched around her coffee cup. "I'm sorry," she whispered.

His breath caught. He hadn't expected her reac-tion. He hadn't meant to shame her, for heaven's sake. He'd just been hesitant to let things get out of hand before he could get up his nerve to ask her if she might consider staying at the ranch—she and Blake. He started to speak when a thunderous knocking at the front door broke the spell.

He jerked it open and a man was standing there, a very old one in a ragged hat. "Sorry to bother you, boss, but Katie Bess is due." He grinned. "I knew you'd want to be there."

"Yes. I do. Thanks, Baldy."

He closed the door and turned. "Katie Bess is one of my Shetland sheepdogs," he explained. "We use them to help us herd cattle. Katie Bess is our newest, and she and her pups are purebred."

"Christmas babies," Maggie said with a smile, trying to live down her humiliation. "Can I come, too?"

"Sure. But not in that," he said with a faint grin.

"I'll hurry and change."

"What's going on?" Blake called as they went past his door.

"Never mind." Maggie peeked in his door and told him, "Go back to sleep. Santa may come while we're outside, but only if he thinks you're snoring."

"I am, I am!" he promised, snoring loudly.

Maggie laughed as she closed the door. She got into her red flannel shirt and a pair of jeans, thick socks and boots, grabbed her parka and rushed out into the hall. Tate was already ahead of her, his boots making loud thuds as he went toward the hall closet and jerked out his shepherd's coat and hat.

She followed him to the stable where the mother sheepdog, who resembled a small collie with her fluffy tan and white fur, was lying in a clean stall. There were already three tiny furry bodies nuzzling close as the puppies nursed. And even as they watched, a fourth and fifth were born. Tate and Baldy spoke encouragingly to the dog, of which they were both obviously fond, and commented glowingly on the pups. They were like patchwork in color, beige and brown and white and brown and tan and white, and Maggie would have loved to pick them up and cuddle them. But they were too tiny just yet, and she satisfied herself with watching, adoring the tiny things with her eyes.

When she was a child, her parents had always kept her away from the animals when they were about to give birth. Far from thinking it would be an interesting experience for her, they were horrified at the thought that it might frighten her. But this wasn't a frightening experience; it was a humbling one.

The dog bent, licking the soft little coats. Her liquid brown eyes were as tender as a human mother's, her tired body shivering a little in reaction.

"I'll get some milk for her," Baldy said, moving away.

Tate's lean hand found Maggie's in the semidarkness under the central hanging light bulb. "She's been sick," he explained, "and we were afraid she might need help. But as you can see, she was up to it. That's a fine litter, Katie Bess," he said gently to the dog, who wagged her tail and looked up at him as if she loved him. "Good girl."

Baldy came back with milk and some fresh meat. "I'll take care of her now, boss. Looks like more snow coming, but Merry Christmas anyway."

"Merry Christmas, Baldy," Tate chuckled. "I guess we've both got our presents tonight."

"Guess we have, although yours looks a mite prettier than mine, but just a mite, mind," the old man said with a smothered chuckle.

Tate didn't seem to take offense. He wished the old man a good night, and he and Maggie went back toward the house.

The snow was coming down softly, but the wind was calm. They could see for miles in the white landscape, the snow lighting the way as surely as a lamp. Tate stopped to light a cigarette and slid his arm around Maggie's shoulders as they walked.

"Was it hard for you, when Blake was born?" he asked unexpectedly.

She looked up at him. "You mean, was it hard physically?" He nodded, and she let her eyes slide back to the house, silhouetted against the snow and the mountains and the dark sky. "I guess it was. But it's his face I remember, not the pain. Life is like that, isn't it? We may remember the cut, but it's the kiss that came afterward that stays in the memory."

"Profound thoughts on a Christmas Eve," he murmured.

"Yes. It's a profound night." She sighed, feeling his strength near her, dwarfing her, supporting her. "A night for miracles."

"I haven't celebrated Christmas since the accident," he said. "I haven't cared about much. But you and Blake have made the color come back into the world for me," he added, looking down at her. "You've brought me out of the past, out of the shadows. I think I'd forgotten how to smile until you came along."

She smiled up at him, but her heart felt heavy. Was that a way of saying goodbye and thanks for the hand? Or was it more? She was afraid to ask him for anything.

"I'm glad you've remembered how again," she said, forcing her eyes back to the path.

"About what I said in there," he murmured, nodding toward the house. He hesitated. His dark eyes cut down to hers. "I didn't mean to embarrass you. Maggie, if you want me, all you have to do is say so."

The blatant shock of the words stunned her. She couldn't even answer him for a few seconds. Yes, she did want him all right. But he made it sound matter-of-fact, like offering a thirsty traveler a drink of water. She flushed violently.

"I...I'm sleepy," she faltered. "I'd better get some rest so that I can cope with dinner tomorrow. Thanks for letting me see the pups!"

She practically ran up onto the porch and through the quiet house to her room, tears glistening in her eyes. She couldn't look at Tate, and that was a shame, because the look on his face would have told her everything she needed to know.

After she'd put on her pajamas, the same blue ones she'd worn at the cabin, she paced the floor with the lights off. She paused at the window, looking out into the snowy darkness with eyes that didn't see. Christmas was tomorrow. Then, in two days, they'd be gone.

She closed her eyes on a groan and got into bed. She had to forget. No, she had to make plans. She'd been coasting, loving Tate, getting to know him. But there was no future in it, and she'd been making dreams, not plans. Now she had to decide. Did she keep the ranch? Did she send Blake back to school? Did she go back to Tucson?

She worried the question for hours. Finally, in desperation, she got out of bed. Surely Tate would be asleep by now, and she needed a cup of coffee and an aspirin for the headache she'd given herself. Hopefully she wouldn't run headlong into Santa Claus out there, she mused.

But when she went into the dark kitchen and collided with a warm shape, she let out a faint gasp until she saw Tate's face silhouetted in the light from the Christmas tree.

"What are you doing up?" she faltered.

He let his dark eyes run slowly over her body in the pajamas, and he smiled because she was so obviously embarrassed at not having on a robe.

"I'm about to make coffee," he mused. "But now that you're up, you can do it while I put some clothes on."

That was when she realized that he didn't have anything on. She kept her eyes on his face with wide-eyed apprehension that tore a deep laugh from his throat.

"My God, is it that much of a shock?" he whispered wickedly.

"I've never even seen a naked man!" she screeched, and it was true because she'd never looked at her husband, not once.

His eyebrows arched in the faint light from the tree. "And you were married? Well, lady, you're overdue."

"No, I'm not." She closed her eyes tight, and he laughed as he turned back down the hall.

"All right, coward."

But she peeked. Just as he went into his room, the streaming light from it silhouetted him and she got an eyeful. He was the most magnificent man she'd ever seen, with or without clothes. She turned into the kitchen feeling poleaxed. He could have been a centerfold, all right, she thought dazedly.

He was back in less than five minutes, but only clad in his jeans. His feet were bare, like hers, and so was the rest of him.

"I thought you'd gone to sleep," she murmured. She plugged in the percolator, having already filled it with water and coffee and laid out cups and saucers and cream.

"I couldn't sleep," he said quietly. "I wanted you too badly."

Her eyes lifted. "But . . ."

He shrugged his broad shoulders. His lean hand touched her cheek. "I know. I frightened you off. Maybe I meant to." He sighed heavily. "I'm still in the learning stages about seduction."

"I thought you didn't want me."

"I finally realized that," he said on a soft laugh.

She managed a tight smile and let her eyes fall to his chest, but the bare expanse of it disturbed her, so she averted her gaze to the tree.

"I forgot to call Michael," she mentioned.

"Is it too late?"

"The time zones are a couple of hours apart," she recalled, "and it's later on the East Coast. I guess he's asleep. It's just as well, anyway. I haven't quite decided what I'm going to do."

He caught her waist and leaned back against the kitchen counter, bringing her lazily against him. "Decided to do about what?"

"About the ranch. And Blake." She stared at his chin. "And me."

"Well, I can't see any real problem, honey," he said carelessly. "I want to buy the ranch, so that gets it out of the way. And Blake doesn't want to go to military school; he wants to live here and learn the cattle business. That takes care of him. Which only leaves you and me."

She swallowed. Her heart was going wild. She looked up hesitantly, her eyes faintly pleading. "You and me?"

"Mmmhmm." He bent, brushing her nose with his. He smiled softly. "And that means," he whispered at her lips, "that you're not going anywhere until I say so, pretty girl."

"But I can't...my job...responsibilities..." she protested weakly, the words muffled by his lips.

"Hush," he chuckled, and his mouth opened lazily, taking her lips with it. She made a faint sound, but he held her close until she gave in, and then he unbuttoned her pajama jacket.

"Tate!" she·protested against his hungry mouth.

"God, you're soft," he whispered as his hands tenderly took the soft weight of her breasts. He eased the fabric away from them and pulled her against him, holding her there, drawing her lazily from side to side so that the thick hair on his chest made delicious patterns on her softness, so that the hunger got worse by the second and she began to make noises that he liked.

Her nails bit into his shoulders and she clung, her mouth as eager as his.

His lean hands slid down to her hips and pulled them gently against his thighs, pressing her to him so that she could feel how much he wanted her. "I go crazy when I get close to you," he said huskily. "Eventually I'll give in to it, and so will you. We have to do something about it."

Her hands slid over his broad chest, savoring the feel of it, adoring him. "Yes."

He bit at her mouth. "When?"

Her eyes opened. "What?"

"When do you want to get married?" he asked simply, his black eyes soft, tender.

She stared at him blankly. "You...you want to marry me?" she stumbled.

"Of course I want to marry you." His shoulders lifted and fell and his mustache twitched. "Can you see us living in sin with Blake around?" he chuckled.

"But, marriage," she said quietly. Her pale eyes searched his dark ones. "You haven't wanted anyone around you..."

"Yes, that's true," he said honestly. "But you know how it's been for the past week. You have opened doors for me." His hands slid up her bare back and down again, smoothing her breasts against him, shuddering a little with the sweet pleasure of it. "Maggie, I've learned that I can't live in the past. And I don't want to, not anymore. I want a family. I want you. And Blake. I don't want to spend the rest of my life alone, and I don't think you want to, either." His dark eyes narrowed. "Or have I read it wrong? Is it just a physical thing with you?"

"I want you like crazy," she admitted without embarrassment. "But it isn't just a physical thing. I love being with you. I feel safe and happy." She stared down at his chest, where her fingers were buried. "I..."

"Don't stop now, for God's sake," he whispered huskily. "Say it."

She looked up, flushing. "You didn't."

"I won't—not until you do," he said. "What's the matter, city girl, balking at the last fence?"

Her chin shot forward and she glared at his smug expression. "Well, you know already, don't you?" she challenged.

"Of course I know," he said with barely concealed impatience. "You were trying to seduce me before we went to see the pups, weren't you? That isn't the kind of thing a virtuous woman does unless she's pretty stuck on a man."

Her blush got worse. "Maybe I just got hot and bothered," she muttered.

"Fat chance. Say it." He nibbled at her mouth and his hands slid up her sides, smoothing blatantly over her breasts and making her moan. "Say it, woman, for God's sake!"

"I love you," she murmured. "I love you, you horrible, wonderful man—" His hard lips cut her off, and her mouth was taken, possessed, absorbed, the second the last word was dying on the air, his hands strong and warm and tender on her soft breasts as he made them burn with pleasure.

He bent, lifting her, his big body shuddering with unconcealed hunger. "It's been years," he whispered roughly, "and I want you like hell. But I'll be gentle with you."

Her arms tightened around his neck and she buried her face in his throat, trembling. "I don't care if you aren't," she whispered. "I love you so much. I want you just the way you are, Tate."

He groaned, laughing, as he carried her down the long hall. "My God, this is going to be sweet," he whispered.

She flushed, laughing. "I go all giddy and wild when you touch me."

"Just remember that Blake's a light sleeper," he whispered.

She nibbled at his jaw as he carried her, savoring the feel of his broad, warm chest, the clean scent of his body. He was going to be her lover, and she could hardly wait. This was like nothing she'd ever experienced, not even in the excitement of her first marriage. This was the promise of heaven and only the beginning of a long, achingly sweet relationship....

"Santa Claus!"

They'd just passed Blake's room and were at the door of Tate's when the sleepy young voice froze them in place. If Tate hadn't been quite so hungry, the look on his face would have been comical as he swung around with Maggie close in his arms to see Blake ambling slowly toward the living room with his crutch under his arm and the cast bumping the floor.

"Santa Claus!" Blake called again.

"Damn," Tate whispered huskily. "He thinks he heard Saint Nick."

"Thank God," Maggie whispered back, frantically buttoning buttons while her face blazed with embarrassment.

He put her down, smiling faintly at her panic. "Calm down," he said gently. "Nothing happened."

"By the skin of our teeth," she moaned. She looked up at him and her heart stopped. "Oh, I love you," she breathed huskily. "And if it had happened, I wouldn't be sorry."

"I wonder," he mused. He bent and brushed his mouth gently over hers. "I lost my head, but I think it might be a good idea if we do it by the book. For Blake's sake."

She smiled dreamily. "That sounds nice. Too bad your heart's giving the show away," she added, pressing her hand over its hard, heavy beat.

"My body and my mind don't always agree," he confessed, but he was smiling, too.

Lights went on in the living room. "Wow!" came a hearty exclamation from a young voice. "Mom! Mr. Hollister! Wake up! Santa's been here!"

"Make that Mom and Dad, Blake," Tate called down the hall.

There was a short, shocked pause, a gasp, and then a yell that could have awakened the dead.

"I think he's pleased," Maggie murmured.

"Do tell," Tate said, grinning. "I am, too. Well, we might as well go and open our presents, since we aren't going to give each other our best one just yet."

"There'll be time for that," she replied.

His dark eyes searched her gray ones. "All the time in the world," he agreed. "But we get married first."

"Yes, Mr. Hollister," she whispered.

Blake was already through his first two packages when they joined him, his eyes bright with love as he showed Tate and Maggie his new copy of the *Stockman's Handbook* and the software for his computer.

"But my best present," he told them, "is my new dad."

Tate ruffled his hair affectionately. "I hope it was worth that broken leg," he murmured dryly.

Blake flushed. "You knew?"

"I used to be a boy myself," Tate chuckled. "Yes, I knew."

"But how?" Maggie asked gently.

He gave her a rueful glance. "Well, you see, honey, while he was trying to get himself lost, I was busy sabotaging your generator so you'd have to spend Christmas week with me."

"Tate!" she gasped.

He smiled at Blake, who was laughing openly. "A man gets lonely. Maybe old Scrooge had a humbug attitude toward Christmas, but I wanted a tree and someone to help me enjoy it." He shrugged. "Hard to find company up here in the mountains, unless you trap it."

Maggie hugged him on one side, and Blake did on the other. He held them both gently, fighting the sting of moisture in his dark eyes. Christmas had brought him gifts he'd never imagined, and he had them in his arms.

A week later, Blake was in school in Deer Lodge, crutches and all, and Maggie and Tate were just home from the justice of the peace's office. They'd just been married, with Blake as a witness and had dropped him off at school on their way back to the ranch. Maggie and Tate were alone for the first time, and she was afraid.

It was harder than Maggie had realized, the newness of belonging to a man after so many years of being alone. She felt like a beet when she glanced at her husband and hated her own feelings of inadequacy and nervousness.

He took her gently by the waist and looked down into her soft, frightened eyes. "Listen," he said gently, "I'm just as nervous as you are. Probably more, because I've got to set the pace. So just relax, Mrs. Hollister, and we'll kiss each other stupid and see where it gets us. Okay?"

She lifted her face to his, smiling shyly, and closed her eyes as his mouth settled gently on hers.

As he'd thought, once she relaxed and stopped being shy with him, everything fell into place. Minutes later, they were on his king-size bed, fighting the clothes that separated them until nothing did, not even the faint chill of the air.

"Slowly," he whispered, stilling her movements, holding her. "Slowly, honey. Yes. Yes, like that," he murmured against her mouth as she shifted, letting him guide her. His lean hands caught her hips and held them as he moved. His mouth became demanding then, his hands insistent. He paused, breathing roughly, and felt her trembling. Then he moved again and it was easy. So easy. So sweet.

She clung to him, feeling his movements, feeling him breathe, feeling the wildness of his heartbeat over her breasts as his body slowly merged with hers. She'd been afraid, but there was nothing to be afraid of. He was her husband and she loved him, and this was the most beautiful expression of love that she'd ever dreamed of.

Her eyes closed as he shifted again and she opened her mouth against his throat as she heard him whispering, heard the words, burned with the passion in them. She arched, trembling, clinging, and heard his breath catch even as her body began to echo the sweet rhythm of his. And all at once they were soul to soul, as close as flesh could get to flesh. One.

She could barely breath at all, and she was still trembling in the aftermath when she felt his eyes on her face. She opened her eyes, looking up, fascinated, into the black tenderness of his gaze.

"I love you," he whispered huskily.

"I love you, too." She reached up, clinging to him, shuddering in completion. "Tate, it was...it was never..."

"Never like this," he finished for her. He nuzzled her cheek with his. "I know." He wrapped her close, savoring her soft warmth in his arms. "You know," he whispered, "if we do this enough, you might get pregnant."

She smiled into his throat. "I've heard it said that a ranch needs lot of sons."

"Well, we've got lots of time," he whispered, lifting his head. "And I'd like to give you children,

Maggie," he said, bending. "I'll love you all my life. All the way to the grave. Good times, bad times, all the times we share. You're my world."

"Oh, Tate, you're my world, too," she whispered brokenly, burying her face against him.

"Come here," he whispered. "Show me."

She tried to answer him, but there was so much emotion in her that she couldn't speak for it. Two lost, lonely people had found a miracle this Christmas. And as she pressed against him, she managed to smile through tears of exquisite joy, her heart brimming over as she thought of all the Christmases yet to come that she and Blake would share with him—Christmases bright with laughter and filled with love.

* * * * *

A Note from Diana Palmer

I learned to cook from my grandmother, who used the pinch-of-this and dab-of-that technique and never wrote anything down. I still can't write recipes, and I don't have the talent, sadly, for crafts. So the only thing I have to share with you is nonedible—it's a little history about hard times and sweet lessons. And I hope you'll enjoy it and accept it in place of the recipe or craft I was unable to give you this Christmas.

I spent the first few years of my life with my mother's parents on a small sharecropper's farm in southwest Georgia. Like the previous four generations of my family who worked the land, my grandparents butchered hogs and cattle, they made their own sausage, they churned their own butter, they cared for livestock, picked cotton, hoed corn and peanuts, chopped wood for the stove and fireplace. They went to bed by kerosene lamp and got up by the first light of dawn. It was a hard life—there were no regular hours, and they didn't get paid overtime. They got half of whatever they made on the crops. But I learned a profound lesson from them the last Christmas I spent there.

The Christmas tree that year didn't come from a tree lot—they never did. My grandfather would hitch up the mules to the wagon, then we'd go to the nearby woods and Granddaddy would cut down a small pine tree. When we got it home, Granny and I would mix up Lux flakes (a detergent) to make "snow" to go on the tree. We'd put candles on the branches, and we'd string popcorn and make colored paper chains.

Christmas morning there would always be presents under the tree. There were fruit, nuts and the usual magnificent Christmas dinner. But the most incredible thing was that, even though we lived in a house with a leaking tin roof and rough wooden floors and no conveniences at all, I never knew I was poor. Until that Christmas, when I overheard my grandfather telling my grandmother that he thought he'd given me a pretty good Christmas for a poor man. I never told anyone what I'd heard, but I was shocked. There was so much love in our house and so much happiness that I didn't know we were poor until I heard my grandfather say it.

Because I had so few material possessions, I appreciated every little thing I got. And that's what I want our son, Blayne, to understand about Christmas. That it's people who count, not things. I want him to know the beauty of a family circle, the magic of love, the joy of fellowship in church. I want him to grow up looking for the small, hidden pleasures, for the sparkle of beauty in an ugly place, for the hurt under the cold attitude, for the scream in the laughter. I want him to find wealth in poverty, as I did so long ago. And that is, after all, the real message of the Christmas season. Love is the gold—everything else is just tinsel.

Diana Palmer

If you enjoyed the Silhouette Christmas Stories, DON'T MISS THESE OTHER WORKS BY THE SAME AUTHORS:

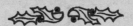

MIRRORS by Linda Howard

Terribly injured and temporarily blinded, Steve Granger needed Jay's help, and, inexplicably, Jay found her ex-husband more compelling now than when they'd first met. But there were memories haunting Steve, memories of another life, one he couldn't share with Jay—one that might tear them apart again.

May 1988 Special Edition

FATE TAKES A HOLIDAY by Dixie Browning

Sophie Pennybaker won her all-too-attractive boss at a charity auction and was *forced* to go on a romantic vacation with him. It was fate . . . and the opportunity of a lifetime!

February 1988 Desire

FOOLS RUSH IN by Ginna Gray

In tracing her missing twin, Erin Blaine's first find was dashing Max Delany, her sister's supposed beloved. Dodging gunmen and double-crossers, Max and Erin sought clues...and stumbled onto unwanted desire.

November 1987 Special Edition

BETRAYED BY LOVE by Diana Palmer

Kate had loved Jacob forever, but he had always considered her off-limits. She couldn't risk telling him her true feelings—but then Jacob started taking some risks of his own....

December 1987 Desire

Take 4 Silhouette Special Edition novels
and a surprise gift
FREE

Then preview 6 brand-new books—delivered to your door as soon as they come off the presses! If you decide to keep them, you pay just $2.49 each*—a 9% saving off the retail price, *with no additional charges for postage and handling!*

Romance is alive, well and flourishing in the moving love stories of Silhouette Special Edition novels. They'll awaken your desires, enliven your senses and leave you tingling all over with excitement.

Start with 4 Silhouette Special Edition novels and a surprise gift absolutely FREE. They're yours to keep without obligation.   You can always return a shipment and cancel at any time. Simply fill out and return the coupon today!

* Plus 69¢ postage and handling per shipment in Canada.

Silhouette Special Edition®

Take 4 Silhouette Desire novels
and a surprise gift

Then preview 6 brand-new Silhouette Desire novels—delivered to your door as soon as the come off the presses! If you decide to keep them, you pay just $2.24 each*—a 10% saving o the retail price, *with no additional charges for postage and handling!*

Silhouette Desire novels are not for everyone. They are written especially for the woma who wants a more satisfying, more deeply involving reading experience. Silhouette Desire nove take you beyond the others.

Start with 4 Silhouette Desire novels and a surprise gift absolutely FREE. They're yours t keep without obligation. You can always return a shipment and cancel at any time.

Simply fill out and return the coupon today!

* Plus 69¢ postage and handling per shipment in Canada.

Gary Hart, former Democratic senator for Colorado,
has written a frighteningly authentic tale
of man's race toward destruction.

GARY HART

The
Strategies
ZEUS
of

In a world of international power politics, it becomes a race
against time as conspiracy and intrigue surround forces in Wash-
ington and Moscow that are attempting to sabotage the arms
negotiations.

"*well-placed plot twists and sharp, believable dialogue*"
—Booklist

"*an intriguing plot*"
—Philadelphia Inquirer

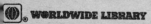

FOUR UNIQUE SERIES
FOR EVERY WOMAN YOU ARE.

Silhouette Romance

Love, at its most tender, provocative,
emotional ... in stories that will make you laugh and
cry while bringing you the magic of falling in love.

6 titles per month

Silhouette Special Edition

Sophisticated, substantial and packed with
emotion, these powerful novels of life and love will
capture your imagination and steal your heart.

6 titles per month

Silhouette Desire

Open the door to romance and passion. Humorous,
emotional, compelling—yet always a believable
and sensuous story—Silhouette Desire never
fails to deliver on the promise of love.

6 titles per month

Silhouette Intimate Moments

Enter a world of excitement, of romance
heightened by suspense, adventure and the
passions every woman dreams of. Let us
sweep you away.

4 titles per month